Among
the Tin Cans
and
Broken Glass

By
T.A. Novak

Enjoy your ride.

T. Novak

ISBN: 978-0-9885051-5-5
This printing updated in 2015

This book is printed on acid free paper.
Printed in the United States of America.

Cover art by
Carter Lake, Iowa artist
Keith A. Goc

Alley Cop Publishing-Est. 02/08

Dedication

This book is dedicated to the past and present officers of the Detroit Police Department, men and women that daily risk their lives for the citizens of Detroit. While this book might depict some officers in a bad light, I want to stress that this type of officer is in a very small minority. I admire and salute the police officers of Detroit for their willingness to serve. I further admire those men and women I served with that remained to retire from a job I truly loved.

I would like to especially dedicate this work to the memory of men that I personally knew that were killed in the line of duty: Sergeant Stanley Sech, killed in February, 1963 while answering a "Family Trouble" run; Patrolman Jerome Olshove, killed in July, 1967 during the riot; and Patrolman Stanley Rapaski, killed during a bar hold up in January, 1969. Stan was off duty and a customer that chose not to take action because his wife asked him not to. Stan followed the orders of the criminals and died when one of the holdup men shot him when Stan's badge was found in his wallet.

There's one more that I would like to add to this dedication, a man who I worked with and greatly admired. His name is Richard Dungy who retired as Detroit's Deputy Chief after serving twenty-five years. He died in September of 2015.

Requiescat In Pace.

Prologue:

In the 1960's Detroit Michigan had a population of approximately 1.5 million people. Their police force numbered around 5200 men and women. This is the story of one of the officers that served on that department. He was no super-hero, just a man who loved being a police officer. The time he served spanned the 1967 Detroit Riot, a trying time in that man's life and the city's history.

This book is based on actual incidents occurring during the 1960s. Names and places have been changed with the exception of that of Richard Dungy, a close friend.

This book does contain street language and street jargon, not intended to offend or alienate the reader, but to depict the reality in the day-to-day life of a police officer.

Chapter 1

Jake was assigned Beat 22—Joseph Campau from Conant to the City of Hamtramck boarder on the afternoon shift, May 21, 1962.

It was dark by the time he finished four rounds on his beat. He had walked the front side of the businesses, tugging at door handles and making sure they were all secured.

Now, he was in his favorite place—the alley. The moonlight glistened off of the shards of glass, the resident jewels on the concrete-paved alley running on the east side of Joseph Campau. The soles of his brogans crunched as he walked. His toe accidentally kicked a can. When it stopped rolling, Jake's flashlight beam caught the label: *DelMonte Peaches*.

The night was warm. Jake crossed Burnside and checked the back of the abandoned TV repair shop. It had plywood nailed over the rear door and window. He walked a few more steps, looking through the bars on the back door of Bill's Barber Shop. The three empty pump-up barber chairs were silhouetted against the faint light filtering in from the street. The owner always fastened the back door with two padlocks. Jake's nightstick dangled loosely from his right wrist, twisting on its leather thong as he pulled on the locks. He walked a few more steps edging around three garbage cans and tugged at the back door of Ziggy's Market.

"Umph."

What was that?

The noise was a guttural sound. It scared him. He froze, straining to hear more. Someone was in the alley with him; somewhere within earshot. He turned, slowly scanning all that he could see in the dark. A power pole was six feet to his right. Across the alley, he made out the fence surrounding the backyard of the home facing Burnside. Jake felt that the noise came from beyond the power pole to the south of him. To his left front, another alley teed off, running between Burnside and McPherson. His eyes slowly panned the area from where the sound came from;

1

pausing to make sure it was a garbage can he saw in the night. Twenty feet up the alley was the back door of the Seven-Eleven Bar. *No, the sound didn't come from there. Maybe from just beyond?* But he wasn't sure. His mind raced. *A muffled voice? Maybe. But where?*

His eyes backed up; covering everything he could distinguish between the direction of the sound and the pole next to him. Again his night-eyes searched past the dim light bulb that barely illuminated the back entrance of the bar. Further down the alley the back of the Sunoco Station looked quiet. The old stake truck that was always parked blocking its back door was in place. *Maybe a rat? No, it wasn't a rat,* he convinced himself. *Maybe if I take a step or two? Wait!* He tried shutting his mind off.

Headlights and the sound of an engine pierced the night. It was a car turning into the alley from behind, heading toward the officer. He pressed himself against the building, keeping his badge toward the wall. The car turned left into the alley heading east, went down four houses and stopped. The driver got out, rolled open the garage door to the side, got back in the car and drove in. The door rolled closed.

In seconds Jake heard the man-door on the garage close. Silence returned. He stood still. *Shit! Whatever I heard, kiss it good-bye.* He relaxed, wondering if his mind was playing tricks on him. His heartbeat returned to normal.

Jake took a couple of steps and leaned against the power pole, staring into the darkness. His night eyes caught sight of movement. He was sure a head bobbed above the stakes on the bed of the old truck, then back out of sight.

Jake searched his memory, trying to visualize the truck he had seen a dozen times in daylight. It was an early 50s red Ford ton and a half with a stake bed. Frank Burns, the owner of the gas station, kept old tires in it. The truck was parked parallel to the back of the station using it as a barricade to the rear door and most of the rear windows, a deterrence to would-be burglars.

2

Jake worked his way toward the truck, trying not to let loose stones or broken glass crunch under his feet.

Questions were rushing through his mind. *What would anyone be doing in the back of that truck? Stealing worn-out tires?* Time and again, Herbie White told the class at the Police Academy: "Crime isn't always obvious. Sometimes it's an out of place noise, a movement, something that just doesn't fit. Be nosy. Earn your pay."

At the front of the truck Jake pressed against the wall of the gas station. He strained, listening. He heard some movement in the bed of the truck, he drew his revolver as he slowly, he tip-toed to the back of the truck. He turned to face whatever was in its bed while flicking on his flashlight.

The beam exposed the face of a boy turning to look over his shoulder into the light. Sweat rolled off of his forehead, the beads glistening on his dark skin. "Police...Freeze," yelled Jake. Underneath the boy was a skinny, shaking, wide-eyed girl. She began to cry. Another order followed: "Get up, slowly. Keep your hands where I can see them."

****

On January 8, 1962, a forty-some-year-old police officer walked amongst the classroom filled with casually dressed men and women. His dark, wavy hair was parted on the left. The navy blue shirt he wore was neatly pressed. The three vertical military creases ironed into the back of the shirt were straight and sharp. The Sam Browne rig he wore was spit shined including the holster he wore in cross draw fashion. The matching navy blue trousers showed not a wrinkle ending crisply at the black shoes reflecting the overhead lights. The embroidered gold bars on his left shirtsleeve just above the cuff indicated twenty-plus years of service. The silver badge over his left breast bore the numbers seven four seven. The officer stopped halfway down the second row looking at the silent class.

"What's your name recruit?" he barked.

3

"Bush. John Anthony Bush, Sir."

"You can cut the 'sir' shit, kid. You're not in the Army."

"I was a Marine, sir."

"And I supposed that you can give me fifty push-ups, Mr. Ex-Marine?"

"Probably a hundred."

"Bullshit."

The officer turned toward the rest of the class. "How many ex-Marines have we got in here?" Eighteen hands went up out of the forty-eight men and two women in the Detroit Police Academy class of January 1962. He thought for a minute; then continued walking between every row in the class. "Must be my lucky day. Over a third of the class are jarheads."

With a wry smile he shook his head and walked among the desks in the classroom. "Let's get to back to business. I'm Patrolman Herbert White. You'll be looking at my handsome face for the next thirteen weeks here at the academy. While others will try to drill some basics into your head on criminal law, the code of ethics and such, my main job is to try and let some of my twenty two years of street work rub off on you." He reached the front of the class and stopped pacing. "So you don't get your ass killed." He smiled. "Better yet, to keep you and your partner from getting killed." Patrolman White started moving again. "Oh, and by the way, I do run the self defense and the physical training classes." He stopped in front of Bush's desk, smiling. "And I will see if this Marine can in fact do a hundred push ups. Right, Mister Bush?"

John Anthony Bush was a skinny 168 pound five foot eleven inch recruit. For sure, not an imposing figure for a future police officer. He was born in Detroit; two generations removed from Poland. His father, Ted, changed the last name from Buszewski to Americanize it. "So it would be pronounced right."

Jake, as he liked to be called, was raised in a strict home where, krauts were Germans, nips were Japanese, Italians were

4

whops or dagos —depending on what Ted Bush wanted to call them that day—and blacks were niggers.

Jake's dad never finished the 9th grade and he never remembered his mom and dad not working as he grew up. Ted worked in a tubing factory and his mom worked there too. By the time Jake got into high school, his mom's job was eliminated and she never went looking for another job

A brother and two sisters made up the rest of the family. They all had their household chores and they had to be done or a belt across the ass was the first warning. Sometimes mom preferred using an ironing cord, or a broom; whatever was handy. Dad was always called on for the heavier punishment. Home was not the quietest place. Jake's mom and dad fought a lot.

A Catholic education gave Jake further training on doing what was told. The nuns at Ascension parochial school in Baseline Township, before it became the city of Warren, did not spare the rod. The priests of Notre Dame High School in Harper Woods did not need a rod. A student did not question the authority of a Marist Father more than once. Father Boulanger—all five foot two of him—showed one six foot three Allen Davis the quick way to the floor one occasion. Lesson learned. No more sass. No more questions. The fathers were respected; some feared. All of Jake's school years were spent with other white kids.

Jake worked from his sophomore year on, slinging pizza at Tina's, working at J&J's Sporting Goods, or washing dishes at Ciro's Restaurant. At Ciro's Jake worked side by side with Sims and Sonny, one an ex-boxer and the other a seventy-year-old grandfather. Both were black. Jake liked them.

The last two summers before graduating Jake worked two jobs. If he wanted a car, he had to buy it. If he wanted it to keep running, it came out of his pay. There were no free rides in the Bush household.

Jake's jobs meant no real time for sports. Oh, a bit of football at the local park or a hockey game at Hielmann Field could be worked in, but no organized going out for the team at school stuff.

Work also meant no beer parties with the boys and very few dates. The fights Jake had growing up were mainly with his younger brother, Dave. So, he was not born and raised on the streets. He was just an average kid with average grades from an average home.

Hank, a friend growing up across the street, was planning to go into the Army the summer he and Jake graduated. "Wanna go in on the 'Buddy Plan', Jake?" asked Hank.

"I was in the Boy Scouts once and didn't like Mr. O'Danny's oatmeal. I'm joining the Marines."

Ted Bush laughed and said Jake did not have enough guts to join the Marines. That made him more determined. On June 18, 1958, Jake was sworn into the United States Marine Corps. That same night a train had him on his way to Marine Corps Recruit Depot, San Diego, California. Between twelve weeks of boot camp and four additional weeks of Advance Infantry Training at Camp Pendleton, Jake learned how to fight the Marine Corps way. That is: kick ass, or get your ass kicked. Jake lost as many fights as he won.

After two weeks leave, Jake reported to Naval Air Station Moffett Field located in the bay area of California. He was a member of the Marine Barracks in the Marine Guard Company. The Marines didn't call them MP's, but that is what they were. This was Jake's introduction to law enforcement.

A Marine Guard on a naval air station meant instant authority along with a colt forty-five automatic in the hands of men as young as seventeen. Some marines, no doubt, were too young. In the first six months Jake was at the base, two on-duty marine guards were shot by other marines. They were playing fast draw with their pistols. Both the shooter and the wounded marine spent time in the brig.

Six months later another young marine shot up the main gate. No one got hit. One private named Shannon was looking for a discharge. He got jail time. Jake was a witness to this one and learned to duck and dive as one round from a Colt .45 missed the Corporal of the Guard by less than a foot. Jake heard three other shots as he hit the ground inside a temporary plywood shack. Splinters were raining down on him and he chambered a round into his own .45.

"Shannon, you bastard..." Jake remembered yelling as the marine ran into the night with him and another marine guard after him. Shannon was arrested in Mountainview, California, by the local police.

Months later, the four-man crew on the main gate was arrested for being drunk on duty. Jake was under house arrest for two days until fingerprints on a broken gallon jug of burgundy wine and twenty-four empty Schlitz cans proved that at least one Polack from Detroit did not drink. The other three marines went to the brig.

Even though he was just a PFC, Jake became the NCO in charge of the gate. Jake's new crew were all privates, black, and fresh from boot camp. Their names were Sweets, Miller and Davis. To them Jake was the "Roos-key". Nicknamed by Miller who thought Jake was Russian. To Jake, they were his work mates, his fellow marines and in time, his friends.

The Marines had American Indians, Japanese Americans, Hispanics and every kind of WASP from every corner of the U.S. Jake didn't even want to think of what his dad might have called any of his fellow Marines.

Later in his Marine Corps career, a burglary arrest at the base golf course clubhouse cemented Jake's future direction. Jake wanted to be a cop and planned his life with this goal in mind.

Jake married a girl he met as she was going through his gate. Her name was Anne. Her father was in the Navy. At age nineteen Jake became a father. A few months after Deborah was born Jake landed a straight day job in the Marines. He was the Motor Transport NCO and shortly later became the father of a second daughter, Michelle. The new job allowed him to attend Foothill Junior College part time as he took every correspondence course that had a law enforcement slant to it.

The last year as a Marine Jake spent two hours every other day in the base weight room. He was determined. He also started applying to police departments; first to Los Angeles, then San Francisco and lastly Detroit.

Los Angeles and San Francisco sent their entrance exams to the Marine Barracks. A Major, James Burns, second in command of the Marine detachment, administered them. The two tests were passed. The City of Detroit sent a letter to Jake that briefly said: to pursue a career as a police officer in Detroit, he would have to apply there in person upon his discharge. Los Angeles wanted Jake and San Francisco put him on a waiting list. Jake opted to return home to Detroit and try there.

On June 17, 1961 Jake was honorably discharged from the marines. He, his wife and two daughters, one and a half and six months old, drove to Detroit. On June 21st he was filling out an application for the Detroit Police Department. Written tests, physical agility tests, then a physical exam followed.

Police department investigators interviewed old neighbors and school administrators. The background investigations took forever. In the meantime Jake picked up a job as a bartender at the restaurant he worked at prior to joining the Marines while he waited.

An envelope with the Detroit Police letterhead finally arrived in mid-November. The letter was to the point. It directed John Anthony Bush to report to the Detroit Police Academy located at 100 Clinton at 8 a.m. on January 8, 1962.

Jake showed his dad the letter. Ted Bush may have been proud of his son, but never showed it.

"I heard that they give out a trophy to the best shot at the Academy. Bet you twenty bucks you can't win it."

"I learned in the Marines that I'm just an average shot with a pistol," Jake answered. "But if they give one for the best grades. I'd bet on that."

The thirteen weeks of training passed quickly. And yes, Jake did get the opportunity to do his one hundred push-ups for Officer Herbie White. The graduation from the academy was held at the Detroit Fine Arts Building auditorium on March 16, 1962. At 1:00 p.m. diplomas, badges and assignments were handed out.

Jake ended up second in the scholastic standings. He lost the $20 bet with his dad. Ted wouldn't take the money. He bought Jake a slapjack as a graduation present. "Here's something to even the odds in a fight." Ted may have been too tough for hugs, but the tear in his eye told Jake he was proud of the son in blue wearing badge number Two-Four-Four-One.

Jake Bush, Frank Prudent and Elmer Lambroux were assigned to The Eleventh Precinct from the January class. They were now officially a part of a department of fifty two hundred men and women police officers in the City of Detroit.

Graduating officers were ordered to report to their assigned precincts after the afternoon ceremony. Frank, Elmer and Jake planned to meet in the Eleventh Precinct parking lot. As Jake drove into the lot behind the precinct, he looked over his assignment. It was an early 1900 vintage concrete two-story building located at the southeast corner of Conant and Davison.

Officers Lambroux, Bush and Prudent walked into the garage just off of the parking lot in the back of the station house. Their orders were to report to Inspector Harlan Brushaber.

The two overhead garage doors were open. Inside a silver 1960 Plymouth idled with the driver's door open. Each side of the car had a large, sweeping wing painted on it with "Detroit Police" stenciled under the wing, both painted dark blue to contrast with

9

the silver. A red bubble light sat atop the car. The radio could be heard calling out car numbers with locations and short messages.

An officer with a cigar in the corner of his mouth came out of a door as the three entered the garage. The cop pulled the cigar out from his mouth and yelled over his shoulder to the door ajar behind him. "Hey Dick, come look at the new uniforms Herbie White sent us. Damn they get smaller all the time. Bet not one weighs a hundred seventy-five."

From behind the door appeared another officer with his hat on the back of his head and a clipboard in his hand. "New guys reporting in?" He saw the nods. "Welcome aboard. Dick Van Harron here. The cigar with a mouth is Larry. Larry Horvath." The three rookies shook hands with the two officers as the radio sounded.

A radio message blasted out, "Eleven-Four, meet a man Seven Mile and Van Dyke. Property damage hit and run."

"That's us. Gotta go," the cigar smoker said as he jumped in behind the wheel.

"Can you tell us where to find Inspector Brushaber," Prudent asked as Van Harron climbed in the passenger side.

"Right through that door. See the Sergeant." The car tires screeched as Horvath hit the gas.

The three went through the door Van Harron motioned to and walked down a short passageway that opened up into a high ceiling room. To their left was an elevated four-foot high dark mahogany desk. It ran nearly the full width of the room. There was a four-foot opening at each end. The off-white plaster wall behind the desk was twenty feet high. An eight by six foot map of the Eleventh Precinct with the scout car territories outlined was centered on the wall behind the desk. At the end of the desk, on the right, stood the American flag while to the left, the State of Michigan flag.

A bald officer wearing glasses shuffled papers on the left side of the desk. In the center sat another officer with sergeant stripes on both arms, and glasses on the end of his nose, making notes on papers in front of him. Standing behind the sergeant leafing through a binder was a tall, slender officer in a white shirt with gold lieutenant's bars on his collar. He was referring to the map on the wall from information in the binder. To the far right, a young man in a light blue shirt worked a switchboard. The patch on his shirt read, *Police Cadet*. Bush, Lambroux and Prudent stopped in front of the sergeant, removing their hats.

"Excuse me," Lambroux said. The sergeant looked up, his right hand pushing his glasses higher on his nose.

"Our new officers, right?" the sergeant asked as he leaned back in his chair.

"Yes sir." Lambroux added, "We're supposed to report to Inspector Brushaber."

The sergeant turned toward the cadet at the switchboard. "Ring the inspector, Bill. Tell him the new guys are here." He turned back to the three, motioning with his head. "The door just past the cadet."

Inspector Brushaber was hanging up his phone as the three new officers approached his open door. He stood from behind his desk and took two steps around it. The inspector had a starched white shirt with a metal gold oak leaf on each collar. He wore a dark navy blue tie that stopped precisely above his belt buckle. The badge over his left breast was a smaller gold shield.

"Come on in, men. I'm Inspector Harlan Brushaber." He extended his hand, shaking with each officer as they officers lined up in front of the desk.

"Frank Prudent, sir."

"Elmer Lambroux, sir."

"John Bush, sir."

The Inspector motioned the men to sit as he walked behind his desk. He remained standing, all six foot two of him. Jake's eyes scanned the room. The office had two large windows. One behind the desk faced west toward Conant. The other was facing north.

Brushaber walked to the north window staring out to the traffic on Davison. He watched a few cars go by. When he turned, he came to a rigid parade rest with his hands clasped behind his back. The silence made the seconds drag.

Jake was thinking, *He either has a board stuck up his ass or was a drill instructor.* Jake gave the inspector another good look, and then decided the inspector was no doubt *a sea going bellhop*—what they call a Marine stationed aboard ship. From top to bottom, not a hair was out of place, not a wrinkle was in his shirt nor in the navy blue trousers. He had a small spit-shined holster worn on his right hip. It held a nickel-plated snub-nosed revolver. Jake's eyes were checking the shine on the Inspector's shoes when he spoke.

"I'll make this short and to the point. You officers have just spent thirteen weeks at one of the finest police academies in the country. You are now a part of the Detroit Police Department. A department I have now served for over thirty years. The badges you now wear make you a part of what I think is the greatest job in the world." The inspector paused. "You represent fifty-two hundred members of this department as you wear that uniform." The inspector walked to the rear of his desk. "Remember this—if you tarnish the badge you're wearing, you tarnish me and every other officer on the department. Keep this uppermost in your minds as you start your new careers." The Inspector slowly looked into the eyes of each young officer before him. "Keep something else in mind—you're on probation. The sergeants and lieutenants will send me a monthly report on your progress and work ethic for your first year. Any misstep and I'll guarantee that your career will be a short one." The Inspector paused again. The three young officers noted the stern look on his face as he let his last sentence sink in. "Any questions?"

Heads bobbed, the three officers looked at each other. "No sir," Prudent answered for the group.

"Good. See the lieutenant at the desk for your shift assignments." The officers stood, thanked the Inspector and exited, closing the officer door behind them.

They took a deep breath and went to the front desk. The lieutenant turned away from the map, looking at the three as they approached. "I'm Lieutenant Robertson. This is Sergeant Fitzmaurice and that's Jim Bollis, the clerk." A brief exchange of hellos followed. The lieutenant continued. "Take a minute to relax. The Inspector's speech is probably close to the one I heard when I reported in three years ago." He smiled. "The boss likes to let you know that he is in charge." He put down his binder and took a sip on a cup of coffee. "Which one of you is Bush?"

"Here sir," Jake replied, shaking the hand the lieutenant was offering.

"You are on my shift, afternoons."

"Prudent?"

"Frank Prudent, sir." Frank stepped forward. "You're on nights working for Lieutenant Jines." He looked at the remaining officer. "You must be Lambroux. Days, Lieutenant Ruggles' shift. Roll call for all shifts is fifteen minutes to the hour. Prudent, your shift starts Sunday night at midnight. Lambroux and Bush, you start on Monday. Any questions?" He turned to the sergeant. "Fitz, would you show the men their new home?"

"Sure." The sergeant stood and walked around the desk. "Anyone interested in a coffee? It's there in the corner," his head nodding toward a coffee pot. "Grab one and follow me for a quick tour." He pushed his way through the double doors on the opposite side of the room from the desk. The three rookies passed on the coffee and followed in to what turned out to be the squad room. "This is where we hold roll call."

The fifteen-minute tour of the station that included the holding cells through a door behind the desk and the detective offices upstairs. There was a pistol range in the basement.

The tour was wasted on Jake as his mind was drifting off counting the hours until his first shift. As he made it to the parking lot he looked at his watch and calculated.

68 hours until Monday, 3:45 p.m. He climbed into his '55 Ford and headed home.

13

Chapter 2

On Monday March 19, 1962 at 3:00 p.m. sharp John Anthony Bush entered the squad room of the Eleventh Precinct. He grabbed a hanger and hung his winter dark blue coat on the long, empty rack in the back of the room. He adjusted the newly issued Colt, six inch, nickel-plated .38 caliber pistol in its holster. He wore it in cross draw fashion; the holster glistening with a good Marine Corps spit shine. He wandered around the empty room. A Ping-Pong table took up the north side of the room that paralleled Davison. The four eight foot high windows let in some light to the room. He found the switch and turned on the overhead fluorescent lights to completely illuminate the room. Jake walked to the Teletype machine in the corner, reading the latest messages on the six feet of paper hanging off of the top of the machine. The last two were on missing persons, one from the Eleventh Precinct, and the other from Number Twelve. Three other teletypes were on robberies in Number Six, Ten and Seven. A bell rang and the paper started moving; a message was coming in. While the latest was being typed out, Jake picked up the binder labeled "Information Circulars," seeing that the more current ones were to the front.

Another officer entered the room, threw his coat over a chair and tore off the long paper on the Teletype machine. He used a paper cutter to separate each message as he read them. Jake looked up, catching the officer looking at him.

"Bush is that you?"

Jake looked more closely. "Malone? Bob Malone? What the hell are you doing here?"

"From the looks of the uniforms, I'd say the same thing as you." Bob reached out to shake Jake's hand. "It think the last time I saw you was graduation day at Marine Corps Recruit Depot, San Diego. What was it, September, 1958?"

"How long've you been at Number Eleven?" Jake asked.

"Three years next month. Remember, I was only in the Corps for six months."

"Yeah. Weekend warriors Sergeant Akers called you guys."

They quickly renewed a friendship that the thirteen weeks of Marine boot camp formed. It was easy since they shared the same Quonset hut and the same squad just about three and a half years before.

Other police officers started to arrive. Card games began along with a Ping-Pong game. Bob said no to a card game choosing instead to go over the teletypes and circulars with Jake. Bob took notes in a small steno pad. Finally, he started working on his stolen car board, showing Jake how to update it. "We may be a pretty slow precinct," Bob added, "but crooks travel. Some might even live here. Remember that as you go over this stuff."

"What about the others?" Jake asked, as he looked around at the rest of the men either visiting, playing cards or playing Ping-Pong. There were four other officers now taking notes at the table.

"Usually one guy on a car will take care of the board and the teletypes. We take turns."

Promptly at 3:45, Sergeant Fitzmaurice burst through the double doors yelling, "Roll Call!" Lieutenant Robertson followed. Cards were dropped, chairs squawked and conversations subsided as all the patrolmen fell into two ranks facing the podium. "At ease," the Sergeant said as soon as semi-straight lines were formed.

The lieutenant opened a binder, resting it on the podium. "Eleven-One, Hall and Van Harren. Eleven-Two, Broadnax and Barnes. Eleven-three, Malone and Horvath..." The lieutenant continued until ten cars were assigned. He paused briefly. "John Bush, Beat 22." The two lines of officers bobbed heads, getting a look at the new officer. The lieutenant continued, "Warneke, you're Bush's partner for the night. Show him what walking a beat's about." He looked toward the sergeant. "Anything else, Sarge?"

15

"Just a couple items," the sergeant said as he opened a note pad. "Outer Drive, between Van Dyke and Seven Mile. Make yourself seen a bit more often, Eleven-Four. Complaints of drag racing between nine and ten at night. Eleven-Seven, special attention to 19877 Dearing; people on vacation for two weeks." The sergeant put the note pad into his pocket. "That's all I have, boss."

"Okay, let's hit it men." Lt. Robertson turned and left the room followed by the sergeant.

Jake knew he would have a walking beat with a partner until the bosses felt he could be on his own. Richard Warneke, the junior officer on the shift had the task of breaking in the new man. Warneke was six months out of the academy. Dick, as he liked to be called, was slightly taller than Jake with a thin face. Jake found out that Dick was assigned Beat 34 for the month, but normally filled in on a car. Even though each scout car had three men assigned with one man normally off, a car was a man short when someone called in sick or took vacation.

There were a total of thirty-five walking beats listed for the precinct. Only five were walked on a regular basis and then only when all ten cars were manned. Seniority got you assigned to a car. With no seniority Jake knew he would walk for a while.

"Hey Barnes, can you give us a ride to our beat?" Dick shouted out to the group of officers heading toward their cars."

On the way out, Dick showed Jake the map over the back of the main desk. The precinct was outlined in black on the map that included Highland Park and Hamtramck. "Our precinct covers close to twelve square miles." Jake could see that Number Eleven was bounded by the City of Warren on the north side of Eight Mile Road, the Twelfth Precinct to the west starting at the Chrysler Freeway, the City of Hamtramck to the south and the Fifteen Precinct to the East, just below Van Dyke. Warneke added, "The ethnic make up is about 40% Polish, 40% Black, 15% Italian and the rest of every other claim to fame."

While walking the various beats Jake found out that Number Eleven, along with the Twelfth, Fourteenth, Fifteenth and Sixteenth Precinct were inhabited by the more affluent or working class citizens of the City of Detroit. Their crime rates were low. They were good pre-retirement precincts. Not really what Jake wanted.

It was Jake's eighth day on the job. There was a cold drizzle falling; not a good night to walk a beat thought Jake as he stood for roll call. He just about had the names and the car assignments down pat in his mind when he heard the Lieutenant call out, "Eleven-One, Hall and Bush. Eleven-Two, Broadnax and Barnes..." The rest of the assignments faded as Jake realized he was on a car.

Finally!!! Who's Hall?

Patrolman John Hall greeted Jake with a big smile after roll call. "You won't mind riding over walking in the rain, would you?" Jake just laughed in response and followed John to their car.

Eleven-One was a Plymouth station wagon that had two folding stretchers behind the rear seat. John went over the car's equipment so Jake would know where the switch for the siren and flashing red light were. "The radio's the big thing. But you'll catch on as we go. Normally, we split the shit behind the wheel. The man in the jump seat handles the radio, does the log sheet and handles the reports. The best way to learn the territory is to drive. If you want you can drive all night."

"I know how to type if we have any reports," Jake answered.

"Good, then you can do both jobs."

Number Eleven had ten cars assigned to specific areas. Five were station wagons that doubled as ambulances. The rest were two-door sedans. Eleven-One's territory took in the northwest corner of the precinct. Jake followed Hall's instructions on getting to their territory. The Eight Mile Road boarder to the north was easy. Jake was raised just off of that road only to the east in the Fifteenth Precinct.

Jake cruised the outer perimeter of their area with John pointing out the important business places on Dequindre, Mound, Seven and Eight Mile Roads. "If the radio is quiet, we normally find a light to sit on, write a ticket or two then cruise the main streets. On midnights we check the alleys behind the businesses, but there's no routine."

"Any hold ups in the area lately," Jake asked.

John Hall thought for a moment. "Before Christmas, we had one at the Top Hat at Van Dyke and Eight Mile. I think that's the last one close to our territory. Dick, my regular partner, and I were right on it." He chuckled a bit. "Spent the next few hours looking for someone that the night manager described. Turns out it was a phony. The guy made it up. Guess he needed some extra money for the holidays." John showed Jake where to park to watch a light at Mound and Eight Mile. "Time to get you your first mover, Jake."

Ten minutes of silence and watching cars come and go passed when the radio sounded. "Eleven-One, see the man at 20230 Caldwell on a barking dog. Five-Two, Jefferson and Seminole, see the woman on a purse snatching."

"Eleven-One on the way," John Hall acknowledged into the mic. He gave Jake directions to Caldwell just off of Eight Mile and their barking dog.

The radio sounded again, "All cars and Thirteen-Cruiser, This is information on a car used in a robbery armed in Number Thirteen. A black Buick, License, Mary Boy one-zero-two-two. Last seen heading west on Alexandrine from the scene. Two white male subjects armed with revolvers."

Jake had a short course at the academy on the radio system in Detroit. There were three frequencies. East Side Dispatch covered the 5th, 7th, 11th and 15th Precincts. Central Dispatch covered the 1st, 2nd, 10th and the 13th. West Side Dispatch took care of the 4th, 6th, 12th, 14th and 16th Precincts. The calls Number Eleven normally heard were just for their side of town. Chases and hot runs could be broadcast citywide. The dispatchers worked out of Police Headquarters. They took the incoming phone calls and dispatched the radio cars. There were usually two to three dispatchers for each radio frequency. When the cars acknowledged receiving the call, they answered to radio operators that were in different locations than the dispatchers. The radio operators kept written and audio taped records of all radio traffic in case they were needed in court.

Eleven-One's radio blasted, "Radio to all cars. Thirteen-Six is in a chase. Thirteen-Six, what is your location?"

A scout car siren could be heard in the background along with screeching tires, "...heading north on Woodward, just crossing West Grand Boulevard. In pursuit of a black Buick, license Mary Boy one-zero-two- two."

"Thirteen-Six and all units, this vehicle was involved in a robbery armed..."

Squealing tires and sirens were heard over the radio transmission. "They just turned east on Holbrook. They're blowing every light."

"Thirteen-Three is at Chrysler and Holbrook."

"Thirteen-Cruiser is approaching Oakland and Holbrook."

"They're spinning out." Gunshots were heard over the radio. Then silence.

Jake and John sat in their car. Jake's heart was pounding as he listened for more. Eleven-One was four miles away as the crow flies, and for sure not paying attention to their barking dog run.

"Ever get in a chase, John?" Jake asked as his racing heart settled down.

"Once. Some speeder thought he could outrun the radio. He didn't."

The radio came alive again. "Attention all units. Suspects in the hold up in Number Thirteen have been apprehended. Thirteen-Six, Thirteen-Seven-Oh is on the way along with a tow truck."

Jake looked at John. "Ever work in Number Thirteen?"

"No. I kinda like it quiet. Been here at Eleven since the academy...Twelve years. I'll take our five or six hold ups a year. Don't need any more excitement, thanks."

19

John took out a blank report and penciled in "Barking Dog" in the complaint box. "Let's go see a man about a dog."

"Maybe we'll read about what went on in tomorrow's *Free Press*," said Jake as he started out of the car.

"Probably not. Sometimes they have five or six hold ups a night in Number Thirteen. It's not news."

Jake was finally walking a beat without a partner on April 1, 1962. In March a posting had gone up in the squad room asking for volunteers to work the afternoon shift. Jake put his name on it. Jake's beat assignment was 34, Van Dyke from Outer Drive to Davison. He liked that beat since it covered the place where he used to work while in high school: J&J Sporting Goods. Mr. And Mrs. Nowicki, the owners, always smiled when they would see him walk in the door.

"You grew up into a nice young man, Johnny," the Mrs. would say in her broken English every time he stopped.

Jake was relieved that he did not get Beat 35 on Seven Mile Road. That's the beat where Libby, a hundred fifty pound Mastiff, was in charge of a fenced in junk yard. Dick Warneke had told Jake to walk as quietly as possible and to the farthest side of the alley to hopefully sneak by just in case the seven foot high fence would not hold her. That didn't always work. Libby had great hearing.

The weather started getting better with a bit of sunshine finally becoming less of a rarity. It was a bright afternoon on May 3rd and Jake was walking Beat One and Two, Conant Avenue. It was the station beat. He was thinking about seeing what the men at the fire station were cooking for supper. He joined them when he could. A dollar thrown into the pot got you a seat at the table.

As he walked he saw a man sitting on a folding chair at the corner of Fleming and Conant. The man was strumming a guitar and singing. There were some people on the porches of the first houses on Fleming taking in the entertainment. A yellow Cadillac was parked just east of Ray's Party Store with the three passengers moving with the music.

The man can sing, Jake thought recognizing the Frankie Lyman song. "Do that for a living?" Jake asked as the man paused when he stopped to listen.

"Like to," the man answered, standing and folding up the chair.

"Don't stop 'cause of me," Jake quickly added. "Your neighbors seem to like what they're hearing."

"Need to take a break and check the pig anyhow."

A short conversation and a few questions later Jake found himself four houses down Fleming looking at a pig cut in two grilling on a chain link gate that had been removed and set over a hole in the middle of the back yard. The coals were glowing under the pig. Jake's new acquaintance, Willie McAdoo, was liberally adding his own "special sauce" with a one-inch paintbrush.

"Ever have real southern Negro bah-bee-que?" Willie asked.

"Can't say I have," Jake said as he dipped his finger in the bowl of sauce that Willie was offering.

"Pig's been goin' for 'bout twenty four hours now. Be ready at eight. Want to join me and the neighbors?"

At eight Jake was sitting on Willie's back porch with a plate in his hand heaped with potato salad, collard greens and a generous cut of pork. Willie was singing as his wife, Louree, was serving up the food with Coletta, the neighbor from next door. About twenty adults and children filled the yard. It was the first time Jake felt odd about being white.

Jake licked some sauce off fingers. *This beats the fire barn cooking all to hell.* The kids seemed curious about the man in uniform, but the older folks didn't seem bothered in the least. Of course it helped when the host introduced Jake as an old army buddy.

21

Chapter 3

Jake's normal shift was afternoons the month of June. Eleven-Two, manned by Barnes and Broadnax, dropped him off at the north end of Beat 22. Jake had walked the Joseph Campau beat the most of any in the precinct. The ten-block stretch once had seventy-two thriving businesses supported by the surrounding neighborhood. Now, only twenty-five were still operating. It was Sunday. He knew one gas station and the two bars would be the only places open. Jake had over seven hours of shaking doors and walking alleys in front of him, and he loved it.

The sun was shining with temperatures in the 80s as Jake, wearing a summer light blue shirt, walked to the first door to start his day. His light colored shirt and navy tie was smartly set off with his spit shined thick black belt, holster on his left in cross draw fashion and a cross strap over his right shoulder. He tugged at the locked main entrance of Globe Furniture. He continued, rattling the three doors along Joseph Campau. The building had once been a movie theater. That was when nearly every neighborhood had a corner movie house. Large plate glass windows replaced the marquees where coming attraction ads once hung. Now the windows were filled with tables, chairs, sofas and lamps for a whole city block. Jake climbed the fire escape on the south side of the building and checked the door at the top. It too was secure.

Crossing Grant, Jake headed for the one sure sign of life on his beat that day; the Clark gas station. He saw a friendly face, Levi Pierce, wearing a white shirt with red vertical pin stripes and a "Clark" emblem over the left breast pocket. Levi was singing as he wiped off the white globes that sat atop the two pumps on the ramp. He looked up as the officer approached. "Hey Jake, my man. On for the evening?"

"Yeah. I'll be around," Jake smiled as he stood to watch Levi finish wiping down the pump.

"Time for a Coke?"

"Next trip, maybe. And you know its Pepsi."

Levi laughed. He was the regular afternoon attendant. His days off changed from week to week, and sometimes he filled in on nights when someone got sick. Jake was glad to see him working. The other black attendants did not talk to cops. "See you the next time around," Jake said as a Chevy pulled onto the ramp.

Jake walked toward Dearing. The three other businesses on this block were boarded up. At Dearing, Jake could hear music blaring from across Joseph Campau behind the Krajenke Buick garage. He decided to check it out and crossed the street. The Buick service garage faced Joseph Campau, the north end starting at Dearing. The garage covered a full block. The dealership showroom and used car lot took up the next block to the south. As Jake made his way to the alley behind the garage, he noticed that the first house facing Dearing had the yard and fence decorated with maroon and white crepe paper. The Hi-Fi was cranked right up. Jerry Lee was doing "A whole lotta shaken' goin' on." Card tables and chairs were arranged throughout the yard. Three women were scurrying around, two setting food at a couple of larger tables while the third, a forty-something blond in a yellow flowered dress pumped up a keg in a washtub of ice. She spotted Jake as he turned into the alley. "Hey girls," she yelled above the music, "We have police protection tonight." She stopped pumping and walked toward the four-foot cyclone fence that bordered the yard. "You gonna come to our party tonight officer?"

"What you celebrating?" Jake asked as he got close to the fence.

"Graduation. My kid finally got outta high school. Plenty to eat and drink. Care for a beer?" She leaned on the fence making sure she showed the tits that barely fit in the top of her dress. "Gotta name, officer?"

"No, nothing for me," adding, "The name is Bush. Jake Bush."

Hey girls, come on over. Meet officer Bush. My sisters, Margie and Kate. I'm Paula." The two sisters smiled and moved toward the fence. Both were within a year or two of Paula and both dressed in their Sunday finest, definitely not church attire though. Like Paula, they were making sure a lot showed.

Margie spoke. "Bush. You Polish?" Jake nodded. "Girls, looks like we got a nice, young Polish cop on the beat tonight." She flipped open the top button of her white blouse as she talked.

Kate chimed in, "Maybe the stud in uniform we've heard about. You a stud?"

Jake started walking toward one of the back doors on the service garage with retreating steps, fumbling for words. "Gotta go check the rest of the beat. Have a… have a nice party."

"Make sure you stop back by," Paula added. "We've got plenty for you."

Jake gave a cursory tug at the closest overhead garage door as he hastened on his way. He just wanted to put the party scene and the three beauties behind him. He checked the side of the building, then the front and re-crossed Joseph Campau.

Three real beauties and me a Polish stud. That's all my pregnant wife would need to hear about. He quickened his pace.

He slowed once across the street and started checking the front doors again. The vacant shoe repair was secure. The owner died two months ago. *Still no buyers.* Jake glanced in the window. The pedal-driven leather sewing machine stood silent against the back wall. Stan, the owner, proudly showed Jake the workable antique a few months before. Jake remembered the cigarette that bobbed up and down as the man talked. Now, all that was left were the old shoes still piled where Stan last put them, tags running through the eyelet of each pair. The owners still hadn't claimed them.

"Gotta go past that yard all night," Jake mumbled to himself as he left the shoe shop and thoughts turned to the backyard party. *Drinking kids and wild women. Polish stud. Yeah, right.* For a second he felt a twinge in his loins. "Last thing I need," he mumbled as he dismissed the thought.

He kept walking. The Blackberry Bar was open. Jake stood on his tiptoes to see through the high small window on the door. Two people sat at the bar nursing beers. The bartender, clad in a stained, white apron, was leaning in the corner. A cigarette was hanging in the corner of his mouth as he watched the TV mounted above the rows of assorted whiskey bottles. Jake thought of showing his head in the door, but bars were not his kind of place. *A badge in a bar tends to send customers out the door,* he reasoned. That thought stopped Jake for a minute. *What am I afraid of?* "Gotta change that," he said under his breath and turned and stuck his head in the door. "Afternoon guys. Tigers on TV?" A grunt was all he heard from the bartender. The two at the bar never turned as they sipped on the brown bottles of Stroh's. He turned and let the door close behind him. *There. Did it.* Three months on the street and Jake was still getting used to wearing a badge.

Balls will come with time.

Jake continued checking every door and building on the east side of Joseph Campau. Just past McClean stood a vacant dress shop. The three old mannequins against the back wall were the only clues left of the store's previous business. Next-door was Bill's Barber Shop. It too was secure. Jake got to Ziggy's and rattled the door. He looked through the glass toward the meat counter in the back. A single fluorescent light was on. This was Jake's lunch stop on days and afternoons except Sundays. Ziggy was a happy-go-lucky Pole that welcomed Jake to the beat the first time they met. "Ever want a sandwich, stop in. I make the best," were the first words Jake heard from the 300-pound butcher that was shaking his hand. The sandwiches were the best too. The normal fare was a fresh onion roll, about a quarter pound of sliced meats topped with tomato, lettuce and mayo. That with a jellyroll and pop ran sixty cents. *No sandwich today.* Jake kept walking down the street.

He pulled open the screen door of the Seven-Eleven Bar. He had gotten the owner out of bed one night when he found the front door unlocked. Walter Szepanski, the owner, asked Jake to make sure he stuck his head in the door when he was on the beat. Four men were sitting at the bar watching the TV. The game was on here too. Jake saw that Al Kaline was up to bat. Walt was tending bar and waved the white bar rag, signaling everything was okay. Jake watched Kaline bat then let the screen door slam behind him.

He walked up the ramp of the Sunoco station next door. It was never open on Sundays. He checked the two overhead doors on the front, then the door to the counter area. He walked around the back to check all the windows, glancing at the red Ford stake truck that blocked the back door. He felt himself blush, remembering all too well the rape he thought he interrupted just two weeks before. It was just teenagers screwing among the old tires in the back of the truck. *Two weeks later and the guys were still laughing. Some day, that too will pass.* He hoped.

Jake crossed McPherson and walked among the sixteen cars they kept in the Rambler dealer's used car lot. The small sales office had only one door with a large window on each side of the three-step porch. Through the windows he could see two desks and matching chairs. The desks were bare except for a phone on each. The main dealership was two blocks down in Hamtramck. Jake looked at a station wagon, thinking he would need to replace his '55 Ford soon. His third child was due in November. He stopped at the light on the corner of Carpenter. When it changed, he crossed to the west side of Joseph Campau. There was a Hamtramck police car turning. The two officers inside waved. His beat and theirs met at the border of the two cities. Jake touched the bill of his cap with his nightstick, acknowledging their wave.

On the other side of the street Jake continued to rattle doors heading back to the north. They were either locked or boarded up. Some days, on rare occasions, he would find a place unlocked. It was a good way to kill time, checking for a burglar that was never there, and then waiting for the owner to come and lock up. He'd be able to claim one report on the monthly activity sheet. No arrests. It was always just a forgetful owner. At the corner of Burnside Jake checked the abandoned Polish restaurant. It went out of business the month before. *Too bad. They made a good pot of duck soup.*

Jake hated Sundays on Beat Twenty-Two. With Ziggy's closed, there wasn't a place to eat. He had to call for a car to take him somewhere, that is, after getting permission to leave his beat. *Of course, I could always go to the greasy spoon a block east of my beat.*

He put that out of his mind, remembering the bad case of the shits he got the first and last time he ate there. Levi still laughs, remembering Jake making a dead run for the men's room key that night. *Then there's that party behind Krajenke's and those forty-something year old broads...* He shook his head and said aloud, "No; bad thought Jake." *I'm not that hungry.*

The second last block on this side of Jake's beat had three more abandoned buildings and a gas station converted into "Ray Tate's Bump and Paint." The empty buildings and the doors leading to the vacant apartments upstairs were all nailed shut. Jake walked cautiously as he approached the bump shop.

Ray could leave this place unlocked.

Ray had a German shepherd that lived in the garage. Jake, as well as anyone else, gave the building a wide berth when Ray wasn't around. "Oscar" did not like people, except maybe Ray. If anyone got too close to the building, Oscar's snarling, barking and snapping fangs would remind you he was around. Those from the neighborhood even knew to stay out of that particular alley behind the bump shop. Jake remembered daydreaming one night and got the shit scared out of him as Oscar hit the alley-side overhead door windows with his blood curdling growling and barking. Jake didn't think the glass would hold the dog's vicious attack. It did. Jake was still shaking two blocks later. Oscar's territory became etched in his mind.

The Davison Elementary School took up the last block of the beat. The front of the school faced Davison. The school property was bounded by Maine to the west, Joseph Campau on the east and Grant to the south. The graveled schoolyard had a twenty-foot cyclone fence around the playground on the Joseph Campau and Grant Street side to keep the balls and the kids off of the street.

Jake entered and crossed the playground through the gate at Grant. Schools were prime targets for burglaries. For some reason the kids thrown out during the week would break in at night, or weekends. He circled the school. The tall windows ten feet above the ground were covered from top to bottom with heavy cyclone fencing; some to keep the balls from breaking them, the rest to keep people out. The second floor had the fencing just on the playground side. His check this round assured him the school was secure.

Jake cut back across Joseph Campau heading for the Clark station and a break with Levi. "What's happening, man?" Levi asked as he pulled a Pepsi from the cooler. Levi grabbed a Coke for himself; motioning with the bottles, "Let's go out on the ramp. Gotta couple of pop cases we can sit on."

Jake grabbed the bottle Levi offered looking around at the close quarters inside the gas station building, "Good idea. It's nice out tonight."

Levi took a pull on his Coke as he positioned the wooden case under him. "What's goin' on behind the Buick garage?

"Krajenke's?"

"Never could pronounce that name. Saw you hot footin' over there the las' round."

"Some woman and her sisters are putting on a graduation party for her kid. Guess it's an open house. Mom was pumping up a keg of beer."

"Mama serving up the beer. Hm, hm, hm. Doesn't surprise me none. First house on the left off'n the alley?"

"Yeah. No kids there yet." Jake took a swallow of his pop. "You know the family?"

"Just know of them. Her ol' man is in Jacktown, serving five to fifteen for a couple of stick ups."

"Thought I'd steer clear of the place. Ma and her two sister's sounded like they were pretty well on their way and already flashing too much tit for me."

"Hell man, handle the pumps and give me that badge. I'll do party patrol for you." Levi flashed a toothy grin as he tipped his Coke. "Never say no to some tits I say."

Jake stood and finished his drink. He offered a quarter to Levi. Levi shook his head as he grabbed the empty bottle. "This one's on me. Besides, I like the company. One of these days when someone has a gun stuck in my face, I'm hopin' you sneak outta the alley like I see you doin' all the time."

"Thanks. I'd better be getting back to them alleys." Jake walked around the building and disappeared. He popped back out when he got to Meade. Jake unlocked the blue box and put the phone to his ear, pulling the lever inside. When the cadet answered, Jake said, "Beat 22, Badge 2441." This beat pulled in the last quarter of the hour. He returned to the alleys. Jake avoided the party for the next couple of hours, staying out on Joseph Campau.

It was after nine and getting dark when Jake checked the school again. He reversed his route, slipping into the alley behind Ray's and headed toward Krajenke's. He stayed to the far side of the alley so Oscar didn't hear his footfalls as he tiptoed past. The party was in full swing as he started checking the overhead doors on the Buick garage. A voice rang out from behind. "Remember me, honey?" He turned and there was Paula in the yellow flowered dress. "Thought you were going to stop and visit?"

"Can't right now. Got the rest of the alleys to check."

"Better stop next time. Least you can do is be sociable." She smiled, raised her drink in a mock toast and turned walking back to a group of kids surrounding the beer keg. She put a little extra shake in her ass.

Jake quickly turned around the corner of the building and out to the main street. He checked the side door of the garage as his mind was working overtime. She was teasing and Jake knew it. His male ego liked it, and didn't. *Drunken women and yard parties were not covered at the police academy.*

29

Truth be known, this Detroit born, ex-marine had to ask during a class what a Blind Pig was. When the rest of the class laughed, he knew he had led a sheltered life. A classmate, Dick Norman, whispered that it was an after-hours illegal drinking establishment. Of course, Dick's father was a lieutenant at the Twelfth Precinct. Jake's father was a factory worker at Bundy Tubing and did most of his drinking at Lefty's Bar or at home. How was he to know?

Jake normally preferred to stay in alleys when he walked a beat. The object of walking a beat, according to Herbie White, was to let people know you were out there, thus hold down crime. Jake's theory was to stay in alleys and catch a bad guy who didn't know you were out there. Today he was following Herbie's advice so he could stay away from the party as much as possible. Jake walked facing traffic. That is the way all beats were to be walked, according to Herbie, so you could see the cars coming at you. Maybe spot something suspicious, or, to cover your backside. As Herbie put it, "Who knows how pissed some guy might be after you just hung a parking ticket on his car. He just might want to jump your ass over it."

At Meade Jake crossed Jos Campau to make another pull. There was one call box on a beat, the walking cop's contact with the station. Whenever you pulled the lever inside the locked call box, a bell would ring on the precinct switchboard as well as having the call box number punched out on a paper tape. Conversations were short, the cadet normally answering, "Number Eleven."

Jake gave his beat and badge number, hung up and slammed the call box door. If a beat officer failed to make his pull during the assigned quarter hour, a car would be sent to check on him. Of course, the cadet, trying to be a pal would generally give the officer an extra fifteen minutes before sending a car to check. That might be all right if the beat cop just lost track of time. It wouldn't be if somebody were playing tug-o-war with the officer over his gun. In 1962 hand held radios were still on the drawing board.

It was near ten when Jake was due to check the back of Krajenke's again. The three sisters were sitting around a card table with a couple of paper cups in front of each of them. About twenty high school age kids mingled around, closer to the house, some talking, some dancing. Jake tried to look busy as he passed, looking at the overhead doors to make sure all the glass windows were still intact. "Hey girls, our sweet, young police officer is back." Jake recognized the voice. "Time for a drink honey, and no excuses this time."

Jake acknowledged the woman in the flowered dress. "How's the party going?" His own words, *Balls and boldness,* crossed his mind.

"Kate, get the man a drink. What'll it be, honey?" Paula said as she walked toward the fence.

"Nothing, thanks."

"At least a pop." She paused, adding, "Forgot you're on duty."

"Got a Pepsi or root beer?" Paula opened the gate, stumbling in her high heels as she reached for it. "Damn shoes," she kicked off the white heels as she opened the gate. "Come on in. Did I introduce my sisters?"

"Yes, you did, earlier." He hesitated just inside the gate. Kate showed up with a Faygo Root Beer. The party never missed a beat even with a uniform in the yard. The kids still hung out near the keg on ice. Jake grabbed a folding chair and sat next to the fence as he took the offered bottle. The sisters gathered around, pulling chairs closer. Jake eyed them up, one at a time. Paula for sure was past forty with Kate maybe a year younger. Margie looked about thirty-five. Kate stood quietly off to the side as Margie and Paula started throwing questions at Jake. It was small talk that Jake wasn't paying too much attention to as his eyes scanned the yard. He just grunted an "Uh-uh" a time or two when they waited for a reply.

As Jake was thinking that this was not where he wanted to be with the kids more concerned with the keg than a uniform, Kate blurted out, "You one of those cops that can fuck all night?"

Paula chimed in, "Bet he's not one to leave a woman wanting…"

Jake stood as Margie added with a giggle, "I'd sure bet he's one of them Polacks that can pour the kielbasa to you."

Her words faded in the background as he caught a glimpse of movement to his far right. He saw a dark figure running off of Dearing and down the alley toward Ray's Bump Shop. Without a word, Jake leap-frogged the fence, not knowing what he was running after. The party, the music and the women's voices where quickly in the background as he started closing in on the running figure. Oscar hit the door on the back of Ray's with high-pitched yaps, barks, snarls, and growls. The running figure stumbled to the left as if trying to avoid the charge of a dog he couldn't see. Jake was gaining and less than twenty yards behind when Oscar sounded off as he passed Ray's back door.

"Police! Halt!" Jake yelled over the noise. The man looked over his left shoulder, dropping something from his right hand. He went into high gear. The alley dipped slightly, then rose to the crown of the cross street. The runner failed to make the quick ups and downs stumbling, and then tripping over the curb. He fell into the base of the twenty-foot cyclone fence at the school Jake dove on the fallen figure, rolling as the man tried to get up. Jake forced the man's head against the sidewalk and got the right arm twisted behind, pinning the man for a brief moment. He grabbed his handcuffs, cuffing the arm he had twisted in front of him. A sharp pain erupted in Jake's left thigh. Teeth tore through Jake's trousers as the man bit into solid meat. A siren was faintly heard in the background as he slammed the cuffed arm as far as he could in an upward motion. Jake pushed with all he could muster, leveraging with his right leg. On Jake's second thrust the teeth let go with the man's face skidding on the concrete and stopped by the bottom of the cyclone fence. The man went limp. Jake finished applying the handcuffs and dragged him to his feet.

"I think you dropped something back there. Let's go see what it was."

"I ain't dropped nothin'," the muscular, black male answered, as he spit out a piece of dark blue trouser material. Fifteen feet away in the middle of Grant Street lay a patent leather purse. Jake picked it up by the broken strap as he passed keeping a tight grip on the handcuffs. "Hey, I ain't never seen that before. You ain't hanging that on me…"

"Just shut up. Time to see where you came from." A scout car with its red light flashing and siren waning passed the corner as Jake was leading his prisoner back onto Joseph Campau.

At the front of the Buick garage Jake saw Barnes and Broadnax getting out of Eleven-Two. Sitting on the sidewalk was a woman reaching out to the officers as they approached. Barnes and Broadnax started lifting what appeared to be a seventy-year-old black woman to her feet. Her dress was torn and her knees were bloody. Jake heard her crying, "Mah purse. Someone got mah purse…"

From the left Jake saw Levi running across the street toward the police car. Levi slowed when he saw Jake. "Cool man. You got the asshole." Levi flashed broad smile. "That's him. The one who grabbed the purse. Called it in as soon as I saw it." Levi gave a friendly slap to Jake's back. "Damn, Jake. Where'd you come from?"

"Where do you think?" Jake answered with his own smile.

Broadnax opened up the rear passenger door on their car. "Nice grab, Bush," guiding the prisoner into the back seat. "Barnes, call for another car for the lady," added Broadnax.

Barnes started to reach for the mic as he slid into the jump seat. "What the hell happened to your pants?"

"The bastard bit me."

"Better get in the back with your man, here. 'sides the report, the boss'll want that leg looked at. "Radio from Eleven-Two."

"Go ahead, Eleven-Two."

"Need another car to assist at Dearing and Joseph Campau."

"Okay, Two. Eleven-Three; meet the officers, Dearing and Joseph Campau."

33

"Three on the way."

The prisoner was booked. Barnes and Broadnax sat around while Jake finished typing the report on the Robbery Not Armed and arrest of James McGee. Barnes put down an empty coffee cup. "You 'bout done, rookie? The boss wants us to take you to Receiving Hospital to have that leg looked at."

Jake handed in the report and followed Barnes to their car. Barnes and Broadnax started talking as they pulled into the night.

"Man, did you see his pants?" asked Barnes.

"Damn that hadda hurt," said Broadnax.

"Probably needs stitches. I hate stitches," laughed Barnes.

"Glad it's him that's gonna get shots. Man, I hate shots," Clarence Broadnax added as he lit his pipe. The tall, slender black officer turned his head smiling at Jake, removing his hat revealing tight gray curls on his head. "Good catch, kid. This is one you can be proud of."

Barnes turned onto the Chrysler Freeway heading to Receiving Hospital. He looked up into the rear-view mirror catching Jake's eye. "We're just ribbin' you. Welcome to the world of cops and robbers, Jake. Even looks like the good guys are one up on this one." Eleven-Two abruptly stopped after the turn onto the hospital's emergency ramp.

Jake slid out of the car, looking at the double doors in front of him. Broadnax hung his head out the window. "I'm comin' with you. We get off in a half hour. I want to make sure you don't keep us past quittin' time. Mama's waiting up for me."

"Damn. Hope my woman's waiting up for me too," chimed in Barnes.

His laugh faded in the background as Jake and Clarence climbed the short porch under the red neon sign that read, "EMERGENCY ENTRANCE".

Chapter 4

It was a sultry afternoon on August 25, 1962, when Sergeant Fitzmaurice bellowed out "Roll Call" as he pushed his way through the double doors. The uniformed patrolmen shuffled into two ranks as Lieutenant Robertson walked passed the sergeant and reached the podium. The lieutenant opened his binder and waited for silence. He spoke when the only noise was the beat of the overhead fans.

"Eleven-One, Hall and Van Harren. Eleven-Two, Broadnax and Bush. Eleven-Three, Horvath and Malone..." The Lieutenant read off the names pausing only to hear the responding "Here Sir." The two fans barely moved the hot muggy air. At every other pause, the lieutenant wiped his brow with his handkerchief. His tie was gone and the collar on his white shirt was open. He read the last assignment, "Eleven-Ten, Reilly and Maples." He turned toward the sergeant. "Any special attentions, Sarge?"

"Family vacations are in full swing. Give a good look at 19982 Stotter, 20362 Anglin and 19880 McCay. Cancel 19642 Rogge and 20211 Klinger." With each address, the corresponding car covering the address would answer.

The sergeant looked up from his notes. "Pay attention to this, all of you." He gazed up and down the two ranks of officers to make sure they were listening. "Give special attention to your late operating and all night gas stations. Two have been hit recently. In Number Five on the first of July and last week in Number Fourteen. We don't have much to go on except the cash drawers were empty, and both occurring between 11 p.m. and 1 a.m. The attendants were killed. A shotgun is the weapon of choice. Whoever it is doesn't leave a witness. Check all your gas stations, especially the all nighters like Clark Stations. Let them know we're around." Jake thought of Levi at the station on Joseph Campau. The sergeant continued, "By the way, moving violations are down for the month. Sit on a light if you have to, but let's get the numbers back up. That's it for me, boss."

Lieutenant Robertson closed his binder. "Okay men, let's hit it... and be careful out there."

Bush found Eleven-Two on the east ramp to the garage. It was one of the station wagons. The day shift driver, Joe Brinkman, was waiting for his relief. "Did you get the oil changed yet?" Clarence asked Brinkman.

"All done, Clarence. Had 'em put new rubber on it too."

"Thanks, Joe." Clarence saw Bush approaching. "You got the wheel, Bush."

Before Jake could say anything, Clarence dropped his briefcase into the passenger's side window of the Plymouth Station Wagon. "I thought I heard Barnes say you wouldn't let him drive much," Jake said as he slid behind the wheel.

"You'll learn the streets faster driving," Clarence answered as he sat back, crossed a leg and lit his pipe, bringing it back to life. He took out a steno book out of the briefcase. "Besides, Barnes is a wild driver. Scares me sometimes."

Jake glanced over as he backed the car off of the station ramp. Clarence was writing the date with the name Jake Bush following it.

"A special log you keep?"

"Yes. My own. I jot a note in it when anything happens. Just in case I go to court or something. Then too, I might write a book some day." Jake pondered that thought as he drove to Eleven-Two's territory.

Take off the uniform and give him a sweater, he could pass for a college professor. Especially with the pipe clenched in his teeth.

The afternoon turned to evening, then to darkness as they cruised the main streets of their territory. Half way through the shift, Clarence took over the wheel. Clarence did not talk much. If Jake asked a question, it was answered briefly and to the point.

As Clarence drove past the Clark Station Jake could see that Levi was on duty. Levi looked up and waved as the police car drove past. "Think we ought to stop and visit with the attendant? Maybe tell him about the robberies?"

"Probably knows," Clarence answered. "Then too, we don't want to scare him. We'll just be seen more."

The radio ended the conversation. "Eleven-Two, meet a man at 18120 Arlington. Neighbor trouble."

"Two on the way," Jake answered into the mic.

Jake saw porch lights on up ahead as Clarence drove north on Arlington. "Numbers should be 'bout where the porch lights are," said Clarence. He slowed the car.

"You think that's our trouble?" Jake asked as he saw a woman standing on the porch. She was totally nude.

Jake heard her through his open window. "Hallelujah! Praise the Lord. I say; praise the Lord!" The woman was beating on the front door as she sang out.

Jake and Clarence walked to the porch with Clarence leading the way. The curtains were parted on the front window of the house, a man and a woman were looking out.

"Hallelujah! Praise the Lord. I say; praise the Lord!"

"Ma'am...Lady..." Clarence shouted above the singing.

"Hallelujah! Praise the Lord and be saved," she sang as she turned toward the voice behind her. "Praise the Lord, brother; cleanse yourself. Rid yourself of your worldly garments and be saved."

Clarence reached for her outstretched arm guiding her off of the porch. "Where do you live, Ma'am?" He turned to Jake. "Go grab a blanket from the car."

Jake ran to the car and returned with a blanket. He started to put it around the woman and she shrugged it aside. Jake looked at Clarence, then back at the nude woman in front of him. She was white with short dark hair and a distant gaze in her eyes; a pair of light blue slippers were all she had on. He tried putting the blanket over the woman's shoulders again.

Other porch lights came on. People seeing the police car came out of their houses.

"Hallelujah! Praise the Lord," the woman sang out as the neighbors gathered. She looked straight into Jake's eyes. "Do you want to be saved, brother?" He tried holding the blanket in place as Clarence led her by the arm toward their car. The question and a touch of her skin made Jake's hand flinch back and the blanket fell again. Clarence picked it up and held it firmly over the woman's shoulders.

A man approached from across the lawn. "I'm the one who called. She's nuts."

"And you are?" Clarence asked as he steered the woman toward the rear door on the police car.

"Her brother-in-law. She blessed me, then her sister, and tossed off all her clothes. She's been running around the neighborhood, just as you see her, praising God and blessing everyone."

"Stick around, mister. Need some names and addresses."

"Hallelujah! Praise the Lord. Repent, all you sinners," the woman sang out as Clarence and Jake tried to ease her in the back seat of the car. She threw her arms high and shed the blanket again.

"Climb in beside her, Jake," ordered Clarence. "And try to keep her covered as best you can."

In short order Eleven-Two was driving toward Detroit Receiving Hospital on the Chrysler Freeway. The psycho ward was the next stop. They had her admitted, leaving the information on her sister and brother-in-law.

As they approached their car to leave, Clarence suggested Jake drive. "I'll do the report. Then I need to make some notes on this." He chuckled, then took out his pipe.

Jake headed the car back toward their precinct. "Thanks a lot for sticking me in the back with Lady Godiva."

"Better you than me. How would it look for a black officer to sit next to a nude white woman?" He chuckled again. "Besides, I saw how squeamish you looked, trying to put the damn blanket on her. You needed the experience."

"Thanks for the experience, partner," Jake mumbled as he drove.

"Gonna get a lot more as time goes by. You're gonna see white ones, black ones, live ones, dead ones, naked and fully clothed, as well as some that shit or puked all over themselves...and maybe on you. Think you can handle it?"

"I can handle it," Jake answered sharply.

"Good. That's what being a cop is all about. Being able to handle it all." He smiled at Jake and closed his little book. "Stop at the Top Hat. Time for a coffee. I'm buyin'."

"Coffee's free for cops."

"Then pretend I'm buyin'."

August turned to September and September to October. An occasional day in court brought Jake into contact with some of his academy classmates. War stories were shared with Jake doing most of the listening. The Eleventh Precinct did not have too much activity. In November Jake put in a written request for a transfer to the Thirteenth Precinct. He would not have a year on the job until January, but he knew he wanted to work in a precinct where he could do more police work than write tickets. Number Thirteen was one of the action precincts. Jake wanted action.

December, 1962 came with Jake back on the afternoon shift. Officers were on vacation or off for other reasons and he found himself filling in on just about every car in the precinct. He still walked a beat at times, but did not mind it. On the eighth day of the month he heard his name at roll call.

"Eleven-Six, Horvath and Bush..."

Well, I finally get to work with Horvath and his cigar.

Jake wondered what was really behind the smoke and the loud laugh as Larry took the wheel. Jake's eyes scanned the meticulous car board that Larry hung in the center of the dashboard. "Lotsa assholes on the street and a lot of them use a stolen car," Larry boasted, "and I'm about the best there is in this precinct." Smoke filled the car as Larry drove off the ramp. "Check my stats with the boss if you doubt that," he added with a laugh.

39

He blows more than cigar smoke, concluded Jake.

Within an hour Larry spotted a car turning off Seven Mile onto Stotter. It was stolen. A young black male was behind the wheel. As Larry was forcing the car over, Jake could hear him muttering under his breath. "Go ahead and run, nigger. Just give me a reason…"

Jake was out of their car before the driver could attempt to run. The sixteen year old was handcuffed and taken to the station. A second car brought in the stolen car. As Jake typed the report, Larry paced, gnawing on this cigar. He seemed pissed. One sentence over lunch confirmed what Jake thought. "One of these days I'm going to get my chance to shoot one of them black bastards."

"You serious?" Jake asked.

Horvath laughed. "Just kidding kid."

Jake wondered if Horvath talked like that around Barnes and Broadnax.

Probably not. Barnes would crush the asshole's head. Broadnax would probably re-light his pipe and calmly make a note in his little book while asking Larry why a man of Jewish descent would feel such hatred toward another human being. Jake made a mental note to keep a wary eye on Larry Horvath.

It was Christmas Eve and Jake was working. Any holiday, especially Christmas meant that all the senior men were off. The boss at roll call paired the most senior officers with the most inexperienced.

"… Eleven-Five, Malone and Bush. Eleven-Six, Reilly and Bates…" the lieutenant kept calling off the assignments. Jake was relieved when he heard he was with Malone. Horvath was working and Jake had spent three days on his car already that month. Jake was tired of Larry and tired of checking all the lover's lanes in the precinct. That was Larry's biggest thrill—catching lovers screwing in a car by sneaking up and putting a flashlight beam on them.

Malone was in the jump seat as Jake got to the car. "What's this, my Christmas present?" Jake asked as he slid in behind the wheel.

"Yes, you get the pleasure of working with me today. Let's see, the last time we were together you were my squad leader at boot camp. You remember San Diego, don't you?"

"Hope I didn't do anything to piss you off."

Jake steered the car onto Conant, heading toward Van Dyke as Bob replied, "Don't remember anything..." He paused and added, "Yet."

The radio was virtually quiet as most of the air transmissions involved minor runs. There was a fender bender here and a noisy party there. Jake drove, checking all the business places on the territory's main streets. The car, Eleven-Five, covered the northeast end of the precinct. Eight Mile Road was quiet. The Top Hat, a 24-hour burger joint, was closed for the holiday. Jake turned onto Van Dyke. Near Outer Drive Bob spoke up, "Pull through the ramp at the Clark Station." Jake did so. Bob waved at the attendant keeping warm inside. "Hell of a day to be working," mumbled Bob as the attendant waved back.

"Heard another station was hit on the west side," Jake said.

"Yeah. I try to keep an eye on this one even when I'm on another car. The only way this shit's going to stop is someone catching the bastard in the act."

"That's gotta be a tough job. Alone, pumping gas and worrying about whether you'll live through the night," Jake added. Thoughts we going through his mind about Levi on his old beat. "One of the Clark station attendants on Joseph Campau is working two jobs, nights and sometimes afternoons. Says he's got kids to feed, so he tries not the think too much about the risk."

"Oh well, it's Christmas. Maybe even the bad guys take a day off."

"Speaking of Christmas, you just reminded me. My uncle Al lives on Spencer just off of Lantz. They want me to stop for some good Polish cooking if I'm in the neighborhood. You hungry?"

41

"You bet. Stop at a call box and I will put us out of service."
Bob smiled as Jake made a U-turn toward a call box he had
spotted.

Smiles, kisses, handshakes and Christmas wishes greeted the
officers. Then Aunt Ceil fussed over them, making sure Bob and
Jake had enough to eat. Father Stan, the parish priest from Queen
of Heaven, was there as well as Uncle Al and Ceil's daughter,
Doris and her husband, George. Jake and Bob met the rest of Aunt
Ceil's brothers and sisters who were in the midst of a late-evening
meal.

The officers ate their fill succumbed to a second slice of
pumpkin pie. Bob was trying to say no to the bag of Christmas
cookies that Jake's aunt was offering.

"Take it to the station if you don't want them. Al has more
than enough to keep him fat and sassy. I gave Jake some too," she
said as she pressed the bag into Bob's hand.

"Merry Christmas," Bob and Jake said in harmony as the door
closed. Bob took the wheel and drove to the call box so Jake could
put them back in service.

"We're back in," Jake said as he slid in the passenger seat.
"Nothing for us from dispatch." The radio remained fairly quiet as
Bob retraced the route they drove earlier. He drove in the curb lane
as Jake looked into the closed shops. On Van Dyke, a block south
of Seven Mile, they passed the closed J&J Sporting Goods. "Use to
work there," Jake said as they drove by. "Between my junior and
senior year at Notre Dame."

Their conversation turned to their boot camp days and Staff
Sergeant Akers. Both agreeing that the only time the drill
instructor seemed human was after graduation when he sat with
them and lit the smoking lamp. "I didn't know the man could talk
in a normal tone," Bob laughed. "He always had a cadence to his
voice."

"You-fucking-shit-head..." Jake tried his best to mimic the
drill instructor's monotone voice. "On the grinder-in five minutes-
for calisthenics, you shit maggots."

Bob laughed. "Glad those days are over. Too much running." Bob drove toward the Clark Station on Van Dyke again. "Time to check my man one more time."

"Speaking of that… Mind going back to the station by way of Joseph Campau? I know it's not our area, but I'd like to see if Levi's on. Maybe give him my bag of cookies from Aunt Ceil for the kids and wish him a Merry Christmas."

"We'll do that right now," Bob answered while he waved at the attendant as he drove through the ramp. "It'll be about quitting time after we check your friend."

Jake knew his request would be out of line if he was working with Horvath, but Bob was an old friend and a good cop.

Bob turned off of Davison and passed the Globe Furniture Store. The Clark station was well lit. Both saw there was a white man in the small building with the attendant. "Just drive by. Don't pull in," Jake suggested. "It's Levi and I want to see something."

The police car headed south on Joseph Campau. Levi was looking out the station's plate glass window as the police car passed. Eleven-Five continued down Joseph Campau and out of the attendant's line of sight. "Something's up. Levi would have waved. He always waves." Jake knew his old beat. "Take a left at the next corner." Bob made the turn.

"Let me out and take the car through the alley. I'll hoof it from here and meet you at the gas station." Jake hoped he was wrong as he jumped out of the slow rolling car.

He ran back toward the Clark Station. His nickel plated .38 in his right hand as he rounded the corner and slowed as he reached the station ramp. The man had Levi outside the building, pulling him toward the alley. "Drop the fucking gun," Jake commanded as he saw a shotgun pressed against Levi's head.

"Don't come another step or I'll blow this nigger's head off." The man had his sawed off shotgun against Levi's left ear.

Jake started to lower his colt for a second, then threw it back up, pulling the hammer back and aiming at the robber's head. "He dies, you die."

The gunman's eyes darted to his rear. The shotgun moved from Levi's ear, swinging toward the alley. Two shots broke the silence. Levi screamed and stumbled forward, falling to the pavement. The gunman crumpled where he stood. The shotgun clanged on the concrete as it fell between Levi and the gunman.

Officer Bob Malone was crouched at the curb near the side of the small Clark Station building. A slight wisp of smoke was rising from the gun in his hand. Jake ran to Levi looking for blood as he turned him over.

"Oh God! Oh God," Levi was sobbing. Silence filled the night. Jake helped Levi to his feet. Levi stood, his hand tightly gripping Jake's. He slowly looked at the man lying a few feet from him. A pool of blood trickled from under the still body. Levi looked back at Jake. "This was too close, man. Too fuckin' close."

Bob Malone checked the prone body, and then holstered his gun. His voice cracked as he spoke. "Call for the sergeants, Jake. Get us some help here."

Flashing red lights and police cars filled the station ramp at Joseph Campau and Grant. Homicide detectives showed up to assist the Eleventh Precinct detectives. The Clark Station was closed for the last half hour of Christmas Eve, 1962 and well into the next morning.

It took that long for Jake's heart rate to calm down. He began wondering if he put in for a transfer too soon.

Chapter 5

The Thirteenth Precinct was a two-story building built in the 1950s. It was located at the southwest corner of Woodward and Hancock. At ten thirty in the evening on February 3, 1963, Jake walked in from the garage toward the desk. The desk faced Woodward Avenue, the main entrance to the precinct house. Jake stopped in front of the patrolman filing some papers. "Hi. Can you help me out?"

"What cha need?" The balding clerk shoved the papers aside.

"I'm Jake Bush. Transferring in from Number Eleven. I'm starting the midnight shift tonight."

"Butch Walters," the clerk answered as he extended his hand to Jake. "Kind of early aren't you?" He added as he glanced at the clock over the back of the desk.

"Guess I am," Jake replied, "but I thought I'd get a look around, get caught up on the teletypes and that kind of stuff."

Officer Walters looked back at the sergeant. "Boss. A new man reporting in. Mind if I show him around?"

The sergeant looked up briefly from a logbook. "Yeah, go ahead." He glanced over his shoulder at the clock and just shook his head and smiled.

"Right this way," Butch said as he walked around the desk. He pointed at the hallway at the far end of the desk as he walked. "The Dick's offices are on the left." He opened the door with the words stenciled on the glass, *Thirteenth Precinct Detective Bureau.* "Normally these guys are just around on the day shift. You'll find them here working a bit of overtime when the load demands it. This way." Jake followed the clerk. "Across the hall is the bullpen." Butch peered through the barred opening on the steel door. Jake took a look through the bars as the clerk moved out of the way. "It's our temporary holding room for prisoners being booked," Walters offered over Jake's shoulder.

Jake could see the room was at least twenty feet by thirty with another cell door on the far side to the right. The room had a continuous bench secured to the four walls of the entire room. The walls were covered with four by eight inch cream-colored tiles. The floor was concrete with a drain in the center. The overhead lights were recessed behind heavy wire cages. Jake looked at Butch. "The door on the other side; where does that go?"

"That's where you bring them in. There is a room on the other side of that door where the doorman fingerprints them. You come in off the garage." Butch leaned on the barred door for a moment. "Don't bring your prisoners to the front of the desk. The bosses don't like that. Women are the only prisoners you bring to the desk." Butch turned continuing down the short hallway, stopping at another large steel door with bars on the small opening at eye level. "In here we have ten individual cells. Nothing fancy. Just to hold someone for the Dicks or those waiting to go downtown. Once they are printed, we move them from the bullpen into here."

Butch turned back down the hallway toward the desk area. "From Number Eleven, eh? What made them send you here?"

"I asked for a transfer."

Butch paused, put his hand in this shirt pocket and pulled out a cigarette. "Let me hear this again. You asked for a transfer? To here?" He lit it and offered one to Jake.

Jake waved off the offer. "I thought this would be a good place to work. Number Eleven is a bit slow."

A laugh got Butch coughing as he tried to inhale a puff. He hacked a couple of times before adding, "The only way one comes this place is to fuck up...or gets assigned here out of the academy. This is a new one on me."

Jake was not laughing. He followed as Butch led on. As they got to the front of the desk the clerk pointed to the door just past the main entrance to the precinct house. "That's the old man's office. Inspector Loftus. The hall in front of you is to the report room." He turned walking to his end of the desk. Jake knew the tour was over when Butch lifted the hinged end of the desk to get behind it. He motioned with his head, "The Teletype room's behind you, out the door is the garage, and up the stairs is the locker room and squad room. Roll Call is fifteen minutes before the start of the shift. Any questions?"

Jake hesitated, and then asked, "Locker's assigned, or grab what's empty?"

"Grab an empty." Walters dropped and latched the desktop. He turned his chair and sat. "Hope you know what you got yourself into asking for this place." He smiled and put out his cigarette in an ash tray. "Anything else?"

"Not right now."

Jake took the steps that Walters had pointed to and found the locker room. He hung his winter coat and nightstick in an empty locker and went out the side door and found the squad room.

It was a normal police squad room, equipped with a pool table, a ping-pong table, a couple of tables for card games, some extra chairs and a small podium.

Jake went down to the teletype room. He started making notes as he went through teletypes and bulletins sent out since his last day at Number Eleven. He found a big binder with Detective Bureau circulars and took some notes. At eleven thirty he went back up to the squad room.

At the south end of the room a Ping-Pong game was in full swing. It was a game of partners. Jake heard an officer shout out, "Sam and I got the winners."

At the pool table a game of eight ball was in progress, another game of partners. Small groups of police officers stood or sat around the room talking and laughing. Near the pool table was a row of chairs occupied by six black officers. They watched the game. At the next missed shot one spoke to his friends, "I'd have banked it."

"Not me. I'd cut the nine in the side, then went for the twelve." Jake noticed that none of them called to play the winners.

Jake was sitting off by himself. He did not see a soul he knew. Jake had hoped one of his classmates from the academy would be there. He knew Arbanas, Norman and Prell were assigned to

47

Number Thirteen. None were apparently scheduled to work that night. Jake passed the time by reading the notes he took earlier, glancing up only when he heard shouts of triumph from the pool or ping-pong table

At 11:45 p.m. the door on the north end of the squad room opened with the first of two sergeants entering calling out, "Roll Call." Pool sticks thudded on the table and the ping-pong ball bounced on the floor in the far corner until it ran out of steam. Thirty patrolmen shuffled to line up in two ranks. Jake found a spot in the back rank. A lieutenant in a crisp white shirt stood at the podium and started calling out names and cars. "Thirteen-One, Douglas and Jones." Two voices responded, "Here Sir." In minutes, the lieutenant assigned twelve cars before a pause. He checked his notes, and then proceeded. "Robertson and Henson, you got the ticket car." Two more voices responded after hearing their names. "Beat One and Two, Franks and Singer." Two voices responded. "Beat Twenty-three and Twenty-four, Titcomb and Bush." Jake looked to see who answered as Titcomb before responding. The lieutenant paused again, looking at the two men beside him wearing stripes. "Anything else?"

One sergeant stepped forward. "We are starting a new month. We need some movers written. Get them early and I won't be on your ass the end of the month. In January we were down 15% from last year." He stepped back. "That's all I have, Lou."

The second sergeant just shook his head when the lieutenant looked his way.

"All right. Let's hit the streets." He grabbed his notes and went out the door followed by the two sergeants.

Jake caught up to Titcomb as he was reaching for his winter coat off the back of a chair. "I'm Bush. Jake Bush."

"John." Titcomb took Jake's extended hand and shook it. "Just out of the academy?" Titcomb walked toward the locker room.

Jake followed. "Transferred in from Number Eleven." Jake heard a chuckle from John's way as they went into the locker room. Jake grabbed his coat and nightstick.

"Why'd they move you?"

"I asked to move." Before John could say anything, Jake added, "I take it nobody asks to come here." Jake followed Titcomb down the stairs and into the garage.

"We'll talk more later. Got all night. Let's grab a ride with Thirteen-Three." John quickened his pace and hailed a car before it could pull off of the north ramp.

Beat twenty-three and twenty-four was Woodward Avenue starting at Boston Boulevard to Alger. As they started walking, John talked. "You'll notice that things are a bit different out here." John started shaking doors as they walked.

Yes, Jake saw a new world compared to Number Eleven. There, the traffic slowed to a crawl after midnight. Here, people were on the street, waiting by threes and fours in the bus stops, and the traffic on Woodward was more like mid-day on Seven Mile rather than midnight. The busiest was the southwest corner of Woodward and Clairmount. There was an all night drug store complete with a lunch counter and a bank of phone booths in the back. On their first pass Jake counted fifteen people in the place. Various small businesses were the primary make up of the beat with the exception of three massive churches. They each took up a whole city block. One was First Baptist; another was The First Congregational Church of the Lord and lastly the Blessed Sacrament Cathedral. Jake and John shook doors on all the businesses and the churches, walked the alleys and made two pulls to report in to the station.

At two in the morning Titcomb and Bush were checking the First Baptist Church for the second time. The main entrance to the church consisted of two oaken doors that stood fifteen steps above the street. Black, wrought-iron railings graced both sides of the concrete stairway leading to the doors. Tall stained glass windows stood twenty feet above on each side of the doors. The steps, doors and stained glass were all part of the base of the steeple. Jake pulled the handles of the double doors at the top of stairs while John waited on the sidewalk below. They were secure.

The pair in blue checked the south side doors and windows, then the rear of the church on the alley side. All the windows, except those on the front of the church, stained glass or not, were encased with heavy cyclone fencing. *So much for trusting in the Lord*, thought Jake.

They walked around the north side toward Woodward, checking the last door. John spoke up. "Not much different than Number Eleven, eh Bush? Walking and shaking doors."

"I think we had a lot smaller churches. None for sure with fifteen doors and a building that covered a full city block."

As they reached Woodward, a black and green Checker Cab was in the middle of the street. Three of its four doors were open. The lights were on and the motor running. They instinctively ran to the cab. The radio's mic cord was cut.

"You check the alley we just came out of. I'll be on the other side of the street," Titcomb barked.

Jake wheeled and ran to the rear of the Baptist Church. The alley was silent as he slowed to listen for footfalls. To the north in the next block under a single alley light Jake saw a woman in a red coat walking. He circled the church, flashing his light in the bushes around it. Nothing. When he reached Woodward again, he looked to the south and back north. Nothing. It was after two in the morning and traffic was still steady, but no cars stopped at the cab abandoned in the middle of the street. Jake saw his partner coming out of the alley across the street.

"See anything?" John yelled to him.

"No cab driver. Nothing." Jake answered. He leaned inside the cab, combing the front seat with his flashlight. "I don't see any blood on the seat. Where's the driver?"

"Who in the hell knows? This is Number Thirteen. Maybe he quit." John was talking as he started to check out the back seat.

50

Jake was kneeling on the pavement, bent inside the front of the cab shining his light under the seat.

"Fuckin' crazy woman. She tried to rob me." Jake hit his head on the bottom of the dash as the voice startled him. The cabby was standing behind him; the radio mic with a short piece of wire was in his right hand.

"What woman?" Jake asked as he stood up.

"Some black bitch in a red coat. Picked her up at Pingree. Said she was going to Highland Park. Then a block back, said she wanted all my money. I put on the brakes. She leaned over the seat as I grabbed the mic. When she swiped at the mic cord with a big fuckin' knife, I ran."

John came around the cab. "She get any money?"

"Not a cent. And I wasn't waiting to see if she would use that knife on me."

The Thirteenth Precinct sergeants' car pulled up as the cabby was talking, Jake grabbed at their back door and slid in. "Attempted hold up. I saw a woman fitting the description in the alley heading north." He looked over his shoulder, toward his partner, "Be right back."

Sergeant Anderson drove north down Woodward. "Which way, son?"

"She was on the east side in the alley, heading north."

"What she look like?" Asked Sergeant Howard from the passenger seat.

"Don't know. Just someone in a red coat. She was a block away from me when I was looking for the cabby in the alley."

Anderson reached the Clairmount-Clay intersection three blocks to the north. He slowed, all three officers looking one way then another. On the west side of Woodward next to the drug store three people were waiting in the bus stop, two men and a woman. The woman was wearing a red coat.

"Bingo!" Anderson said as he made a quick U-turn and gunned the car toward the bus stop.

The two elderly black men at the bus stop quickly raised their hands as the three officers came out of the car with guns drawn. "You, lady. Up against the car," yelled Sergeant Howard as he grabbed her left arm.

"Get your mutha fuckin' hands off of me," she screamed as the two sergeants each had a hold of an arm, pushing her onto the hood of the police car.

Sergeant Anderson reached into her right coat pocket. He brought out an ebony-handled switchblade knife. Howard handcuffed her behind her back.

"Not so tight, you fuckin' bastard."

A bus approached the stop as the sergeants put her in the back of the car. The two men climbed onto the bus without saying a word.

Sergeant Anderson drove off with his three passengers. He talked over his shoulder. "I'll drop you off at the cab, Bush. We'll make the report."

Titcomb had the cab moved to the curb across from the Baptist Church. He and the cabby were leaning on the trunk. The sergeants pulled in behind it.

"You want us to come in with you?" Jake asked as he climbed out of the police car.

"No. We'll see you at the end of the shift," Anderson added.

"And thanks for the tip," chimed in Sergeant Howard as he slipped in the back of the car to sit with their prisoner. The sergeant's car slowly pulled up alongside the cab. Sergeant Howard opened his window.

"That's her. That's the bitch," the cabby yelled as he looked into the back seat of the police car.

"Follow us to Number Thirteen, Woodward and Hancock," said Howard. "We'll need a statement."

The cab and the police car drove off, leaving Titcomb and Bush standing at the curb.

Jake and John were eating a burger and washing it down with coffee at the counter in the Daley Drug Store fifteen minutes later. Jake spoke first. "Thought we'd at least get to go to the station to make the report."

"You do know that we won't even be mentioned in the report, don't you?"

"What do you mean?"

"Like we weren't even there," added John as he finished his coffee and rose, grabbing his coat.

"I was the one who saw the red coat…"

"Just forget it. Anderson and Howard will probably put themselves in for a citation for this." He put on his coat and gloves as he walked, Jake tagging behind him. "Welcome to Number Thirteen, Mr. Volunteer."

John led the way out into the cold February night. He was turning up the collar on his coat. "I got one tip for you. Here you watch your own ass and cover your partner's back. And trust no one." John spun his nightstick on its leather thong as he walked. "Remember, you picked Number Thirteen. And this is a place where no one knows who the bad guys are."

Chapter 6

The area that the Thirteenth Precinct covered was half the size of Jake's old precinct. It was home to The Detroit Historical Museum, The Institute of Arts, Wayne State University, Harper, Woman's and Children's Hospitals, the General Motors Building, the Vernor's Ginger Ale Plant, the Fisher Theater with WJR 760 on your AM dial broadcasting from the top floors, Blessed Sacrament Cathedral and the biggest churches of just about every religious denomination in the city.

Interspersed among these noted institutions were some of the more infamous ones like "The Willis Show Bar," the hub of activity in the white enclave in the southwest end of the precinct; "Dancing Dolly's," a dime-a-dance hall above the small businesses on the west side of Woodward near Alexandrine; and "The Diplomat Lounge," a bar featuring female impersonators called "The Jewel Box Review." It was on Second just off of West Grand Boulevard. Added to these there were a few houses of ill repute— whore houses—at 101 Edison and a few others on Arden Park, Chicago and Boston Boulevards that catered only to elite clientele, like doctors, lawyers and Indian chiefs. There were also innumerable Houses of Illegal Occupation—Blind Pigs. That's not to mention, the 100 or more street girls just working Brush, John R and St. Antoine from the Boulevard to Canfield on any given night. The Thirteenth Precinct was, if anything, diverse.

For the month of March Jake moved onto the afternoon shift. Afternoons were the busiest and the precinct assigned extra officers to work it. Volunteers were sought. Naturally, Jake volunteered to stay on it. Though assigned to a walking beat, Jake filled in on cars on a fairly regular basis. There were only four beats in the precinct that were walked with one man. The rest were two man beats.

One of Jake's frequently walked beats was the precinct house beat. This was a solo beat and extended from Warren to Alexandrine. The beat had one restaurant. It was at one time a real

Detroit streetcar that was bought, parked and converted into a restaurant. Thus it was aptly named: "The Streetcar Diner" and stood at the corner of Warren and Woodward. The place was a twenty-four hour favorite of the local winos. It served breakfast anytime, greasy hamburgers, Coney dogs and a stew that was always listed as 'Today's Special'. The coffee that came with an oil slick was free with any meal. Seniority and maybe a touch of ptomaine taught you not to eat there. Jake tried it once. He decided he would pack a lunch if he knew he'd be on that beat.

It was on March, 1963 and the flashing neon lights were shouting "Dancing Dolly's" over a door that was sandwiched between a barbershop and a second hand store. It greeted Jake right after dark the first time he was on that beat. Out of curiosity Jake opened the door and climbed the creaking, old wooden eight-foot wide stairway. He could hear the music coming from above. At the top the landing a set of double doors opened to a huge dance floor. A doorman was sitting on a stool just inside the door. The man was at least 300 pounds stuffed into a white short-sleeve shirt, red tie and black pants held up by two inch wide red suspenders.

"Any problem officer?" The doorman asked as he slid off of his stool, straightening his tie and puffing out his chest as he towered above the officer.

"Nope. Just seeing what's on my beat," Jake replied as he eyeballed the room.

The music was blaring from overhead speakers placed in the ceiling above a large, spinning mirrored ball that reflected the red, white and blue lights lining the walls. There was just enough light so Jake could make out the people. He barely could distinguish males from females at first. The song lasted about thirty seconds and the only two couples on the floor parted. Each man quickly offered a ticket to his partner as Frank Sinatra's voice started the couples dancing again. Jake's eyes became better accustomed in the dim-colored lights.

Inside a small glass enclosed booth a blonde sat with her hair piled on top of her head. She was selling tickets from a roll on a spindle. The sign above said dances were a dime apiece. *That might be Dolly if there was such an owner.* Dolly or whomever wore a see-through pink blouse with a black bra underneath. The bright, red lipstick she wore was thickly applied, extending beyond her normal lip lines.

A disheveled old man turned from the booth and tried to straighten a stained, light-colored tie as he eyed the five ladies sitting on stools at a small bar. The sign above the bar advertised Coke and coffee for twenty-five cents. The ladies, illuminated by extra lights in the ceiling, showed the rough miles that couldn't be hidden by the extra make up they wore. Jake checked the chairs that lined the walls. Only one was occupied. The occupant, a fifty-something male held a few tickets in a trembling hand as he slicked back his graying hair with the other. The Sinatra song stopped, and a Perry Como number started after a short pause. Jake turned to the doorman as the man with the hand full of tickets got up and walked toward the dance hall girls. "Not very busy tonight, is it?"

"It'll pick up later," the doorman answered as Jake headed for the stairway. "Once those in the local bars drink enough courage."

Jake did a fast count after his first round. Beat #1 consisted of four churches, five bars, the ptomaine diner, the Vernor's Plant, Dancing Dolly's, two smoke shops, two law offices, one bail bondsman, a sundry of other small businesses and the Thirteenth Precinct house. This beat did not have too much action or attraction. His first shift and many others on it were pretty quiet.

"Thirteen-One, Canfield and St. Aubin, at the store, a B&E in progress." It was April 16, 1963 with a little rain falling. There'd be no walking tonight. Someone called in sick.

"Thirteen-One on the way." Jake answered.

Bill St. Lawrence drove their silver Plymouth east on Canfield across the Chrysler Freeway. "It's a mom and pop grocery on the southwest corner. You grab the front; I'll cover the back." It was just after eleven. "Just so you know, there's a recessed front door with plate glass windows on either side. The owners live above the store." Bill brought the Plymouth to a stop on Canfield just before the corner.

Jake jumped out of the car, cutting around the corner to the front. The glass was out of the door. A figure in black came out the hole and Jake grabbed him. Twinkies, cigarettes and red licorice flew. It was a kid so Jake holstered his gun. Another kid came out and Jake reached and grabbed him by the arm and swung him around. In the dim street light over the corner, Jake could see that neither could be fourteen. "On the ground he commanded." He pushed the two toward the sidewalk. Jake found himself falling right with them. Someone jumped on his back. He grabbed an arm, pulling a fourth kid with him as he fell.

"Get his gun and shoot the mutha-fucker!" A voice shouted.

Jake felt a tug at his holster. He let go of everything and held on to the butt of his pistol. Two sets of hands were working at the leather strap over the trigger guard. He hung on to the pistol and holster. Fists were pounding on the back of his head and into his rib cage.

"That's it, get the gun. Shoot 'im!"

Rubber squealed as a car stopped. The punches subsided while bodies started flying. At the same time, Jake was hearing three heavy thuds. Whomp, whomp, whomp.

"On your fuckin' bellies. Now!"

Jake started to stand as he recognized the two cops. They were Frank Simms and Pete DeAngelo from Thirteen-Two. Frank had his gun drawn. He booted a kid in the ass.

"I said on your belly." To Jake's right were two kids and to his left another two. Pete pocketed his blackjack and got out his handcuffs.

57

Bill came around the corner holding two more teens. He had them handcuffed together. Bill pushed his two prisoners to the sidewalk. "Join your friends. On your bellies."

The six kids ended up lying side by side. Jake connected two with a pair of handcuffs while Pete DeAngelo cuffed the other two.

"Twinkies, licorice and a couple of cartons of cigarettes," Pete said as he snapped the last cuff. "And they're ready to blow your head off, Bush."

Jake checked his holster. The strap was still snapped. "Thanks guys." His head, back and ribs ached from the punches. "They're only kids." Jake bent over and retrieved his hat.

Pete smiled. "This ain't the Eleventh Precinct. Here, they'll kill you and never bat an eye."

"I got plywood already cut fo' the door," said the owner, Malcomb McGee. "Third time in two months me and the Mrs. been broken in to." There were splashes of gray on the temples of the black owner. "The till is open, so they know there's no money. Still they come in, take the same thing. Same bunch of hoodlums I'll bet. Twinkies, red licorice, and Camels."

"They ever try to come up to your apartment?" Bill asked.

"The door is double bolted at the bottom of the stairs out back. An' if they do, I got me a twelve gauge double barrel loaded with buckshot to greet them."

Bill St. Lawrence put the fifteen dollars worth of evidence in the truck of his car. Jake finished getting information for their report. The six boys, ages twelve and thirteen were turned over to the Detroit Youth Bureau for Breaking and Entering.

After two hours of overtime the paperwork was done. Bill signed the report that Jake had typed. "How 'bout stoppin' for a beer on the way home, Jake?"

"Don't drink."

"Hell then, have a red pop or a root beer."

"Where?"

"Ike's on Third."

"Past last call isn't it?"

"Ike always takes care of the boys with badges."

"See you there."

Jake drank a root beer while Bill put away two bottles of Stroh's. "Gotta tip for you, kid."

"What's that?"

"Get a hold of Jim Breedlove. Tell him to make you one of his special blackjacks."

"I have the slapjack my dad gave me."

"You need one of Jim's 24 ounce specials. Fuck a slapjack. Like tonight, when you get in to something where you need to turn the tide," Bill's blackjack thumped on the table. "This'll do the trick."

Jake picked it up and got the feel of it. "Looks like it'd hurt."

"Supposed to. Them kids woulda killed you tonight. That's a fact. Five bucks is cheap insurance."

By the end of May Jake had a full taste of the precinct. The bosses moved him around a lot. This day, May 25th, 1963, he and Don Gilbert were assigned two single beats that crossed each other. They decided to walk together. Each beat covered the Willis Show Bar. He had heard about the fights, the shootings and was warned to watch his back if ever inside.

Don decided to show Jake the Willis Show Bar just for the hell of it. "Sometimes they have some pretty nice looking strippers," Don said as he led the way through the front door. Jake and Don found fifteen men at the bar staring at a redhead riding a blue-feathered boa to the music. The bartender and the bouncer were the only ones to notice the two cops. Neither liked the presence of a uniform in the place. They gave the officers a "fuck you copper" look and Don gave it right back. A slow stroll through the bar brought more attention before the officers exited the side door.

"Looks like a friendly place," Jake said as the door closed behind him.

"Mighty friendly. A fight run there draws three cars." Don smiled. "Just start swinging your stick or blackjack as you go in the door 'cause you're fair game to all of them."

"And you just had to show me the place?"

"So you know where the exits are—in case of a retreat." Don laughed as they crossed Third Avenue.

Don was and ex-minor league ballplayer in the Yankee system. He said eight games in seven days for six years took a toll. The buses, cheap hotels and his pay topping out at $600 a month with very little chance to make the big leagues convinced him to try something different. "Besides, with kid number five on the way, the decision was easy." Don had started the academy three months after Jake graduated. His assignment to Number Thirteen gave him the street smarts Jake still was learning.

The small talk was stopped by the sound of breaking glass as they entered the alley on the west side of Third Avenue. Both stood still, eyes peering through the darkness as they waited for more sounds. A door squeaking as it opened on a back porch above the back of a furniture store alerted them to movement. Don whispered. "Watch the porch while I take the steps—in case the son-of-a-bitch jumps."

Don quietly opened the wooden gate to a small yard and started up the steps. Near the top the wood groaned as Don put his weight on it. A head bobbed out of the open door. "Freeze asshole," Don commanded gun in hand. The figure dove for the porch railing with one motion and hurled to the ground fifteen feet below.

Jake was there to greet the man as he rolled and tried to make it to the wooden seven-foot fence. Don came down the steps and helped with the handcuffs. "I guess he doesn't know what freeze means, Jake."

"Man, I think I broke my ankle," the man moaned.

"Tough shit," Jake said as he raised the man up and leaned him against the fence. "Too bad you didn't break your neck."

"If you got 'im, I'll see what he was doing in that upstairs apartment," Don said.

"He's not going anywhere."

The paperwork took an hour. Their prisoner was a small-time burglar two blocks from home trying to make a few bucks from someone who really didn't have much to steal. The loot consisted of a broken-down television and a radio.

Cass Avenue, Second and Third, heading south from Wayne State University to Alexandrine, made up the white enclave of the precinct. Some of the residents were students rooming near the campus. But most were just white trash separated from more of the white trash living around Tiger Stadium when they put in the Lodge Expressway.

The afternoon of May 25th had Jake walking and admiring his surroundings: old apartment buildings, large homes turned into rooming houses, a few run-down small businesses and the cockroach-infested flats above the businesses. Jake's thoughts were broken by a voice as he passed a brick two story apartment building. "Hey, officer! Hang on. I need to talk to you." Jake turned to greet the short, balding man wearing a dirty under shirt and black, baggy pants.

"Whatcha need?" Jake asked, looking down as the man motioned for him to come closer so he could talk quietly. Jake bent and moved his ear closer.

"I'm the manager of these apartments. There's a woman in number eight that doesn't belong there. She's a trouble maker, and I want her off of the property."

The stale beer breath made Jake move back a bit. "She's not a tenant?"

"No, just trouble. She's trying to sue the owner, saying she hurt herself on the ice last winter. The owner don't want her around. She's just a fuckin', drunkin' whore."

Jake looked at the man. "Number eight? You do know I just can't make her leave if she's visiting the tenant."

"Look officer, she's trouble. I want her outta here!" The manager had stopped whispering.

"Hang on, hang on. I'll check, but if the person paying the rent is allowing her to visit, there is nothing I can do."

"What do we pay taxes for? I am asking for you to do me a favor and I get some lawyer bullshit."

Jake sighed. "Where's the place? I'll see what I can do."

"Around the back. Downstairs."

Jake went around the building and knocked on the door with the painted over eight on it. The manager followed. A strong smell of whiskey and smoke greeted Jake as the apartment door opened. "You the owner of the apartment?" Jake asked the man at the door.

"Bill, a cop is looking for you," the man opened the door fully to a dimly lit living room. He motioned for Jake to enter. Jake took two steps in.

On the couch sat a legless man, blotches of uncombed gray hair on his head, a stained yellow shirt hanging over black trousers that had each leg pinned half way between the hip and where the knees should be. The legless man spoke. "I'm Bill. Whatcha want?"

Jake's eyes panned the room. Another sloppily dressed man in his fifties sat beside Bill. A skinny mid-fortyish looking woman was sitting on the far arm of the couch, wearing a white T-shirt, jeans and ratty old tennis shoes. Two other chairs held male occupants, each in need of a shave, a bath and some clean clothes. Beer bottles littered the floor. Glasses and whiskey bottles were scattered on the two end tables. Jake knew they were all drunk.

The manager yelled out from outside the door. "The broad. She don't belong around here. I want her out."

Jake turned and pointed to the manager. "On the sidewalk, mister. I'll do the talking." The manager moved back as Jake turned to Bill. "You heard him. He doesn't want the woman in here." Jake looked at the woman as he spoke.

Bill answered, "Look officer. I don't want no trouble."

"There's no trouble. If you want her here, that's your business. You are paying the rent, right?"

From beyond the door the manager was yelling, spit spewing from his mouth, "Bill, the bitch has got to go, or next month you won't live here."

Bill looked over at the woman and shrugged his shoulders. "I guess you gotta go, Loretta."

Loretta stood, all 98 pounds of her, snarling at Bill. "That ain't what you were saying ten minutes ago when I was sucking on your cock." She threw a beer bottle at him, missing his head as it shattered against the wall behind the couch. "What do you mean, I gotta go?"

Jake moved between Bill and Loretta. "Come on lady, let's just leave." He reached to grab her arm.

"Don't you touch me, you fucking prick. I am not leaving." She backed into the corner behind her. Two of the drunks fell out of their chairs scrambling to get out of the way. "No cop is telling me what to do."

Jake stepped toward her. "Just take it easy, lady. It's time to leave. You don't have a choice..."

Loretta lunged, her fingernails going for Jake's eyes. Jake parried her advance with a swat of his left arm. The move knocked Loretta off balance and to the floor as one set of nails grazed his cheek. Jake jumped on her, attempting to hold her still. "No more bullshit, lady." She went limp under his weight. "Now when I let you up, I want you walking out that door."

As Jake rose, she grabbed at his leg and tried to bite it. "You fucking pig!" She was twisting and, kicking. Her teeth were snapping at any part of Jake near her. Jake twisted her left arm around and snapped on one handcuff. "Let go of me you fuckin' son-of-a-bitch." She was screaming and kicking. More chairs flew as the rest of the men got out of the way.

Jake twisted the right arm avoiding her teeth again and got the other handcuff secured behind her back. Jake paused to catch his breath, and then lifted up the screaming woman. Her head was snapping from one side to the other as she was biting at air.

The manager was standing, watching from the open doorway. "Call for a car for me!"

Jake turned toward the nearest drunk. "You, pick up my hat and put it on my head." The man obliged. Jake, firmly holding Loretta by the handcuffs with a little lift, pushed her out the door. "A little tip, lady. Walk with me, or I will drag you like a dog."

She hissed, snapping her teeth and kicking back with her right leg. "I'll cut your balls off..."

She was lying on the sidewalk as Thirteen-Nine pulled up. Jake was holding her down so she wouldn't hurt herself, or him. Charlie Mangus broke into a toothy grin as he got out of the passenger side of the scout car. He opened the back door.

"Bush, I see you've met the Mad Dog of Third Avenue, Loretta Sweet."

Lieutenant Rose looked up as Jake brought Loretta in front of him. He apparently had seen her before.

"Take her right to Women's Division, Mangus. I don't want to hear her screaming all afternoon."

Jake made the trip with Thirteen-Nine to Women's Detention on the ninth floor of Police Headquarters. There he got a glimpse of her rap sheet. It was three pages deep. Loretta was twenty-five with arrests ranging from prostitution to narcotics and was currently on parole for attempted murder. The jail matron requested Jake to help escort Loretta to a cell, adding, "I fought with this crazy bitch before and was off a month with a broken nose."

All summer, Jake was formally assigned a beat, but when he did fill in on a car, it was usually with someone new. Jake always remembered what John Titcomb told him the first night on a beat at Number Thirteen; "Trust no one."

Jake was naïve but knew how to add two and two. For instance, when your partner parks the scout car in an alley, saying he has to see someone on business and goes in the back door of a bar; or another parks after dark behind a fancy house on Chicago Boulevard, something's not right. One partner pointed out what back door to knock on, "Just in case we get a run." Jake kept mental notes as to who was drinking on the job or doing whores.

By working straight afternoons, Jake also took note of who the real cops were. He ran into them while keeping up a stolen car board or making notes on teletypes before to roll call. There were plenty of good cops to offset the ones Jake chose to stay clear of. The drinkers and whore chasers might have referred to cops like Paul Arbanas and Fred Greening as hot dogs, but Jake knew better. Jake also knew they probably put him in the same category. He didn't care.

Jake also noted that on all three shifts, the black officers kept together and to themselves. None played pool or ping-pong. Jake never asked why.

On July 30, 1963, Jake was casually checking the bulletin board to see what beat he would have the next month. His name was not with assigned beat officers. He checked the other shifts. He was not there either. Then he saw it. Platoon #3, afternoons, Scout Thirteen-Seven, Lucius Diamond, Ozell DuBois, and John Bush. Jake was assigned his first car.

The names did not ring a bell. Bill Johnson came in and started checking the list. Jake asked, "Who are Diamond and DuBois?"

Bill smiled as he turned to leave, "The Coal Car, buddy. Big Lucius and Ozell. As black as they come."

65

Chapter 7

Jake looked over his shoulder as an imposing voice answered, "Hear Sir" to the lieutenant's call of the name "Diamond." Jake gave the same response when his name followed. When roll call was over, a jumbled line of men in blue filed down the stairs, heading to the ramp on the north side of the station's garage. Jake did not know what kind of a car Thirteen-Seven had, so he kept his eye on the tall, heavy black officer in the middle of the pack.

Diamond found the 1963 four-door, black Plymouth sedan on the ramp. Jake saw that the day-shift officer waiting for relief at the car did not speak to Lucius Diamond. He just left when Lucius got near the car. Diamond climbed behind the wheel. Jake opened the passenger door and climbed in. Diamond started the car and headed off of the station ramp. "The name is Bush. John Bush, but I go by Jake."

"Hmph," was the only reply. Jake's hand was extended to shake, but the black officer did not even look over. *Welcome to the Coal Car.* Jake could cut the silence with a knife. A mile down Woodward, the Plymouth stopped at the southwest corner of Clairmount and Woodward in front of the Daley Drug Store. Diamond climbed out of the car. "Ah'll be in makin' a phone call. Get me if we get a run."

Diamond was gone before Jake could answer. He rolled down his window, letting the thick smell of Aqua Velva out.

Musta bathed in the shit.

After fifteen minutes of just sitting, Jake checked under the seats looking for a stolen car board or a circular book. He found neither. He grabbed the keys and checked the trunk. Nothing. Jake sat and waited, listening to the occasional radio transmissions. Forty-five minutes later a call finally came for Thirteen-Seven.

Jake went into the drug store and saw his partner's big body crammed into one of the three phone booths along the back wall. The bi-fold door wouldn't close with Lucius' ass hanging out. Jake tapped on the glass and his partner looked over his shoulder. "We gotta run. I'll be in the car." Jake turned and went back outside. Five minutes later Lucius Diamond climbed behind the wheel and hit the key on the Plymouth.

"What we got?"

"132 Pingree, see the man on a complaint."

Lucius turned off the engine on the car. "You came and got me for a 'complaint' run?"

"Should I have made the run without you?" Jake looked at Lucius, thinking, *You arrogant son-of-a-bitch*, but bit his lip.

Lucius Diamond re-started the car. "Fuckin' rookies," he mumbled.

"Hey, I don't know what this shit is, but we got a call on the radio. I came and got you. That's what you told me to do. If that makes me a fuckin' rookie, I guess I am."

"Let's get one thing straight, Bush. This is my car. I'm in charge. I call the shots and what I say goes."

The tires squealed and the car rocked as Lucius took the turn onto Pingree too fast. The car screeched to a halt in front of 132, a green two story wood sided house. Jake grabbed the clipboard and followed. Lucius rapped on the door with a massive fist, then rang the bell. An elderly black man opened the door. Lucius barked, "What's your complaint, mister?"

"I, uh, four kids in the alley. They knocked over my trashcans, been breakin' glass, makin' a mess. I asked them to stop and all I got from them is 'fuck you ol' man' "

"They still there?" Lucius asked, turning from the porch.

"Were when I called 'bout an hour ago."

"Get his name. Ah'll be out back." He banged through the gate into the yard.

"I'll be right back, mister," Jake called over his shoulder as he ran to catch up.

Lucius went from the yard into the alley through the back wooden gate. Four teens were rolling dice against the garage. "Leave the dice lay and grab you some wall," he barked.

"What fo' man?" A kid in a dirty T-shirt wearing a red, do-rag asked.

His answer was a massive black hand at his throat, picking him up and slamming him against the garage wall. The kid's tennis shoes were two feet off of the ground. "When the Black Diamond says, grab you some wall, it means up against the mo- fuckin' wall nigger." He dropped the teen. The other three scrambled off of the paved alley floor and lined up facing the garage wall. "Get the car, Bush. These punks are goin'to jail."

"Jes' stay outta mah way, rookie," was all he said on the way into the station with the kids. Lucius wrote the report and did all the talking. The kids were seventeen, so they went into the bullpen joining two drunks sleeping on the benches.

When Jake signed his name to the bottom of the report,he saw that the heading read, "Investigation of Robbery Armed."

Lieutenant Brooks did not question the arrests or the report. Jake didn't either. For the next two hours, Thirteen-Seven was parked in front of the drug store and Lucius was crammed in another phone booth.

What the hell have I gotten into? Jake just sat and waited.

The next day Jake worked the car was three days later. He went in to check the latest teletypes and stolen cars in the room just off of the main desk. A black officer was updating a stolen car board. He looked up as Jake came in.

Jake spoke first. "You wouldn't be DuBois, would you?"

"Yes, Ozell DuBois."

"Jake. Jake Bush." Jake extended his hand to shake.

Ozell grabbed it. "Glad to meet you, Jake."

"You keep up a board? I couldn't find one in the car."

"Lucius thinks it's a waste of time. But I keep one."

"Where?"

"There's a place in the locker room. I leave it there. Can't leave it in the car. Someone would toss it."

"Mind if I use it when you're off?"

"I'll show you where I keep it." Jake smiled as Ozell went back to updating the board. "By the way, Lucius is off today, so you're stuck with me."

Jake already knew he was going to have a better day.

When Ozell was done, Jake followed him up the stairs to the roll call room. Once inside Ozell found a seat among four black officers watching the pool game. Jake looked for a partner among those near the ping-pong table. He called for the next game.

Bill Malcom was standing next to Thirteen-Seven's car when Jake came out. "You're clear with radio." Without saying anything more he brushed past the approaching DuBois.

Ozell headed for the passenger's side, his board and book underneath his left arm. "You drive, Jake. I'll do the paperwork."

Jake slid behind the wheel and headed off of the ramp. "Lucius didn't let me drive, so give me a little help on the territory."

"Is he bein' a jerk again?" Ozell asked as the car headed north on Woodward. Jake nodded. "He's tryin' to impress you."

"I was really impressed when he had one kid by the throat dangling two feet off of the ground with one hand. I still don't know what touched him off."

Ozell was hanging the stolen car board off of a bent piece of coat hanger in the center of the dashboard as he answered, "Did the kid ask 'why' when Lucius told him something?"

"Yes."

"Lucius doesn't let any one question his authority. 'specially our kind. I've had to pull him off of a few people. He's tryin' to get a reputation. Even tellin' everyone to call him 'The Black Diamond.' "

Jake turned left onto Clairmount. "Finally getting assigned to a car after a year and a half made my day. But Monday I had second thoughts. Does he ever have a day when he is not playing Mister Badass?" Jake looked to Ozell for an answer.

There was a pause. "We don't hang onto too many partners. White ones for sure. They normally just last a month." He motioned for Jake to turn right on Hamilton Avenue. "I'll show you the territory. Not a whole lot of businesses, mostly homes. The old, swanky part of Detroit." He laughed. "And by the way, Lucius is not that bad. You just have to stand up to him."

"And have him grab me by the throat?" They both laughed. "How long have you been with him?"

"Three years give or take a month."

In one afternoon and ten radio runs Jake found out that Ozell had three kids, a wife that teaches school, and that he was working on a teaching certificate himself. He had seven years on the job, but wanted to be a teacher. He added that Lucius had sixteen years and no friends at Number Thirteen. "He's the kinda guy you don't get close to." At lunchtime Jake asked Ozell where he wanted to eat. "I brought my lunch. Just drop me off at the station."

Jake took the car to the Taystee Barbecue here he ate alone. Lucius had dropped him off there the day they worked together. Lucius did not say what he did for lunch and Jake didn't ask.

August went by quickly with Jake working the car every day he was scheduled. Ozell took Tuesdays and Thursdays off for school. He was going to the University of Detroit. The tension between Lucius and Bush eased somewhat the third time they worked together. Lucius pulled a traffic offender out of an open window of his car. A passenger jumped from the back seat and got ahold of Lucius' arm. The man drew back to throw a fist when Jake sent him sprawling. Lucius let Jake drive when the arrests and the reports were done.

"You're pretty quick getting outta the car when them niggers started jumpin' on me."

"I'm your partner."

"Yes you are." His voice lost its gruffness.

A bit of peace came over the *Coal Car* that day.

In the first three months on Thirteen-Seven, Jake was involved in 94 arrests. That was about three times the number of arrests he had in ten months at Number Eleven. He made the best of the days he worked with Lucius and looked forward to the days with Ozell. Lucius would spend 3 to 4 hours a shift on the phone at Daley's Drugs on the corner of Woodward and Clairmount Jake talked to Ozell about i. "Don't know what he is doin'. None of my business. But he does it with me too."

Jake thought of a plan to inflate Lucius' 285-pound ego and minimize the phone time. When he called Thirteen-Seven back in service by phone, he'd talk to the dispatcher. Voices become familiar.

" 'spatch," was Frank Bellows' normal answer when he picked up the phone at headquarters.

"Frank, this is Bush, Thirteen-Seven. I've got Lucius today, what can you do for me?"

"Got three, Jake. They'll keep you busy for a while."

Of course, when Jake got in the car Lucius would complain about their car getting all the runs. Jake's answer was simple, "Frank says he's got them backed up a mile. Besides, this makes the boss happy. We write our share of tickets and make a lot of reports. We fill up the log sheet every day. I know the sergeant made the comment last night that we were among the best on his shift."

"We are the best!" beamed Lucius. "Where to, patnah?"

Jake was working when both Lucius and Ozell were on. It was October 26th. As junior man, Jake worked another car with someone off. He was working Thirteen-Two with Joe Hebert. Joe didn't waste time or mince words.

"How's the 'Coal Car' coming?"

"Okay," answered Jake wondering what prompted the question before they left the ramp.

"Didn't anyone tell you that you're supposed to call in sick?"

"What for?"

"To let them niggers know you don't like working with 'em."

By then end of the shift Jake knew the unwritten rules: No eating with a black partner, do as little as possible and to call in sick often. Jake didn't have to ask why the blacks didn't play pool or ping-pong. No doubt there was another unwritten rule. Jake wondered if Broadnax and Barnes from Number Eleven knew about these rules.

It was two o'clock in the morning on October 26th when the radio blared, "Thirteen-Seven, family trouble, 117 Gladstone." Jake turned the car toward the address. Lucius was his partner.

A woman answered the door as they heard a man's voice yelling from behind, "Don't open no fuckin' door fo' no police."

She motioned for Lucius and Jake to enter.

"What's the problem, ma'am?" Jake asked as Lucius moved to the other side of the room.

"Who the fuck let you sons-a-bitches in?" A medium sized black man wearing boxer shorts and an undershirt walked into the living room.

"He's been drinking and…" The woman answered.

"Get the fuck outta my house," the man shouted as he pushed past Lucius, reaching into a hall closet. Lucius jumped on the man's back. As they wrestled, Jake saw the man's left hand on the pistol grip of a shotgun. Lucius had his enormous left hand covering the trigger guard and his right arm was around the man's neck. Jake pried at the shotgun with both hands. The twisting and turning of Lucius and the man pulled Jake into the three by three closet on top of the heap. He reached behind into his back pocket. A flash of black leather encased lead caught the man along the left side of his head. The shotgun came loose in Lucius' hands. He handed it to Jake, rolled the man over and handcuffed him.

An hour later, they were done with the paperwork. Charles Knight, age 43, had been booked for Attempted Felonious Assault.

Lucius took the wheel of the '63 Plymouth as they left the station.

"Where do you want to eat, patnah?"

Jake thought for a second, and then answered. "Don't you mean where do *WE* want to eat?"

Lucius' head snapped toward Jake at the word *we*. "Don't start no shit, Bush. You know the whites don't eat with their black partners."

"Lucius, just over an hour ago we were crammed in a fuckin' closet fighting with some guy over a shotgun. Why can't we sit across a table from each other and eat?"

"You're askin' fo' a bunch of trouble."

"I can take it. Pick a place, I'm buying."

"This is mah car, Bush. Ahm buyin'." White teeth flashed a wide smile on his dark face. "How 'bout the Disc Jockey Lounge?"

"They fry eggs?"

"There won't be a white man in the place."

"Will you watch my back?"

"Bush, you're with the Black Diamond. Nobody'd dare fuck wichyou."

A week later, Jake got a phone call from Frank Prudent, an old academy classmate. He, Jake, and a few others from Number Eleven still got together for a monthly card night.

"I just wanted to tell you some guy is lying about you. He said that some black cop named Lucius and you are swapping wives." Frank laughed at the absurdity as he talked. "It was a cop named Hebert at Recorder's Court. When I told him he was full of shit, he got a bit red and left."

Jake told Frank about the different rules at Number Thirteen and the night he had lunch with Lucius. Someone no doubt saw him and Lucius leave the Disc Jockey Lounge.

Thirteen-Seven swung onto days for the month of December. Jake dropped Ozell off at the station for his normal lunch break, but instead of going somewhere to eat he just waited for ten minutes. He was picturing his partner eating a cold baloney sandwich with a cup of coffee. Out of curiosity, he went into the station to see what Ozell did for lunch. After searching all the back rooms and offices he went upstairs. He heard the sounds of a ping-pong game in the squad room, and got on his tiptoes and looked through the high window on the door. Ozell was playing Lieutenant Zimmerman one-on-one. Jake didn't interrupt them.

When Ozell got back in the car at the appointed time, Jake merely asked, "How bad the Lieutenant beat you?"

"He couldn't beat me on his best day." There was a pause. "How'd you know?"

Jake told him what he did and why.

"I am tired of the bullshit stuff said behind my back and tired of being called a nigger lover because I don't call in sick. I like being a cop and like to work. And I think you're just as good as me. Who gives a fuck about whether you're black or white?"

"Boy, you gotta lot of stuff welling up inside you, Jake."

"Yes I do. And I can't see why you can't be my partner on the ping-pong table or that you have to sneak around playing the lieutenant or anyone else."

" 'cause that's the way it is 'round here. That's the way it will always be. And that is why I'd rather teach than be a cop."

The next day, Jake called for the next game of ping-pong. Joe Hebert and George Puckett were the winners. Hebert spoke up, "Who's your partner, Bush?"

Jake grabbed the pair of paddles on the empty end of the table. "Ozell, come on up here."

The room went silent. Ozell started waving his hands and shaking his head from side to side.

"Ozell, we can do this. It's all legal." Jake reached into his pocket and pulled out a ball that he had dipped in ink. Half of it was black. "See, I have a ball for integrated games." He pulled another totally black ball from his pocket and let it bounce on the table. "This one is for when it's only black officers playing, or should I say, niggers?" As Jake smashed it under his paddle, he added, "Of course, we will have to handicap you, won't we?" Hebert never said a word as he put his paddle down. He just stared at Jake. The game was over. The squad room was silent. Roll Call followed ten minutes later.

As their car rolled north on Woodward, Ozell finally spoke. "That took a lot of guts, Jake. You're not going change them, but you got them thinking." Ozell was smiling as Jake turned onto Clairmount. "I think you're crazy, but..."

From that day on any run that a car with Jake working it , whether he was with Lucius, Ozell, or any other partner, a second or even third car was near with the black officers making sure a Polish cop's back was covered. Jake stopped playing ping-pong.

Jake sat in Thirteen-Seven parked in front of the Daley Drug Store. It was two in the morning on January 29, 1964. A radio broadcast gave out three stolen cars. He added a fourth to the board that was wanted in a burglary in the Fifth Precinct. Jake passed the time watching traffic, checking license plate numbers on the board to pass the time.

A half hour went by when the plate on a 1957 Chevrolet brought him to attention. He looked at the drug store, couldn't see Lucius, and then drove off after the Chevy. Jake flipped on the red light and hit the siren. He forced the car onto a ramp of a closed dry cleaning store three blocks away. The driver started to run as Jake yelled, "Freeze!" The man glanced over his shoulder and saw the nickel-plated revolver pointed at him. He stopped.

Another car pulled onto the ramp. It was a crew of detectives working overtime. Detective Stuart Walker asked, "Whatcha got here?"

"Came over the radio 'bout an hour ago. Car and occupant wanted in a B&E in Number Five." They helped Jake search and handcuff the prisoner. "How about taking this guy in for me?"

"Where you going?" Walker asked as he and his partner put the man in the back of their unmarked car.

"Back to the drug store and get my partner. I'll bring the car in."

A smile broke across Walker's face. "You're working with Lucius, eh?"

"You got it." Jake put his car in gear and drove back to Clairmount.

Lucius took care of tagging the items recovered from the trunk of the Chevy. There were three car batteries, thirty-four packaged spark plugs, sixteen sets of windshield wipers and a cash register.

"Here's the information Walker and Mullis gave me on your prisoner," Lieutenant Rosema said as the handed Jake a notepad. "You're going to type the report, right?"

"Ah'll do it," Lucius said from the end of the desk as he was filling out the last evidence tag.

"I think Bush knows more about this than you do, Diamond."

When Jake came in for his next shift, he found out that Lucius Diamond was off of the car. He was the first Detroit Police Officer assigned to patrol the halls of a school. Northern High was his new beat; straight days, weekends off and no midnights. Lucius said he got promoted. Jake knew better.

Chapter 8

February 1964 found Jake assigned to another car, Thirteen-Nine. The two senior members were Charlie Mangus and Bill Fabrera. Jake had been riding to work in a car pool with Bill and he suggested to the bosses that Jake be put on his car. They needed a third man. It was an easy move. Ozell had two new partners too, both white.

Nine's territory was the southwest corner of the precinct. The first half of the month went fine. Just after Valentine's Day, Bill was driving on Third Avenue with Jake in the jump seat. Bill stopped at Canfield and Forest where a woman was standing.

"Lola, have a seat." Bill motioned for her to climb in the back of their Plymouth.

"Hey sugar, I can't afford another DPI arrest. It's too early. I ain't made no money."

"Well, we can negotiate that." Bill drove a couple of blocks and parked in an alley behind the Third and Alex Diner.

"Jake, why don't you go have a cup of coffee while I get my system drained."

Jake went in the back door to the restaurant and ordered a cup of coffee. Sipping it, he had time to think. His Catholic upbringing started weighing on his mind. *Allowing someone to commit a mortal sin was the same as you committing it,* so said Sister Mary Antoinette, a teacher he remembered. While nowhere near sainthood, Jake tried to stay free from mortal sin, just in case he bought a bullet. Flashes of Bill's wife, Charlene, kissing him good-bye as they left for work that afternoon just pissed him off all the more. He pushed the cup out of the way and left a quarter on the counter. The wrinkled waitress behind the counter yelled after Jake, "Uniforms don't pay for coffee, honey."

"Buy a pack of smokes on me," he called over his shoulder as he let the door slam behind him. "I shouldn't have let this happen," he mumbled to himself as he walked toward his car.

The woman was spitting out of the back window of the car as Jake approached and Bill was outside the car zipping up his pants. The girl then took a slug out of a small Listerine bottle, and spit the fluid out. "You're next honey."

"I don't do whores. Take a walk."

"Who you callin' a whore?" She screamed as she climbed out of the police car and slammed the door.

"Just hit the road," Jake commanded.

The scraggily haired woman straightened out the slip under her red skirt and threw her short black fur wrap over her shoulders as she turned toward the diner. "I don't know 'bout you white, honky cops. Don't even know how to treat a lady." Her hips had an exaggerated sway as she walked into the night.

"Jake, what the fuck you pullin'?"

"Maybe I should have told you. I don't do whores."

The subject never came up when Jake worked with Charlie during the month and Bill never talked about it again. March's schedule had Jake on another car and he just figured the two senior men on Thirteen-Nine decided he was not a good fit on their car.

Thirteen-Seven had a new crew as well as a new Ford Station Wagon as of the first of March. Jake's new partners were Ronnie DiPonio and Jim Breedlove. Ronnie was a seven-year man and Jim had five years on the job. They both came to Number Thirteen straight out of the academy.

Jake's first lunch stop with Ronnie gave him a clue about his partner. Ronnie took five minutes to comb his jet black, wavy hair before he walked into The Pecan Grove Waffle Shop on Second and Lothrup. Ronnie greeted one waitress, "Hello, gorgeous" and turned to take a menu from another with a, "Well beautiful, what can we do together tonight?" The women giggled as Ronnie slid into a booth. "They just love that hot Italian blood of mine," he explained to Jake without being asked. Ronnie was married with five kids.

James Breedlove stood six foot two but carried only 170 pounds in full uniform. He spoke with a firm, but soft voice. Jim was a shopper. If you needed new shocks for your car, he could tell you where the best deal was. If you needed some clothes, he knew a wholesaler that sold to policemen at discount prices. Jim was married with no kids. His sideline business was making his special 24-ounce blackjacks.

The month was filled with normal radio runs and the car handling school crossings in the morning and after school.

On April 2, 1964, after a month of writing routine tickets and answering radio calls, Ronnie saw a black woman walking up onto a porch at two thirty in the morning. He rolled to a stop and cranked down his window. "Ma'am can I talk to you?"

She walked down the steps and toward the car with a quizzed look on her face. "I was just wondering what a pretty, young lady like yourself was doing out this time of the night?"

The small talk lasted ten minutes before Ronnie asked her have a seat in the back of the new 1964 Ford Station Wagon. Jake just sat in the passenger seat.

What's this Casanova up to?

"Aren't you a bit afraid to be roaming the streets this time of the night?" Ronnie asked as he drove around the block and pulled into an alley.

"Why should I be?" She answered as he put the car in neutral and twisted around and folded his arms over the back of the seat.

"For one, you are sure built. What are those, thirty-sixes?" Within minutes Ronnie talked the woman out of her sweater and bra. "Now those are some very nice breasts. Jake, aren't they nice?"

Jake just sat in his seat, his eyes staring into the night. *What the fuck you doin' Ronnie? I'm going to lose my job.*

Jake was trying not to pay attention to the line that Ronnie was giving the woman when he heard, "Jake look at these tits…"

79

Ronnie poked Jake in the arm, "Just look at these wonderful, beautiful tits."

"I don't want to look. I don't want..." Jake paused for a second, then blurted out, "No, I do want her out of the fuckin' car. Now!" Each word got louder as he spoke.

The woman was fully clothed and back in front of the address where Ronnie picked her up within minutes. "Sorry, lady. My new partner does not appreciate pure beauty." She blew Ronnie a kiss as she walked up the porch. "What the fuck, are you queer or something?" Ronnie was spitting mad as he pulled away from the curb.

"Am I queer? Did you happen to notice that there is a big gold wing painted on the side of this black car that has the word 'Detroit Police' under it? And damn it, I have a wife and three kids at home. All I would need is for someone to drop a dime in a phone and my family and badge are gone." Jake's heart was pounding like he just sprinted six blocks after a car thief. "And you want to know if I am queer?"

The car went silent as Ronnie drove around their territory. The bars were closed. The traffic was light. Ronnie just drove. After an hour he pulled into the Algiers Motel. This was his regular coffee stop. "Listen for the radio," he snapped. He left and went into the lobby to join Maria, the attractive Hispanic woman who worked most of the night shifts. A half hour passed before he got back in the car. "What I can't understand about you, Bush, is the word was out that you and Lucius were swapping wives and here, I can't have a little fun..."

"That was a bullshit lie just because I worked the 'Coal Car' without calling in sick. Yeah right, I'm gonna swap wives with my partner—any partner." Jake shifted around to look at Ronnie. "Did anyone say why I was bounced off of Thirteen-Nine after just a month?"

"Didn't ask," said Ronnie as he drove slowly along the curb on Hamilton Avenue.

Jake started shining the spotlight on the business fronts, looking for signs of broken glass or forced entry on the doors. He continued the conversation.

"Because I said no broads. No whores, no bullshit. If you want me off the car, do as they did. Tell the boss we don't get along." Jake hung the spot light back under the dash. "There is something else you better know about me. I don't drink and I don't steal. If any of these faults undermine the way you or your partner operate, then you better see the bosses and get me moved. It's your choice."

Two days later, Jake was working with Jim Breedlove. "He did what?" Was Jim's response when Jake told him about the girl in the back seat of their car. "Why that slick little Dago. Don't worry about me Jake. I don't do that shit."

Near the end of the month, May's assignments were posted. Jake checked the board. Ronnie must have decided he could tolerate Jake because he was still on the car.

Jake was finishing updating the stolen car board on April 25th when the bell on the Teletype machine sounded. He tore off the paper the machine had spit out and read it, making notations in the car's log book.

The teletype was on a Robbery Armed Tenth Precinct. Wanted was a 1963 Buick Electra "225" Black over gray with three male Negro occupants. Two of the men entered Racey's Drug store at 12546 Dexter at about 10:35 PM April 25, 1964. Jake paused and checked his watch. *Just over a half hour ago.* He continued reading. One subject shot an eighteen-year-old customer when he didn't move fast enough. Two clerks and twenty-one customers were robbed of cash and jewelry. Also over $1,000 in assorted bills was taken from the two cash registers. The perpetrators were described as #1, Male, 35, 6'3", 220 pounds, dark complexion, wearing a dark stingy brimmed hat and a brown zippered waist length jacket. He was armed with a nickel-plated revolver and he was the shooter. #2, Male, 35, tall, medium build, light colored

81

skin. He was armed with a dark revolver. There was no description on the driver of the car.

Jake waited at the wheel of his car after relieving the afternoon crew. Bob Harford was filling in on the car while Ronnie and Jim were off. Bob was a fourteen-year veteran who traded to work straight midnights. He climbed in the car, tossing his hat on the dashboard. "I had to call home before we took off to make sure all's right on the farm."

Jake drove the car north on Woodward. "The board is up to date, and the book has a couple of new teletypes in it. I'm going to sit on a light for a while."

"Right to business, eh?" Jake pulled to the curb on Woodward near Euclid. Bob continued, "You'll need to handle any court cases that come our way. I have a foal due tomorrow."

"A what?" Jake glanced over at his partner. Bob was buffing the toes on his black cowboy boots with a handkerchief, as he propped them up one at a time on the dash.

"A foal; a colt. My mare's ready to pop. May even be tonight. That's why I called home. Wife's calling the station if things change."

While watching the light, small talk enlightened Jake. Bob had a horse farm near Twenty-five Mile and Van Dyke. Bob's plan was to work midnights another ten and a half years. If he kept his nose clean he could keep playing cowboy during the day. His eighty-acre farm would be paid off by then. His only concern was someone reporting that he lived outside of the city. Then he would have to decide between his badge and cowboy boots.

Jake and Bob wrote four movers and went over to the S&C Restaurant. Jake sat with the car while Bob was out having a coffee.

The radio sounded: "All units. This is an update on teletype 6750, Robbery Armed and shooting Number Ten..." The description of the car and men were repeated. "Approach with caution. The men are armed and dangerous." The radio message tailed off as Bob got into the car.

"What was that all about?"

"The teletype info in the book on a R.A. Number Ten," Jake answered. He put the car in gear.

"Not having coffee?" Bob asked as Jake started driving north on Second.

"Maybe later. I want to check the area first."

A Black over Gray Buick pulled onto Second Avenue off of Hazelwood. It was 2:15 a.m. "Bob, check out the Buick. It's like the one wanted in Number Ten." Jake stayed a block behind the Buick. "Quick, read the descriptions to me again."

Bob picked up the book, before opening it he said, "Look Jake, I have a colt due. I don't want any trouble."

"Just read me the Teletype."

"Robbery Armed, Number Ten. Three Black males. 1963 Black over Gray Buick Electra 225." Bob continued reading the physical descriptions.

"Well we've got two men in that Buick and I'm going to pull 'em over," Jake said as he hit the gas to catch up to it.

Jake flipped on the flashing red light while Bob motioned the car over to the right curb on the one-way street.

The driver rolled down his window as Jake approached. "Turn off the ignition," Jake commanded. "Both of you, you're your hands where I can see them."

"What the fuck you stoppin' us fo'?" the driver snapped. He started to open his door when Jake had his pistol pointed at him.

"I said hands where I can see them!" In the corner of his eye, Jake saw Bob covering the passenger side of the Buick. "Slowly, I want the passenger out of the car. Hands first." Jake watched the driver as the passenger started to move.

Bob barked, "Out and put your hands on the roof." The passenger slid out of the car and did as told.

Jake watched the driver as Bob patted down his man. When this was done, Jake spoke again. "Okay you. When I open your door, move out with your hands showing."

"I don't know what the fuck is going on, but my lawyer is going to hear 'bout this..." The man shouted as he slid out of the car. His six foot three muscular frame slowly turned and he put his hands on the top of the car. He wore a brown zippered jacket and a short brimmed black hat. "I am going to have your white, honky ass. You ain't fuckin' with some dumb assed street nigger."

Jake kicked at the inside of the driver's feet to spread them apart, keeping his pistol on him. He patted the man down with his free hand. The man was clean. "Okay, both of you. Move to the back of the car and put your hands on the trunk."

"I'm gonna sue your ass. Your kids won't have milk for their cereal," the driver added as he moved to the back of the car. "If you didn't have that gun you'd know who you were fuckin' with." The passenger never said a word. Jake and Bob each handcuffed a man and they sat them in the back of Thirteen-Seven.

"Bob, call for a car to assist while I check the car."

"The Teletype said two men, about thirty-two. The one ain't close to that," Bob said out of earshot of the prisoners.

"Maybe they ditched one of the guys and this young guy's the driver. No description was given on him." Jake turned and went back to the Buick. The car was clean. No guns. No money. Jake popped the trunk. It too was empty.

Thirteen-Five arrived to transport the car. Bob crowded into the back with the two prisoners. The driver of the Buick was yapping as Jake got behind the wheel, "There's going to be hell to pay over this. I have my rights..."

Jake adjusted the car's mirror to look into the eyes of the man doing all the talking. "There's been a hold up and a car like yours was used. Someone was shot. If you're clean, you have nothing to worry about."

At the station the identification produced showed the driver of the car to be Melvin Camak, 32, of 136 Connecticut, Highland Park. The passenger was Thomas Leslie, 20 of 1218 Glynn Court, Detroit. Camak was yelling in the background from the bullpen as Bush talked to Lieutenant Rosema.

"Here is the teletype, Lou. Hold up and shooting Number Ten. Ten thirty or so last night."

Lieutenant Thaddeus Rosema read the Teletype. "Any guns? Money?"

"The driver's got a couple of hundred dollars on him, but the car is clean. No guns."

"Make a report on information and boot them."

"But Lou, take a look at them. The driver fits the description of the shooter."

"You could find twenty-five guys in Buick Two Twenty-five's that fit the description. Make your report and boot 'em."

Jake left the lieutenant and grabbed the phone off the wall. He had heard that this lieutenant was quick to boot suspects. Jake dialed the number of the warrant desk at headquarters.

"McCray, Warrants."

"This is Bush, Number Thirteen. Do you have anything on Camak. A Melvin Camak of 156 Connecticut, Highland Park. That's C-A-M-A-K. DOB, 12-15-32. And please—look hard. My boss wants to boot him and I think he's a shooter in a hold up. The Dick's should see this guy before he walks."

There was a long pause on the other end of the phone. "Bush, I have a warrant for a Camak, same address, first name of Lawrence. Larceny from a building. Write this down. Warrant number 153224, Number Ten Detective Bureau."

"You said Lawrence?"

"Probably a brother. Use this warrant number and my name. That'll hold him for the detectives. Any questions come up, let's just say it's my mistake."

"What the fuck you mean a warrant on Camak? I told you to make a report and boot the bastards" The lieutenant was red in the face as he talked. "Might as well hold them both for Investigation Robbery Armed. Use the warrant number as a back up." He paused for a moment, adding, "Next time, when I say boot them, I mean boot them."

"Sorry boss, just trying to do my job." Jake turned, *Thanks you Mr. Warrant Clerk.* Jake had a feeling. And the only good description was of the shooter. The driver of the car, Melvin Camak, fit that description.

The next night Jake checked with the afternoon detective crew. Camak was released on a writ at 5:30 a.m., the same night of his arrest. He walked after all.

It was late May when the sergeant handed Jake a subpoena as his name was called at roll call. Jake opened it when he got to his car. It said that there would be a Preliminary Examination for Melvin Camak, at Detroit Recorders Court scheduled for June 9, 1964. Jake checked his notes. Camak was the driver of the Buick he arrested on the 26th of April.

Jake found Detective John Krok before they started hearing the morning cases on June 9th, and told him he thought the guy walked scot free.

"You mean no one called to tell you that you arrested the right guy?"

"Not a word until I got the subpoena. I had to look back at my notes to see who Camak was."

"He did get out on a writ before we could put him in a line up, but your doorman already got mug shots. I used them when I was interviewing the witnesses at the drug store. Bingo! They all fingered Camak out of the twenty or more pictures I flashed." The detective looked at Jake, "He was the shooter. It took us another two weeks to find him again. Jake smiled as he thought of Lieutenant Rosema.

The detective continued, "We made him on another Robbery Armed too. He got cocky and pulled another after you arrested him. By the way, good work Bush."

"My boss wanted him booted. Ol' Rosie will never know."

"He'll know. I'll make sure I do a write up on this. I'll send the lieutenant a copy."

Detective Krok was good on his word. Harford and Bush received Citations for "Meritorious Police Work." Lieutenant Thaddeus Rosema gave Bush his at roll call two months after the original arrest. He didn't smile when he shook Bush's hand. His voice cracked as he said, "Good work, officer."

A jury trial found Camak guilty of robbery armed six months later. He was sentenced to Jackson Penitentiary. His accomplice in the drug store robbery was identified through mug shots as Edward Collins, 32, of 609 Hague, Detroit. Neither would finger the driver of the get away car. Judge Davenport sentenced them the maximum time allowed. Jake did the math. They'd be in until 2004.

Chapter 9

"Thirteen-Three, alarm at 9044 Russell, ADT man is on the way."

"Want to back them up, Ronnie?" Jake asked as he neared the corner of Woodward and Kenilworth. They were working days and it was a Sunday morning.

"That's one place you do not want to go, Bush, believe me," Ronnie answered. "It's the Morris Store's Warehouse."

"Sunday may be a good time for a B&E."

"Trust me on this Bush, let Don and Rudy handle it."

Jake drove slowly north on Second Avenue, and then checked the few businesses not boarded up on Hamilton. It was a beautiful day, a good day to cruise with the windows down. The minister was still talking and shaking hands on the steps of the Second Congregational Church of Jesus Christ. He saw the police car and waved, flashing a smile at the officers.

"Friend of yours, Jake?" Ronnie asked while returning the wave. Some of the people in suits, hats and fancy dresses waved too.

"That's the Black Diamond's church. And yes, I met the preacher. Nice guy." Jake smiled; knowing nobody knew what all went on a year ago. "The church ladies make some fine Sunday dinners too."

"Don't tell me Lucius took you to one of them?"

Jake thought he'd throw a bit of gossip for Ronnie to pass around the station. "Gotta eat somewhere, right? They make fine southern fried chicken and sweet potato pie."

The radio broke the small talk. "Thirteen-Seven-O. Thirteen-Seven-O. Shots fired at 9044 Russell. Meet Thirteen-Three." There was a slight pause in the radio. "All cars in Number thirteen. Thirteen-Three is looking for a Negro male, 17-18 years old. 5-8, 150 pounds, wearing jeans and a green short sleeve shirt. Last seen running north on the railroad tracks at Caniff and Greeley."

"Damn, I should have cruised down that way," Jake muttered as he turned east on Woodland. "Maybe we can find this guy roaming the streets."

"Still not a place you want to be, Jake," Ronnie added as he wrote the description on the clipboard, " 'specially you."

The afternoon ended with Thirteen-Four picking up the man wanted for the burglary. Jake walked into the squad room as Rudy Ruediger was telling those within earshot, "Yeah, I saw him stumble as I let a round fly his way. Thought I hit the nigger." Rudy was in a crouched position mimicking with his finger as if it were his Colt. "Bastard leaped a fence and was gone in a heartbeat."

"Was he the guy Four got?" Ambrose asked.

"Yeah, that was him," Rudy shot back.

"Next time how 'bout a better description, Rudy ol' boy." Ambrose took the floor. "Thirteen is a long way from seventeen, and five-two is a ways from five-eight."

"Who gives a shit? They all look alike anyway," answered Rudy as Jake left the crowd.

Roll call was held and Jake was making his way down the back steps to the parking lot. Rudy yelled to him. "Hey Jake, we'll meet you at Tom Babcock's house. Don, Bill and I'll ride home with him."

"What the hell are you talking about?"

"Just meet us at Babcock's," Rudy answered.

Jake walked to his car confused. As he neared his Rambler station wagon it became obvious. The car was full except for the front seat. A crate filled the back of the station wagon right to the rear of the front seat. Small boxes were stacked in corners. Jake read a couple of the boxes. One was a drill the other an electric frying pan.

He yelled at the blue uniforms climbing into Babcock's station wagon. "Hold it, Rudy." Jake ran between cars in the lot to get to

Tom's. Rudy looked up from the back seat of the car. A smile vanished from his face as Jake spoke. "The only thing I'm taking home are the guys I drove to work with, nothing else."

"Oh Jake, just meet us at Tom's." Rudy smiled as he spoke.

"You don't understand, Rudy. In five minutes if my car is not empty of all that shit, I'm going in to the station and make a report of found property. And I don't think it'll take a Dick Tracy too long to figure out where that stuff came from."

Bill, Don and Rudy climbed out of the car. Don spoke. "Don't do anything stupid, Bush."

"I'll say it one more time, the only thing riding in that car with me are the guys in the car pool. Nothing else."

"Jake, be a sport, just meet us at Tom's…"

Jake cut Bill short. "Someone shot at a kid running from a B&E. And now someone wants me to haul more shit than six kids could carry." Jake looked his car then added, "I'm going in the station to have a coffee. When I come out my car had better be empty. Your choice."

Jake's gut ached as he re-entered the building. His hands were shaking as he tried to pour a coffee in one of the paper cups sitting next to the pot. "Shit!" The hot liquid burned as he slopped it on his left hand.

The ride home was tense. Bill was bidding from the front seat of the Rambler with Rudy who was sitting behind Jake. "Give you fifty bucks for that above ground pool."

Oh, that's what was in the crate.

"Hell, it'd cost you three hundred at Wards," Rudy retorted.

The bid went back and forth three times when Jake jumped in. "Bill, your dad retired from the department, right?"

"So what?"

"How many things did he bring home where you wondered where it came from?" Jake's question brought a halt to the bidding.

"How in the fuck did we get this saint in our car pool?" Rudy poked Jake in his shoulder as he talked.

"I'm not a saint, but I am not a crook. And by the way, this is my last day in the car pool. You won't have to worry about me again." Jake finished the sentence as he pulled onto the twenty thousand block of Dresden. Tom's red Rambler station wagon full of stuff was already parked in the driveway.

The crew got out and Jake drove around the block to his own house. His three kids were playing in the back yard as he came around the corner and parked the Rambler in the garage. Deb, the eldest, grabbed at his hand as he pulled the garage door down. "Daddy, you put any bad guys in jail today?"

Mike bumped into Michelle as he tripped grabbing for his father's leg. Jake picked him up. Mike poked at the badge on Jake's chest, squealing, "P'liceman. Daddy's p'liceman." A tear rolled down Jake's cheek. It was a day he couldn't share with his wife.

Jake became at ease working Thirteen-Seven since there was an unspoken rule of "No naked women." Ronnie still teased all the waitresses and had his coffee with the midnight girl at the Algiers Motel, but he kept things on the up and up while working with Jake. What happened the rest of the time, Jake didn't care.

Jake's other partner, Jim Breedlove, asked Jake to join him in the leather business he had going. They made holsters and blackjacks. The main product was the 24-ounce blackjack and filled orders as fast as they could. Jim and Jake also took on odd jobs to make extra money such as painting houses or doing electrical wiring. They also went in on a small fishing boat. Jim and Jake became partners both on the job and off the job.

Jim's aunt needed her house painted. Aunt Martha poured the coffee at her kitchen table as she talked about getting the trim painted. After a tour around the two and a half story house Jim sent Jake to pick up some paint from the Glidden Store on 6 Mile. "Get a five gallon bucket of the white oil based stuff. Have Frank put it on my account. He gives policemen a break on the price. Here's a list of some other things we'll need."

Jake left for the paint store, knowing Jim would get them a good wage for the job on the 2½-story house. He started in the door of Frank's Paint Supply, and then remembered the list over his visor. He caught a glimpse of Louie Begin, his old pistol instructor from the academy cutting through the parking lot in a non-descript Chevy. Jake waved, but Louie looked away. He grabbed the list from over his visor and banged back into the store.

Guess he don't remember me. Oh well, lots of guys going through his classes no doubt. Jake forgot about Louie, got the paint, two four inch wide paintbrushes and a couple of two inchers. He checked the list then found two wire brushes and scrappers for knocking off loose paint.

Sultry summer nights meant writing a ticket or two to pass the time and please the bosses. It was close to four thirty on a Sunday morning. Jake was driving and next up for a ticket when a maroon Caddie blew a red light right in front of him. Within a block he caught up to the car and motioned the driver over. Jake walked up to the car as the driver rolled down the window. "Sir, can I see your license and registration?"

"There a problem officer?" the middle-aged driver asked as he handed the papers to Jake.

"You kinda blew that red light back there at Clay."

"Well, you see officer, I had a very late business meeting. And my wife always goes to six o'clock mass on Sunday mornings. She doesn't drive, so I am rushing to get her to church. Sorry."

Jake looked at the license and registration and handed them back. "I don't want to hold you up. I know what it's like trying to keep a wife happy. Have a safe trip." The Cadillac drove off as Jake climbed into his car.

"What are you doin', Jake?" asked Ronnie. That was a good red lighter."

"He's got to get his ol' lady to mass at six."

"You are shittin' me, right?"

"I guess you didn't see it?"

"See what?"

"I'll show you." Jake gunned the Ford and caught back up to the Cadillac as it got into Highland Park. "Look at the passenger door."

There, just below the door handle was a spent rubber clung to the door just above the chrome molding. "I am betting it makes it all the way for Mr. Melton to get the missus to mass." Jake dropped his speed back and made a U-turn to get back to his territory. "He probably thinks I'm a nice guy. If the rubber makes the trip—he will pay."

"Bush, you're a bastard."

"Yes, I am."

Jake and Ronnie were eating breakfast at the S&C on Second Avenue. It was just after five a.m. on July 20, 1964. They were sitting at the counter. To Jake's left sat a man with a smooth voice. Jake recognized the voice as that of Jay Roberts, Captain of Night Flight 760, the disc jockey on WJR. That was the station Ronnie always played on his little transistor radio sitting in the corner of the car's dash.

The music was soft and smooth, just as Jay's voice. Every night Jay, the Captain, would take the listeners on a make-believe flight to some far off place. Altitude, speed and destination weather forecasts were part of the trip as well as what to see and explore in Spokane, Albuquerque or wherever the make-believe flight was headed.

Jay was talking to a very beautiful blonde to his left eating breakfast. Jake could hear the conversation.

"So what is a pretty lady like yourself do that you eat breakfast at this hour?"

"I'm a call girl."

"You know, that's got to be hard work. Answering calls for Doctors, Dentists and…"

93

"You don't understand," she interrupted. "Call girl, like in prostitute."

Jake leaned over the counter looking past the Captain of Night Flight 760, "One-Oh-One Edison?"

"Yes, that's the place, officer. Come and see us some time..." She dropped a ten to cover her breakfast and left the restaurant. All eyes watched as she walked with the elegance of a model.

"Call girl? Her? I can't believe it." Jay's face was flushed as he signaled the waitress for more coffee.

Jake added more sugar to his cup as she poured. "I'd never have guessed it either."

"She can take my calls anytime," Ronnie chimed in.

"By the way, Jay, I hear it's a two hundred dollar a night place," Jake added.

"I'm a happily married man, officers." Jay paid his bill and got up to leave. "News is about over, got to get back behind the mic."

"There goes my hero, the captain," Ronnie said as he finished his coffee.

"Maybe we ought to take him on one of our night flights, Ronnie."

"Yeah, to far off and erotic places, like Canfield and John R."

Jake pulled into his garage only to remember he was supposed to pick up some milk on the way home. He quickly backed out, cutting off a non-descript Chevy. He tried to motion he was sorry, but the driver looked away as if not caring about the close call. It was Louie Begin, the pistol instructor from the academy.

Strange, seeing Louie twice in two weeks.

The no naked women rule was intact until Thirteen-Seven got a run. "113 Chandler, Apartment Fourteen. See the man, family trouble." Ronnie knocked at the door and a black man motioned for the officers to come in. He wore a yellow short-sleeved shirt, dark pants and a pair of house slippers.

Ronnie asked, "You call the Police?"

"Yes sir, I did. My wife has had a bit to drink and she's raisin' a ruckus..." His soft voice was interrupted.

"What the hell you callin' the po-lice for, Edgar?" She walked in with an exaggerated sway wearing a peach-colored robe with a fluffy feather-like collar. "Well hello there Mr. Po-licemen." She walked around Ronnie and Jake, looking from head to toe.

"Now Naomi, don't you go..."

"Hell, las' time they sent a couple of big ugly suckers. Ah like the looks of these two guys." She circled around Ronnie and Jake again. "You know I'm half white. My daddy was a Polack."

"Don't listen to her officers. Naomi, don't..."

"Just hush, Edgar. These two just might want to feast their eyes on a real woman." The robe fell to the floor and all she had on was her light colored skin with a pair of high-heel slippers that matched the robe at her feet. "What'cha think? Like to try on a little half Polack?"

Edgar grabbed at her wrist. "Naomi, get the damn robe on. You're embarrassing me."

"Take your fuckin' hands off of me!"

"Get your damn robe on!"

"I can show my ass to anyone I want."

Edgar slapped his wife across the face. "Get the damn robe on!"

Jake had the woman by the arms as she started kicking at her husband.

"Hold onto her, Jake. I'll get Edgar out," Ronnie yelled as he grabbed Edgar and started out the apartment door.

Naomi was spitting and yelling, "Ain't no man slappin' my face. Come back here Nigger!"

Jake held one arm and tried picking up the robe. "Here lady, put this on."

"Let go a me. I'll kill that mutha fucker." The robe fell back onto the floor as Jake held the woman trying not to touch her exposed parts. "Come back here, you chicken-shit mutha fucker!"

Jake was hoping that Ronnie had Edgar down the two flights of stairs and into the car before he let Naomi go. He ran out of the apartment and held the door shut for a few more seconds until he felt she wasn't trying to pull it open. He ran down the stairs and into the car. The window above the street was open and Naomi and her tits were hanging out, yelling, "Hope they throw you ass in jail an' never letchew out." Ronnie drove into the night.

Jake had the clipboard out. "Can I have your name, sir?"

"Edgar Simons."

"Age?"

"Thirty-five."

"Wife's Name?"

"Naomi Simons. She's thirty-three."

Ronnie asked, "Got a place to stay for the night?"

"You're not takin' me to jail?"

"What for?" Ronnie asked.

"Thought the police had to take you to jail when they see you hit a woman."

"Well, I don't know what we saw," Jake said. "If you' promise not to go home 'til tomorrow, we'll just make a report and call it good."

"I've got a sister on Alexandrine. She'll put me up."

Edgar Simons was dropped of at 144 Alexandrine.

Jake was making out the report over coffee at the S&C when Ronnie spoke. "Thought you didn't like tits, Jake."

"What are you talking about?"

"I saw you eyeing up ol' Naomi's jugs. Damn they were nice weren't they?"

"They were there, but I wasn't eyeing them up."

"Sure Jake. Didn't get a good feel either when you were wrestling with her I'll bet."

"Ronnie, I…"

"She had a cute nose too. Kind of a Polish nose. From her daddy no doubt." Ronnie laughed and finished his coffee. "Did you make a date to meet her after work?"

"That's enough, Ronnie."

It was November 4, 1964 and Jake was pushing a cart up and down the isles of the local Chatham Super Market. His wife made the list and he did the shopping. He grabbed two gallons of milk from the refrigerated case. As he let the door close he caught movement in the corner of his eye. Someone was coming out of an isle and ducked when he saw Jake turning. *Louie Begin.* Jake left the cart went down another isle and caught sight of Louie making it out the front door. He yelled as Louie got to the door of a nondescript Chevy. "Louie, hang on." The man in a small brimmed fedora stopped and turned. *Yes, it was Louie.*

"Once, I can buy it," Jake said, not waiting for Louie to say anything. "Twice, pure coincidence. Three times? Louie, you're following me."

"How do you know me?"

"You were my pistol instructor at the academy. Early 1962. Still a cop I'll bet."

"Yes, only with CID."

"CID? You investigate cops?"

"Got somewhere we can talk? Have a coffee?"

"My house. Two blocks over… I guess you already know."

"Anyone there?"

"The wife is working. The kids are with a sitter. I had court this morning."

Louie got into his car. "Grab your groceries. I'll wait on the street by your place."

"You'd better be there. I want some answers."

"I'll be there."

Over coffee Louie spilled his guts.

"Not a word of this can be leaked. Not to your wife, and for sure, not to anyone on the job. It'd be my ass if word got out and we'd have our case blown wide open. Something we're not ready for yet."

Jake sipped his coffee as Louie told him that he had been followed for the past two and a half months. Jake's entire shift was being watched while they were at work and on their days off.

"Why?"

"I have your word on this, right?"

"You do."

"First off, I want you to know I know you are on the up and up. Otherwise we would not be talking."

Louie then unfolded the story behind the reason for the tail: The Morris Store's warehouse. He told Jake about infra red, nighttime films of police cars going to the 10 foot cyclone gate, an officer rattling it, then the car moving off until they no doubt got a radio call to "Meet the man from ADT." When the guard from the security company arrived, he would open the gate and along with a scout car crew or two, search the three-story structure for burglars. The films showed officers loading material into the trunks of their cars or in their back seats. Sometimes two or three trips on one radio call.

"We got positive ID's on a couple of guys. My boss put the tails on to see who all is involved. After two and a half months of living and working with you, I know I can scratch you off of the list."

Jake thought for a minute. He knew Don and Rudy worked the area that covered the warehouse. Two and a half months did not take them back to that Sunday when his car was full of merchandise from the warehouse.

"When you gonna nail them?"

"Some day when they slip up. The Morris brothers, do not want to drag the name of the Detroit Police Department in the mud. They won't prosecute as of now. But, we'll get them." Louie finished his second cup of coffee. "The alarm on the gate has been fixed. No more false alarms. No make believe radio calls on a burglar. But, they'll slip up." Jake took the hint and led Louie to the door. "Remember, not a word."

"Don't worry. Just don't get caught by the next cop you tail." The non-descript Chevy drove off with Jake noticing that one brake light was burned out. He thought of calling CID to report it, but put it out of his mind.

It wasn't until December 14th that Don and Rudy made the headlines of the *Detroit Free Press* and *The Detroit News*. Two weeks before Christmas, they tried to shake down a local electrical supply business. A demand for a case of Crown Royal for the scout car crew working the area brought in a special squad from the Commissioners office. They were fired. It was termed a suspension in the papers, but they never returned. Half of the Thirteenth Precinct officers said they were set up. Jake knew better.

1964 ended with Jake involved in just over two hundred arrests. Robberies, burglaries, and stolen car arrests were the norm in the Thirteenth Precinct just for showing up, answering radio runs and paying attention.

Chapter 10

The snow had stopped. About five inches were turning to slush under the tires on Woodward Avenue. It was a January night Jake was cruising Chicago Boulevard just after bar closing time when the radio broke the silence. "Thirteen-Seven see the Manager, 10244 Woodward."

"It's that restaurant just off of Trowbridge," Jim said after he acknowledged the run.

As the door of the restaurant closed behind the officers, they could hear a woman's voice.

"I ain't payin' for no fuckin' swimp dinner. They tasted like shit."

"Fine," the man answered, his tie was loosened and the top button undone on his white shirt. "The police are here."

"What've you got going mister?" Jake asked.

"This woman comes in and orders a shrimp dinner. It's $5.50. She eats all of it and now won't pay."

A plate was on the table in front of the blonde. Six tails from deep fried shrimp lay among a smattering of rice pilaf and green beans. She wore a fur wrap dangling off her shoulders. "The fuckin' swimp were rotten, and I'm not paying no five fifty for it."

"Looks like they were good enough to eat, so they're good enough to pay for. That, or it's off to jail." Jake looked into her heavily painted eyes, "Your choice."

"So take me to jail. I am not paying this asshole a dime." The blonde threw her napkin on the table; stood and straightened the tight purple slacks tucked into her high, black patent leather boots.

Jake looked at the manager. "See the Thirteen Precinct Detectives at eight in the morning. You'll have to appear to get a warrant. If you don't show, she'll be bounced."

He took the arm dangling under the fur wrap, "It would be a lot easier paying the five and a half bucks than spending the night in jail, don't you think?"

"I am not giving the bastard one cent."

Jake tugged at her elbow. "Come on sweetheart, I guess you can digest the shrimp in the ladies lockup."

"You don't need to pull at my arm, an' I'm not your sweetheart."

"Just a phrase, lady, I wouldn't have you either."

Jim stayed behind to get the information needed for the report. Jake had the woman seated in the back of their car when Jim came out. Jim slid in beside the prisoner. Jake got behind the wheel and made a U-turn on Woodward, heading to Number Thirteen.

The woman spoke, "Just let me off at the corner of Euclid, darling, by the Disc Jockey Lounge."

"For one, this is not a Yellow Cab," Jake said over his shoulder. He adjusted his rearview mirror to look into the back seat. "What makes you think that I'm just gonna drop you off on the next corner?"

She was applying another layer of lipstick using a small mirror as she answered. "Because I am the best at getting a cop's gun off, isn't that right Jim honey?"

Jake's eyes shifted in his mirror to the face of Jim Breedlove. In the night-lights of Woodward Avenue shining into the back seat he could see the blush rise on the cheeks of his partner. The nose of the police car dove toward the pavement as Jake hit the brakes. He jumped out and opened the door behind him. "Out bitch!" He grabbed the blonde's arm and jerked her out of the car.

"Who the fuck you callin' a bitch?" She yelled over the screeching tires as Jake jumped behind the wheel and made another quick U-turn on Woodward.

Jim Breedlove sat there in the back seat as Jake pulled up to 10244 Woodward. He didn't turn around, speaking in a low tone. "Get in there and pay the money she owes."

"Say she had a change of heart."

"Jake, I..."

"If you don't the guy'll be in to see the Dicks in the morning and someone will have to explain what happened. It won't be me."

Jim bought out Jake's interest in the boat and the blackjack partnership was dissolved. They had agreed, when the boat was bought, that when one wanted out of the partnership, the other had first choice. Jim wanted the boat. Jake asked the bosses for a transfer to another car.

Jake was in the bosses office before roll call. "Sarge, I asked off of Seven, what happened?"

"Sorry Jake, it was too late to make changes for the month. I don't know what's going on between you guys, but you're there for another month."

"Put me on a beat then. Let one of the rookies ride in my place."

"That serious, eh?" Sergeant Knight scribbled on a pad. "It's February and damn cold out there."

"I'll wear my long johns."

"Okay, I'll pencil you in on Beat 33. Higgins can take your place on Seven.

"Thanks." Jake went out and waited for roll call.

The March roster came out with Jake working Thirteen-Three with two new partners. Michael Mulligan was the senior man.

"Thirteen-Three, Oakland and Holbrook, a man doing traffic."

"Three on the way." Jake hung up the mic and wrote the run down on their log sheet.

"Must be Tommy," Mike Mulligan said as he turned onto Oakland off of East Grand Boulevard.

"You know him?"

"Yeah. He's got cerebral palsy and lives with his mother. Every now and then he likes playing traffic cop. He grabs a whistle, dresses as close to police blue as possible and starts directing traffic somewhere in our territory."

Holbrook came into view and there in the middle of the intersection under the overhead traffic light was a mustached man in his mid-forties. He wore a dark blue wrinkled jacket and a light blue shirt. He had on a dark navy tie and black pants. He stopped the Holbrook traffic with a long shrill blow on his whistle when he saw the black police car approaching. Mike pulled the car to the curb, swung open his door and waved to the man in the street. "Tommy, time for a coffee break."

Tommy approached the police car. Mike pointed a thumb over his shoulder toward the back seat. Tommy slid in. "A-ah, Th-anks f-for the br-eak, O-Office-err Mull-lligan. C-Cars ke-eep co-oming. Mu-ust be the Dodge Plant le-etting out early." Tommy had to force most of the words out, the volume rising and falling as he talked.

Mike started to drive away. "Tommy, this is my new partner, Jake Bush."

A wide smile came across Tommy's face as Jake reached back to shake his hand. "Does th-the rookie bahh-y the donuts?" asked Tommy.

"That's the rules, right Tommy?" Mike laughed. "Donuts on the rookie."

Tommy looked back over his shoulder. "O-Officer Mul-lllligan, you su-ure the tra-traffic will be ah-all right without me?"

"Yeah, I think you got it straightened out. The light should handle what's left."

Jake sat there confused with the conversation. The middle-aged man in the back seat had an obvious handicap, but his partner never let on to it. Their car pulled up to the rear of The Donut Hole on Cass. "Jake, let's all go in and discuss Tommy's new assignment."

"Wha-what new ah-ah-assignment?" Tommy's eyes brightened as he held the door open for the two police officers.

The coffee was poured and three powdered sugar donuts showed up when Mike spoke. "There's been a rash of stolen cars in the area. We're moving you up from the traffic department to the stolen car department. Do you think you can handle something like that?"

"Yes sir. Ju-just tell me wha-at to do," Tommy spoke between the three bites it took to down his donut.The powdered sugar had sprinkled his tie like it had snowed.

"We'll meet you about once a week. Give you a list of stolen cars. All you have to do is to check the streets and alleys for plate numbers on the sheet. Call us when you find something. Easy enough?" There was no smile on Mike's face and a serious tone in his voice.

"Ye-Yes sir. Ye-es sir, O-Office-er Mulligan. I ca-an do that. Whe-en do I start?" Tommy's cup was shaking as he moved it to his lips. The splashing coffee washed the white off of the frazzled mustache hairs.

"Tomorrow. We'll meet you on the corner of Holbrook and Oakland. Make it just after eight in the morning. Is 8:15 all right?"

"Ye-es, sir. I'll be the-ere." Tommy was beaming as he finished his coffee.

"But there is one thing that you must do to make this assignment a success, Tommy," Mike paused to look deep into the man's eyes. "You have to give up the traffic duty. No more directing traffic anywhere in the precinct. You're going undercover."

"I ca-an do tha-at, O-Officer Mull-lligan. A-an undercover ah-ah-ssignment." He put his finger to his lips. "Hush-hush. U-undercover."

Thirteen-Three took Tommy back to Oakland and Holbrook and dropped him off. As he climbed out of the back seat, Mike saluted him, adding, "See you in the morning. Right here."

Tommy returned the salute. "8:15 sha-arp, sir."

Mike drove off toward Grand Boulevard. Within a block Jake spoke up. "What's that all about?"

"I've been on this car since Don and Rudy got the ax. I think this is five times that I got a call on ol' Tommy. I've taken him home. Talked to him like a brother. I even talked to his mother.

I've all but threatened him. And still he ends up in the middle of the street doing traffic. He is not all there, but he's harmless."

"I had a hard time understanding him."

"You just have to listen close. The words are there, they just take time coming out."

"Where does he live? Jake asked.

"Three houses off of the corner with his mom. The only whites in the neighborhood. She's getting pretty old. Tommy is all she's got, and his mom is all he has."

"And what's your plan?"

"Simple. We give him a copy of the latest stolen cars about once a week. If he finds any, he can call us. Hopefully, that'll keep him out of traffic." Mike drove around Jake's new territory. Mike talked as he drove. "Tommy's dream has always been to be a police officer. That's how he ends up doing traffic. He'll never be one, but I won't tell him that. I'm just trying to find something he can do, and to keep him from getting run over. By the way, he'll remember your name forever. I don't understand the disease. But he sure has a memory."

"You say they're the only white's in the area?"

"Yes, but the neighbors look out for Tommy and his mom. My guess is they respect her for staying."

That first hour was Jake's introduction to his new senior man, Michael Mulligan. Mike was a ten-year veteran. He had a tint of early gray on the sides of his short cut red hair and a couple of faded freckles on his cheeks. Jake liked Mike's logic and how kind he was to Tommy. Jake knew he was going to like this Irish cop.

Tommy Pine was sworn in by Officer Michael Mulligan as an undercover member of the Stolen Car Recovery Team—the name Mike gave the imaginary job—on March 4, 1965. Tommy turned in his whistle to Mike and Jake gave Tommy the latest printout on stolen cars.

"Remember, you're undercover. A secret assignment."

"Uh-underco-over, yes sir. Ca-an I tell my mo-om?" Tommy pushed the words out as he leaned over to see Mike's face.

"Just your mom. No one else."

"Y-Yes sir. Just my mo-om."

Mike dropped Tommy off at his house. "You know how our shift rotates," Mike said. "Next month we are on midnights. Just call the Police Department and ask them to have Thirteen-Three meet you when you have something for us." Tommy saluted and turned, heading for the alley behind Oakland Avenue.

Jake returned Tommy's salute. "The guy is going right to work."

"Let's see if this keeps him out of the street." Mike laughed. "Hope he don't find too many cars though. I'll get fatter than a hog eating donuts with him."

Just after lunch the radio sounded, "Thirteen-Three, meet a man, Oakland and Belmont."

"Three on the way." In five minutes Jake neared the corner. Just outside of the phone booth by the Oakland Thrift Shop stood Tommy. Jake pulled to the curb.

Tommy looked both ways, and then jumped in the back seat. "Th-the al-ley rear of ni-ine fo-our ni-ine Be-elmont. Bee Zee fo-our-three-ee two-two."

As Tommy forced out the numbers, Jake's eyes glanced at their board hanging from the middle of the dash. BZ4322 was a stolen car. "949 is on the south side of Belmont," Mike said as Jake turned onto Belmont and cut into the alley. Mid-block was a 1962 black Pontiac. A radio check confirmed the number through the Auto Squad. The car was towed to #13. Mike typed up the report. Included in the report were the words, "Location of the car reported by Thomas Pine of 1022 Holbrook." Mike made a fourth copy of the report to drop off at Tommy's house.

Jake was in Recorders Court for a couple of cases on March 5, 1965. He grabbed a coffee and went into the officer's waiting room. Jake was reviewing his notes when he heard a familiar voice.

"Jake, you playing ball for Number Thirteen this year?"

Jake looked up and smiled when he saw Jimmy Gramatico.

"Yes. How about you?"

"I'll start there, but may end up somewhere else."

"You leaving Number Eleven?"

"Yeah, sometime this summer. I don't know when. My uncle, Tony Bertolini, is heading a new unit." He paused. "Haven't you heard about it?"

"No, but then who hears anything at Number Thirteen."

"It's to be made up of ex-paratroopers and Marines. hey you' were a Marine right?"

"Yeh, spent three years in their uniform."

"Letters were sent out to all precinct commanders looking for names to be nominated. Bobby Parkhurst and I already are going from Number Eleven. They are looking for men to start the unit this summer."

"A move would be nice," Jake mumbled. "Thirteen is not what I expected."

"Not enough action?"

"The action is there, but it's taken me a long time to find a decent partner."

"Here, call this number." Jimmy wrote a number on a sheet from his notepad. "Tell the Inspector's secretary you would like to know more about the Tactical Mobile Unit. Give her my name."

Jake took the number. "Thanks. I'll check it out." Jake looked at his watch. "Gotta go I've got three cases coming up today."

As Jake left Jimmy added, "Hey, if you get in, maybe you, Bobby and I can team up on a car."

"Sounds great. See you." Jake headed for Judge DeLuca's courtroom.

Jake was working with the car's junior man. His name was George Sasse. George was six months out of the academy. Jake sized him up as he walked to the car after roll call. He was two inches taller than Jake with shallow cheeks. At 168 pounds Jake knew he was open game for anyone that wanted to roll on the pavement with a skinny cop. Now there stood George, weighing about ten pounds less.

We're sure not a pair to put fear in the hearts of the bad guys making their living on the streets of Detroit.

Jake and George spent the day feeling each other out, talking families and how they became cops between writing a couple of movers and answering ten radio runs. Jake liked his new crew.

Mildred Taylor was rearranging blouses on the counter at The Ideal Resale Shop. It was the middle of the afternoon on March 9, 1965. The bell over the door rang and she saw a mid-thirty year old man enter. He started looking at the rack of ladies coats just inside the door. He grabbed a gray winter coat and brought it to the counter. "You got something like this in red?"

Mildred walked from behind the counter toward the coat rack. She pulled out two red coats. "How do these look?" She asked, holding both up, one in each arm.

The man looked at each, smiling as his eyes stopped then went up and down the older black lady. She had on a navy skirt and a white and blue striped blouse. Her reading glasses hung from a pearl white band around her neck. "Can you try the one on in your left hand? That looks like the one I want."

"Yes I can." Mildred hung up the extra coat and walked toward the counter. A hand grabbed her from behind as she walked past the man. A knife was at her throat.

"Get in the back room." The man pushed her. "Take off your clothes. Make it quick." They were at the curtain to the back room when the bell rang over the door. Mildred let out a scream. "Hush, or I'll kill you. " Two women ran out of the store as quick as they came in when they saw the man with the knife. Mildred pushed at the man as he watched the door close. A quick slash caught her across the right shoulder as she tried to get away.

"Thirteen-Twelve, hold up in progress, 4865 Brush," blared the car radios in Number Thirteen.

Thirteen-Three was on Forest nearing Brush. "That's right around the corner," Jake said as he turned the car onto Brush. "Left side, near Warren." The brakes on the car squealed as they slid to a stop. "I'll get the back," Jake yelled as he flew out of the car. He jumped the fence to cover the rear of the store and drew his Colt.

A man burst out of the rear door running down the alley paralleling Warren. Jake was fifteen feet behind him as he cocked the pistol, yelling, "Police, halt!" The man looked over his shoulder and slid to a stop. Jake motioned with his pistol. "Up against the trunk of that car." The man put his hands on the trunk of the Oldsmobile parked in the alley.

Jake did a quick frisk, holstered his pistol, and put one handcuff on the man's left wrist. The man looked to the right back toward the store, then wheeled to his left. Jake held onto the empty cuff, the steel cutting into the palm of his left hand. Jake jerked the man to the ground with the cuffs, straddled his back and gave him a chop to the back of his neck. The man went limp.

George appeared in the alley. "You all right, Jake?"

"Cut my hand on the cuffs."

George went through the man's pockets. In the right coat pocket he pulled out a bone handled knife. In his left coat pocket was a blood stained envelope and $19.98 in bills and change. "You got our man, Jake."

"I missed the knife, though."

"Happens."

Charlie Dresser from Thirteen-Twelve was coming out the back door of the store as Jake and George walked up the alley. "You guys must have been right on top of this."

"Yeah, lucky, I guess," answered Jake. "You get the call?"

"Yeah. My partner's in the store with the lady and witnesses. She's been cut, so we'll take her to the hospital."

"Maybe we'd better," Jake said. "I'll need a shot over this." He showed the cut from the cuffs on the palm of his left hand. "Can you book the guy for us?"

"Not a problem. Better than getting a shot for lock jaw."

George and Jake worked an hour overtime finishing up the paperwork and tagging the evidence.

The next day Warrant A-124231 was obtained by the #13 Detectives for Robbery Armed on Alvis Lincoln, age thirty-five of 8545 Second. Thirteen-Three was at the Arraignment in Judge Crocket's courtroom. "Man, my first day on a car and a robbery armed arrest. I had a tough time sleeping last night," George whispered.

Jake smiled. "As close to orgasm as you can get, right?"

"What?"

"I mean, when do you get that good, warm feeling? For me it's having sex or when I slam that jail door on a bad guy."

"You're right. Closest thing for sure." George and Jake chuckled quietly to themselves.

Chapter 11

"Thirteen-Three, Mulligan and Bush."

Two voices answered simultaneously, "Here sir."

"Bush, you have some mail," the lieutenant said before continuing. "Thirteen-Four, Reese and Puckett..."

Jake picked up the envelope after roll call. The midnight crews were heading down the stairs while Jake read the letter. It was from the office of Inspector Anthony Bertolini. Jake had an appointment scheduled for 9:00 a.m., April 9, 1965, Office #1022, Detroit Police Headquarters, Beaubien Street.

Jake caught up to his partner on the ramp. He did not mention the letter. Mike was admiring the new 1965 Ford sedan that had been assigned to Thirteen-Three.

"I kinda liked the zip the Plymouths had," said Jake as slid into the jump seat.

"Me too. Guess Ford won the bid after all these years."

It was Mike's turn to drive. The radio stayed relatively silent, no calls for Thirteen-Three. Just after one in the morning Mike saw a blue Buick Roadmaster drop off a woman at Brush and East Grand Boulevard. "That's April Jackson," said Mike as he made a U-turn heading after the Buick.

"Who's April?"

"The girl that guy just dropped off. I'll introduce you later." Mike gunned the Ford and caught up to the Buick, motioning for the driver to pull over. The Buick pulled to the curb. Jake and Mike got out of the car. Jake watching from the back of the Buick as Mike talked to the driver.

"Sir, step out of the car."

"Is there a problem officer?" The man asked as he slid from behind the wheel.

"Step on to the curb," Mike ordered, following behind the man. "License and registration, please."

111

"Did I do something wrong?" Three business cards fell out of the wallet while he fumbled to find his license. Mike picked up the cards and handed them to the man. He took the license and registration from shaking hands. Mike read them in the beam of his flashlight.

"The girl you just dropped off, who is she?" Mike scanned the license as he talked.

"Just—just the baby sitter."

"Your baby sitter?" Mike shook his head and grinned. He looked back down the street, then at the driver. "Mr. Rawlins, do you know that your baby sitter is a convicted prostitute? A whore."

"You're kidding." The man shuffled his feet, looking back toward where he let the woman off. She was gone.

"I don't suppose your wife knows that either." Mike stifled a laugh. "Says here you live in St. Clair Shores. That right?"

"Yes. At 22347 Rosedale."

"Gotta phone number?"

"Lakeview seven-four-two-three-three."

"And how long would it take you to drive to your house from here, Mr. Rawlins?"

"I would guess about twenty five minutes. Why?"

"Because in thirty minutes I am going to call your phone number. Whoever answers will hear about your baby sitter."

"You wouldn't..." The man's face paled.

"I will," Mike interrupted, handing back the driver's license. "Have a safe trip, Mr. Rawlins."

The driver turned and got back into his car, fumbling with the ignition before it started. The Buick turned onto John R and drove toward the Ford Freeway.

As Mike got back into Thirteen-Three, he spoke. "I don't like the johns messing with our whores. When one gets rolled or his throat cut by a pimp, then it's us not doing our job." Mike drove to Woodward and turned right.

"This some crusade to get rid of the johns?"

"Something like that. We wouldn't have a hundred or more girls working the streets if the johns wouldn't be out looking for them."

In exactly twenty-nine minutes the police car pulled up to Woodward and Clay. Mike walked to the pay phone next to Ray's TV Repair. He deposited a dime. Jake rolled down his window to listen. There was a slight pause, then he heard Mike speak.

"Mr. Rawlins, Officer Mulligan here. Hope you didn't break any speed limits on the way home. Have a nice night." Mike hung up the phone and got back behind the wheel. "One thing for sure, he'll be lookin' over his shoulder for me when he picks up his next whore."

The thought of a spent rubber stuck to a Cadillac's door crossed Jake's mind. "I'll have to start getting phone numbers." Jake chuckled to himself, wondering if Mrs. Whomever got to mass that morning last summer.

Inspector Bertolini rose when Jake walked into the office on April 9th. He extended his hand. "John Bush?"

Jake shook the hand. "Yes sir."

"Have a seat," the tall, handsome officer said as he sat down. "Just give me a minute to check my notes."

Jake sat watching the inspector skim the papers in front of him. The man had neatly combed medium black hair with a little gray around the temples. His white shirt was crisp and a gold oak leaf was perfectly centered on each collar. Jake noticed the slight bump on his nose, no doubt broken in a fight years ago. Jake read it as a sign of a street cop.

The inspector pushed his notes aside. "How did you hear about the Tactical Mobile Unit?"

"I ran into Jimmy Gramatico at Recorder's Court, and he told me about it."

The Inspector smiled. "Ah, nephew Jimmy's out recruiting is he?" The Inspector leafed through the file in front of him. "I see you were a marine. An MP."

"Yes sir."

"Just about a year at Number Eleven. Now at Number Thirteen for over two years. Why did you leave Eleven?"

"I wanted more work, sir. I think I had only about thirty-two arrests and most were misdemeanors that first year."

"So, did you find more to do at the Woodward Station?" The Inspector read as he talked.

"Yes sir. More than I imagined."

"I see you have three citations. All robbery armed arrests."

"Yes. One came out of a lucky hunch I had. The car and driver fit a description on a hold up and shooting in Number Ten. The others were being in the right place at the right time."

"The ratings by your supervisors are about where they should be with your seniority." The inspector smoothed the hair over his right ear. "Now I know a bit about you. Maybe I should cover where I am coming from." The inspector leaned back in his chair. "Over the last couple of years things have happened that you might remember, like the near-riot at the State Fair grounds. You remember it?"

"Yes, the Mounted Bureau had to clear the fair grounds when all hell broke loose. I ended up working there for two nights to show a beefed up police presence."

The inspector stood and walked around the back of his desk. "There have been other smaller incidents too, but things died down before they really took hold. If a riot had broken out they had us by the short hairs. We have no riot squad. No way of handling a major incident. The Tactical Mobil Unit will fill that void."

Over the next half hour Inspector Bertolini outlined what he had in mind. The TMU would primarily be a mobile force to combat crime. They'd work city wide, moving from precinct to precinct as the need arose. They would also be the city's riot squad, trained and equipped to handle another problem at the State Fair or any place else.

"Some people in our city government and the department believe Detroit is ripe for a riot. I think they're right."

"The Watts riot sounded like a war in L.A."

"Yes, we want to avoid a repeat of that in Detroit." The inspector took out a folder that he had in a drawer. "We're planning on at least two weeks of riot training before the unit hits the street." The inspector pushed an eight by twelve photo of a 1965 Plymouth toward Jake.

They sure want everyone to see us.

The picture showed a white car with twin bright blue racing stripes from the hood to the trunk. It had a double blue light bar with a speaker in the middle on top of the car; a far cry from the black cars of recent years.

"We want the people to know we are out there. That's why the gaudy cars. We want them to stand out." The inspector pulled back the photo. "We'll be more than a riot squad. We'll flood any precinct at any given time to fight crime. That'll be our primary goal. What's inside those cars is of utmost importance. I want working cops. I want clean cops. I want officers that I can be proud of." He paused. "Do you think you're what I am looking for?"

Jake did not hesitate. "Yes, sir."

"Think about it, Bush. Take a day or two. Talk it over with your family. Then call my office if you're still interested. I am trying to get this off of the ground in July. The cars are on order. I need to fill the seats."

"Yes sir."

The inspector smiled and shook Jake's hand. "By the way, Jimmy, my sister's boy, did put in a word for you. Saw him last Sunday at church."

Jake called the first thing the next Monday morning. The secretary put him through to the inspector. "Sir, I do want the opportunity to work at the TMU."

"That's what I had hoped to hear. You're number twenty-two on the list." Jake wondered if the inspector could hear his heart pounding over the phone when he heard, "My office will send you a letter once the details and the timing are worked out."

Mike and Jake just finished taking a report on an attempt B&E at Woodward and Kenilworth. They were working midnights. "Let's grab a coffee," Mike said as he headed south on Woodward. They drove past a white man sitting on the curb on the east side of the street.

"Make a U-turn, Mike. I want to check a guy out."

"He'll drop a dime in a pay phone if he needs us."

"He's a white boy on Woodward and it's almost 2 a.m. Probably too scared to use a phone in this neighborhood."

"Yeah, you're right." Mike made the turn, looking for the white guy. "There he is."

The man was sitting on the curb. He had a dark mustache and his shirt was hanging half out. He was kitty corner across the street from Daley Drugs at Clairmount and Woodward. Jake rolled down his window as they stopped next to him.

"Got a problem, mister?"

"Yeah, they stole my truck." The man started to get up as Jake climbed out of his car.

"Who stole your truck?"

"Some colored dude."

"How did he get it?"

"I gave him the keys about two hours ago. Said he needed to go get groceries for a sick auntie. He never came back."

Jake opened the back door. "Have a seat."

Jake climbed back into his seat. "Got a name?"

"They call me T-Bone."

Mike started driving as Jake spun around. "Okay, Mr. T-Bone, start with your real name."

"It's Tom. Tom Bradley. T-Bone is my CB handle." Jake turned to an empty page on his clipboard. "I'm a truck driver. Drive for Wide Eye Express."

"You gave some guy the keys to your semi?"

"No, no. I am not that dumb. He's got my '60 Chevy pickup." Mike snickered as he drove slowly down Woodward while Jake took notes. "Let's start from the beginning, Mr. Bradley."

"I was at this bar in Highland Park, having a few beers and grabbing the end of a Tiger's game. This girl slides onto the stool next to me and we started talking."

"Just out of the blue, she's hitting on you. What she say her name was?"

"Man, you got it all wrong. She's a nice girl."

"Her name?" Jake pressed.

"Jackie. Short for Jacqueline, I think. A real cutie. Legs up to her..."

"Save the description for later. On with your story."

"We got to talking. She says there's this really cool blues band playing at a lounge in Detroit."

"The Disc Jockey Lounge?"

"Yeah, that's the place. So we end up there about nine. Man, it was really a cool band all right. A few tunes later, a black guy slides into the booth with Jackie and me. Says he's Jackie's cousin. I bought him a beer."

"Jackie's black?"

"No, no. She's white. Hell, I don't know. She's real light skinned if she is."

"Is this the same guy who got your truck?"

"Yeah."

"How did he get your truck?"

"He starts layin' it on us how his auntie is sick and needs some groceries. He got into what kind of cancer she has and all that stuff. Then Jackie starts crying."

"The aunt. Was this Jackie's mom?"

"I don't think so. The guy says the auntie lives around the corner and he wants to borrow my wheels for a quick run to the store. I said no and Jackie bawls even more. Hell, I gave him the keys. He promised to be back by the band's next break."

"What's his name?"

"Don't know. He never said what it was."

Mike adjusted his rear view mirror to look into the back seat. "You gave your keys to a guy and you don't even know what his name is?" He was laughing before he finished the question.

"What happened to Jackie?" Jake asked.

"She went to the powder room when the band went on break. I haven't seen her since. I even had the waitress go in and yell for her. She wasn't in there."

Mike was laughing his head off and Jake was trying to stifle his as he asked, "What's the plate number on the truck?"

"It's 1032 DW...or DH. I don't really remember. Wait, the numbers may be 2103."

"DW for dumb whitey, or DH for dumb honky?" Mike said as he glanced into the mirror again.

"Tom, what's the color of your truck?" Jake interrupted.

"It's a two-tone. Black and silver."

"Got someone you can call on the plate number?"

"No. I live alone. The papers are in the truck."

"I'm going to check the Clark Station on the Boulevard." Mike said as he made a left turn. "They might be using it for something like a hold up."

Jake turned to face their passenger. "You do know there aren't any stores open after nine. A&P, Kroger's. They're all closed. You're not very smart, Tom."

T-Bone didn't respond to the comment. "I hope Jackie got home okay. Wonder what happened to her?"

"In case you haven't figured it out Mr. Bradley," Jake interrupted. "Jackie's probably riding with her cousin as we speak, looking for another easy mark. How about giving me your driver's license so I can start a report?" Jake held his hand over the seat while T-Bone dug for his wallet.

"Hey, my wallet. My fuckin' wallet is gone. I had it when I paid for the beers."

"Nothing going on at the Clarke Station, Jake," Mike said. "Got any ideas?"

"Oakland, Hamilton? Somewhere where it's dark and dreary. Maybe they are planning a B&E."

Mike turned onto Oakland and headed north. "On second thought, Mr. Bradley, you said you picked her up at a bar in Highland Park. What bar?"

"I don't know. It's on Woodward. That's all I know."

Mike took Boston Boulevard to Woodward and turned toward Highland Park. "Jake, what we have here is a pigeon drop." He looked in his rearview mirror again. "That's larceny by trick, Mr. Bradley, a felony." Mike drove into Highland Park as he talked. "We don't have a license number, just the color of the truck, but we have Mr. T-Bone here that can identify the truck."

Five blocks into Highland Park at the corner of McLean stood the What's Up Bar. "That's the place, officers." Mike circled the block looking for a black and silver Chevrolet pick up.

"Back up, Mike. In the alley." Jake saw the rear end of a truck in the alley.

Mike backed up and pulled in behind the tailgate protruding into the alley. "Your truck T-Bone?"

"That's it. They're probably in the bar. Let's get 'em."

Jake lifted the mic from the dash. "Thirteen-Three to radio."

"Go ahead, Three."

"Contact Highland Park and have them send a car to McLean and Woodward at the What's Up Bar. We need their help on a larceny."

The radio was quiet for a minute. "Three, Highland Park is en route."

119

"Three out." Jake hung the mic up. "Mr. T-Bone, or better yet, Mr. Bonehead. Wanna bet that Jackie and her cousin are drinking a few more beers on you and your wallet?"

"No. Can't be. She's a nice girl. And damn, she got legs. Nice tits too."

"Bradley, do all truck drivers lose their minds when their dicks get hard?" Mike asked as he backed their out of the alley.

"No blood left in the brain with legs and tits on his mind," Jake added. "By the way, is your mind clear enough now to give us a description on the man you gave the keys to?" Jake jotted down the description: A black man wearing a black and white striped shirt and a small brimmed black hat with a small red feather in the band.

In five minutes, a Highland Park Police car turned onto McLean. Mike flashed his headlights as he and Jake slid out of their car. "Sit tight, T-Bone. We'll be back in a minute."

T-Bone Bradley watched as the four officers brought out Jackie and her cousin in handcuffs. They were placed in the Highland Park Police car. Jake and Mike waved at the officers as they pulled onto Woodward.

Jake flipped a set of keys to Tom Bradley as he climbed into Thirteen-Three. "Here, follow us to the Thirteenth Precinct. We'll make a report on this fiasco. Highland Park will hold your sweetheart and her cousin until our detectives sort this out and see what if anything to charge them with."

Tom Bradley climbed out of the police car as Jake added, "Oh, by the way, here's your wallet. I think they bought a round for the house on you. There's no money in it."

Jake was excited about his upcoming transfer. He started to tell Mike, but decided to keep it to himself. When the radio wasn't busy, Mike always found something to do.

"Time to check the blind pigs, partner," he mubled.

Jake remembered the embarrassment at the police academy when he asked what they were. "How many do we have in our area?"

"Two. Found them just watchin' traffic after two in the morning. Most don't get going 'til the regular bars close." Mike cruised passed both of them. One was on John R just off Piquette. It was above a candy store. The candy store was only open at night. Mike pointed the man out on the sidewalk. "He's the doorman; the one who looks over the clientele coming to the joint."

A second man was behind the counter. "By the way, the guy inside's not there to sell Tootsie Rolls." Thirteen-Three rolled bye as Mike talked. "His job is to warn them upstairs if the cops are coming."

Mike drove around the corner and onto St. Antoine. "Here's another. It's a private home that's so tucked away it doesn't have a man outside." Mike cruised back onto Harper. "Booze, broads, some dice and maybe a bit of drugs are their specialty."

Without asking, Jake figured that Mike didn't like them any more than the johns, and figured Mike had a way to deal with them. He found out just how when they got back to John R.

Both John R and St. Antoine were posted "No Parking" between 2:30am and 6am. The signs were there to expedite snow removal. It didn't matter if it was almost May.

The blind pig customers parked anywhere they wanted, and they never looked for signs in the middle of the night. Normally a scout car crew never wrote a parking ticket. But Mike's theory was to "harass the bastards," even if it meant writing parking tickets. Thirteen-Three wrote twenty that night.

As Mike wrote the first ticket he added, "This is like my own little fun tax that I put under their windshield wiper." He laughed, "If they can frequent these places, they can pay the ticket." Jake agreed and took turns writing parking tickets.

It was the third night in a row of writing the parked cars in front of the candy store that brought the doorman out. Jake rolled down his window as the man approached. He was wearing a small brimmed black hat and a black topcoat. His massive dark brown hand reached into the car with a bill folded lengthwise between his first two fingers. The five zero caught Jake's eye. A deep voice said, "I think it is time I bought you two gentlemen a little breakfast."

Jake pretended he did not hear or see the man. He just forcefully swung his door open as if the guy wasn't there. The black hat and the fifty-dollar bill hit the sidewalk as the man scrambled to get out of Jake's way. Mike climbed out from behind the wheel. "Jake, I think it is time we kicked in the door of this asshole's business."

Jake saw the man inside fumbling under the counter. Before Jake and Mike reached the steps going up the outside of the building people were coming down. Others were heard jumping out the upstairs back window over the alley.

"Line up and let's see some identification," barked Mike.

"Right here," Jake pointed to the front of the building. "Driver's licenses, please."

The lights on the store went out. Jake heard the lock turning in the door.

A radio check found two out of fifteen people wanted for traffic warrants. They went to jail. The others bitched about "the cops pissing on their party."

"It didn't look like you appreciated that fifty in the doorman's hand," remarked Mike as Jake drove away from the station after locking up the two.

"Damn, I forgot to say, 'No Thank you' to the guy," Jake laughed. "The last I seen of that fifty was when the guy was trying to catch it as the wind blew it under the car." Jake pulled into the rear of the S&C for breakfast. "Oh, I put the address into Precinct Vice's book. Maybe they can get someone in there, bust the place legally and close it down."

"It'll open in a week if they do..." Mike paused, adding, "You poppin' for the meal since you turned down that fifty?"

"I thought you were buying with the cut you get from your whores."

"Yeah, right. I'm just glad the S&C includes the coffee with their ninety-five cent special," Mike laughed as he sat at the counter. "The girls have been holding out on me lately."

Chapter 12

Cops need to have a little levity as they try to do their job. They do this to combat the day-to-day seriousness that could get to you in time. Jake appreciated the fresh look on things, even the humor in not so humorous events that Mike Mulligan was injecting into their work.

The run was a simple call with the words, "Family Trouble," following the address on Liecester. Such was the case as Thirteen-Three cruised the streets on May 3rd.

An open door allowed them to hear the screaming and enter unannounced.

"I'll cut your mutha fuckin' ass," the wild-eyed teen-ager lunged, grabbing the old man by his ragged T-shirt.

"Start cuttin' then, you punk-assed son-of-a-bitch."

Jake jumped in between the two. "Hold it! Hold it! No one's cutting anyone." He pushed the two men apart. The younger of the two had a knotted cut-off piece of a nylon stocking on his head to keep his "Do" in place. He wore a long sleeve pink shirt with a wide collar opened down to the third button, black and gray striped pants and a pair of black wing tip shoes. Jake's eyes went from one man to the other looking for a knife. He didn't see one. "Just settle down for a minute."

The older man's shoulders slumped as his bloodshot eyes looked past Jake toward the younger man. "I didn't raise my kids so they turn out to be a pimp."

"Who you callin' a pimp?"

"Hold it. Hold it." Jake pushed the two further apart. "Who called the police?"

"I had mama do it. This is my fuckin' house and this sorry excuse for a son with his fancy ass clothes says he don't have to do nuthin' 'round here."

"Who the fuck you callin' sorry, old man?"

Mike Mulligan pulled at the young man's arm to put more distance between the two.

"Doncha be grabbin' at me!" The youth jerked his arm out of Mike's grasp.

"Just cool it, kid," Mike snapped back.

Jake took out a pad from his pocket and looked at the older man. "Name sir?"

"Milton Latchman. And I want that son-of-a-bitch outta this house. I am done with him." He pushed past Jake to shake his fist in the boy's face.

Jake caught a flash of movement. "I'm tired of you ol' man." The younger man had grabbed the arm of his father spinning him and had a knife at his throat.

Mike's Smith and Wesson appeared in the younger man's right ear. "Drop the knife!" The hammer was slowly cocked back. "You got two seconds before I test your hearing."

"CJ...CJ," a woman's voice screamed. "Please officer, don't shoot my baby." Tears gushed down the woman's cheeks, her hands folded in prayer.

"I told you he's crazy," the older man blurted out. His eyes widened as he felt the pressure of the knife just below his Adam's apple.

Mike repeated slowly. "Drop the knife, CJ!"

"CJ, do as he says. Please, son." The mother was on her knees. "Please, oh please CJ."

CJ felt the pressure of the gun muzzle in this ear, looked at the woman on her knees, then at Jake. The blade fell to the kitchen floor. Jake and Mike turned CJ around and squeezed a set of handcuffs on him. Jake grabbed the knife off of the floor for evidence. It was a street-common bone handled knife with a two and three quarter inch blade.

Mike slid into the back seat of Thirteen-Three with Charles James Latchman, "CJ." He was nineteen with bad case of moonshine breath. He came home drunk and started a fight with his father. Jake was finishing taking information from Mr. Latchman. "We'll hold him for felonious assault.

Milton Latchman leaned over to look into the back seat of the police car. He looked back at Jake. "I know what you're gonna do to him on the way to the station." He looked back into the eyes of his son. "He's not really a bad boy. Just gets a bit rambunctious when he drinks. Please don't hurt him too bad."

"What do you think we're gonna do?" Jake asked.

"I know you police like to beat on people."

"Mike, how 'bout we let CJ out of the car?" Jake turned to Milton Latchman. "The charge is felonious assault, him having that knife at your throat. Not mine, not my partner's, but yours."

"You gonna press charges?"

"No, sir."

Mike had CJ out of the car and was taking off the cuffs as he said, "We just don't beat on people."

Jake went to the driver's side of the car. "If you don't want to press charges that's your choice. Call us back when someone really gets hurt." Jake and Mike drove off into the night.

"Should I just pull around the corner and wait?" Jake asked.

"No, maybe another car will get the run." Mike was writing on their log sheet. *10:05pm, Radio Run. Family trouble 1230 Liecester. T/T Milton and Charles Latchman of same address. They decided to settle dispute on their own.*

Jake checked the traffic on John R, then on Brush. When he turned onto St. Antoine the radio sounded, "Thirteen-Three at twelve thirty Liecester, a man has been cut."

"Thirteen-three on the way," Mike responded into the mic. "What Jake, a half hour since we left their house?"

"If that. Wonder who cut who?"

"You still have the knife?"

"Yep."

A week later, Mike was cruising East Grand Boulevard, ready to turn onto Oakland. The radio operator was broadcasting a description on a Robbery Armed and stolen car in the First

126

Precinct. Jake wrote the information down. Mike made a U-turn heading back toward Woodward then south.

"Time to check the hot corner."

"Where?"

"Canfield and Brush. He probably got a few bucks with the car, and now he's lookin' to get laid." He turned onto Canfield, heading toward Brush, talking as he drove. "On any given night thirty girls can be found working that area."

Mike slowed for the yellow light changing to red at Brush. Jake checked the plate on a Pontiac pulling away and heading north. "That's it. The Pontiac. Charlie Lincoln Ten-forty-two."

"Just like I planned," Mike beamed. He casually turned left onto Brush to catch up to the Pontiac. "Just be cool, Jake. Make like it's just a traffic stop."

Jake threw his hat off and put one foot up on the dash. He rolled down his window. Against the inside of his door his pistol Colt was in his right hand. The police car pulled next to the Pontiac. Jake's voice rang out, "Hey buddy, pull over to the curb." The Pontiac started to pull to the left curb on the one-way street, but Mike did not let him move in. "Over to the right." Jake yelled.

Tires squealed and the Pontiac's taillights fishtailed. It was a half of a block ahead of the police car in an instant.

"Put a bullet into it," Mike yelled with his foot in the carburetor. "Fuckin' dog-assed Ford."

Jake leaned out his window, cocking his pistol. Mike screamed, "Hold it! Hold your fire—pedestrians." The Pontiac was speeding down Brush, just missing four kids.

By then Jake knew a shot would have been fruitless as the Pontiac was putting more distance between it and the police car. Jake grabbed the mic, "Thirteen-Three is in a chase. North on Brush. A '63 Pontiac. Charlie Lincoln one-zero-four-two." Their siren and light was on and the Pontiac two blocks ahead of the police car.

"All units clear the air. Thirteen-Three, what is your location?"

127

"North on Brush. He just blew the light at Forest, now at Warren."

The radio operator repeated, "Thirteen-Three is in pursuit of a '63 Pontiac, Charlie Lincoln one-zero-four-two. North on Brush, north of Warren."

"He's still going north, crossing the Ford Freeway." The siren was wailing in the background as Jake spoke into the mic. "Holy shit, I see one of our car's coming toward us."

"The son-of-a-bitch is going ninety." Mike yelled to Jake as he slowed at every red light before crossing.

A police car with red lights flashing was coming the wrong way on Brush, heading toward the Pontiac with Thirteen-Three now four blocks behind. The Pontiac swerved right to miss the police car, bottoming out with the sharp dip as Brush Street went under a railroad viaduct. The traffic light ahead at Baltimore and Milwaukee turned red, the Pontiac never slowing. A yellow Cadillac nosed out from Milwaukee, heading east. The stolen Pontiac cut to the right, glancing off the Cadillac's front bumper, and went into a sideways skid. Taillights and headlights were spinning as Thirteen-Three was making up ground. The Pontiac's front end went to the left, as it's back end hit a parked car. That threw it into a one-eighty. Sparks and debris flew as the Pontiac smashed into two parked cars.

"Thirteen-Three to Radio. He just cracked up south of the Boulevard..." Jake dropped the mic as their car screeched to a halt.

He ran toward the Pontiac as the driver reached over and locked the passenger's door. "I'll call for the Fire Department," Mike yelled from behind. Through the windshield Jake saw the man grimace in pain. Smoke was coming from under the hood of the car. "Fire Department's on the way," Mike said as he walked up, while Jake was heaving a chunk of concrete through the passenger window. He reached in and unlocked the door. "They'd better hurry. The guy's leg is pinned under the dash."

"I see you found a way to unlock the car." Mike threw the beam of his light to assess the driver's problems. "You almost hit the fucker in the head with the key."

Fire trucks, sirens, lights and hoses filled the southeast corner of Brush and East Grand Boulevard. A tow truck moved the Pontiac so the firemen could cut the occupant out.

Frederick Louis Smith III, 24, of 2131 John R was taken to Receiving Hospital as a police prisoner. He was charged with Robbery Armed and Unlawfully Driving Away an Automobile. For fifty-three dollars and a ride in a Pontiac he lost his left leg just above the knee.

At a much later court appearance, as he leaned on a set of crutches, he got five to ten at Jackson State Penitentiary. He was a three-time loser.

Wednesday afternoon, May 16th was Thirteen-Three's day to work with the tow truck clearing parked cars from the rush hour lanes on Forest and Warren Avenue. Dave Purdue was filling in on the car with Jake. The Whitney Tow Company's driver was hooking onto an old Studebaker pickup as Jake wrote the ticket.

The driver, Randy, came back after he had the front end in the air. "There's a toolbox in the bed of the truck. It'll be gone five minutes after I drop it on Third Street."

Dave leaned from the passenger's side to look out the driver's window at Randy. "Throw it in the back of your truck, or I'll take it home if you don't."

"Yeah, Randy, and I'll have to take you to jail for doing it," interrupted Jake with a forced laugh. Jake finished the ticket, noting on the station copy where the truck would be towed. He climbed out from behind the wheel and put the hard copy under the wiper on the Studebaker. On the way back to his car he grabbed the metal tool box and put it in the back seat of Thirteen-Three.

"You know I called for that," Dave said. Jake did not answer. Once the hour-long follow-the-tow-truck routine was over, Jake drove to the station. He grabbed the toolbox and started into the station. "Where you goin' with my toolbox?" Dave asked.

"It'll be in the property room under a safekeeping tag." Jake paused. "For the owner."

"What a fuckin' hot dog."

Jake did not acknowledge the remark. He gave nine tickets to the clerk so the owners could find their towed vehicles. In the proper space on the Studebaker's ticket Jake wrote: Towed to Third, North of Warren. Safekeeping tag #77813, gray metal Stanley toolbox, #13 Property Room.

By the end of May, Tommy Pine had called in two stolen cars. Over a plate of lamb and rice at Sophie's, Mike talked about Tommy. "What's that, fifteen cars the guy's found for us?"

Jake was buttering another hunk of the Hungarian flat bread. "Yeah, about that many. And he's stayed out of traffic. Maybe we should bring him here some night and buy him dinner."

"I don't think he can handle Sophie's spices. He's more the donut kind."

"Mike, I need to talk to you about something."

Mike sopped some bread in the juice on his plate. "Sounds serious…"

"I'm being transferred."

"Where to?"

"A new bureau. The Tactical Mobile Unit."

"Never heard of it."

Jake spent the rest of the meal going over how the transfer came about, what he knew on the unit and why he was going.

"Just when I was starting to like working with a Polack." Mike poured his third glass of water to ease the fire Sophie added to her dishes. "When's this going to happen?"

"I just got a letter the other day. We start training on June 21st." Jake looked across the table at his partner. "Mike, you'd work well there. Let me put in a word for you?"

"Sorry Jake. I am too old to start over. Been here at Thirteen since the Academy. Besides, I'm having fun."

"The part I don't like is leaving a partner like you," Jake pushed his empty plate aside.

"Don't get all teary eyed, kid." Mike got up from the table. "I'll just have to break in another rookie."

"George'll move up to my spot. He's pretty good." Jake handed his bill and a five to Sophie at the till.

"Maybe I'll get lucky and get a good Irishman for a change. They're easier to train."

Jake drove to the nearest call box. Mike spoke into the phone. "Sam, this is Thirteen-Three. Put us back in service." He jotted down a number and slammed the blue steel call-box door. "Sixty-seven Melbourne, see the manager," Mike said as he climbed back into the jump seat.

Five minutes later, they were in the manager's apartment. It was just inside the door at the Melbourne address, a brown two story brick building. "Yes, I called. Name's Leroy Jones. I went to number five to collect the rent and this is what I got." He took the wet towel off his left wrist. A two-inch wound slowly oozed blood once the pressure was off.

"Who cut you?" Mike asked.

"Mabel Stokes. She's the one renting number five."

"You mean just for trying to collect the rent, she cuts you?" Jake asked as he helped the man put the compress back on.

"This is 'bout the third time this week I been by to collect. She just busted out the door and takes a swipe at me with a butcher knife. Says she's tired of me bothering her when she is busy."

Mike put away his notebook. "Keep the towel on that and wait here. We'll go talk to Mabel.

Twenty feet down a dark hallway Jake pounded his fist on number five. The door opened six inches and a woman's face looked through the opening. "We're here on a complaint," Jake said to the face. "Can we come in and talk?"

The door was opened fully by the woman. She was barefooted, wearing a faded blue housecoat and a head of wild red hair. As Jake walked in the open door he saw three other women sitting on a couch facing the door. To the right, on a stuffed chair, slumped a man with his head back and eyes fixed at the ceiling. Newspapers, cups and trash covered the coffee table in front of the couch. "Who called you all?" The woman asked as she grabbed a cigarette off of the coffee table and lit it.

"Are you Mabel Stokes?" Mike asked as he crossed the room toward a doorway next to the couch.

"Donchu go lookin' 'round my house!" The woman rushed past Mike and down the hallway. Mike and Jake ran after her. The hallway led to a kitchen. She was at a sink emptying a syringe as they grabbed her by the arms. "You're hurting me! Let go." The syringe fell into the sink as Jake twisted her right arm.

Mike finished putting handcuffs on Mabel while Jake went back into the living room. The three women and the man were right where he last saw them. He started to ask questions, but noticed they all were in a trance. Mike pushed Mabel into the room. "Jake, call for some back up. I think we walked into a drug pad."

Jake looked around the room. There was no phone. "I'll get the manager to call." He stepped out the door and into the hall, yelling, "Mr. Jones...Can you hear me?"

The manager's door opened. "Yes, officer."

"Call that police number again. Have them send Thirteen Cruiser. Let me know what they say."

Jake stood in the open door. Mike had Mabel sitting on the arm of the couch. "I need some names." Mike tapped the woman's arm with his notebook. "I'm talkin' to you, lady."

She lifted the frizzled, red head of hair and smiled. "I don't think I have to tell you a mutha fuckin' thing."

"Suit yourself." Mike looked at the first woman sitting next to Mabel. "You, in the flowered blouse, what is your name?" She didn't answer.

Mr. Jones came up the hallway. "They said a car's on the way, officers."

"Thanks. If your arm's Okay for now, we'll take you to the hospital."

"It'll keep."

"Good. Stay in your apartment. I'll knock on your door."

In less than five minutes, the apartment had four more guests: The crew of Thirteen Cruiser. Ralph Vanderbush, the crew chief, was the first in the door. "What'ch got, Mike?"

"I think we got Mabel Stokes dabbling in drugs. She was emptying a syringe when we caught up to her in the kitchen."

Vanderbush started directing his men. The uniformed driver, Larry Muzzy, was posted at the apartment door. Jake went to see Leroy Jones to get more information for his report. Mike stayed with Mabel as Patrolmen Muste and Briggs were emptying the pockets and purses of the four stoned visitors.

Once all were identified, the kitchen, bathroom, bedroom and the living room got a complete search by the members of the cruiser crew.

"Found this taped under the toilet bowl." Matt Briggs walked in with a green plastic soap container. He pried it open. White capsules filled the container. He broke one capsule open, and touched the powder with his index finger, then to his tongue. "I'd guess heroin."

Vanderbush spoke, "Mike, have your partner, what's-his-name, call for another car to help transport prisoners."

"His name is Jake."

Vanderbush barked again. "John and Matt, make sure you check the bottom of every drawer. Turn this place upside down. Mike, when we get these people out, have Jake bring the manager in. Find the knife he was cut with. That's our in for a legal search and seizure. And make sure the manager goes to get that cut sewed up."

Two hours later Jake and Mike were putting their initials on the last piece of evidence, a twelve-inch butcher knife. It still had a blood smear on the blade.

"Smart move, Jake, calling for the cruiser."

"I don't know much about drugs. Figured they would."

"You're right. They may be a bit fat and old, but they've seen it all. Ralph's an old partner." Mike smiled. "Taught me that dime in the phone bit with the johns."

Jake read from his note pad. "In case you're interested, Mabel Stokes is really Mabel Wilson, wife of Pinky Wilson, a red-headed pimp that's trying to corner the heroin market in this part of town."

Mike handed the report to Jake. "You sure you wanna leave us? We're on a roll. A Polack and an Irishman. We might even get promoted to the cruiser crew someday."

"Sorry, I've got the first half of June on vacation. Then it's Belle Isle and the TMU Boot Camp." Jake smiled as he signed the report "Friday's my last day."

"Well, the Tactical Mobile Unit probably needs a good Polish cop—one trained by Mike Mulligan."

Chapter 13

The sun was shining brightly on June, 21st. Jake was early reporting in to the brown brick building that served as the Detroit Police East Side Radio base on Belle Isle. He leaned against a tall oak, one of many that lined the graveled parking lot, lit a cigarette, and a bit apprehensive about his future.

The new assignment was heavy on his mind. He was facing the unknown with the new job, new partners and new bosses. By the third drag on the cigarette, he was able to put that aside, rationalizing that he survived the giant leap from the quiet Eleventh Precinct to Number Thirteen. He knew he could handle this. But his dad had him worried, even more than the new job.

Jake cut his family vacation short to make the training for the Tactical Mobile Unit. He and his family were sharing a two-week stay on Round Lake with his parents and a younger sister, Marie. He left everyone at the cottage. The night before an ambulance brought Ted Bush home. He could not walk on his own, and his speech was slurred.

When Jake left for Belle Isle at six that morning, his mom was going to make a call to Dr. Bookmeyer.

Ol' Doc will know what to do, Jake reasoned as he lit another cigarette, fighting off the thought that he should be there. *No, I need to be here. This is my life.*

Cars started pulling into the parking lot. Crew-cut types started gathering; all new recruits for the TMU. Jake looked for familiar faces and spotted Jimmy Gramatico climbing out of a black Dodge. He headed for him.

Mom and my brother, Dave, can get dad to a hospital.

"Hey Jimmy. When did you get the new car?"

Inspector Anthony Bertolini was under the portico of the dark brown brick building. He smiled as he looked at the eager faces on the men sitting on the grass in front of him. "Welcome fellow officers. This is the start of what I feel will be the best outfit in history of the Detroit Police Department, the Detroit Police Tactical Mobile Unit." Applause and cheers broke out. The inspector raised his arm after letting the cheers drift across the island for a few seconds. "And next month, when we hit the street, Detroit will soon realize that you are the best." Another round of cheers rang out.

The Inspector turned to the officers standing behind him, "These Lieutenants and Sergeants will be your street bosses. They'll take over as soon as I get off of my soapbox. Gentlemen, introduce yourselves."

Each stepped forward with a short introduction.

"Chet Sylvers, Lieutenant, fifteen years of service."

"Alan Orth, Lieutenant, seventeen years."

"Ralph Ostachowski, Sergeant, eighteen years."

"Gerhardt Kempf, Sergeant, fifteen years."

"Chester Stasik, Sergeant, sixteen years."

"Charles Erdmann, Sergeant, fourteen years."

The Inspector took the floor again. "Now it's your turn. When I call your name, stand and state your full name and give your former precinct and time on the job. Arbanas, start it off."

"Paul Arbanas, Number Thirteen, three plus years."

Jake eyed up his old classmate. *One of the best cops in the precinct.* Then he heard, "Bush."

"Jake Bush. Number Thirteen, same class as Paul."

Other officers stood when their last names were called. Jake heard a few familiar voices among the sixty. Gramatico, Parkhurst and Preemo from Number Eleven. Jake remembered Parkhurst was there when Sergeant Seckora got killed the summer of 1963. Seckora was Jake's shift sergeant when he was at Eleven. The killer lived through the ensuing shoot out and got five to ten for manslaughter. Jake planned on asking Bobby about that.

More names were called until the last one stood. "Dick Whyser, Number Five, seven years on the job." An unlit cigar was clenched in his teeth as he spoke. He took a seat on the grass.

First there was a loud chirp, chirp, and then a siren's whine followed by the two-tone sound the English Bobbies use. The noise made heads turn to see Lieutenant Sylvers and Sergeant Kempf drive up in a new 1965 Plymouth. Whyser's voice could be heard, "Damn thing's got a three speed siren." The car was just like the picture, white with two royal blue racing stripes running the length of the car on the hood, roof and trunk lid. The side panels were in the same bright blue and Detroit Police was stenciled in white on the doors. Tactical Mobile Unit was in smaller print on the rear fenders.

"Okay, take a quick peek at one of the new cars. We're taking delivery of fourteen of them this week," announced Inspector Bertolini. "We'll reconvene in fifteen minutes."

"Step, stomp. Step, stomp. I want to hear them feet hit the ground." Sergeant Ostachowski was demonstrating the drill for the sixty patrolmen sitting on the grass. "Half of the battle can be won psychologically. The more noise you can make with your feet, the more menacing you will be." Again, he posed, using his police baton and holding it like a lance. He led off with his left foot and brought the right sharply up to the heel of the left. Step, stomp. Step, stomp. "All right, I want you to fall in. Make two ranks shoulder to shoulder. Give yourselves about five yards between the front and back rank. It's time to practice."

The patrolmen milled around, finding friends or precinct buddies. Two ranks were formed on the grassy field. "Close it up. Remember, no one's to get between you," Barked Sergeant Stasik from the rear. "Hold your baton like you are going to drive it into the gut of anyone in front of you."

Sergeant Ostachowski moved to the side to watch. "Remember, short steps. Lead with the left and stomp that right foot. At the ready, forward, march!"

Sixty men in T-shirts, jeans and sneakers started to step and stomp their way across the field. Ski, as he was soon to be called, ran from side to side, yelling, "Don't race. Shorten those steps. More noise with the feet."

"Keep your lines straight," Stasik yelled from behind.

Nine more days of drills followed, along with short chalkboard sessions showing "V" formations for clearing a street and daily practice at step and stomp with some hand-to-hand combat exercises thrown in. The formations turned green grass to a brown dusty field by day three.

Jake spent every evening at Harper Hospital in room 421. He ran into Doctor Bookmeyer the first evening. "I called in a Neurologist, Doctor Frank Shipman. I believe your dad had a stroke. Doctor Shipman will be able to take care of him." Jake looked past the doctor into the room. Ted was asleep. "I gave him something to keep him down. He needs to stay in bed."

The second week Sergeants Erdmann and Kempf spent the morning reviewing how the TMU is to stop a car and transport prisoners. "One officer's job is to approach the driver. The other better not be on his ass," said Kempf. "Your job is to be on the passenger's side and to the rear watching through the rear window."

"The second man is there to protect his partner." Sergeant Erdmann added as he walked among the men sitting on the grass. "We are working two men crews, and expect both men involved in every stop. I repeat, every stop. If we drive by and see one guy sitting in the car while the other is out investigating, you'll win your ticket out of this bureau the first offense."

"Any questions?" Kempf asked. "Now, how to transfer prisoners." His presentation was short and sweet. There were no cages or protective screens between the front seat and the rear. The prisoners were to be handcuffed behind their back and the second officer is to ride with the prisoner behind the driver. "This is to prevent a kick to the head by some unruly bastard. Questions?"

Another tool was introduced to the men of the TMU. Each car would be assigned a Motorola hand-held radio. This would enable the passenger in the car to keep in communication with his car, or other cars in the bureau. "The range is a mile," added Sergeant Ski. The radios were another first for the city.

Sergeant Erdmann added, "Remember, with the car-to-car radios we can talk to each other without tying up a radio frequency. Use the car-to-car frequency to call for help in transferring prisoners or assist on an investigation. We are a team." He looked around. "All right, take a break. Be back in fifteen."

Right after training on June 29th, Jake met his mom and brother at Harper Hospital. Dr. Shipman arranged the meeting to explain his findings on Ted Bush.

"Your husband and father has a weak spot in a blood vessel on the left side of his head. Through surgery, I can correct it. With Ted's and your permission I will schedule surgery. In the meantime, he has to stay in bed. I'm having a tough time convincing him that complete bed rest is in his best interest."

"I'll talk to my dad as soon as we are through here," answered Jake. "When can you do the surgery?"

"I hope to set it up as soon as possible."

The next day, the new officers of the TMU car-pooled from Belle Isle to the Rouge Range on the west side of Detroit. Folding chairs were arranged in rows facing a target range. There were ten evenly spaced silhouette targets with a dirt berm behind them. Sergeant Erdmann stood at the podium and a table was to his side where ten shotguns were displayed. "This is the Model 97 Winchester, a sawed-off, pump shotgun." The sergeant held one aloft. "Each one of our cars would be carrying two of them in a specially designed box. That is where they are to be stored. They are never to be left inside your car. That is not to say that you cannot make the decision on the street as to when to break them out. Now without further ado, I turn the class over to the range officer, Dennis Kline." The sergeant found himself a seat next to the inspector, lieutenants and sergeants in the back row.

Patrolman Dennis Kline, dressed in dark blue fatigues with bloused boots picked up a shotgun and loaded it as he moved to the podium. "To give you a little background, I was a Ranger in the U.S. Army during Korea. I owe my life to this, the Winchester Model 97." A chilling story of killing before being killed followed.

"The Model 97 is a twelve gauge pump shotgun that holds six rounds between the chamber and the magazine. It was a trench gun in World War I. Today, fifty years later, it still has a place, mainly as a riot gun. A unique feature of this weapon is that when the trigger is held, a shell will fire with each rack of the action."

For emphasis, Patrolman Kline turned toward one of the silhouette targets behind him and emptied the shotgun. The target was cut in half. "Use this weapon wisely and it will serve you well." Kline reloaded and stepped to his left and fired one round into a new target. This silhouette showed nine holes when the range instructor fired a load of double-O buck from ten feet. "Each pellet is equivalent to a .32 caliber bullet. And, as you can see, it'll blow a man to bits."

His words became etched in the minds of each patrolman when they took their turn firing from the hip at a target. The cardboard silhouette was cut in half by the fourth shot Jake took.

Ted Bush's surgery was set for July 1st. Jake went to the hospital for a visit right after his last training day. Ted was in the corridor on the pay phone three doors down from room 421.

"Dad, what are you doing out of bed?"

"Gotta go, Buttons. That mean ol' cop you have for a dad caught me. Love you. Tell Deb I love her too. Bye."

"Dad, the doctor said no getting out of bed."

"I wanted to call your kids. I miss them."

"They miss you too, but you won't be able to bribe them with M&M's if you're dead."

"Who told you about the candy? Anyway, tomorrow at this time I'll be as good as new. Here, help your old man back to his cell."

"I want you to stay in bed. It's for your own good. The doctor said..."

"Ah, bullshit," Ted interrupted. "I think I could walk out of here right now. I'm OK."

"If you were OK, I wouldn't have to help you back to your room."

Ted Bush, age 52, fell into a coma during the night. The next time Jake saw his dad, he had a machine breathing for him and wires running to four other pieces of equipment.

TMU's first day on the street was July 3, 1965. The Detroit News and The Detroit Free Press ran special sections covering the introduction of the Tactical Mobile Unit to the citizens of Detroit. Words like: "Elite strike force," and "Hand picked officers," trumpeted their arrival. Jake already knew his father would never read the articles about his new assignment.

The TMU was given the numeral radio designation Eight since Detroit did not have an Eighth Precinct. There were two shifts, days and afternoons. The afternoon shift's crew of Eight-Six was Jimmy Gramatico, Jake Bush and Bobby Parkhurst.

As Jimmy suggested, the three officers who met at Number Eleven teamed up. Parkhurst put it best, "Partners on cars are like marriages. Some work out, some don't. Only we won't need a lawyer if we want to break up."

James Gramatico was a hard working, young, energetic police officer that wanted more challenges than the Eleventh Precinct could give him. He was six foot and skinny as a rail, not an ounce over one seventy-five. What he may have lacked in size, he made up with his fleet feet and agility. He had five years on the job.

Robert John Parkhurst was the junior man on the car. He had moved to Michigan as a youth, and still carried a bit of a North Carolinian drawl. He had hired on a year and a half before Jake, but the Sergeant Seckora killing in 1963 took a toll on him. He resigned from the department, only to return nearly two years later.

For the next two weeks Jake split his time between Harper Hospital and working. Jake read the articles to his dad during his visits to the hospital, but never knew if his dad heard a word.

All ten TMU cars were working the First Precinct on July 7, 1965. Eight-Six strayed a little north into Number Thirteen. Jimmy was driving. An occasional streetlight or the headlights of a passing car broke the July darkness. As they turned off Third onto Willis, Jimmy caught a glimpse of movement. "Jake, you see someone in the alley?"

"Missed it." Jake turned to look behind.

"Does Willis have an alley that tee's into the one on Third?"

"It does."

"I'll swing around the block and drop you off. I thought I saw someone duck into the shadows when he saw our car." Jimmy maintained his speed. He turned left on Second. "He's in the alley on the south side. See if you can see what he's up to."

Jake jumped out of the slowly turning car and waited for Jimmy to drive out of sight. He looked down Willis into the darkness, took off his hat and covered his badge with it. He crossed the street, went to the alley and headed back toward Third. Jake pulled the small radio from the case on his hip and turned it on. "Eight-Six, how do you read?"

"Loud and clear. I'm sitting on Canfield just off of Third."

"I copy that," Jake answered, as he moved down the dark alley. He checked his watch. Eleven-forty. He reached the tee in the alley and saw a man standing to his right at the alley mouth that emptied onto Willis. Jake stayed against a fence and watched. The man was looking to his right, and then glanced back to his left. He wore a dark rag on his head, a white T-shirt and dark pants. Two girls crossed the street and came into view. Jake crept closer.

"Hey girls, you want a real man's cock?"

A girl's voice answered. "Say what?" The girls froze within ten feet of the man.

"How 'bout a taste of my dick? Or maybe my knife?"

"Run Rita!" The taller girl grabbed the other, running back toward Third

The man quick stepped across Willis and to the door of an apartment building. Jake whispered into his radio as he moved. "Eight-Six. Two girls are running your way. We need them."

The man kept watching the girls while Jake stayed in the shadows. The man opened the outside glass door of the apartment building and leaned against the wall near the mailboxes. He lit a cigarette. Jake ducked behind a parked car to watch. "Six, Jake here. Got the girls?"

"Yep. What you got?"

"A possible attempt rape. Perp's just inside the door of an apartment on Willis. I need you to come up the alley from Canfield in case he runs. It don't look like he lives there. He's just smoking a cigarette and waiting."

Jake heard Jimmy's faint voice over his walkie-talkie. "Eight-Six to any TMU Unit. Anyone in the area of Third and Willis?"

"Nine is at Woodward and Alexandrine."

"Meet us at Canfield and Third. Stay off of Willis."

"Roger, Six."

Minutes passed. Jake was kneeling next to the parked car when he spotted Jimmy moving in the alley. Just then their man casually came out of the doorway, looked around and tossed his cigarette aside. He started to walk west toward the alley.

Jake jumped up from behind the car as the man walked by. "Freeze asshole!" The man bolted and cut into the alley. Right into Jimmy's leveled Colt.

"Goin' somewhere?"

Timothy Howard, 25, of 5922 Fischer was conveyed to Number Thirteen by Eight-Six.

Eight-Nine took statements from Rita Coolidge and Beverly Abernathy. Nine's report said that the same man had tried to stop Rita, age 11, when she was on her way home earlier. She went back to her aunt's house to get someone to walk with her because she was scared. Her cousin, Beverly, was 18. Timothy Howard was held for Assault with intent to rape for Women's Division.

"I sure like those walkie-talkie's," Jimmy was saying as they left the station.

"Yeah, I think Timothy thought we fell outta the sky." Jake laughed.

"The girls' mothers said they just love them po-lice in the fancy white cars."

"You're Uncle Tony said they would."

At 7 p.m. Jake met his mother, two sisters and brother at in his dad's room at Harper Hospital on July 7th. Dr. Shipman was due in to talk to them. Jake looked at his father. They had cotton taped over each eye. A nurse came in a lifted the cotton and applied liquid to Ted's eyes.

"That's to keep them from drying out," she explained as she went back out of the room.

Doctor Shipman came in a few minutes later. Jake was the first to speak. "Doc, I think it's time to tell us what is going on with my father?"

The doctor's words confirmed what the family already surmised. Without the machine, Ted Bush would die. The only warmth in his body was in the vicinity of his heart. Jake took a deep breath and asked, "Can you give us a minute to talk, please."

The doctor stepped out of the room.

On July 18th, the phone woke Jake at 4 a.m. It was the hospital. The end came less than eight hours after they unplugged his father's respirator. The funeral three days later put an end to Jake's mind being in two places.

Chapter 14

Jake re-read the announcement posted on the bureau's bulletin board saying there's been a departmental policy change due to recent retirements. All patrolmen with four or more years of service by January, 1966, would be eligible to take the promotional exam for the rank of Detective. It had always been five years. Jake jotted down the exam date of January 16, 1966. Mike Mulligan had said it took a good year or more to study for the exam. He had six months. *I'll just study twice as hard.*

Bobby and Jake were working the Thirteen Precinct. "You know Jake, you and Jimmy got three stolen cars already. When's it my turn?"

Jake was driving south on St. Aubin. "Just have to keep your eyes open, Bobby." As Jake crossed Warren a Cadillac was heading north on St. Aubin. Jake made a U-turn.

"What've you got?"

"The Cadillac. The one with the top down. Four kids. The driver gave me a look." Jake caught up to the Cadillac as it turned onto Forest.

"Nothing on the board," Bobby said as Jake pulled alongside.

Jake hit the siren and pointed to the curb. The driver didn't look over. Jake pulled further in front of the Cadillac and hit the siren. The car pulled to the curb and stopped.

Bobby approached the driver. "Let me see your license and registration, son."

Jake was to the rear of the car watching the passengers. "It's my uncle's car. I don't have the registration."

"One at a time, out of the car!" Jake commanded. "Up against the building."

Jake had the four teenagers spread eagle as he patted them down one by one. Bobby stood guard. Jake pointed toward the car. "I say it's stolen. Check the key, Bobby."

145

Bobby climbed in the passenger side of the car and pulled the key. It was a dummy key broke off just to fit in the ignition. He looked under the dash and saw a couple of wires dangling.

The car was towed into the Thirteen Precinct. The four occupants were turned over to #13 Youth Bureau.

Jake was on the phone as Bobby was listening to the one-way conversation. "Is this the home of Ross Frank? Can I speak to Mr. Frank? This is Patrolman Bush of the Detroit Police." There was a pause as Jake listened. "Can I have his work number?"

Jake hung up the phone and re-dialed. "This is Patrolman Bush of the Detroit Police, can I talk to Mr. Ross Frank? Okay, I'll hold." Jake put his hand over the mouthpiece. "He's at work. Chrysler's. Probably doesn't even know his car isn't in the lot." Jake dropped his hand from the mouthpiece. "Hello, Mr. Frank. Do you own a 1963 Cadillac license Edward Boy 4-9-6-3? Did you let anyone use it? Well, I have it at the Thirteenth Precinct, Woodward and Hancock. It'll be here for you to pick up. Yes sir. No damage. Just see the desk officer with the registration or title. You're welcome, sir."

Eight-Six was heading out of the station parking lot. "Where do you want to have lunch, Bobby?"

"Your choice."

"How 'bout the American Coney Island on Michigan?"

"How'd you know the car was stolen?"

"Didn't. But the driver gave me a quick look."

"Just a look?"

"Well, maybe I can smell 'em." Jake pulled in front of the restaurant. "The American has the best Coney's. By the way, you asked for a stolen car. I delivered. You buying?"

"No, but thanks for lettin' me in on the action."

While downing three Coney Islands, Jake asked, "Bobby what happened the night Sergeant Seckora got killed? I know you were there."

"It was a family trouble run. We got the call. Sergeants Seckora and Jamison were near and got there just before us.

Seckora went to the front door and knocked as I moved to the right of the porch." Bobby stopped. His hands were shaking. He put down his Coney dog.

"The screen door exploded and the sergeant flew off of the porch." Bobby's eyes were watering.

"Bobby, let's save the rest for later."

"It could have been me. I would have been at that door…"

Jake waved at the counter person, George. "Bill, please," and drained his Pepsi. "Let's go, Bobby."

Jake and Bobby were cruising the Seventh Precinct the evening of August 8th, 1965. Number Seven bordered the southeast corner of Number Thirteen. A new Pontiac Convertible drove past Eight-Six going in the opposite direction on Chene Street. Bobby was driving. Jake checked the plate number with his board.

"Bobby, make a U-turn and get that Pontiac."

"Whatcha got?"

"Charlie Young Seventy-five Fifty-two is listed as stolen. That was just one letter off."

"It doesn't match."

"Just get the car."

The Pontiac turned off of Chene onto Garfield. When Eight-Six made the turn, it was gone.

"Dammit, Bobby, I think we lost one."

"It wasn't the number on the board."

"I don't care. It was close enough for a check." Jake looked around every corner as Bobby drove. "How 'bout slowing it down and drive in circles. Go a block wider with each swing."

"Jake, you're chasin' ghosts."

"Bobby, just do it."

For twenty minutes Bobby drove in circles. "Where's the boundary between Seven and Thirteen?"

"Don't worry about the boundaries."

"We're supposed to work Number Seven today."

"Hell, I'm worried about why that car got away so fast. Fuck what precinct we're supposed to be in." Jake looked down Garfield as Bobby drove on Russell. "There it is!"

Heading east was the Pontiac. Bobby hit the brakes, backed up and turned down Garfield.

"You sure about this, Jake?"

"Just stop the fuckin' car!"

Jake checked the numbers again as Bobby closed the gap. The plate read Charlie Victor and the board had Charlie Young.

"What do you wanna do, Jake?"

"Take a guess." Jake flipped the switch on the blue lights and let a short wail out of the siren. The driver pulled to the curb.

Bobby approached the driver while Jake covered the passenger side of the car. "Can I see your license and registration, sir?"

"Sure officer, but I lost the registration." He handed over his license to Bobby, and then leaned over to open his glove compartment. Jake moved his hand to his pistol as the man opened it. "I already got a couple of tickets for no registration."

Jake watched as the driver retrieved some traffic tickets from the glove box. "I'll take those," Jake said. He grabbed the three tickets. They all were written over the past month for "No Receipt of Registration."

"You want to step out of the car, Sir?" Jake moved around to the driver's side as he talked. "Is it Robinson? Leonard Robinson?"

"Yes sir."

"Have a seat in the back of our car." Jake handed Bobby the tickets. Jake stopped the man as he reached the curbside of the police car. "Got any weapons? Like knives or guns?" Jake started a quick frisk of the man.

"Hey man. I just lost the registration. Just write the ticket and I'll get a new one tomorrow."

"You didn't get a new one after three tickets, though." The man was clean. "Just have a seat, Mr. Robinson." Jake put him in the back seat.

"Jake, I don't know about this. He's got three tickets already for no registration."

"Think there's a possibility of a mistake on the hot sheet?"

"Someone had to check before writing the tickets."

"So, we'll check again." Jake reached in for the mic. "Eight-Six calling radio."

"Go ahead Eight-Six."

"How about a larceny check on a Charles Victor seven-five-five-two?"

"Wait one, Eight-Six."

"Bob, can you get me the VIN while we wait?"

Jake grabbed his clipboard penciling in the name of Leonard Gary Robinson along with the information on the car and the time. He heard radio calling.

"This is Eight-Six."

"That is a stolen 1965 Red Pontiac Convertible, Charles Victor seven-five-five-two. Give Lambas a call at Auto Squad."

Jake thought for a couple of days on what he wanted to say to Bobby. He talked to Jimmy, the senior man. "The guy's working scared. A quicker response would have gotten the car earlier. We almost lost it."

Jimmy stood by Bobby. "He'll catch on. He's been through a lot."

The next time Jake was working with Bobby came on August 12th. He decided to talk to his partner.

"Bob, I think you're being too careful out here. Is there a problem?"

"I just like to know what I am getting into. I saw what knocking on a front door could bring."

"Bob, I think you have to bury Sergeant Seckora. If you're working scared it might get us both hurt. I need to know that you'll cover my ass, and I'll cover yours."

"Sometimes I think you go too fast. I like to take my time and know what we're doing. I don't want any trouble."

"I don't think I'm going to get you into trouble. Sometimes you have to react and can't think too much. And by the way, trouble comes with wearing a badge. That's just my thoughts though."

Jake's off time was spent tape-recording the Detroit Police Book of Procedure. He thought he'd try something he heard about when he was in the Marines—*Sleep Learning.* Once he had the book of procedure on tape he'd play it back as he slept.

Anne was thankful he only did this while working the night shift, or when she was sound asleep. When he worked days, he'd play the tapes while he re-read the book once the kids were in bed.

"Why is that book so important to you?" Anne asked.

"Making detective is my next goal. Bear with me on this."

"I told the girls at the bank a year ago that you eat, sleep and dream of police work. I was joking at the time. Guess it wasn't a joke."

Jake made the mistake of mentioning his studying methods at work.

"Sleep learning, give me a fuckin' break," Dick Whyser butted in. "You'll write a 72 to 75, no matter what kind of magic trick you try."

"Are we on a hot streak or what, Jake? Our car has got fourteen felony arrests in the last five days," Jimmy said.

They were talking before roll call. Bobby overheard the conversation. "Save some of those arrests for when I'm on the car, guys."

"I'm off through the end of the month, so it will be up to you two," said Jake. "I'm goin' deer hunting. Oh, by the way, the

150

bosses asked for volunteers to help break in the new guys when they come on board. I threw my name into the hat."

"I hope it wasn't because of me," Bobby said.

"Not really. It's just time for a change."

1965 ended with the TMU featured in the papers again. They were doing the job that Inspector Bertolini and the rest of the Detroit brass wanted. Crime was dropping dramatically wherever the Tactical Mobil Unit worked. Ten more cars were ordered and the men to fill them were interviewed. Jake knew he was doing his part. He also knew his dad would've been proud of him.

Chapter 15

The new cars and men arrived. Crews were reassigned to put newer men with the original officers that formed the TMU. The new men's riot training would be put off until the summer.

Some of the original men were given the chance to return to their previous assignments. Paul Arbanas was one of them. Paul liked knowing his area like the back of his hand. He knew Number Thirteen. The TMU never knew where they were working, so learning the entire city would take years.

The addition of ten more cars and sixty men gave Jake the opportunity to move to another car without raising an eyebrow. The bosses assigned Jake to Eight-Twelve, Whyser and the new man coming in from Number Five, Jesse Scott. Jake moved down to third man on the car since Jesse had more seniority than him.

If nothing else, the change in crews balanced the scales a bit more. Dick was 6-2 and weighed in at 215 pounds. Jesse was six foot and his 225 pounds was all muscle. Jake noted that Jesse's arms were as big around as his legs. Jake was still tipping the scales at about 175 pounds.

There were now twenty TMU cars patrolling the streets of Detroit. Ten cars assigned to the east side of town, the other ten to the west side. Each set of ten cars had a car of bosses working the street with them, two sergeants in one car, a lieutenant and sergeant in the other.

New Years Day 1966 had Jake and Jesse working the 7 p.m. to 3 a.m. shift. The Fifth Precinct was the assignment. Jesse was driving as Jake tried to make conversation. "You're from Number Five, right?"

"Yes."

"Do you prefer Jess or Jesse?"

"Either."

Jesse turned off St. Jean onto Mack.

Not very talkative, thought Jake.

"Watch the guy in the gray coat!"

"The guy in the bus stop?" Jake turned in his seat to keep his eye on the man.

"Yeh, him."

Jesse slowed for a car to pass on his right, hit the brakes and squealed tires as he backed up to the bus stop. He jumped out. "Just keep your hands where I can see them!" Jesse had his hand on his pistol and he approached and Jake was right behind.

"Man, I'm just waitin' on the bus."

"I know." Jesse pushed the man's left arm up and reached inside of his coat. A blue steel automatic appeared in Jesse's hand. "This your bus ticket?"

Eight-Twelve spent the next two hours scanning old wanted circulars and teletypes looking for a description that might match that of Lennie Warner. They came up dry. "All we'll end up with is a CCW unless the Dicks can find something," sighed Jesse as he signed the report that Jake had typed.

"What tipped you off that he was carrying something?"

"When he saw us, his left elbow moved. He was making sure his piece was tucked away."

"You saw that?"

"Gotta watch the street people. Their moves might tell you something."

Jake didn't ask any more questions. Jesse was street smart. He had learned well in the years he spent at Number Five. Jesse was head and shoulders above any partner Jake had 'til now, maybe even Mike Mulligan.

It was a few days later when Jake was back with Jesse Scott. There were no long conversations with him. A snap of a finger and jerk of Jesse's thumb got Jake's attention. Jake made the right turn into an alley, to where the thumb was pointing. Their passenger door flew open and Jesse was off running. He was chasing a dark figure in the alley. Jake reversed his direction then drove around the block to head them off. Six turns and more than three blocks later Jake was out of the car tackling the running man. Jesse helped Jake apply the handcuffs.

"Let's take our man back to where he started running," Jesse said as he slid in the back seat with the prisoner. "I think it was by a Chevy at the mouth of the alley."

Beneath the trunk lid of a Chevrolet was a pry bar. Jake checked the trunk. No damage. He then ran his flashlight across the small sign over the back door to the right of the Chevy. "Norm's Hardware." With the light he checked the door. The hasp for the padlock had pry marks under it. The broken padlock was on the alley floor. Jake picked the pry bar up by its hooked end to keep from disturbing any fingerprints and put the bar on the front seat floor.

Without Jake asking Jesse offered. "Saw him from two blocks back cut into the alley. I check alley walkers."

In just days Jesse showed Jake that there was more to police work than checking license plates. Though words were not spoken, Jesse was teaching Jake how to be a complete cop.

Jake was paired with the senior man, Dick Whyser, on January 13th. A cigar was always clenched in his teeth as he talked. "Yeah, I spent a few years on Five Cruiser—involved in two fatal shootings, too. I did everything I could to keep out of the limelight, but things just happened."

Jake just listened as the cigar bobbed up and down in Dick's mouth with each syllable. "One time there was this run on a bank hold up. We were three blocks away..." The words kept coming hours on end. With one partner there wasn't too much said, with the other, there was no end to it. "We busted the grease ball before he knew we were there."

"Dick, the green Ford turning right, let's talk to him."

"What for?"

"His brake lights aren't working."

"You gonna write him?"

"No, but I want to talk to him. See if he's got anything else going."

"I'll stop him if you are gonna write him. I ain't in no mood to jaw with some spade just to pass the time."

"Forget it." That was the fourth car that Dick would not stop in the two days they worked together. On Eight-Six they'd stop a lot of cars and talked to a lot of people. Minor traffic violations opened the door. It was a legal stop. Jesse and he did the same. Jake soon learned that when he worked with Dick, most of the stops that were made, happened when Jake was driving. Dick drove and talked. Jake started doubting all Dick's old war stories.

Mid-January brought the Detectives exam. Jake studied for the past six months. Dick told him he didn't have a snowball's chance in hell of passing it. "You'd need a year or two to study for it, so you're wasting your time."

"You taking the exam?"

"For the second time. Last time I wrote a 72. I think I should break 80 this time."

Jake smiled to himself.

Probably wrote a 60 and hopes for a 70.

Grand River was quiet and it was almost two in the morning. The speedometer needle was not registering as Jake drove the parking lane heading northwest with his headlights off. The few parked cars on the street were skirted in the very light night traffic. Jesse patrolled the streets that way and Jake did likewise.

"Can you see the guy in the next block?" Jesse asked.

"Uh-huh." Jake put the car in neutral and let it coast to a stop. They were a half block away and watched the man get out from behind the wheel and walk to the trunk of his car. The trunk was opened and it looked like he got something out. He closed it and got back behind the wheel.

Jake got comfortable in his seat. "There's a bar across the street. You think he's going to hit it?"

Jesse ran his hand across his chin. "The timing is right. They're announcing last call by now."

Jesse looked at the string of buildings on the other side of Grand River. "Must be a back door to the bar off of the alley." He thought for a few seconds. "When he goes in through the front, one of us can be right on his ass, the other can come in the back."

"By the cars parked in front, could be at least four or more people in the bar." Jake's heart started pounding.

The inside of Eight-Twelve was quiet for a minute. "You're right. Too risky. It'd be nice taking him down in the act, but not the smartest."

Jake put the car into drive. After a couple of months with Jesse he knew what to do. The Plymouth moved ahead, its lights still out. Jake stopped the car with the parking brake, and he and Jess slipped out of their car.

Jake went up the driver's side, his pistol out against his pant leg. Jesse was covering from the curbside, his .38 leveled at the back window. "Keep your hands where I can see them," Jake barked. He opened the driver's door slowly to get a full look at the man behind the wheel. "Step out, sir, over to the curb. Keep your hands in sight."

"Man, I was just sitting in my car. What's the problem?"

Jake walked with the man as he climbed the curb. "Hands on the roof."

"You can't just yank a guy out of his car…"

"Hands on the roof," Jesse ordered. He pushed the man to lean him forward and patted him down.

"You looked interested in the bar across the street. Any other reason for just sitting here?" Jake asked.

"I don't know what you're talking about."

"I'll check the car." Jesse moved to open the passenger side door.

"Man, you ain't searchin' my car." The man reached out for Jesse's left arm.

Jesse made a quick pivot and with an underarm swing of his right forearm, caught the man between the legs. The force of the blow put him over the top of the car and onto the street flat on his back.

Jake was around the parked car with his gun on the man when he heard, "Go ahead an' search the fuckin' car."

"Come on. Back on the curb."

Jake guided the man as he limped back around the car.

Jesse was running his flashlight under the front seat of the car when he spoke. "Cuff him, partner."

Jake applied the cuffs, while Jesse came out of the car with a .44 magnum Smith and Wesson and a piece of a nylon stocking. "We guessed right."

Lloyd Burroughs, 37 of 15234 Glynn was locked up for Investigation of Robbery Armed at the Tenth Precinct.

Eight-Twelve headed for the Bureau. "The Dicks might find a hold-up they can make this guy on," Jake said as he turned the car onto Jefferson to head for the bureau. "At least I hope they can."

Jesse finished writing the entry on their log sheet. "Well, it turned out better than swapping bullets with him in that bar."

Jake mumbled a low, "Uh-huh."

"I'm going to have to get me a bigger gun, Jake. My .38 is like a pea shooter when the bad guys are packing something that big."

That was the first time Jake remembered hearing two sentences in a row out of Jesse.

The Detroit Police went modern producing stolen car sheets and the latest teletypes and making copies available. On the way out for the day shift, one of each set of ten cars would swing by Police Headquarters and pick up the latest of these for the TMU cars. The afternoon crews would just pencil in any updates.

A slight drizzle was falling as Jake retrieved the computer printouts from Eight-Eleven. Whyser was driving, heading for the assigned Second Precinct. Jake put the stolen car sheet on the board in the middle of the dash and started reading the teletypes. "Says here there was a strong arming during the night in Number Two."

Dick was cruising past Tiger Stadium. "Tell me something important, like when's the home opener for the Tigers?"

A few more turns and Eight-Twelve was heading down Myrtle. A group of men were coming off of a porch on the north side of the street as they drove by. Two men looked at the Blue and White police car and turned the opposite way from the group.

"Dick, make a U-turn. There's a couple of guys we should talk to."

"Why?"

"Make a U-turn. It's about the strong arming last night."

"What about it?"

"It happened here on Myrtle."

Dick made the U-turn. "Jezus Christ, kid it's raining."

"It looked like a blind pig letting out. Two guys separated themselves from the rest when they saw our car." Jake started reading the descriptions of the two men aloud. "#1, Negro Male, 27, six foot, 225 pounds. Has a mustache, wearing a blue short jacket and dark work pants. #2, Negro Male…"

"We can round up a whole bunch of niggers and find a dozen that'll fit the descriptions."

"I just want them two further up the block. One of them has a blue waist length jacket and work pants."

Eight-Twelve coasted to a stop beside the two men.

"Your show, Jake. Have at it."

Jake slid out of the car. "Hold up, guys. I need to see some ID from you." Dick stood off to the side.

"Aw, man, what's this shit?" The man in blue started searching his pockets for his wallet.

"Where you coming from?" Jake asked.

"A party. That a crime?" The man in blue shoved his driver's license at Jake.

Jake took the other man's ID. He stepped back toward Dick. "The guy in blue fits #1 to a Tee."

"So, what's your next move?"

"Let the Dicks talk to them at Number Two."

"That's bullshit, kid."

"Dick, the guy fits the description."

"What about the other guy?"

"They both split from the pack. I say we take them in and let the Dicks sort this out. A quick line up will either make them or boot them."

Jake turned to the pair. "Guys, we are goin' for a ride. There was a hold up last night in this neighborhood and we need to check this out further."

The man in blue spoke. "What if I don't want to play your fuckin' game."

"Ain't no game," Jake took a quick look at the ID. "Dudley Smith, you and your pal are under arrest."

"Might get your ass kicked, Mr. Po-lice."

Dick stepped forward. "Boys, boys. Humor my rookie partner. It'll just be a quick trip to the station and I am sure the Lieutenant will kick you loose. Come on, get in the back of the car." Dick said as he opened the back door.

The ride to the station was pissing Jake off all the more as the man in blue work clothes talked about breaking backs for a pastime and Dick making jokes about some cops pushing their light asses around too much for their own good.

Jake showed the Teletype on the Strong Arming to the Lieutenant on the desk. He took a look at Dudley Smith Jr. and Aaron Thornton. "The one in the blue sure fits. Might as well hold them both for the Detectives."

Dick made a brief report on two arrests for Investigation, Robbery Not Armed, per Teletype 4927, listing their names, ages and addresses. Nothing more.

The rest of the day was quiet except for the repeated remarks by Dick. "You know that was just a bullshit arrest, don't you?"

Jake never answered. He just hoped that a line up would make one or both of them.

Fuck you and your ego, Dick.

The next day, Jake and Dick were in the ranks for roll call. Their ten cars were working Number Two again.

"Eight-Eleven, Marcomb and Wiles, Twelve, Whyser and Bush." There was a pause. "Twelve see a Detective Lieutenant Morrow at Number Two first thing. Thirteen, DeComillo and Wright..."

Jake drove straight to the Second Precinct and led the way into the Detective Bureau. "Lieutenant Morrow, we're Eight-Twelve. You wanted to see us?"

"I need some statements on the fight with Dudley Smith and Officer Williams, the doorman." He looked up from his desk. "You were the ones that helped Williams with the prisoner, right?"

Dick stepped forward. "No, we weren't involved in any fight. Musta been another TMU car. The Doorman OK?"

"Got a broken hand and some pulled muscles in his back."

Dick turned and looked at Jake. "See, your chicken shit arrest got another officer hurt. You happy now?"

The Lieutenant stood. "Whoa now. You the car that brought in Smith?"

"Let's just say he did," Dick said as he lit the stub of his cigar and motioned with his head.

The Lieutenant looked down at the report in front of him, then at Jake. "You Bush?"

"Yes sir."

"We made Dudley Smith in a line up. We've got him downtown now. The Robbery, B&E Bureau is questioning him. He may be wanted on a few other muggings." He smiled, then looked over at Whyser. "I think your partner's got himself and you in line for a citation."

Back at the Bureau, while waiting for off-duty roll call, Jake was playing Euchre. He could hear Dick Whyser talking to his usual cronies.

"Yah, we nailed this fucker to the cross. Number Two Dicks made the guy on one mugging and lookin' at him on some more. Hey, who was that crew that helped the Doorman out in the bullpen? I wish I woulda been there to get a piece of that shithead."

Jake looked forward to the days he worked with Jesse Scott. There wasn't a lot of talk between them, but a lot of work got done.

Jake broke the ice as they cruised the streets of the Seventh Precinct. "Jesse, how you getting along with Dick?"

"Okay."

"I don't know if it is just me or what. I ask him to stop a car and he wants to know why."

"So?"

"He's driving me nuts..."

Jess interrupted, "See that little kid in the Mercury we just passed?"

"Yeah. All by himself."

"White kid in a black neighborhood. No one else in the car. Something's up." Jesse made a U-turn and parked a block down to watch the car. It was just after two in the afternoon. Ten minutes went by when a white woman cut across the street and got in the Mercury. As she drove closer, Jesse got out of the car and flagged her down.

"Ma'am, your license please."

"What's wrong?" She fumbled with her purse and dropped the wallet as she fished for her ID.

"Want to step out of the car?" Jesse opened the door for her. She stepped out and staggered; her eyes were glassy and looking off into space. Jesse turned her right arm over and saw the tracks.

"Just got a hit, eh?" He turned to Jake. "You see where she came from?"

"The brown shingled house on our right."

Jesse jumped in the Mercury and pulled it into a parking spot at the curb. "Call for one of our cars. Tell them to look for our Unit." He put the woman's keys in his pocket as he put her back in her car, handcuffing her to the steering wheel. "Just stay where you are. Take a nap or something."

Jess drove Eight-Twelve to the brown-shingled house. "Time for a daytime raid, Jake."

One kick and the back door swung open. Jesse was leading the way with his gun in his hand. The toilet was heard flushing as he and Jake went through the kitchen into the living room. Another kick and the door of the bathroom opened. A grinning black man held down the handle on the toilet, saying, "Too bad mutha fuckers, the shit's all gone."

The grin disappeared as Jesse had him upside down, head first in the toilet bowl. The water was rising as he tried pushing himself up with both hands on the rim of the bowl. Jesse had him by the legs, pushing his head into the bowl. Jesse flushed the toilet. "Better tell me now where the rest of the stuff is." The water started to rise again as Jesse used the man's head like it was a plunger.

"Hold on man, blub, blub…" His arm strength was no match for Jesse's. The water rose covering his nose and mouth. Air bubbles rose in the bowl as he thrashed his head.

Jesse flushed the toilet again. "One more time. Where's your stash?"

The water rose a third time. Air and words came out of the man's mouth, "In the wabb, blub, blub…"

The water receded. "Where?"

"In the bedroom wall."

"Eight-Fifteen to Eight-Twelve."

Jake grabbed the mic on his walkie-talkie. "Go, Fifteen."

"Where you guys at?"

162

"I'll be right out." Jake left Jesse with their prisoner handcuffed and sitting on the couch.

Eight-Fifteen called for Women's Division to turn over the two-year-old boy in the Mercury. Irene Prathers, the driver, was held by the Detroit Police Narcotics Division as a material witness in the case against Nathan Weems. Five bags of pure heroin were found behind the full-length mirror in the bedroom wall.

The reports were made and evidence tagged. Eight-Twelve had a late lunch at Sophie's. "How far do you think this case'll go, Jesse?"

"Let's see, a decent lawyer and bond posted by his supplier—he'll be back in business in a week or two."

"And the court case?" Jake asked as the waitress put the plate of Lamb and Rice in front of him.

"Probably never make it past the prelim exam. Illegal search and seizure."

"Guess we knew that up front."

"Yeah, but a lot of heroin is off the street, and ol' Nathan will be looking over his shoulder for a long time."

"Bet ya he'll be toilet shy for a while too."

Jesse laughed as he dabbed the flat bread into the sauce of his Beef Paprikash. "You didn't like my interrogation methods?"

"Just sayin' it was different." Jake washed Sophie's spices down with a tall glass of milk.

163

Chapter 16

"Eight-Twelve'is chasing a stolen car in Number Ten." The radio operator's voice broke the silence of the day shift on April 25, 1966

"They're going east on Collingwood, now north on Lawton!" Jake was shouting into the mic.

Jesse made a power turn. Jake grabbed street names as Jesse closed the gap between their white Plymouth and the red Buick.

"Your location, Eight-Twelve."

"Lawton, crossing Monterey."

Tires screeched and doors flew open. Jesse went after the driver. Jake took the passenger. The young black male ran east down an alley with Jake was paralleling him on the street. He felt he was ahead of the guy and cut through a yard. He slowed, listening for footfalls. Jake looked over the cyclone fence. A city worker was emptying a garbage can into the back bin on a DPW garbage truck.

The man with the thrash can in his hand pointed to the garage to Jake's left and mouthed, "In there."

Jake quietly opened the gate and moved up the alley, leapfrogging the fence. He walked around to the front of the garage. The overhead door was up. A black Desoto was parked in it. He looked under the car.

"All right. Get out. Hands in the air."

The passenger from the stolen car slowly crawled out. He had a three-foot hunk of a two by four in his right hand. "Drop it," Jake commanded.

There was no response, only an empty look in the eyes of a boy of about fifteen. "I said drop the board." Jake drew his revolver.

Shit kid, don't do anything stupid.

"Drop the fuckin' board!"

The boy took two more steps and his arm with the 2x4 came up. Jake sidestepped and swung his pistol to deflect the blow. The

2x4 caught Jake on his left shoulder as the barrel of his Colt caught the side of the boy's head.

The kid landed in a heap at Jake's feet and he put away his pistol before handcuffing his stunned prisoner. There were pieces of something stuck in his skin on the left side of his forehead.

"Saw everything," Willie McGraw stated. "He dove across the fence, headfirst into that tree." The DPW worker pointed to the Elm growing next to the fence. "Then crawled into the garage."

Tree bark; that's the pieces in his forehead.

"Got a badge number for my report?"

"Yes. DPW 1342."

Thanks, Mr. McGraw. Appreciate the help." Jake pulled his handcuffed prisoner up. "We'll call if we need you."

Jake walked the young man back to Eight-Twelve. Jesse was waiting for him. He had a second youth in the back of the car. "Where you been?"

"Had to get him out of a garage. We need to call the Sergeants. Mine is hurt. I hit him in the head when he wouldn't drop a two by four. A witness said he dove headfirst into a tree before I got there."

"He's really having a bad day."

Thomas Boyton, 15 of 1377 Seward and Henry Leland 16 of 1788 Blaine were handed over to #10 Youth Bureau. Boyton, Jake's prisoner, was transferred to Receiving Hospital under guard. He was an escapee from Boys Training School in Lansing, serving time for armed robbery.

****

Drugs, guns and crooks were taken off the streets in record numbers as the TMU's first full year on the street ended. Jake learned to tolerate cigar smoke and bullshit while he waited his turn at the wheel when he worked with Dick Whyser.

The Tactical Mobile Unit's twenty cars were working the quieter precincts of Number Fifteen and Sixteen. This was more of a public relations move rather than a need. Jake was behind the wheel cruising the area where he and Dick Whyser lived in the Fifteenth Precinct.

It was 11p.m. when a figure came out of the alley as Jake turned off of Strasburg onto Bringard. He drove up alongside and jumped out of the car.

"Hold it, mister; I want to talk to you."

The twenty-something white male just looked over his shoulder as he walked, "Fuck you."

Jake grabbed him by the arm. As he turned the man around, he found himself falling under the man. Jake struggled, but couldn't budge him, as he tried to get at the blackjack from the small pocket on the rear of his right trouser leg.

"Hold it, Bush," Whyser said as he was pulling the man off. "You, hit the road." Dick gave the man a shove.

Jake got up from the sidewalk. He stammered as his face flushed, "W-What the fuck…"

"Lesson number one, you want to stop someone, you better be bad enough to do something about it."

"Eleven at night. Coming out of an alley—and what about my partner?"

"Wasn't bothering me."

Jake brushed off his trousers. The man disappeared around the next corner. "What's going on Dick?"

Whyser did not answer as he climbed back in the car.

Jake got back in behind the wheel and put the car in gear. "Talk to me, Dick."

"Nuthin really to say. You just think you're some hotshot cop. I say you're not." Dick dug out a new El Producto.

"And you let this guy knock me on my ass to prove something?" Jake started driving.

"Yeah. You flunked the test."

"This was a test?"

"I think I made my point."

"And your point is that you call all the shots on this car."

"Somethin' like that."

"Dick is your ideal partner one that just follows you around and idolizes you?"

"Respects me is more like it."

"Respects you?"

"Yes respect. Remember how you made me look in front of that lieutenant at Number Two?"

"You did all the talking."

Jake turned a few more corners. "You're pissed 'cause I was right." Dick did not respond. "So was this just a good opportunity to put me in my place?"

Dick just puffed on his cigar as Jake turned west onto State Fair.

The radio sliced through the silence that followed. "All units, officer in trouble, Hoover and Eight Mile. At the motorcycle club."

"We're five blocks away!" Jake slid into a right turn on Hoover.

The Harley club was on the left. They were the first TMU car at the scene. A black precinct car was there with the doors open.

Jake and Dick burst through the black door with a white skull and crossbones painted on it. Bodies and chairs were flying. Jake pulled his blackjack as a glancing fist caught him above his ear. He lost his hat, but recovered and clipped his attacker across the shoulder with the 24 ouncer. A second swing caught the man alongside the head. The leather jacket went down.

Garcia and Cesarz waded in the front door swinging clubs. Jake saw the odds turning in their favor. Two black leather jackets were on top of a uniform to his right. He caught one between the shoulder blades with his blackjack, and then let a foot go at the side of the head of a mop of red hair under a bandana. When that one rolled, Jake saw that Dick Whyser was the uniform underneath. Jake helped Dick to his feet while giving another attacker a swat with his blackjack.

More uniforms came in the narrow door. The last standing leather jacket dropped a broken beer bottle, raising his gloved hands. "I'm cool man. Just havin' a little fun."

167

The precinct officers were searching the fifteen bikers leaning spread-eagle along the walls. The four crews from the TMU stood guard. There were seven more bikers lying on the floor with handcuffs tightly secured in the small of their backs.

Sergeants Ski and Erdmann were taking notes. "Who knows what happened?" Ski asked.

One of the men from Number Fifteen spoke up. "We tried to stop one of these bikers just outside this place for running a red light and he ran inside."

His partner chimed in. "I called for help before we went after him."

The Fifteenth Precinct paddy wagon was used to help transport some of the twenty-two people arrested. Three were women. Jake noticed each of the girls outweighed him by at least fifty pounds. He recognized one as the redhead that he knocked off his partner.

The rest of the night was filled with reports on the arrests and injured prisoners. Jake kept copies for his bosses and climbed in the car. Dick drove down Gratiot heading for the Bureau.

"Guess we kicked some ass tonight," came out of a cloud of smoke.

Jake was filling out the run sheet. "Yeah, we did."

"By the way, thanks for, er, you know…"

"I didn't know it was you under the pile." Jake chuckled. "If I did, I'd a gone the other way."

Jake put away the run sheet.

Embarrassing, isn't it? Being on the bottom.

"Dick, about earlier tonight…"

"Let's just forget about it. Cigar?"

"Don't smoke 'em."

"A cigar and a beer or two and you might make it as a cop."

"Don't need to make it. I'm here."

In 1965 the Watt's riot took place in California. The question was when would something like that happen in Detroit? Radio runs started coming over the air as a group of young blacks started breaking windows along a string of businesses on Kercheval Avenue in the Fifth Precinct. Those arrested said that guns and reinforcements were heading in from Chicago.

"You think Watts was bad, wait'll you white honky mutha fuckers see what we have coming."

Ten cars from the TMU were already working in the next precinct, Number Seven. In thirty minutes all twenty blue and white cars were there in and around Kercheval.

All units were put on 12 hour shifts. The TMU patrolled that area day and night for five days, stopping any cars containing more than two people. That may have had something to do with nothing happening.

A small clipping in the *News* and *Free Press* dubbed it as the "Kercheval Incident."

It was a warm, September evening. Bob Maples was driving Eight Twelve. "It has been a long time since you broke me in on the beat at Number Eleven, Jake."

"Four years or more."

Bob was in the second group of officers that came to the TMU. Bob was filling in while Jesse and Dick were off.

At Canfield and Rivard fifteen young blacks were hanging around the front of a corner grocery store. Bob drove to the curb alongside the group. He climbed out and so did Jake. "All right kids, move along," Bob commanded.

From the back of the crowd a voice shouted, "Fuck you Uncle Tom."

Bob moved through the crowd like a cat and had one black youth by the throat. "It's Uncle Tom, SIR! You understand that?"

"Yes sir."

Bob pushed him along. "And when I say, there ain't no corner hanging, I mean just that. Now get your asses out of here." The crowd of black youths looked back at Officer Maples, all six-four of him. They mumbled, but kept moving.

Jake watched the group slowly walk past the next corner as Bob got back in behind the wheel. Jake climbed in. "You get that much?"

"Hell, they don't like cops, white or black." Bob drove past the Wonder Bakery on Russell.

Jake changed the subject. "How'd you leave things at Number Eleven?"

"Same. Nice and quiet."

"Does that German Shepard still live on the roof of the Turtle Soup Inn?"

"And ol' Oscar's still at Ray's Bump Shop scaring the shit out of everyone." Bob laughed. "Yeh, I remember that day we were walking past the Turtle Soup Inn. I think we both thought that dog was coming off of the roof."

Jake remembered the flat roofed restaurant. "Hell, I remember beating you to the corner."

"And I was worried that the chain he was stretching would break," Bob said as he threw his hat on the dashboard. "That Precinct has more bad assed dogs than anywhere. Remember that one in the junk yard on Seven Mile?"

"I sure do."

A plate of ribs at the Taystee Barbecue cut the night in half as Bob and Jake talked about the old days. Their kids were the next subject as Jake cruised Woodward, and then turned onto the Edsel Ford service drive heading west.

A Lincoln was parked at an angle toward the curb and two men were beating on a third. A pregnant woman was standing at the side of the car screaming.

"Street hold up!" Bob said as he started out of the car.

Jake was closer and got there first. He turned his back to the man that was being hit, moving him away from his attackers.

Jake felt a sharp pain behind his left ear. He looked up between a pair of legs when he heard, "Get up Jake. Get the fuck up!"

Bob was straddled over him, jabbing with his 24 oz. blackjack. Before Jake could get all the way to his feet the pregnant woman was on Bob's back. A grab, a push, a shove, and swinging blackjacks had things back under control. He and Bob lined the three men and a woman against the wall of the Wayne State University storage building.

Jake backed toward their car and grabbed the mic. "Eight-Twelve needs help Ford Service Drive west of Woodward."

As the last word came out of his mouth the four were coming off of the wall swinging at Bob. Jake joined the melee, parting one man's hair with his blackjack.

Sirens sounded in the background. It sounded like the bugles of the cavalry to Jake. In seconds Blue and white cars and policemen were all over the area.

Jake made sure he grabbed the man who hit him behind the ear. He handcuffed the man and slid in beside him in the back seat of Eight-Twelve.

Bob drove down Cass toward the Thirteenth Precinct. Bob adjusted the inside rearview mirror, looking into Jake's eyes. "Well Jake, what're you waiting for?"

"He'll get his in court," Jake answered.

Bob eased the car over to the curb and slowly turned in his seat. "You may have broke me in on a beat, but here's one thing I need to teach you." A three-cell flashlight caught the prisoner over the bridge of the nose. "The only justice is alley justice."

The next day Sergeant Ski accompanied Jake and Bob to recorders court. The Assistant Prosecutor wanted the charges to be Assault and Battery on a Police Officer, but the defendants' attorney talked the prosecutor into charging them with disturbing the peace.

It took seconds for Judge Gillis to throw out the charges. "There is no such thing as disturbing a policeman's peace." The gavel went down, "Case dismissed."

The predominantly black onlookers in the courtroom were mumbling as Jake and Bob left.

Bob whispered to Jake, "See what I mean?"

When Jake, Bob and Sergeant Ski got to the elevator the three male defendants were there waiting.

"Fuckin' Uncle Tom," said one as Ski grabbed Bob's arm.

"We'll walk down." Ski pushed Bob and grabbed Jake at the same time. "This is not the place."

"I liked that turban you put on that one dude, Jake. Kinda set off his new suit."

"I don't know Bob, the one with the flat nose and puffed up eyes impressed me."

"Learn something Jake?" Bob looked past the sergeant at Jake.

"Yes, I guess I did."

On September 14th, Eight-Twelve was assigned to Number Two. It was quiet and dark. Jake was cruising the alleys with his lights off. They were in an alley off of Michigan Avenue. Two men dropped a cash register and were off and running when the tires on the white and blue police car crunched some glass. Dick took after the man on his side as Jake was in a race with the other. Jake's man turned a corner and crossed Michigan onto 12th Street. He cut between two houses. As Jake made the same turn, his man was bouncing off of a seven-foot high cyclone fence. Jake caught the sleeve of the man's jacket as he went down. They rolled twice and the man was able to get to his feet with Jake hanging onto a jacket sleeve. There was a kick to the ribs, a stomp to the back of Jake's legs, and another kick as Jake hung on to the sleeve.

"I'm gonna stomp your fuckin' ass," were the words Jake heard as he caught another foot in the small of his back.

Jake would not let go of the sleeve, working out his 24 oz. blackjack and taking one swing at the side of the leg of the guy dancing on him. Jake followed with another to the man's hip as he got to one knee.

As the man pulled out of his jacket the blackjack glanced off of his shoulder catching him in the side of his head. The dancer had his hands over his head, yelling, "I give. I give." When the man's hands dropped, Jake's blackjack hit its mark. "You give when I say you give."

Dick was waiting at the car when Jake got back.

"Who the fuck walked all over you?"

"My friend here. I hope he feels worse than I do."

Jake ended up at Receiving Hospital for X-rays. The dancer was handcuffed to a nearby gurney getting ten stitches in his head before being booked for Breaking and Entering.

It seemed like every day the TMU was into something. On this day the high number cars were working Number Ten, the Livernois Station.

Jesse was cruising Linwood approaching Elmhurst. It was near two in the morning the time to head back to the Bureau. They had stopped fourteen cars and had nothing to show for it.

Another night was done until a man came out of The Bow Tie Bar with a bottle of beer in his hand. He crossed the street in front of Eight-Twelve and into a parking lot. Jess didn't say a thing, just turned the blue and white into the parking lot, fixing his headlights on the man.

Jake climbed out as Jess brought the Blue and White to a stop. Jake put the beam of his three-cell light on the man and watched him bend down to put the bottle against the back tire of a parked car. A broad smile came across the man's face. Jake drew his Colt and took aim at the rising figure. A blue steel pistol had replaced the beer bottle. It was coming from the man's waistline toward Jake.

The decision to squeeze the trigger was already made when Jess came up behind the man. "Freeze," Jake screamed as he took the pressure off of his trigger.

Jesse came over the back of the man grabbing the cylinder on the pistol and with a flip of his wrist wrenched it out of the man's hand.

"Damn Jess, I could have shot you."

"Hoped you wouldn't."

"I don't know whether you saved my life or his," Jake said as he was tightening the cuffs.

Jake turned the man around. "Got a name?"

"Harris."

"First name?"

"Harris."

Jess retrieved a wallet out of the man's back pocket. He pulled out a driver's license. "Says here his name is Harris Harris."

"That's what I said." The man smiled, revealing a gold metal blade in place of his left upper front tooth.

"Easier to remember, I guess, Mr. Harris Harris." Jess opened the back door of the car and guided the man in.

Harris Harris was held in the Tenth Precinct for "Investigation of Robbery Armed" with a hold for "Carrying a Concealed Weapon."

It was Jake's turn to take court cases. He was at the Prosecutor's Office for the CCW warrant at eight in the morning. Jake waited for an hour and did not hear his name or the name "Harris." He asked at the desk.

The clerk checked his log. "Sorry, nothing for you Bush. No prisoner by the name of Harris Harris either."

"Can I use your phone to call Ten DB?"

"There it is," the clerk turned the phone and Jake made the call.

By noon Jake was standing listening to Inspector Bertolini. "This Harris is supposed to be a snitch on a big narcotics bust going down in Pontiac. He called his contact with the Feds. They bounced him."

"He was drawing a gun on me."

"They thought you might have been flowering up the report a bit."

"He was coming up with the gun. I almost shot my partner. This is total bullshit."

"Just let it go, Jake. Let it go."

"Yeah, and that weasel might shoot the next cop that stops him. They didn't even call us. Fuckin' Feds!"

"Want me to have them come down here to talk to you and Jesse?"

"What? Talk to somebody in a $300 suit that's bought with drug money? I wouldn't waste my time." Jake slammed the door on his way out.

Jake re-lived the gun coming up in his dreams for weeks. More than one dream had Jesse falling when Jake took a shot at the man. In other nightmares Jake awoke to the pain of a bullet burning in his chest. Every dream had Harris Harris with the gold metal blade in place of a tooth, smiling as he turned and walked away.

Chapter 17

The Patrolmen formed three loose ranks when Sergeant Kempf yelled out, "Roll Call". It was the end of September and he had a stack of envelopes in his hand. "I've got the promotional exam results to pass out before the assignments. Listen up for your name. Bohy."

"Yes, sir."

"Pass this back to him." The sergeant handed the envelope to the first rank.

"Breed."

"Yes, sir."

"Here Dunn, to your right."

"Bush... Hell, he's Polish. We know he flunked." The sergeant flipped the envelope back over his shoulder. It landed on the floor.

Most of the forty men in the ranks broke into a laugh.

"Bet you twenty bucks I wrote the highest exam among those here." Bush pushed his way to the front and bent over to pick up the envelope.

"Just teasing, Jake."

Jake handed the envelope back to Kempf. "I'm not. Twenty bucks."

The sergeant raised his hand at the offer of the envelope. "It was a joke."

"No Sarge. Open the envelope." Jake pushed it at Kempf.

"Bush, er, ah, it's personal."

"You made it public. Remember? I'm just a dumb Polack. Open it. Twenty Bucks."

The sergeant had the envelope in his hand when Lieutenant Chester Sylvers came out of his office. "Hope you got twenty bucks, Gerry."

The Lieutenant took the remaining envelopes and silently passed them out to the men. "Bush called you, Sergeant. Open the envelope."

Kempf's face flushed as he slowly tore it open. His voice cracked, "Eighty-seven." He cleared his throat. "Anyone beat an eighty-seven?"

Envelopes were opened; results unfolded. He asked in a pleading voice. "Anyone?"

The room was silent. Sergeant Gerhardt Kempf pulled two tens out of his wallet and handed them to Jake.

The Lieutenant walked to the podium. "Now that the bullshit is over, here's tonight's assignments. Eight-One, Cesarz and Garcia..."

The TMU officers filed out of the squad room into the basement garage toward their cars. Richard Dungy fell in alongside Jake. "Damn good score, partner. Where'd you end up on the Detective's list?"

"Thanks. So far back they're pumping in daylight to me. How'd you do?"

"Not too good on the list, four-seventy-five, but I wrote a ninety-one."

"Ninety-one? Why didn't you speak up?"

"And make that Kraut happy? Besides, I knew we'd have lunch on his dime."

Jake put his arm over Dick's shoulder laughing, "Where do you and your partner want to eat tonight?"

"Let's do Chinese. The Wok on Second."

Dick, Norville, Jesse and Jake ate well thanks to Gerhardt Kempf.

****

October brought many changes to the TMU. Inspector Anthony Bertoloni was promoted to District Inspector and Lieutenant Sylvers made Inspector. Sylvers was put in charge of the Tactical Mobile Unit. Lieutenant Alan Orth took over Jake's shift.

Jake got a letter through Inter-Department mail. It read: "Officer John Anthony Bush, Badge #2441 is ordered to appear on the 18th of October, 1966, 9 a.m. at the Internal Affairs Office, Room 398, 100 Beaubien for a hearing concerning the arrest of Thomas Boyton."

An Inspector Reese of the Internal Affairs, Detroit Police Department, signed the letter.

Jake scratched his head, trying to remember the name. "Remember arresting a Thomas Boyton?" Jake asked Jesse as they walked out toward their car.

"No."

Jake read the letter aloud up as Jesse drove out of the garage. "They aren't telling you much. You don't remember the name?"

"Not a clue."

"First thing you want to do is call the DPOA."

"Why?"

"You may need a lawyer. They provide them free."

Jake called the Detroit Police Officers Association that afternoon.

On October 18th, Jake met Attorney John Aberdash on the third floor of the Detroit Police Headquarters. Jake showed John Aberdash the letter. "Do you remember the arrest?"

"I'm not sure. I'd have to see my report."

"They'll have a copy," he assured Jake as they entered room 398.

Jake removed his uniform hat and straightened his black tie. His light blue dress shirt had military creases running down the front and rear. The spit shined Sam Brown cross strap and holster glistened under the fluorescent overhead lights. "Uh-hem…" Jake cleared his throat as he stood in front of a girl at the desk. "Jake Bush."

She nodded at the door behind her. "Right through there, officer."

The door opened up to a conference room with an oblong mahogany table. Jake and the attorney entered. Jake sized up the room as he held the door. There were eight chairs around the table. At the head of the far end of the table sat a man with graying temples wearing a dark blue suit—*A cop.* There was a tape recorder in front of him and a tray with glasses and a pitcher of water.

On his right was a second man wearing a close crew cut and a bulge on his left hip under his mint green sport coat. *Another cop. Maybe a detective.* Next to him were two empty chairs.

On the left was a woman in a maroon suit and two men in dark pinstriped suits. None of them looked like police. The man at the head of the table stood. "Officer Bush?"

"Yes sir."

"Have a seat." He indicated the first empty chair to his right. "I'm Lieutenant Fox. Inspector Reese asked me to take the lead in this matter. I see you brought John Aberdash with you."

"Sorry, I should have introduced him."

"No need. We've met many times. Have a seat John."

Jake and his attorney sat down.

The Lieutenant pressed a button on the tape recorder, and started introducing the rest of the people in the room. "Officer Jake Bush, this is Mrs. Mary Blades, Dr. Roy Johnson and Arnold Horwitz. They are part of the Detroit Citizens Committee for Race Relations. To your left is my partner, Sergeant August Sonfeld."

"I'd like to interrupt, Lieutenant," John Aberdash said as he stood. "Since you have the tape recorder going, Officer Bush and I would like to hear the complaint that is being made against him."

"Oh, there's no complaint. This is just an informal hearing concerning the arrest of Thomas Boyton by Officer Bush."

"If there is no complaint, then I guess we don't have to be here." John stood and put his yellow-dog tablet into his attaché case. "Come on Jake, we're leaving."

"Wait. We have some questions."

179

"Lieutenant, you have a tape recorder going. My client vaguely remembers the arrest of Thomas Boyton. If there is no complaint, or no charges, there'll be no questions answered."

The lieutenant hit the switch on the tape recorder. The reels stopped turning.

"Okay, let's start over. Please sit down."

Jake and John sat down. John took out the pad of yellow dog and put it in front of him. John clicked the pen in his hand. "Your show, lieutenant."

Lieutenant Fox hit the switch on the tape recorder. He cleared his throat. "At approximately 2 p.m. on June 23rd of this year you arrested Thomas Boyton, colored male, 15 and Henry Leland, colored male, 16 for UDAA in the Tenth Precinct. I have a statement by Mrs. Natty Boyton, corroborated by another witness that she happened to be driving behind your police car after the arrest.

Mrs. Boyton's statement claims that the officer in the back seat of the white police car was pistol-whipping her son while in route to the police station. As a result of this, Thomas Boyton ended up in Detroit Receiving Hospital with a major concussion."

The lieutenant poured some water into a glass and took a sip. "Now this is just one account of what happened. We want to hear your side."

The serious head injury jogged Jake's memory. "You say it involved a stolen car?"

The lieutenant thumbed through some papers in a manila folder. "Yes. A Red Buick. Boyton was a passenger in the car."

"Do you have a copy of my report?"

"Yes, I do."

"If it's the one I am thinking of, I had a witness to the arrest."

John Aberdash stood. "Can we see the report, lieutenant?" The lieutenant handed a copy of the report to the attorney. John scanned it then handed it to Jake.

"Is this the report you are referring to?"

Jake took the report and read it. "Yes sir. I noted the witness's name, Willie McGraw, and his badge number. He's a DPW worker."

John took the report and read it again. "Why did you note this on your report, Officer Bush?"

"Because he saw the kid running and told me where to find him. Then after I had the kid handcuffed he was still there watching."

"And you had to use force to subdue Boyton?"

"Yes sir. He came at me with a hunk of two by four. I entered it in as evidence."

"Anything else you remember?"

"Yes, the witness saw the kid dive headfirst into an elm tree then crawl into the garage."

The attorney looked at the lieutenant. "Did you get a statement from..." he looked at the report, "Mr. McGraw?"

"We haven't got that far yet."

"Judging by the report that Officer Bush wrote and signed, I would suggest that you interview Mr. McGraw prior to going any further with this inquiry."

The lieutenant clicked off the tape recorder. He looked at the people around the table. "Do any of you have any questions?" There were none. "I think we have covered all we need to. Thank you, Officer Bush, and John, good seeing you again."

John Aberdash and Jake headed for the elevator.

"It's good I called the DPOA," Jake said as he pushed the down arrow next to the elevator.

"Never answer a letter from any of these guys without calling the Detroit Police Officer's Association." The door of the elevator slid open and Jake and John entered. "Never think you're alone. That's what you pay dues for. I may be wrong, but I don't think you'll hear from Lieutenant Fox on this again."

Days later Jake walked into the squad room and heard Lieutenant Orth call out. "Patrolman Bush, "The inspector wants to

181

see you." It was before roll call. The lieutenant followed Jake into the office.

The inspector was seated at his desk as Jake entered.

"Jake, I received a letter from Internal Affairs, a Lieutenant Fox."

"Do they want to see me again?"

"No." The inspector took his time reading the letter to himself. "The bottom line is that they concluded that you used too much force in effecting the arrest."

"You are kidding me, right?"

"No, I am not."

"Too much force. The kid came at me with a two by four."

"We read the report," Lieutenant Orth interrupted. "May I say something?"

"Sure, Lieutenant," Sylvers answered.

"We've made a lot of paper on your injured prisoners."

"Bad guys don't just throw their hands up in the air."

The lieutenant cut Jake short. "Do you know you have only written one ticket this year?"

"How many arrests have I made?"

"We're talking tickets."

"You're talking work. I arrest people." Jake looked at the lieutenant. "Are you telling me you'd rather I write tickets?"

"You have a choice, slow down or find a new home."

The Inspector interrupted, "Jake, all we're saying is to take it easy. Don't bring any heat on yourself. Stay out of the limelight for a while."

The phrase "slow down or find a new home" reechoed in his head as he left the office.

"What'd the bosses want?" Jesse asked. Jake did not answer as Jesse slid behind the wheel.

Never would've thought the Tactical Mobile Unit would be asking me to write tickets. I might as well be back at Thirteen.

Jake glanced at the assignments for January as he walked into the squad room. It was near the end of December. His name wasn't on Eight-Twelve. It took a while, but he found his name assigned to Eight-Four with Ed Bartkowski and Duane Wattles.

Jake caught up to Sergeant Ski. "Someone ask for a change on Eight-Twelve?"

"Whyser saw Orth. He asked for a guy in his car pool to be put on his car."

The higher test score must have sealed the deal.

Jake walked into the garage, meeting Jesse on the way.

"See we don't have you on the car next month."

"Guess Dick had enough of me."

"Looks like it." Jess backed Eight-Twelve out of its slot.

"Yeah, first they ask me to slow down or find a new home. Now they put me with some old duffer from Number Fifteen and an overweight bozo from Six. They're hanging a couple of anchors on my ass."

"Just watch the street people, you'll do all right."

"Well, at least I'll be rid of Dick and his cigar."

"If it'll make you feel better, I asked the bosses to move me to another car."

"You're still with Dick."

"They turned me down. Said it would look bad. I even asked for you as a partner."

"You did?"

"Yes I did. You talk too much, but you're learning."

"I don't know if that's an endorsement or a dig."

There was a slight smile on Cliff's face. A first. "Just show your new crew how a good street cop works."

Jake was filling in on Eight-Thirteen with Richard Dungy the 29th of December. They were working the Fourteenth Precinct.

"Dick, mind if I ask you something personal?"

"What, do I look like a priest?"

"Already saw one. The bosses had me in a couple of weeks ago and told me I needed to slow down. Too many injured prisoners."

"What do you want from me?"

"An honest opinion from a guy I trust."

"You really want to hear what I think?"

"Yes."

"Well, a skinny assed cop like you is always gonna have a brother thinkin' 'Let's see what's behind that badge.' "

"I'm serious." Jake paused a beat. "What brothers you talkin' about?"

"I'm talkin' about my soul brothers. The blacks. Negroes."

"Hell, I've had a few white guys take me on."

"Put some meat on your bones and you might not have to fight so much."

Jake sat quiet for a few minutes. "What's this soul brother stuff? You tellin' me you're black?"

"Yep. Didn't you notice?"

"I thought you were Canadian."

"I am. And just because I play hockey doesn't mean I'm not black."

"Let's get back to what I asked. You think I'm too quick to swing first?"

"No, but the bosses might be taking some heat from upstairs. Sylvers knows you. He probably just wants you to watch your back. Maybe he heard something."

"Okay, 'nuf of the serious shit. Am I still your favorite euchre partner."

"As long as we keep winning."

"Fair enough. Let's go eat."

"Got any soul food in this precinct?"

"Probably not. What about some good Polish food?"

"How do Polacks do ribs?"

"With sauerkraut."

"That's a waste of good pork. Let's get a pizza."

It was the last day of December when Jake knocked on the door and entered at the wave of the inspector's hand. He stood in front of Inspector Sylvers' desk.

The inspector looked up. "You want to see me about something, Jake?"

"Yes sir. I've spent most of the month driving around and doing nothing. This slow down or find a new home mandate has me all fu...messed up. I can't work like this."

"I never told you to slow down. Just to take it easy for a while."

"The lieutenant did."

"Jake, the first of January you are with a new crew. I had Orth move you there. Those guys write a lot of tickets, which is okay, but I'd like their arrest numbers up. I was hoping that by moving you to their car you could help make that happen."

"I'll do my best, sir." Jake felt like a hundred pounds were taken off of his shoulders. "And thanks for the vote of confidence." Jake turned to leave.

"Have a Happy New Year, Jake."

"You too, sir."

Chapter 18

Eight-Four's senior man was Ed Bartkowski, a sixteen-year veteran from the Fifteenth Precinct. Ed was tall and thin with a pointed face and a distinct Polish nose. He went to grade school at St. Hyacinth in Jake's dad's old neighborhood. Bart, as he liked to be called, was driving the first half of the shift. It was the first time he worked with Jake.

"Did you see the look those two gave us? Make a U-turn, Bart." Jake strained his neck to watch a Ford going the other way on East Jefferson.

"What'd you see?"

"Something about the way they looked at us."

"You stop people for looking at you?" Bart made a slow turn to head the way Jake indicated. The Ford was long gone.

Within a couple of shifts Jake learned that Bart was just slow and methodical. He came to the TMU with the second batch of officers. He was ex-regular Army.

Eight-Four pulled out of the garage, heading to their assignment, the Twelfth Precinct on January 6th. Jake was working with Duane Wattles, the second man on the car.

"I heard you were in the 101st Airborne," Jake said.

"Yeh, I was a cook. Got assigned to them."

"So you weren't a paratrooper."

"Hell no. I'm not crazy enough to jump out of an airplane."

So much for the ex-Marine and Paratrooper hype the papers printed about the TMU in 1965. Jake just smiled.

Duane Wattles grew up in South Carolina. He moved to Detroit as a teen and was assigned to the Sixth Precinct out of the academy. He too came with the second group to the TMU. Duane still had a slight southern drawl. His home precinct, the Sixth, was a mix of elderly Polish and working class Negroes on the west side of the city. That's where Jake's maternal grandmother lived.

Duane was six-foot tall with 255-pounds not very well distributed. He was shaped like a pear.

After a slow month with his new crew Jake was able to make an assessment. Bart was a laid back and conservative. He was a good cop that just didn't rush nor take chances. His stops were for traffic violations and tickets were the result. Jake knew he could work around that.

It appeared that Duane spent his time at Number Six doing nothing but finding the right places to eat. He brought that experience with him.

This is the crew that the inspector wants me to make street cops out of. He laughed to himself.

A light cold drizzle was falling. It was the second day of a winter thaw in early February. Eight-Four was working the day shift. Jake and Duane had just got back on the road after a sandwich at Isaac's Ham Shack on Michigan and Livernois. A green Chevrolet made a left turn off of Grand River onto Buchanan.

"I'm going to talk to these guys," Jake said as he motioned the Green Chevrolet to the curb. "No brake lights."

Duane looked up from the paperback he was reading, mumbling okay.

The 1957 Chevrolet with four male occupants pulled to the curb. Jake slid the blue and white in behind them. He got out of the car turning up the fur collar on his jacket as he walked. He glanced back noting that Duane did not get out of the car. Jake approached the driver who was rolling down his window.

"Sir, can I see your license and registration?"

"Any problem, officer?" The driver handed his license to Jake and leaned over toward the passenger's side and opened the glove compartment.

"Your brake lights aren't working." Jake watched as the man dug around for the registration. He saw the end of a green box

187

labeled "Remington" in big white letters. Jake glanced at the papers and handed them back to the driver. "Just make sure you have your brake lights checked. Could be just a fuse."

"Thanks officer," the driver called out as he rolled up his window.

Jake climbed behind the wheel, watching the Chevrolet drive off. It continued west on Buchanan. He followed from a distance. Jake grabbed the mic.

"Any TMU unit in the area of Buchanan west of Grand River?"

"This is Six, Jake. What you got?"

"A green 1957 Chevrolet westbound on Buchanan from Grand River. I'm keeping them in sight. Four black males. I think they have a gun in the car."

"Eight Four, this is Seven-Oh. A green '57 Chev is wanted for a robbery armed in the Twelfth Precinct. Radio just put the information over the air minutes ago."

"This is Eight-Ten we're at Warren and Lawton, heading toward Buchanan."

"What the fuck's goin' on?" The radio traffic had Duane stuffing his book in the glove box.

"I'm making sure I don't get my ass killed while my partner is reading about cowboys and Indians."

Jake keyed the mic again. "Just crossed Lawton and now going over the expressway."

"Six is at 24th and Buchanan. We see 'em coming."

"This is Ten. We're right behind you, Jake."

Jake jumped on the gas and the 318 engine came alive. "Six, block that intersection. Let's take 'em now."

The green 1957 Chevrolet slowed to a stop when they saw three sets of flashing blue lights in front and behind them. Gramatico and Parkhurst stood with sawed-off shotguns leveled at the Chevy's windshield. Jake moved to the driver's side with his .38 aimed at the driver. Scrivo from Eight-Ten was running up behind him. Duane and Joe Breed were on the passenger side of the Chevy.

"Hands where we can see them! Nobody moves!" Jake yelled. He opened the driver's door. "Out, slowly and on the ground." His .38 was pointed at the head of the driver.

Scrivo opened the door behind the driver. "You, out and on the ground."

Breed followed with the front passenger's door and Duane opened the remaining rear door.

Eight-Seven-Oh arrived as the four men were being searched and handcuffed. Sgt. Ski and Kempf stood off watching.

Scrivo and Breed started searching the car once the prisoners were secured and leaning against Eight-Six's car. Jake yelled to Breed, "Glove box's got some ammo in it."

Breed came out from under the front passenger's seat. "And an old Iver Johnson five shot to go with the shells." He had a pencil stuck in the chrome barrel. Scrivo did a slow methodical search. In the crease behind the back seat he found a small brown paper sack with $272 in wadded up bills.

The sergeants offered to help take the car in.

"Nice work, Bush," Kempf said as they were ready to head in.

Jake looked over at the sergeants. "Ask Lieutenant Orth if I should write the ticket for no brake lights?"

Sgt. Kempf smiled. "Always a wise ass, eh Jake?"

Carmen Jones, 33; Alonzo Phillips, 30; Jerome Washington, 35 and Dewayne Anderson, 26 were conveyed to the Second Precinct and held on Teletype 235 for a Robbery Armed in the Twelfth Precinct.

Jake slid in behind the wheel and drove toward Chene and Jefferson. The paperwork at Number Two consumed two hours. It was time to go home.

"You shoulda told me what was going on."

"Where were you when I was talking to the driver?"

189

"Ah, er…"

Jake pulled the car to the curb and looked into his partner's eyes. "I don't know where in the hell you come from or where you've been, but from now on, when I stop a car, you will be outside covering the passenger's side of every, and I mean every fuckin' car."

"Jake I, er, ah…"

"This isn't a discussion. This is what I expect."

"I thought you were writing a ticket."

"Every stop we make, you got one side, I the other." Jake pulled back into traffic.

"It won't happen again."

"It'd better not. I'm not here to get my ass shot off."

Bartkowski and Bush were heading toward the assigned Fourteenth Precinct on the afternoon shift in March.

Ed spoke. "I see Simons already has a car stopped." He passed one of the other TMU cars stopped behind a Ford Convertible.

"Let's make a U-turn, Bart."

"Why?"

"They might need back up."

"Simons is a bit crazy. I like to stay away from him."

"They might need some help."

Bart shrugged his shoulders, but made a double U-turn, ending up behind Eight-Seven.

Simons had the driver leaning on the hood of his police car, going through his pockets as his partner, Hank Raymond, stood off to watch. Jake and Bart were out of their unit listening.

The man turned his head, "You got no cause to search me…" as the officer was digging into his coat pockets.

Simons jumped on the man's back and hit him with two quick chops behind the neck. "Just shut the fuck up, Nigger. Don't make a move." He pushed his face into the hood of the car. "And keep it shut."

"What you got?" Jake asked as he walked up from behind.

190

"Broken tail light and a nigger with a big mouth." He snapped a pair of cuffs on his man. "Hank, put him in our car 'til I can search his."

"What for?" The man asked.

" 'cause you're hiding something."

"Take care of your prisoner, I'll search the car," Jake offered. He did not wait for a response, just started going through the car. He dug under the seats, checked the glove box and even popped up the back seat to look under it. Jake put the seat back in its place. He then ran his hands under the headliner on the convertible top. Jake knew the double folds over the edges were a perfect spot to hide contraband. It was something Jesse Scott had taught him. Jake then searched the trunk. Jake walked to Eight-Seven as Simons was jotting some notes on his clipboard. "The car is clean. Nothing in it."

"Not that I don't believe you, but I'll search it myself." Simons tossed the clipboard on his seat, grabbed the black leather folder that officers carried their blank traffic tickets in and slipped it in his back pocket.

Jake listened as the handcuffed driver talked while sitting in the back seat of Eight-Seven.

"Man, all I was doing is comin' home from work. Been working seven days a week at Chrysler's. I ain't had time to fix that damn tail light." Hank Raymond was sitting next to him. "Then I run into some crazy cop who don't like black people. He's got no right callin' me a nigger."

"Told you he was hiding something," Simons said as he walked up to Jake with two marijuana joints in the palm of his hand.

"You ain't layin' that shit on me, man. Them ain't mine."

Jake looked at the two joints. They were flat like they were pressed in something.

The damn ticket book.

"Where did you find them?" Jake asked.

"In the fold in the convertible top, over the driver's side."

191

Jake motioned Simons to follow him back to Jake's car. When they got near Eight-Four Jake turned. "Bob, I checked the folds on both sides of that car. There was nothing there."

"You missed them, plain and simple."

"Why did you take your ticket book with you to do the search?"

Bob Simons's face reddened. "I was gonna write him."

"Bob, them two joints are flat. Like they'd been pressed in your ticket book. Mind if I look to see if there's a seed or two left in there?"

"Who in the fuck you think you are? This is my arrest."

Jake looked at Bart, then back at Bob Simons. "If you think I'm going to stand by and let you frame some guy 'cause he gave you some shit, you're wrong."

"You ain't takin' over. This is my stop."

"Do you want to call the bosses?"

"Fuckin' asshole Polack."

"Write the brake light ticket if you want and take the cuffs off."

"What you gonna do, take him for a cup of coffee?"

"Good idea, Bob. Thanks. I'm sure he'd like that better than what you had in mind."

"I'm warning you Bush. Next time I have a car stopped, keep your ass moving."

"Or what?"

"Just keep your nose outta my business."

The Top Hat restaurant on Livernois served up two coffees. Ed stayed with the car.

"One minute I'm in handcuffs, the next I'm drinkin' coffee with the police. What gives?"

"I searched your car. I know the joints weren't yours."

"Who's were they?"

"Don't know. They're in a sewer now. That's all that matters."

"Never had coffee with the po-lice."

"Well Willie, we're supposed to be the good guys. I just wanted you to know most of us are. Sorry for the bullshit back there." Jake swung off of the stool and slid a dollar under his cup.

"Thanks, officer. Let me get the coffee."

"No. I invited you. Remember?"

Bart continued the drive to their assignment after the coffee stop.

"You're awful quiet, Bart."

"Jake, you're just too full of piss and vinegar for me."

"Should I have just let Simons railroad the guy?"

"I'm not saying that. I just don't put my nose in where it doesn't belong."

Jake was driving past a Gulf gas station nearing the end of the night shift in the Seventh Precinct on March 25, 1967. It was on East Grand Boulevard and Canton. A white and blue Cadillac was parked away from the pumps. The attendant was pumping gas as Eight-Four rolled by.

"Bart. Did you see the attendant?"

"He's pumpin' gas."

"I think he's worried about the two guys in the Cadillac. He kinda motioned his head toward them as we went by." Jake made a slow left turn two corners down, cut his lights off and turned into the alley to head back toward Canton and eased to a stop behind the last building. They could see the gas station ramp and the Cadillac.

One man was checking the tires on it, and then slowly walked around the car. The second lifted the hood and checked the oil. Customers were pulling in and out. The oil checker went around and opened the trunk. Two more cars pulled in. The trunk was slammed and a man got behind the wheel. His partner climbed in the passenger's side. Their lights went on and the Cadillac pulled out off of the ramp.

"What do you think, Jake?"

"Maybe they were thinking of holding the place up?"

"And found it too busy?"

Jake floored the Plymouth watching the Cadillac's taillights heading north on East Grand Boulevard toward Milwaukee. A red light brought the Cadillac to a stop. Eight-Four caught up as the light turned green. Jake flipped on the blue lights and Bart motioned the driver to the curb.

"They don't look like hold-up men to me."

Jake was already moving out of the car. "What do crooks look like?" He unsnapped his holster and gripped his .38.

"Hands on the dash, both of you!" In the corner of his eye he could see Bart covering the back window from the curb. The driver had his hands on the steering wheel. The passenger looked over his right shoulder and put his hands on the dash. Jake opened the driver's door.

"One at a time, out. Keep your hands in full view."

"You gotta be shittin' me, man." Jake had his pistol half out of his holster. The driver stopped talking when he saw it.

"Both of you, over the hood. Now!" The men leaned over the hood of the Cadillac. Jake did a quick frisk of the driver. Bart moved up and patted down the passenger. He pulled out a bone-handled knife from a jacket pocket and slid it into his own. Jake tapped the driver on the shoulder. "Over to the curb with your partner."

"Man, you just can't pull us over for no reason."

"Lots of hold ups at gas stations in the middle of the night. You never bought any gas."

"Don't know what you're talkin' about," the driver said.

"Bart," Jake called over his shoulder. "Want to check the car?"

Bart did not answer, but moved to the passenger side of the Cadillac, leaning in and checking under the seat, then checked the trunk. He came out with his right little finger in the trigger guard of a blue steel automatic.

"We guessed right, Jake."

John Allen Chendler, 33 of 7840 Girardin, the driver, and James Spivey, 24 of 103 Smith were taken to the Seventh Precinct and held for Investigation of Robbery Armed. The Browning 6mm automatic did have one round in the chamber and four live rounds in the magazine. The gun, ammo and the car were entered in and held on evidence tags for the detectives.

They made the short drive from Number Seven back to the bureau. "That's what happens when you watch the street people, Bart."

"We were lucky."

"Luck's part of the game."

Bart became a little less hesitant as he worked with Jake. Duane just followed Jake's lead, making sure he covered his side of every car they investigated. Jake got comfortable working Eight-Four and their arrest numbers slowly climbed.

195

Chapter 19

The low numbered cars were assigned to the Sixth Precinct. It was May 12th and they were working nights.

"I came here right out of the academy. I know this place like the back of my hand." Duane was driving north on Livernois as he talked.

It was about ten on a warm May evening. and summer was on the way. Jake's eyes were on three white males going in the side door of a bar at the corner of Michigan Avenue. The three were quite visible under the neon lights above the door.

The first of the three started to pull open the door when he saw the blue and white police car. The man said something to his friends and they came off of the three-step porch. They walked back toward the approaching police car. Jake watched as they stared ahead, not looking at the police car.

"Duane, turn right at the corner."

"You see something?"

"Go around the block. I want to have another look at those three we just passed. They were going into the bar and when they saw us, they changed their mind."

"Maybe they're not old enough."

"Nah, they're all over twenty-one."

Duane made the turns ending up heading north again, nearing Michigan. Jake was looking between each house as Duane drove the curb at a crawl. Four houses before the bar at the corner Jake saw some movement on a front porch.

"There they are," Jake said as he started opening the door of the moving car. The three men broke and cut between the houses.

"Halt, police," Jake yelled as he ran after them through an open gate. He passed two of the three, going after the leader. At the back of the yard Jake caught the back of a jacket as the man tried opening the gate. The man turned swinging as Jake ducked the blow and came up with his twenty-four ouncer. It caught the left ear of his attacker knocking his man down. Jake turned to face the two men he passed. A fist was cocked back, starting to come forward. It stopped when Jake's blackjack moved for a backhand swing.

"Hey man, be cool." The man's fist opened and both hands shot up in surrender. Over this man's shoulder Jake could see the third man running back out the front gate.

"Up against the garage, both of you!"

Jake reached down to pull up the one with the bloody ear.

Eight-Four with Duane behind the wheel screeched to a halt in the alley as five people poured out of the rear door of the house.

The first, a dark haired woman, looked at the bloody ear, screaming, "Gestapo! What did you do to my husband?" She started beating on Jake's chest with both fists.

The four others, all older men were screaming at Jake in what sounded like Polish.

Jake pushed the woman aside as Duane came into the yard from the alley. "What you got?"

"I don't know, but let's get these two out of here. Put them in the car."

The woman's fists returned and were pounding on Jake's back. He turned and grabbed a wrist. "One more fuckin' swing and you're going too." He shoved her toward the four screaming men.

Jake grabbed his hat off the ground and backed out of the alley gate. He climbed in with his prisoners saying, "Let's get the hell out of here."

Duane roared out of the alley. "Where to?" Duane asked as he turned onto Michigan.

"Call the bosses and another car to meet us. The one guy's got to go to the hospital and the other to Number Six."

Eight-Eight came by and took the injured prisoner, Tomasz Bogaslowski, to Receiving Hospital. Eight-Seven-Oh said they would meet Eight at the hospital. Duane and Jake took Wadek Pyzyk to the Sixth Precinct.

Lieutenant Arnold Frank listened while Jake explained why he took another look at the three men who started going into the bar.

"...and when I spotted them hiding on a dark porch they broke into a run between the houses. I figured they were going to hold up the bar."

"You see a gun?"

"No. I went after the leader, but he didn't have anything."

"What about the others?"

"One got away as I was taking care of the other two."

The lieutenant was shaking his head, trying to digest what Jake was telling him. His phone rang.

"Number Six, Lieutenant Frank." He looked at Jake and Duane. Then at the man standing handcuffed between the officers. "Yes, sergeant. Yes. They're right in front of me. Okay, I'll hold him. See you in a bit. Thanks."

The lieutenant hung up the phone. "That was one of your bosses. The guy they interviewed at the hospital just couldn't keep his mouth shut. Says they planned on kicking some cop's ass. Guess they've done it before. We'll hold them for Assault and Battery. Your sergeants are inbound."

The next day, Jake was on the stand in the courtroom of Judge George Crockett. The defendants, Tomasz Bogaslawski and Wadek Pyzyk were being charged with Assault and Battery on a police officer. Their lawyer, Melvin Shrewell, was standing in front of Jake.

"Just answer the question yes or no."

For the past ten minutes Jake had been bombarded with questions requiring a yes or no answer. The Assistant Prosecutor assigned to Judge Crockett's court did not pay attention to Jake's plight.

Jake turned toward Judge Crockett. "Your honor, I cannot answer with just a yes or no. I can't tell the court what I saw or had perceived. "

Judge Crockett looked at the papers in front of him, and then at Jake. He then looked at the defense attorney. "I want to hear what Officer Bush saw and why he took action."

"I object..."

The judge's gavel interrupted the attorney. "Officer, you may continue."

Jake retold the story of three men starting to go into the bar, and then stopping when they saw the police car. He then told about the second sighting of the men on a darkened porch, their running and the subsequent apprehension of two of the three men.

Tomasz Bogaslawski, a Pole who emigrated from Germany, grabbed for his heavily bandaged left ear when Jake talked of taking defensive action at the alley gate.

Sergeant Ostachowski was next on the stand. At the request of the Assistant Prosecuting Attorney, he testified from his notes.

"I read the defendant, Tomasz Bogaslawski, his rights to remain silent. He just blurted out, 'Hell you're probably checking my record right now. We planned on kicking the cop's ass. He was just quicker than the last one."

Judge Crockett spoke. "Will the prosecutor and the attorney for the defense approach the bench?" He talked to the two attorneys for a few minutes. They nodded and returned to their seats. Melvin Shrewell turned and talked to his clients. He then nodded to Judge Crockett.

"Does the attorney for the defense wish to address the court?"

Melvin Shrewell stood and cleared his throat. "Yes, your honor. The defendants wish to change their plea to guilty of attempted assault and battery."

Judge Crockett adjusted his dark rimmed glasses and pushed back in his leather chair. "I am going to accept the guilty pleas on attempted assault and battery just to bring this to a close." He picked up a paper from the pile in front of him and pounded his gavel twice.

"I am going to sentence each of you to thirty days in The Detroit House of Correction, and will instruct the Prosecutor's Office to contact the Department of Immigration. I want them to check on Mr. Tomasz Bogaslawski's status here in the United States. Two convictions of Assault and Battery involving police officers don't sit too well with me." His gavel pounded. "Court adjourned."

****

A month and a half passed with Eight-Four stopping a lot of cars with no major arrests coming their way. It was July 10th, a hot, humid night.

Duane threw his uniform hat on the dashboard and wiped the sweat from his brow. It was just after two in the morning. He was driving west on Canfield approaching Brush. The light was turning red so he took his foot off of the gas and coasted.

"Can you believe that?" The slowing police car approached the red light. "That sure is one dumb white guy." He laughed. "Can you believe he's sleeping in his car in this neighborhood?"

Jake looked toward what Duane was talking about. In a Pontiac facing the other direction was a white man with his head back and eyes shut.

"He's getting a head job."

"A blow job? Here?"

"Make a U-turn and see for yourself."

The man's head in the red Pontiac was oblivious to passing cars and the blue and white Plymouth that made a U-turn and pulled in behind him.

Duane took the driver's side as Jake walked up the curbside. "What the fuck?" Were the words out of Duane's mouth as he peered into the open driver's window.

There was a rustle of movement and the passenger's door opened. Spindly black legs in a yellow low cut dress emerged and straighten a hemline, then a red wig.

"Not so fast," Jake said as he grabbed an arm. "Got a name?"

"Ernestine. Ernestine Flowers," replied the yellow dress.

"Flowers, I'm twenty minutes from the end of my shift. But I'll work overtime and bust your ass unless I get your real name,

"Jake's eyes focused on the large hand clutching a yellow paten leather purse.

Jake overheard Duane talking.

"You always just pull off and park just to get a blow job?"

"You know how it is officer; the wife's in the hospital and..."

Jake looked at Yellow Dress. "Well?"

A once high-pitched voice broke in with a deep tone.

"It's Ernest. Ernest Flowers."

Jake was not surprised. He leaned down and spoke through the open passenger window on the Pontiac. "You do know your sweetheart is a guy, don't you?"

The driver's mouth dropped open and he started blabbering, "No, no. Don't tell me that. No wonder she wouldn't let me feel her tits. God, no."

"Out of the car and on the curb, Mr. Papour," ordered Duane.

"I can't believe I had a guy suckin' on me. Man, this is nuts. Hey officers. I am not that kind."

"What kind is that," Jake asked.

"You know, one of those sissy guys. I have a wife and two kids."

Jake faked a laugh. "And while your wife is in the hospital, you are out here looking for a good time. A real family man."

Jake looked at Duane. "Hearing bullshit like this makes me want to work overtime."

"Guys, give me a break." The tears started flowing from Ralph's eyes.

Jake looked at the yellow dress. "Ernest you're clutching that purse awful tight. Let's have a look at what's inside." He grabbed the yellow purse that Ernest had shifted to under his left arm and tossed it to Duane.

"Dump it on the hood of the car, partner. See what we got."

Duane flipped the snap and dumped the contents on the hood. A palm-sized blue steel .32 caliber automatic bounced on the hood at the same time as a bottle of Listerine, a set of keys and a black wallet.

Ernest looked over his right shoulder. "Don't even think it." Jake grabbed a hairy arm and applied his handcuffs. "Even my pudgy partner could outrun you in those pretty yellow high heels."

"I'll call for a car," Duane offered.

"Call for two. One to impound the car. Mr. Papour is going in too."

"What for? I've got to be at Woman's Hospital first thing in the morning."

"As a material witness for starters. Just think. After Ernest here got your gun off, he might have got his off too. Right between your horny eyes."

The reports were made and Duane was driving back to the bureau. "Damn Jake. I see a guy with his head laying back on a seat and all kinds of shit happens."

"Yeah, very observant. Worth the couple of hours of overtime though." Jake checked his watch.

"Damn. I just remembered I have a court case at eight."

"Hey, maybe we got some big-time john killer in grabbing Ernest? They'll run that gun through ballistics, right?"

"More likely to be some queer just carrying a little protection while he makes a few bucks." Jake finished up the entry on their log sheet for the night.

He remembered his old partner, Mike Mulligan, liked messing with the johns. Jake didn't give them any breaks either. "His wife's in the hospital and he wants us to feel sorry for him. Screw the Grosse Pointe bastard," Jake mumbled as he signed the log sheet.

It was a normal July for the Tactical Mobile Unit. Eight-Four made plenty of stops, but most were for minor traffic violations. It pleased the citizens all to hell when Bart, Duane or Jake let them off with a "Make sure you get that light fixed

A couple of minutes on a stop opened the door for things like shoulder movement when an occupant tucked something like a gun under their seat, or talking to a driver worrying about something more than his burned out tail light. A lot of times they did something stupid like tossing something out of the window, thinking you wouldn't see it.

It was about 12:30 p.m. on July 23, 1967. Jake was cutting his lawn after eating lunch. He, his wife and four children went to nine o'clock mass at St. Raymond's. The youngest, Jeanette, fussed a little during mass, but a pacifier calmed her down.

They had dinner over his mom's the night before. She lived across the street and ten doors down on Strasburg. Jake was thinking about her as he cut the lawn. He did her grass, took her to the store and spent as much time with her as he could, but she bitched all through dinner about him not doing enough. His dad had died two years before, but Mom still played her lonely-widow roll for all it was worth. She seemed to forget her other son, Dave, and the daughter still living at home.

Jake stopped pushing the mower when he saw his wife, Anne, waving at him from the porch. He left the Scott's where it was. He had a ten foot swath to do yet.

"Is it my mom again?"

"It's work. An emergency."

Jake was listening to Sergeant Ski, at the same time motioning to Anne to turn on the TV. WWJ was broadcasting. All Jake could see was billowing black smoke coming out of a row of buildings.

"I'll be right in."

He hung up the phone. His wife was still glued to the Television watching the fiery scene as the camera panned Twelfth Street.

"I gotta go hon, we've got a riot on our hands."

Jake quickly changed from shorts to his uniform. He grabbed his off-duty .38 and slid it into his back pocket. He heard Anne behind him.

"You need to take two guns?"

"The sergeant said to bring an extra if you have one."

Jake grabbed his wife and held on for a couple of minutes.

"It looks like the city's on fire." A tear was rolling down her right cheek. "I'm scared, Jake."

Jake looked into her eyes, squeezed her hard and gave her a kiss. "Me too."

He took out the blue steel Colt snub nose from his back pocket. "Here, hang onto this and keep the kids safe."

He turned and went out into the back yard. Jake's three older kids were playing tag while Jeanette played with a rattle in her playpen. He kissed Debbie, Michelle and Michael.

"Be good and listen to your mom." He picked up the five month old Jeanette, hugged and kissed her, then blew a make-believe fart on her exposed belly. She giggled.

He put her back in the playpen and went into the garage. He backed the green Plymouth wagon out and saw Anne and the kids waving, just as they always did when he left for work. Jake waved back like he always did.

But this time, a thought crossed his mind: *I'm sure you'll be safe, but what about me?* He forced that final thought out of his mind as he drove.

A few miles later he turned onto Gratiot. Another thought came from deep within the recesses of his mind. A bunch of black men were rocking and finally turning the car in front of theirs on its side. There were white people in that car. Some of the men on the street headed toward them. They were black. Barbara and Dave were crying. Jake's mom was screaming, "Ted, do something." Jake's dad floored their '42 Buick, running the red light to escape.

That was all Jake remembered from the 1943 Detroit race riot. He was only three then.

Chapter 20

The bureau squad room was crowded when Jake got there at 1:30 p.m. There were no card games being played. It seemed everyone was talking at once, and most had hunting rifles slung over shoulders.

Mike Tennison was racking the action on a new AR-15, Colt's civilian version of the M-16. Walt Couture was standing next to him. He had his normal 8 inch barrel, Smith and Wesson .44 magnum in the holster on the right side, a Smith .357 magnum in a shoulder holster under his left arm, and a .30 caliber carbine with a banana clip slung over his left shoulder. Jake heard Mike saying, "It's the same as the one being used in 'Nam'. I've got a new sear ordered to make it fully automatic."

Jake noticed that the day shift, that normally hit the streets at ten in the morning, was still there. He took a look toward the back of the basement garage, and saw all twenty cars parked in their spots.

Jake shook his head. *This is the Tactical Mobile Unit, the riot squad of the Detroit Police Department. Parked and out of sight?*

"Hey Billy, how long you been here?" Jake asked a man off the day shift.

"Since six this morning."

Sergeant Ski burst into the squad room yelling above the din. "All right men, fall in."

Feet shuffled as over a hundred men and the extra armament tried squeezing into the twenty-five by forty foot room. Violent voices and bold talking voices, the voices of fear, were quickly silenced as the sergeant walked to the front of the room followed by Lieutenant Orth and the day shift lieutenant, Roberts.

Lieutenant Roberts took the podium and cleared his throat. "First things first. You guys on the day shift—we are going to stick around until we figure out some logistics. We have orders to stand by."

Jake could not believe his ears as the lieutenant continued on about orders from on high that said the Tactical Mobile Unit was to stay out of sight "with the hope that this will all die down."

It was now two in the afternoon. According to the radio reports Jake heard on the way in, this all started after a raid on a blind pig on Twelfth Street about four in the morning.

What, ten hours and the cars of the Detroit Police Tactical Mobile Unit—our riot squad—are in hiding?

The lieutenant's voice jolted Jake's wondering mind. "Right now our job is to wait for further orders. That's it for now."

"The town is being burned to the ground and the Mayor and Police Commissioner think this is going to die down. Bullshit."

Jake didn't recognize the voice, but agreed.

The powers-to-be must think that the sight of the blue and white Tactical Mobile Unit might incite those burning, looting and pillaging.

"Yeah, right," Jake said to no one in particular as he turned to leave the room. *They should look at the fuckin' TV. It's already happening.*

Jake saw Jesse Scott in the corner. He was, as usual, alone. "No extra gun?"

"The bosses aren't going to let me on the street."

"Why?"

"I turned in my resignation Friday. Gave them my notice."

"You did. Why?"

"My wife had enough. We're moving to Minnesota."

"Jess, you are all cop. It's in your blood."

Jess went silent. Jake took the hint and walked out of the squad room.

Jake heard the cards being shuffled as the door closed behind him. He walked around the three-story city garage to Jefferson and Chene. He never gave a thought to recklessly chasing a car thief or a holdup man. *But now...* He was thinking too much and knew it.

Jake could see the smoke filling the sky off to the northwest. He watched for an hour, smoking one cigarette, then another. His

206

hands were shaking as he flicked his lighter. Then it dawned on him: he was scared.

He turned and walked back toward the squad room off the backside of the building. Jesse was coming around the corner and he motioned to him.

"Jake, the bosses want us to fall in."

The message from Lieutenant Erdmann was simple. The TMU's afternoon shift was going to move out. They were going to take a designated route, all staying together. They were going to Cooley High School to wait for further orders.

"They're burning Grand River down. Why are we going away from there?" Mike Tennison shouted.

"Because we have orders," Inspector Sylvers answered from the corner of the room. "We are moving closer to the scene. I don't like this any more than you do, but we have to follow orders."

Sylvers nodded toward Lieutenant Erdmann so he could continue.

"The day shift will stand by until Six, then go home. We are going to twelve-hour shifts. The afternoon crews will fill the cars tonight." He raised his hands to silence the mumbling. "Go to your regular unit, three men to a car. Patrolman Scott, you are staying here to guard the bureau." The lieutenant wiped beads of sweat from his forehead as he turned from the podium.

The men in blue assigned to the afternoon shift started moving out to the cars parked in the basement garage. The deer rifles slung over shoulders and extra pistols stood out as they looked for their units. The fact of the matter was that other than the shotguns, the Detroit Police were not equipped with weapons to handle a full scale riot.

In a caged storage area in the basement garage just outside the bureau door were three wood crates labeled: "Made in France."

Ron Breed saw them and said, "Hey guys, our surrender flags are here." There were no laughs, just words of agreement.

The Detroit riot squad, formally known as the Tactical Mobile Unit, drove west on Jefferson across the deserted downtown area and stuck to side streets to stay out of sight, so as not to fan the flames engulfing the city.

The TMU radios were blaring at 4: 30 p.m. with calls about fires and looting. The Tenth Precinct is where it all started—on Twelfth Street. Now the radio calls were to cars in the Thirteenth, Seventh, Fifth and the Second Precincts. Jake shuddered when he heard the call, "Ten-Five and Ten-Eight. Twelfth and Pallister, the firemen are being shot at."

The blue and white units quietly pulled onto the side street next to Cooley High.

The radios continued: "One-Ten and One-Cruiser, Woodward and Montcalm a gang breaking out windows. Two-Five and Six, Michigan and 19th, a car is on fire."

It's spreading. Jake climbed out of Eight-Four and went into the school.

Cooley High and its surrounding streets were deserted on this Sunday afternoon.

"No smoking inside," Sergeant Ski yelled as the men filed up the stairs to the cafeteria. "If you want a cigarette, stay outside. And pick up your butts."

The school was closer to the action only because it was on the west side. Jake stayed outside with the smokers. He didn't feel like playing euchre. Back to the east he could see the black smoke rising in the warm afternoon sun. It covered a wider area than the last time he looked.

"Roll call," yelled Sergeant Ski as he stuck his head out of the door at 6:15 p.m.

Lieutenant Orth addressed the men. "Our orders are to proceed to Grand River and Chicago where we'll meet up with the Michigan National Guard. It's time to get to work."

The men in blue quickly filed out to their cars.

Eight-Four was silent during the ride. Bart, Duane and Jake listened to the continuous radio calls coming one after the other.

"Shots fired from the roof at Linwood and Grand Boulevard. Is there a car in Number Ten that can assist Ten Cruiser?"

The blue and white cars were parked and ten soldiers assigned to guard them. Lieutenant Orth addressed the officers. "We're going to get into our V-formation and clear Grand River. We will leave two National Guard Troops on each side of each block to keep it clear." Lieutenant Orth looked toward the inspector. "Anything to add, sir?"

Inspector Sylvers stepped forward. "These are our orders. There will be no chasing looters. If they get around the corner, let them go. We are here to clear the street and protect the business places on Grand River." Sylvers looked around to let the words sink "Get your shotguns."

Jake opened the trunk of Eight-Four and grabbed one of the two riot guns from the box in the trunk. He crammed two fist fulls of shells into his trouser pockets and took a spot on the left wing of the V formation, five men from the point. He cradled the shotgun, filling the magazine. He counted, *OO Buck, Slug. OO Buck, slug.* He pushed the last OO Buck into the magazine and started to rack the action when Sergeant Kempf approached. "Bush, no one said to load your weapon."

Jake looked at the street filled with people seventy-five yards in front of him. Windows were gone from the storefronts, and two parked cars had smoke billowing out of their windows as the interiors smoldered.

"You want me to go that way," pointing with the shotgun, "with this empty?"

"That's the orders."

"You gonna empty your pistol?"

The sergeant came nose to nose with Jake. "I don't have time for your bullshit, Bush." He looked around. "You know how to use a 30-30?"

"Yes, sir."

"Then fall in the back and grab one of them. Load it and cover the roofs." Jake handed off the shotgun for a 30-30 and a box of shells.

In five minutes the command was given to move out. It was step, stomp. Step, stomp.

Practice was over. *This is the real thing.*

Jake's eyes went from rooftop to rooftop. The cadence of the stomping feet carried down Grand River.

White motorcycle helmets with black plastic protruding brims distorted any sign of fear or anger in the eyes of the men in the formation. The huge V was heading southeast on Grand River. There was still a lot of daylight left. Jake's eyes went from the rooftops to the mob on the streets.

A bullhorn blared behind the stepping and stomping policemen. "You are ordered to disperse. I repeat, disperse. Clear the street. Move or you will be moved."

The street people, rioters, looters and just onlookers did not wait for the formation to come within 100 feet of them. They cleared the street, cutting around the corners of first Ravenswood, then Riviera. Two short blocks had been cleared and four National Guardsmen per block were left behind to cover each side of the street, two to a side.

Step, stomp. Step-stomp. Jake kept his eyes on the rooftops, watching for movement. Step, stomp. Step, stomp. Jake glanced behind when he heard Sergeant Ski yelling, "Stop the platoon, lieutenant."

The four National Guardsmen that were left to guard each block were running toward the formation.

"Platoon Halt," commanded Orth.

Jake saw that Grand River was filling up behind the V as fast as the people could cut around the alleys. The four guardsmen were no match for hundreds of angry people.

I wonder if they have their weapons loaded?

The platoon stood facing the corner of Joy and Grand River. A liquor store was on the southeast corner. The side window was out of it. Jake saw looters inside. On the northeast corner was a drug store. Four men stepped out of the missing plate-glass window next to Patrolman Dan Deacon.

"Up against the wall, all of you," Deacon commanded.

"Fuck you, po-lice." The four men started walking.

Deacon turned one around and barked again, "Against the fuckin' wall."

The "fuck you white mutha fucker" response started Deacon winding up for a butt stroke.

Jake could hear Sergeant Ski yelling as he ran, "Deacon no! Deacon no!"

Too late, the butt stroke caught a jaw. That man fell in a heap and the other three men stopped and grabbed the wall. Patrolmen Breed and Scrivo moved to help Deacon handcuff his prisoners.

The left side of the TMU Vee moved in. People came flying out of both the drug and liquor stores. The right flank guarded the street and the backs of the officers arresting the looters.

Forty-seven men and women were arrested. The TMU had orders not to shoot, but any resistance to arrest, verbal or otherwise was met with force. Notes on injured prisoners overwhelmed the sergeants as they tried getting the names of one with a bloody nose, then another with a bloody ear. This went on until Sergeant Ski threw his note pad into the air after he filled three pages.

"Jesus Christ guys…"

"Kick ass today and they might think about staying home tomorrow," said Jake under his breath.

Sergeant Ski called for a bus to haul away those arrested. They were sitting handcuffed on the sidewalks of Grand River and Joy until it came. The liquor and drug stores were empty for the time being.

Lieutenant Orth had the men fall in two ranks once the prisoner bus was filled. "We'll do an orderly march back to our cars. I want one National Guardsman in each car. This isn't a retreat. Our formation just isn't going to work in this situation."

It was 9 p.m. and was getting dark. Back at the cars, the lieutenant laid out new plans. "We're going to form squads of three cars. We, the sergeants and I, will be with cars One and Two, then Eight-Three, Four and Five will be the next squad. Figure the rest out and I don't want any lone rangers out here. The three car squads will work as a team. The lowest number car is the squad leader. Any questions?"

"Where do you want us to concentrate?" Bohy, the senior man on Eight-Three, asked.

"Work Grand River. If you are going to leave Grand River, call Six-O for permission. And by the way, if a squad is stopping at a store full of looters, call the address out. The squad closest is to back them up. Any other questions?" There were none.

The Tactical Mobile Unit started to move. They had seven squads of three cars each patrolling the streets.

PFC Sean Flanagan, a red-headed Irishman, was in the back seat of Eight-Four. He was out of the Motor Transport Division from Bay City, Michigan.

The first building that Jake's three-car squad came upon was a Federal Department store on the southwest corner of Grand River and Maplewood. The front plate glass windows were broken out. It was a three-story department store, part of a national chain. Eight-Six-O and his squad assisted by surrounding the front and rear.

It took two hours for the officers to go through the clothing racks, changing rooms, cosmetic counter and the toy department. The dim after-hour lights threw shadows that made Jake's heart drop when PFC Flanagan bumped into him on the second floor.

"I said stick close, but not that close, Sean," he whispered. He stood, letting his heart rate drop. Two steps down an isle he caught a whiff of body odor. His flashlight beam slowly climbed a suit display. It was a mannequin in the men's department. Jake panned the blue suit, white shirt and red tie with his flashlight. The wide brimmed hat was tilted over the face. A bead of sweat rolled down from the left temple.

Mannequins don't sweat.

A quick tug of a leg brought the man to the floor and a Winchester twelve gauge commanded no resistance.

"I thought I could get a new set of clothes, an' the only way to get the right size was to try things on," said William Davis after he was handcuffed.

Jake stifled a laugh. "Well, it does fit, but you're still going to jail." Jake and Sean escorted their prisoner downstairs.

Bohy and Cesarz were guarding two other men and a woman arrested inside the store. The breathing mannequin was seated with them on the immobile escalator that went from the first to the second floor.

The manager arrived by the time the building had been thoroughly searched. "I have some of our maintenance men on the way to board up the windows and doors if you can hang around for a bit." He was surveying the damage. It was 11:30 p.m.

Jake walked up to him. "Do you have any food in here?" Eating wasn't in the DPD's plans in case of a riot. Jake had not eaten all day.

"Just a snack bar. Packaged ice cream, drinks and cookies."

"We've been at work since one or so and haven't eaten."

"First floor in the middle. Take all you want. Sorry, but that's all we have."

Boxes of ice cream sandwiches, Eskimo pies, half pints of milk and Oreo cookies were carried out of the Federal Department Store front door. The car-to-car radios of the TMU put out the news that they had something to eat. The lieutenant and sergeants joined them.

As they ate Sergeant Ski spoke. "If you find a looted grocery store, remember, don't take anything that can be contaminated like fresh fruits or lunch meat. We may have to live off the land for a while."

In a half hour the blue and white cars were back patrolling.

"The appliance store. Someone's inside," cracked the car- to-car radio. Men in blue and army dungarees bailed out of their cars. Flanagan was running around the back of the store next to Jake when the PFC's carbine went off. Jake instinctively dropped to the ground. Slowly he looked up. "What the fuck, Sean?"

"It just went off."

"Didn't they teach you what the safety is for?" Jake picked himself off the alley floor, brushing off glass and dirt from his trousers.

"Sorry, sir, but I'm a heavy equipment operator. It's been a long time since I carried a gun."

"Put the safety on and stay here. Guard the alley. And for God sake, don't shoot me, or yourself."

Jake went in the open alley door to the appliance store. The floor was flooded with six inches of water. The overhead sprinkler system was now flowing at a slow trickle.

There were three refrigerators standing against the right wall as Jake walked by. He checked beside each as he passed, then flashed his light across to the stoves on the left. One was pulled out at an angle from the wall. A dark figure was on all fours in the water behind it.

"Get up. Hands on your head." Jake reached for the man grabbing his shoulder. "Up against the wall." Jake patted him down and handcuffed him.

Five more men were brought out of the building by the TMU team. Erdmann shook his head as the prisoners were walked around the upright freezer standing with its doors open on the sidewalk on the side of the store.

"This is the fifth sweep of this business by our cars," the lieutenant said. "Every time we arrest a bunch there are fewer appliances. How in the hell are they carting them off?"

At four in the morning one man was arrested trying to push a washer out of the store's back door. It was the last appliance. The

Good Housekeeping Store, though small in size, held at least a hundred appliances on a normal business day.

PFC Flanagan grabbed Jake by the shoulder. "About the accidental discharge…"

"What discharge?"

"You know."

"Forget it." Jake offered Sean a cigarette. "And learn from it."

****

At six thirty in the morning Jake was driving home. He had no idea how many people he had arrested or, for that matter, how he even got in his car. He pulled into his garage, went into the quiet house, showered and fell into bed.

"You all right?" Anne asked.

"Talk to me tomorrow." He fell dead asleep.

Jake tossed and turned amid dreams of flames and gunshots. He was slouched down in the passenger seat of Eight-Four with just his eyes peering over the window ledge on the car. "Is this door thick enough to stop a bullet?" he asked Bart. Jake felt a hand grab his right ankle. He popped up in bed to see the eyes of his wife filled with tears as she held onto his leg.

"I'm scared, Jake."

He shook the nightmare from his mind and wiped his sweaty forehead with the cover sheet. "So am I."

"I want you to quit. For me. For the kids."

"Give me a year. I've got to see this through."

"You gonna live that long?"

Jake avoided the question. "What time is it?"

"Three."

"Gotta leave at five. We're going on twelve hour shifts, six to six."

215

Chapter 21

The Radio call came out as: "Can any car make shots fired, Southeast corner of Elmwood and McDougal." It was after dark.

Sergeant Kempf was on the car-to-car. "Eight-Three, Four and Five, cover that run at Elmwood and McDougal with us." The scanner in Eight-Four caught Eight-Seven-0 responding to the shots fired run. Kempf and Ostachowski manned Seven-0. The Michigan National Guard troops were not with the TMU, but were assigned somewhere else.

The six TMU cars drove up McDougal with their lights out. The sergeant's car, Eight-One and Eight-Two pulled to the right curb just past Elmwood. The three other cars pulled to the left curb, leaving a car length between each. The patrolmen scrambled out taking up positions using their cars for cover. Jake's eyes went from house to house. He was looking for movement and listening.

Kempf's voice came over the radio. "I'm going to take out this street light. Hold your fire." The sergeant pointed his shotgun up and thirty feet to his north.

Wham! Pieces of glass fell to the street and the street was in total darkness.

Jake was crouched behind the back of Eight-Four looking out over the trunk. Bam! Bam! Bam! Three shots rang out. He fell flat on the concrete between the curb and his car's rear tire.

Bam! Bam! Bam! More shots rang out. Jake lifted his head where he could see the man behind, Bob Cuchak, at the front of Eight-Five. Bob's thirty-caliber carbine with a banana clip was spitting fire into the air. Other shots were fired from Jake's left and right. He just hugged the tire.

"Bob!" Jake was shouting above the gunfire. "Bob! What the fuck you shooting at?"

"Hell, I don't know." Bob pulled the carbine down dropping the banana clip out and slamming in another.

Ski's voice was on the car-to-car screaming, "Cease fire. Cease fire."

The night went silent as Jake raised himself and looked over the trunk lid. "Bob, did you see anyone shooting at us?"

"No."

"Then what are you shooting at?" Jake slumped to the ground resting his back against the fender. "Asshole."

The street was dark and quiet. There were no lights on in the houses on either side of the street. With all that gunfire Jake knew the residents had to be as scared as he was.

The car-to-car cracked again. "This is Eight-Seven-O. Did anyone see any muzzle flashes? I repeat, did anyone see any muzzle flashes?" There was no response.

Ten minutes went by. "This is Eight-Seven-O. Mount up and move out."

Car doors slammed and the blue and white units rolled north on McDougal with their lights out. Three blocks later, Seven-O pulled to the curb. The rest of the police cars stopped behind the sergeant's car.

"Out. Everybody out." Kempf walked from car to car. Spit was flying from his mouth. "On the fuckin' sidewalk."

Sergeant Ski leaned against their car as fifteen patrolmen lined up on the sidewalk.

Kempf walked from man to man, his fingers touching noses as he pointed. "What the fuck do we have here? A bunch of cowboys? I said to hold your fire." The sergeant's eyes were going from one man to another. "I put out a street light and all hell breaks loose. Who in the fuck was shooting?" His eyes kept moving went from man to man.

"We were not under fire. Did anyone see anything? Any muzzle flashes?" There was no answer. Kempf looked at Jake. "You, how many rounds did you fire?"

"None, sir."

He checked the shotgun in Jake's hand, emptying and smelling it before handing it back.

He stepped in front of Bohy. "You?"

"One, sir."

217

His finger lashed out toward Cuchak. "You?"

"Don't know. Maybe ten." Bob's voice tapered off, "Maybe more."

"Jezus Christ." He stepped back looking at the men standing in front of him. "I am going to say this one time. You will not fire your weapon unless you are fired upon. Is that understood?"

"Yes sir," was a mumbled group response.

"Let's get this straight. This riot stuff is new to me too, but I shouldn't need to worry about the guys with badges."

Kempf lit a cigarette, then threw it down and crushed it. "Cuchak, put that carbine in your trunk. You don't know how to use it anyway." He walked back to his car and turned. "The next time I see this shit happen, your asses will be off the street. Understand?"

Another answer in unison:"Yes sir."

"Let's go to Number Seven for a break. Let the fuckin' city burn for a while." He and Ski got into their car and led the way.

The Mack and Gratiot station was bustling with police cars, and policemen leading people in wearing handcuffs. Jake walked inside of the garage attached to the rear of the station house. A group of policemen were standing near a trailer bearing the Salvation Army shield. It was one of their emergency food trailers. Coffee, cokes, sandwiches and cigarettes were offered.

Jake asked for and held out a five to pay for a sandwich and coffee. "No thanks, officer. It's on the house. Thanks for being here for us and God bless you." Jake had no response.

Jake later learned that Salvation Army trailers were also moved into the garages of the Tenth, Fifth and the Thirteenth Precincts. Policemen normally ate in restaurants. The riot and curfew had them all closed. The Salvation Army seemed to be the only ones who realized that the police officers needed to be fed.

Eight-Four's radio blared as Jake leaned on the trunk smoking a cigarette. "This is Eight-Six-O. All east side units report to Number Seven."

One by one, the ten cars assigned to the east side responded. Jake's car was one of the six already there, so he went back in and asked for another ham sandwich and a refill on his coffee.

Lieutenant Orth, Sergeant's Kempf and Ostachowski had the thirty patrolmen lined up near their blue and whites. The lieutenant spoke. "We've been assigned some men from the 82nd Airborne. One man will ride in each car." He turned toward the loose rank of soldiers lined up just inside the garage. "I need ten men, Sergeant Major."

The NCO counted off ten men. "Each of you, pick a blue and white."

A young man in fatigues carrying an M-16 stopped at the side of Eight-Four. Bart stepped forward. "Ed Bartkowski, everyone calls me Bart." Ed offered his hand toward the soldier wearing corporal stripes. "These are my partners, Duane Wattles and Jake Bush."

"Scott Plummer." His look was stern. "Probably not the best of times to meet you guys."

"You got that right," said Bart.

He slid in behind the wheel of Eight-Four while Jake took the front passenger seat. Plummer slid in the back behind Jake. Duane squeezed his way in behind Bart. Jake and Duane had the two sawed off riot guns pointed upwards between their legs. Plummer held his M-16 in the same way.

"Been in the 82nd very long?" Duane asked as Eight-Four fell in behind Bohy in Eight-Three.

"Nuf for two tours in Nam," Plummer replied.

"Well, welcome to our own little war," Jake said as he lit a cigarette, offering the pack toward the back seat.

Stories of Vietnam broke the ice between the policemen and the paratrooper as they cruised the streets of the Seventh Precinct.

Bart was driving south on Chene, the second car in the three-car squad, checking the mom and pop businesses looking for looters and people out past the curfew. The streets were relatively quiet. The mayor had imposed a 9 p.m. curfew. It was after midnight.

Eight-Three turned left onto Canfield, Bart followed with Eight-Five behind them. As Eight-Four reached the alley behind Chene, two distinct cracks and the whine of a projectile followed by the thud of another hitting metal were heard. Bart slammed on the brakes and doors flew open with Jake hitting the ground near the curb. Plummer landed on the concrete to Jake's right. Duane was on the walkie-talkie, "Eight-Four's under fire!"

The night was silent as Jake surveyed the tops of the buildings on Chene against the night sky. Plummer whispered to him. "I'm gonna take out that light down the alley."

Jake looked at the light on a pole half way down the alley. "If you think you can go ahead." *Not on a bet.*

One shot was fired. The light went out. "Hot damn! Glad you're on our side."

Bart grabbed the portable radio from Duane. "All units. Eight-Four took some fire at alley east of Chene, just off of Canfield. Five can you cover the front of Chene?"

"10-4, Four."

"Three, can you whip around and cover the south end of the alley? Make sure no one leaves the area."

"Gotcha, Four." Eight-Three squealed tires to cut around the block. Five backed up to cover the front of Chene Street.

Nothing was moving. The alley was quiet and Jake was still lying on the ground eyeing the building tops, making out at least six dormers against the night sky. He reached inside the open passenger window and stretched the cord on the portable spotlight from under the dashboard. He held the light away from his body and slowly panned the buildings.

He saw the dormers more clearly. They were in pairs stretching across the entire block. It remained quiet. One by one

Jake, Bart, Duane and the paratrooper stood. Bart was checking the front of their Plymouth with his flashlight. He spotted a small bullet hole, just ahead of the front, passenger side wheel well.

Jake looked at the hole. "Judging from where we are, and where we were hit, my guess is it came from an apartment above one of the stores. From one of the dormers." Bart did not answer.

Six other TMU cars arrived to seal off the area. "Plummer, come with me." Jake led the way to the front of Chene. The paratrooper followed.

"Where you goin' Bush?" Bart yelled.

"Find the fucker that shot at us."

"How?"

"Kick in doors if I have to."

The first store was Leonard's TV Repair. A doorway to a stairwell was between it and Stan's Meat Market.

"Let's skip that one for now. Too sharp an angle to hit our car." Jake walked to the next doorway between Stan's and Betty's Beauty Shop and rang the bell. He waited a minute, and then rang again. A buzzer sounded unlocking the door. Jake stuck his head in and saw an elderly black lady in a pink robe and her hair covered by a matching night hat in the open doorway at the top of the stairs. "Ma'am. You alone?" Jake asked.

"Yes sah," she replied.

"Mind if we have a look?"

"No sah. Plenty of trouble 'round here. Heard shots just a bit ago."

Jake and the corporal climbed the steps. "Say you heard shots?" They stopped midway up.

"Yes sah. A popin' sound. From that way." She pointed to the south.

"Thanks." Jake and Scott ran down the steps, went past the beauty shop entrance and stopped at the door leading to the next upstairs apartment.

221

Jake rang the bell. Bart and Duane came up behind as Jake waited. He rang the bell again, then again. Jake stepped back and kicked at the door just above the knob and lock.

"Jake, what the fuck you doin'?" Bart yelled.

"I'm going in there. The woman next door heard the shots." He gave the door another kick.

"I don't know about this. Let's call the bosses."

Corporal Plummer pushed his way in front of Ed Bartkowski. "By the time you get permission the fucker'll be gone."

A third kick opened the door. Plummer was right behind Jake going up the stairs. Bart and Duane followed.

The door at the top was slightly ajar. Jake stopped at the third step below the door and slowly pushed the door open with the muzzle of his shotgun. Plummer had his M-16 pointed just over Jake's left shoulder. Jake's flashlight cut the darkness. The beam slowly covered the room as Jake and the paratrooper eased in through the doorway.

The beam scanned toward an old tattered couch and overstuffed matching chair, then checked behind both. The light danced to a doorway between the couch and chair. It led to a small kitchen. Dirty dishes were in the sink. A small table and two chairs were on the left wall. Three beer bottles stood next to a plate of food scraps. A two-burner stove and narrow fridge were on the right wall. Scott motioned and got a flashlight from Bart. Both beams slowly checked every corner of the small room. The beams met at a closed oak door on the east wall.

The corporal took the left side of the door, Jake the right. Scott turned the knob and pushed open the door. Silence. His left hand ran his flashlight beam into the room. The muzzle of the M-16 followed with the paratrooper's finger on the trigger. Jake followed in a low crouch. Two flashlights swept the room showing a rumpled bed to the left of the door, a small chest of drawers to the right, and in the dormer a single chair tipped over under the window. Jake dropped down and checked under the bed with his light. Nothing. He motioned for Scott to turn on the room light.

Their eyes adjusted to the sudden light from a small bulb overhead. On the floor next to the overturned chair lay two empty .30 caliber casings. Jake picked them up with a pencil in the end and put them in his handkerchief. There was a box built into the window, crudely made from an orange crate.

"What's that for?" asked Duane from the open door.

"Something the Detroit News ran an article on," answered Bart. "It's how a sniper hides his muzzle flash."

The apartment was empty. Jake got the name Gerald Zelinski of 1706 Chene off of a phone bill in the kitchen. A report was made on the shots fired; and the name and address of the person renting the apartment. The shell casings were entered in as evidence.

Eight-Four was cruising back on Chene when the scanner screamed, "John R and Holbrook, officer down."

Jake and Bart stopped talking. Bart switched the scanner to stay on the Central Radio frequency.

"Radio, Thirteen-Seven. Notify Henry Ford Hospital. We're coming in with a police officer that's been shot." The siren could be heard in the background over the radio.

The morning's *Detroit Free Press* headlines shouted "**731 FIRES SET**" in the first two days of the riot. It added that the firemen responding to the fires were being shot at.

Jake read on. *Glad I'm not a fireman.*

He felt some sense of security with a pistol at his side. He thumbed through the pages of the paper over a cup of coffee wondering how this attitude of *Let the riot go and maybe it will burn itself out* got started. He knew unwritten orders were given to the men on the street. *NO shooting unless fired upon.* Jake also knew that the crowds were getting bigger, and more fires were being set. The looting snowballed. He continued going through the paper as he finished his coffee.

Jake caught the lead on an article on Page Three. "Airborne Troops pulled back to Selfridge." *Looks like somebody was worried that the presence of troops fresh from Vietnam might incite the city residents.*

Jake never found anything in the paper on the officer shot the night before. It was the third day since the riot started and was on the way into the bureau, when the news on the radio gave him his answer.

"Jerry Olszowy, Patrolman at the Thirteenth Precinct was pronounced dead just after 3 a.m. today."

Jake pulled his car to the curb and rested his head on the steering wheel. He knew Jerry was a regular on a plain-clothes B&E car in Number Thirteen. A good cop.

Am I going to make it through this?

He turned off the radio and said a prayer. "Eternal rest grant onto him oh Lord, and let the perpetual light shine upon him." Jake put the car in drive and continued on to work.

Jake, Bart and Duane in Eight-Four were patrolling the Tenth Precinct the third night of the riot. They drew the lead car for their three-car squad. Some stores were still smoldering if not burned out except for one here and there that had the words "Soul Brother" whitewashed or painted across the windows.

It was 1:00 a.m. when a pink Lincoln convertible crossed Grand River in front of them. In the open trunk was wedged an overstuffed leather chair. The top was down on the car so that the matching sofa was over the back seat extending beyond both sides. The twin blue lights went on as Jake gunned the police car and turned the corner falling in behind the Lincoln. Mid-block brake lights went on and doors flew open with the driver going to the left and the passenger running to the right.

Jake took after the driver. The driver leap-frogged a four-foot fence and within two steps Jake caught him. They both fell through some sheets hanging on a clothesline. The driver went limp. Jake

224

started handcuffing the man. He was black, about 250 pounds and forty-five years old. The man looked over his shoulder at Jake.

"You got something to hit me with?"

"Why?"

" 'cause I want you to hit this dumb fucker right in the middle of his bald head?" He leaned his head sideways toward Jake, expecting a blow. "I mean, hell. Here I am watching all this looting and shit on TV. So I says, Demetrius, a new sofa and chair would look good in here. Talk about a dumb som-bitch. Gotta good job, good wife. Just too dumb to stay home." His head bobbed. "Go ahead, hit me right upside the head. I deserve it."

Jake agreed, but tried not to laugh as he pulled the man to his feet. "Yeah, being out here is kinda dumb." They walked through the gate toward the pink Lincoln. Duane was behind the wheel and Bart had Demetrius's passenger in cuffs next to Eight-Four.

Bart said, "Duane, take the Lincoln in. Eight-Three will follow you to Number Ten. We'll drop the prisoners at the temporary jail on Grand River. Have Three let us know where we can pick you up."

An empty storefront at 1089 Grand River served as a temporary holding cell for prisoners awaiting transport to a jail. A Detroit House of Corrections bus made a run to different locations picking up and delivering prisoners. The Wayne County Jail and the main city jail downtown at Number One were full. So were the holding cells at Five, Seven, Thirteen, Two and Ten. A bus was the most efficient way to transport prisoners to the outlying precincts or to the Detroit House of Corrections. Jake and Bart led Demetrius Grayson and his brother Jimmy to the storefront. A picture was taken of each prisoner with an arresting officer. They left the prisoners with the two officers guarding the gutted store crammed with others waiting for a bus ride to a jail somewhere.

Jake and Bart were walking back to their car parked on Grand river when they heard,: "Get your ass off the street nigger." A foot went up kicking the black man holding a gas can.

"Ahm just tryin' to get home. I ran out of gas down the block."

"Get off of the street or we'll toss you in jail."

The man stumbled and fell. Jake moved between the two police officers doing the talking.

The man was in his late fifties. Tears were in his eyes. Jake reached for the hand with the gas can, took it and threw it aside. He grabbed the hand.

"I see you've got a prisoner. We'll take this one." Jake reached down and pulled the man to his feet.

"You can have him." The two officers headed toward the storefront with their prisoner.

Jake led the man to his blue and white. "Officer, I ran out of gas. I just wanted to get home."

"All gas stations are closed. Where's home?"

"Burlingame near Second."

"Jake, we've gotta meet Duane." Bart butted in.

"I'm taking this guy home. I don't need some cops bustin' his ass for running out of gas, then have him come back out; only this time with a gun." Jake opened the back seat door. "Come on, mister. This is no place for you."

"My car. What about my car?"

"Come back in the daylight, tomorrow. That's the best advice I can give you."

Eight-Four with Willie Brant pulled up in front of 324 Burlingame as Eight-Three was calling for them. "Gotta go, Mr. Brant. Hope things work out for you."

Bart answered Three on the car-to-car. "Meet you at Chicago and Dexter in five minutes."

"Okay, Four."

Bart wrote on the log sheet as he spoke. "I'll never figure you out, Jake. One minute you're kicking in doors or kicking ass. Then you turn into a boy scout."

"Life's confusing, Bart. We got a race riot going on and some Polack shoots at us. Good cops like Olszowy get killed and others shouldn't even have a badge. Me, I'm just praying I live through this."

The death of a policeman was the main topic of discussion when their shift ended. Both the News and The Free Press had run articles on the shooting. Officer Olszowy was hit by a shotgun blast during a struggle for the gun. The shotgun was his partner's. Nobody played cards prior to off duty roll call.

The bell on the bureau Teletype machine sounded just before on-duty roll call on July 26th, day number four. It read: "Looters are to be apprehended." There were no explanations.

The men on the street knew it meant to put an end to this. No more looking the other way, or hoping things would die down. They knew it meant to meet force with greater force.

Jake and his crew were assigned the Fifth Precinct. Darkness brought out the looters and East Side Radio was calling out one run after another. Midnight came as Eight-Four's scanner picked up the call. "Cars in Number Thirteen, the army is under fire at Virginia Park and Woodward." Eight's scanner then automatically flipped to the next broadcast, "Five Cruiser, Jefferson and Beniteau, man with a gun."

As Duane headed their car to back up the man with the gun run for Five Cruiser, Jake remembered the Algiers Motel at Virginia Park and Woodward where Ronnie had his midnight shift coffees with the pretty desk clerk he was trying to put the make on. Jake knew the motel was noted for pimps, whores and whatever. *Maybe a sniper or two.*

227

Duane turned the corner of Kercheval and Montclair. They saw two police cars and their crews. There were three bodies under a broken storefront window. Eight-Four kept driving. There was no "Man with a gun" at Jefferson and Beniteau. *Another false alarm.*

The squad of Eight-Three, Four and Five spent the night backing up precinct cars, or answering a run when the radio operator called for help. They were involved in thirty-five arrests that night by the time the reports were written.

Jake caught the news when he got home.

"Initial reports are that three bodies were found at the Algiers Motel. Homicide Detectives are on the scene." A lot of Jake's old partners were still working at Number Thirteen. He hoped Mike Mulligan was all right.

The fifth night had the lower numbered TMU cars working in Number Ten. The TV and radio news as well as the papers stated that police and national guardsmen were involved in the shootings at the Algiers Motel the night before. There were questions as to who was there and why no reports were written when three men had been shot dead.

Jake shook his head and mumbled, "No, they aren't that dumb," remembering the blatant racism that greeted him at Number Thirteen in 1963.

That night there were fewer curfew violations and a lot fewer looters than just the night before. Eight-Four and their squad drove down a quiet Grand River. Wisps of smoke could be seen coming from a couple of buildings. Others had roofs caved in and charred walls while a business with the words "Soul Brother" painted across the window still stood untouched. Every block had four or five cars with burned out interiors, flattened tires and smashed windows. Grand River Avenue looked like it barely survived a World War II blitzkrieg. The only thing missing were bomb craters. Only half of the streetlights worked and broken glass was everywhere. The TMU radio scanner reflected a slower night.

By week's end the 1967 Detroit Riot was essentially over, but the scars remained. 7,231 people were arrested for riot related crimes and 43 people died. 34 of those that died were at the hands of armed officials such as police, guardsmen or paratroopers. The news switched from an ongoing riot to coverage of what was called the Algiers Motel incident. Three policemen were suspended and local and federal investigations were ongoing.

Chapter 22

The Detroit Police Department stayed on alert working twelve-hour shifts keeping the patrols beefed up. The TMU started rotating shifts on August 1st to move Jake and his partners to the day shift and those working days to nights. By altering the starting times backwards four hours it took three days for Jake and his crew to swing back onto the day shift. There were still no days off as they manned each car with a full three-man crew. But the worst was over. Normality was returning. Stores and restaurants were re-opening and the curfew was lifted. The radio returned to pre-riot calls: "Thirteen-Seven, 103 S. Boston, family trouble. One-Eleven, Woodward and Seldon, see the man on a fender bender." They were a complete opposite from the previous week's runs on fires and looting.

The low numbered TMU cars were patrolling the Thirteenth Precinct and fully onto the day shift, working 8 a.m. to 8 p.m. The crews were back to noting important teletypes and logging stolen cars on their hot sheets.

Bart was driving; Duane was riding in the jump seat while Jake sat in the back. They just finished lunch at Sophie's on Cass Avenue. Bart was passing time by touring one of their favorite places for finding abandoned stolen cars—the no-man's land under the Ford Freeway off of Russell where the Grand Trunk railroad tracks were.

As Bart turned left to check the area they saw a 1964 maroon Mercury with a white woman in shorts sitting on the hood tipping a brown bottle. Her white male companion was leaning on the left fender, also having a beer. Jake's eyes went to the license plate, then to the hot sheet. *Nothing.*

Bart made a short sweep under the overpass and as he turned to leave the Mercury was moving. The male was behind the wheel and the girl next to him.

"Bart, stop that car," Jake said.

"What for?"

"Something about a maroon Mercury in my memory bank. Just stop him."

"They looked old enough to be having a beer."

"No, it's the car."

"What about it?"

"Just stop them. I'm trying to remember."

The Mercury pulled onto Russell obeying the 30 MPH speed limit. It turned right onto Ferry. At the next corner it took a left.

"Bart, will you stop the fuckin' car?"

"I'm still waiting for a reason."

"Something before the riot." Jake watched the car make a right, and then another left. The blue and white just followed. "Damn, I know there was a maroon Merc involved in something. One of our cars was involved."

"I don't remember anything," Duane piped in.

Jake leaned forward between Duane and Bart and grabbed the mic. "He's leading us up and down the streets. Nice and legal. And too many turns."

"You're grasping at straws," Bart said as he let the Mercury stay a half of a block ahead.

"Switch it to car-to-car, Duane." Duane flipped the switch. "All units, this is Eight-Four. Does anyone remember something about a maroon Merc just before the riot?" The Mercury made the next left, then another right. It was now heading south on Chene.

"Four, this is Six. Had a maroon Merc under the Ford at Russell. Thought it was stolen. Searched it and found a holster for an automatic pistol. We sat on it. Driver returned, spotted us and ran before we could grab him."

"Now will you stop the fuckin' car?"

Bart closed the gap between them and the Mercury. Duane gave a squawk with the siren, motioning for the driver to pull to the curb. The driver of the Mercury complied.

Duane walked up the passenger's side while Bart took the driver's side. "License and registration, please?" Jake was just behind Bart as he made his request.

"What's up, officer? We haven't done anything."

Jake looked over Bart's shoulder at the license. The name Gerald Zelinski jumped out at him.

Jake pushed Bart and grabbed an arm and a shirt. He pulled the driver out of the open window. Both Jake and the driver hit the pavement. Bullets and pills spilled on the street as Jake rolled him over. Jake put his knee in the man's back and was putting on handcuffs when he heard Bart. "What the fuck you doin' Jake?"

"Zelinski. 1706 Chene. That doesn't mean anything to you?"

"Nothing, 'cept you're crazy."

"The sniper. Chene and Canfield."

"Him?"

"Yeah, him."

Duane got the woman out of the car. He had her empty her purse on the hood of the Mercury. She was Betty Ignatowski, 22, of 1833 McDougall. She and the driver were put in the back of Eight-Four while Jake searched the car. He was looking for the .32 automatic that went with the bullets that fell out of Gerald's pockets. The car was clean. He went back to Eight-Four.

"Call for a couple of cars, Duane. Have them take in the car and the prisoners."

"We can take in the prisoners," Bart said.

"Bart, somewhere between here and where we first saw them is a .32 automatic. I am going to walk every inch of that fuckin' route, hoping to find it."

"I never saw him drop anything."

"He ain't carrying bullets to chew on. On one of those turns he or his sweetheart dropped it out of a window. I know it."

The prisoners and the car were transported. Jake walked the route backwards. For an hour and a half he walked while Eight-Four slowly followed. Jake stopped them when he could not see down a sewer grate. He grabbed a flashlight. Fifteen sewer grates and eight blocks later Jake was under the Ford Freeway checking where the Mercury was parked. No gun. He did not want to give up, but Bart pulled up alongside.

"Come on Jake, get in. We got him on the pills and the sniper shooting."

"We would have had him and the gun if you had listened to me." Jake slammed the door shut.

"Either of you guys ever see someone wearing a sign that says, 'I'm a bad guy, stop me'?" Jake looked at the back of his partners' heads and knew he was fighting a losing battle. "Sometimes you have to trust your instincts or worse yet, your partner."

Three days later Gerald Zelinski was given his walking papers. No direct evidence tied him to the sniper fire the night of July 25th. The shell casings had no prints. No gun or projectile was found. The 6 pills confiscated were low-grade uppers. Zelinski coughed up the name of his supplier and the Narcotics Bureau went after the him.

Ed Bartkowski requested and received a transfer back to the Fifteenth Precinct the end of August. Duane was pulling out of the basement garage as he talked. "Told me he liked life at a slower pace than you, Jake."

"I figured that."

"You ain't the easiest guy to get along with."

"I know it." Jake thumbed through the circular book.

"So who's our new partner?"

"Some skinny kid. Justin Shaggert. Just transferred in from Number Four."

"Everyone's skinny to you."

"Fuck you.

"Well, what are you tipping the scales at these days, partner?"

Duane drove into the night cruising Gratiot, heading for the Fifteenth Precinct on September 2nd. Fifteen was their assignment for a few days.

"Don't know what the hell Bart wanted to come back to this for," Jake said as he checked every license plate moving. "Not too much happening. The radio's dead quiet."

"That's what he wants. Something nice and slow."

"I had that at Number Eleven. Drove me nuts."

"Your wife still pressing you to quit?"

"Kind of. I'm checking other departments."

"I can't picture you as a small town cop. What was that, Northville? All they got is a small-time horse track."

"I'm just looking. How did you hear about Northville?"

"You mentioned it to Bart before he left. I can just see you now, guarding a pile of horse shit." Duane laughed at his little joke. "You'll miss the action. I've been watching you too long."

"Fifteen-Ten. One-Nine-Two-Two Van Dyke. At the bar, holdup in progress," was the call. Duane floored the Plymouth.

"That's no more than a block from here," Jake said over the roar of the engine. In seconds they slid to a stop in front of the bar. Jake and Duane burst through the front door, guns drawn.

"He just went out the back!"

"Quick, what did he look like?" Jake paused in front of the bartender.

"White. In his thirties. Tan jacket. He was carrying a blue and white duffel bag and a single barrel shotgun."

Jake slowly opened the door to the alley and slipped into the night. Duane was right behind him. Jake checked a dumpster between the bar and a grocery store. He let the lid down slowly. He was panning the alley with his light. Nothing.

"Duane, grab the car, meet me here." Jake checked more dark corners in the alley until Duane drove up where he could jump in the passenger seat.

"Drive small circles. He's here somewhere."

Duane followed Jake's request. They cruised with their lights out, circling the first block then going wider. "What makes you think he's here?"

"The duffel bag. I'm guessing he's walking."

Ten minutes later the East Side Radio Operator was broadcasting the description: "Fifteen-Ten is looking for a man wanted in the robbery armed of a bar in the area of Harper and Van Dyke. A white male, in his late twenties, early thirties, sandy hair, wearing a tan waist-length jacket and blue trousers. He's is armed with a sawed off shotgun and got approximately one hundred dollars in small bills and change."

Duane drove the curb with his lights out. He was ten blocks from the bar. "I think he's long gone. How long you want me to keep this up?"

"'til quitting time."

"Jake. It's been an hour since the stick up. He's gone."

"We've got nothing better to do."

"Could get a coffee."

"Duane, we were right there. Seconds behind him. No cars were seen or heard leaving. He's hiding somewhere."

"Yeah, where?"

"Go back to the bar. I'll walk the alleys again."

"Bart's right. You're nuts."

"You can sit on your fat ass in the car. I'll do the walking." Jake got out and walked the alley behind the bar. He checked the garbage cans and the yards of the homes off of the alley. A half hour later he got back into Eight-Four.

"Find anything, Sherlock?"

"Two open garages where he could have hidden while we were in the area." Jake thought for a minute. "Let's go back to making circles around the scene."

"It's a waste of time."

"Humor me."

Eight-Four was heading south on Harper just to the east of Van Dyke. Duane was still hugging the curb with his lights out.

235

Jake was eyeing all the recessed doorways to the businesses on his side when he heard Duane. "Hey, what's that description?"

Jake's eyes crossed the street and stopped on the man walking, wearing a tan waist length jacket. "Get him Duane!"

Duane made a power U-turn. The man never looked over his shoulder as he switched a large paper grocery bag from his left to his right hand, and dropped it. He was thirty feet from the bag when Jake jumped out of the car, gun first.

"FREEZE MISTER!"

Jake made a quick frisk and got one handcuff on when he heard Duane from behind. "Hey Jake, we got the gun." Jake glanced over to see Duane back by the bag on the sidewalk.

The man wheeled, trying to twist free from Jake who was throwing a leg over him. Jake rode him like a horse to the sidewalk. The empty cuff cut into Jake's left hand as he hung on for the ride. A quick forearm to the back of the man's head stopped the resistance. Jake finished handcuffing him.

Richard Kajawa, 34, of 12510 E. Eight Mile as conveyed to the Fifteen Precinct. The large grocery bag he was carrying held a Savage shotgun and a rolled up blue and white nylon bag. The shotgun was a twenty gauge with the stock crudely cut into a makeshift pistol grip and the barrel sawed off just beyond the forearm. The total length was less than twenty inches. The blue and white bag with a Greyhound logo held $91 in bills, $1.30 in change and five Remington twenty gauge shotgun shells. In the prisoner's jacket pocket Jake found two more Remington shells.

Before the report was finished the Number Fifteen Detectives informed Duane and Jake their man was an escapee from Jackson Prison. He had been serving time for Breaking and Entering.

The late ride back to the bureau had Duane smiling. "Bart's right. You're nuts and hard headed. But I like the results."

"Still want that cup of coffee?"

"Nah. Had two while you typed the report. You know, you are one lucky son-of-a-bitch. How'd you know that guy would pop out on the street."

"Didn't. But then I knew he wouldn't walk into a coffee shop with a police car parked out in front."

Jake took the written exam for the Northville Police Department. It was November 12th, his day off. He wanted to move his family to the country; yet not anxious to walk away from a job he loved. Passing the exam was not an issue. He knew making a move would be.

Maybe Northville is the place to start a new career? I'd still be a cop.

Jake grabbed the chair across from Dick Dungy, his regular euchre partner and started flipping cards. "First Jack deals."

"Jake, I want to thank you," Dick said as the first Jack fell in front of him. "Made an easy arrest on a purse snatcher today."

"How's that?"

"Lookin' for some kid in a leather coat. Hit some old lady in the eye with a hunk of pipe and grabbed her purse. We turned a corner and this kid sees us and just puts his hands in the air. He just stood there waiting."

"What'd that have to do with me?"

"Shocked the shit out of him when he saw me and Norville get out of the car. Two black officers."

"And?"

"Said he thought the cop in the blue and white might be some white guy named Jake." Richard laughed as he fanned open his cards and looked at them. "Pass. You're the only Jake I know, so it must've been you."

"Still don't know what I did."

"Guess you taught him not to run from blue and white cars." Richard flashed a big smile. "He said he had a steel plate in his head because of you. Name's Boyton. Thomas Boyton."

"Guess I didn't teach him much if he's stealing purses." Jake looked at his cards. "Boyton. Yeah, I remember. A car thief."

"Guess he changed careers."

237

"What's trump and who named it?" Jake asked.

And Lieutenant Fox thought I used too much force. Maybe not enough.

Chapter 23

Jake was trimming his hedges for the last time before winter. One of the cars from Number Fifteen came driving slowly past. Fifteen minutes later he saw it again emerging from the alley behind his garage. He knew the store a block down on Eight Mile had been robbed twice in the last month, so he flagged them down. "I am Jake Bush, TMU. Something happening around here I should know about?"

The driver of the patrol car answered, "Gotta a call on some guy in a ball cap chasin' a kid in the alley off of Eight Mile. The kid was screaming. So far we haven't found anything."

Jake looked across the street at the '55 Chevrolet parked there. "Don't know if this has anything to do with it, but that car," he pointed to the green and white Chev, "doesn't belong there. I've seen it somewhere before, but not around here."

"The name's Troutz. Ray Troutz, this is Bob Billows and we're Fifteen-Three. We'll check the car out. In the meantime we'll cruise the area a bit longer to see if we get another call."

"Let me know if you find out anything," said Jake as he stepped back from the driver's window.

"Sure thing."

Two hours later Jake saw a tow truck hooking onto the Chevrolet. The same two officers were there watching. Jake walked over. "Find out anything?"

"Yeah. Ran a check on this car after you pointed it out. It's owned by a Delbert Young, and lives across from Pulaski school. 19822 Strasburg. We ran a check on Delbert. He's wanted on a traffic warrant."

"Why did he leave his car here?"

"Don't know. He clammed up when I asked about the car and where he'd been the past hour. He's Forty-five and still lives with his mother. Strange dude. Kinda weird and nervous as hell. We got

239

his rap sheet when we booked him. He's a fuckin' pervert. He's had a couple of arrests for molesting kids."

"Maybe he was the one chasing the kid."

"We figured that too. Got flagged down by a Mrs. Melleg over on Hamburg. She was the one who called it in. Her description fit Delbert to a tee, but with no complaint, we have nothing."

"Great. Got some pervert living across the street from the school where daughters go." Jake took note of the license number on the car as it was being towed off.

"We're holding him on the traffic warrant, but as soon as he comes up with the fifty bucks, he's on the street unless we get a call."

Jake leaned in the window of the scout car. "The kid being chased was probably so scared he didn't tell his folks, or they didn't believe him." Jake backed away from the car. "Thanks for the info, and let me know if you find out anything else."

Jake was driving past Casmir Pulaski School on the way to the hardware store two days later. It was November 1st and he was on nights for the month. There in the driveway across the street from the playground was the 1955 green and white Chevrolet. He hadn't heard anything more, so there was probably no complaint filed. Delbert was a free man.

Jake cringed at the thought of someone like that living across from the school that Deb and Michelle went to. *Fuckin' bastard better never come near my kids.* Jake tried pushing Delbert out of his mind but couldn't.

The green and white Chevrolet was backing out of the driveway as Jake was heading home with the screws he needed to repair his screen door. The car waited for Jake in his 65 Plymouth wagon to pass. Jake checked his mirror and saw the Chevrolet pull onto the street behind him. He watched in the mirror as the Chev turned east on State Fair while he continued north on Strasburg.

Might as well see what Delbert it up to.

240

Jake sped up and took the next corner then the next to get back to State Fair. When he got to the stop sign he saw the Chevrolet still heading east just two blocks ahead, so he turned to follow. The driver of the Chevy, who Jake assumed was Delbert, had a constant speed of twenty miles per hour.

Delbert turned onto Goulburn with Jake following and trying to stay a full block behind. The Chevrolet was going so slow he pulled to the curb every so often to let it get further away. Delbert then made a circle around St. Raymond's Parochial School and playground. Jake checked his watch. It was 11:20 in the morning. The kids were just getting out for noon recess. Delbert never topped 20 mph hour.

The green and white Chevy got back on Fairmount and continued east, crossing Schoenner. Delbert made a tour around the Wish Eagan Playfield with the Evans School abutting it. Kids were out playing ball during the noon hour.

Delbert crossed Gratiot and checked two more grade schools; still driving so slow Jake had to work at not getting too close.

At 12:40 Delbert was pulling into his driveway. Jake drove slowly by as Delbert walked to the front door of his house. He wanted to get a good look at him.

Delbert was a white male; no more than five foot two. He wore a brown ball cap pulled down flaring out his ears, and had on bib overalls and a plaid flannel shirt.

At three in the afternoon Jake was sitting in his 1965 off-green Plymouth wagon parked on Manning near Strasburg. He could see the front of 19822 Strasburg. At precisely 3:10 Delbert emerged from his house and got in his car. He backed out of the driveway and headed to State Fair. The Chevy made a right and headed east. The pattern was the same as the morning route. Delbert drove very slowly past St. Raymond's, then Evans, then Gabriel Richard and lastly Pineview. They were all grade schools. At 4:30 p.m. he was pulling into his driveway. Jake headed for home. He was starting nights that day. It bothered him that Delbert, a convicted sex offender, spent his days driving a route around grade schools when kids might be out and about.

Jake set his alarm for 10:50 a.m. before he climbed into bed at 3:40 in the morning. Anne didn't stir as he settled in. It would be a short night for him. He lay there thinking, he had his shift to work, but had kids to watch out for—Deb, Michelle and everyone else's. *Maybe I'll tail him for a few days. It can't hurt.* It was something he just had to do. Jake tried to sleep.

It was 11:15 when Jake parked on State Fair to the west of Strasburg. Five minutes later he saw the two-toned Chevrolet as it slowly rolled up to the stop sign and turned right, heading east on State Fair. Jake cut down Hamburg, and then took Fairmount toward St. Raymond's. He was guessing that Delbert would take his usual route.

Jake parked just off the corner so he could watch down Goulburn. Sure enough, Delbert wearing his brown ball cap showed up two minutes later. He drove slowly around the schoolyard, and headed toward Evans School. Jake was able to get there ahead with no problem, pulling in among the cars parked in front of nearby houses. He caught sight of the Chevrolet in his mirror as he slouched down in his seat. The car slowly passed. Jake drove to each corner to make sure Delbert was still moving, staying a block behind. The route was the same as it was the day before. Delbert cruised past Gabriel Richard and Pineview. At 12:40 p.m. he was pulling into his driveway.

Jake went home for a nap, but couldn't sleep. He did not say anything to his wife about Delbert as he played with Mike and Jeanette in the backyard, waiting for 3 o'clock to come. He made a lame excuse, saying he had to run to the hardware.

Like clockwork the Chevrolet pulled onto State Fair at 3:10. Jake beat Delbert to St. Raymond's, then to Evans. He was parked close to Gabriel Richard when he saw the green and white car coming in his side mirror. Two girls, about seven or eight, were at the corner of Rossini and Crusade waiting for cars to pass. As soon as Delbert went by Jake's parked station wagon, he put it in drive. There were no cars in the curb lane, so Jake had his car inching toward the corner against the curb. He was hoping Delbert was paying attention to the two girls and not watching in his mirrors. Delbert pulled in and stopped next to where the girls were standing and reached over and opened his passenger door. Jake threw his car into park and ran when he heard the girls screaming. They had dropped their books and ran back toward the school.

Jake got to the open door on the Chevrolet just in time to see Delbert's hand working at his hardened cock. His bibs were at his ankles. Jake reached in, grabbed a leg and yanked. Delbert skidded on the sidewalk on cheeks of his bare ass as he was pulling at his bibs, trying to get into them.

In a second, a snub-nose .38 Colt was stuck in his ear. "You twitch and you're dead. On your fuckin' belly."

Two women were running out of the school by the time Jake had Delbert's bibs back on and him leaning on the hood of the Chevrolet.

"Did anyone call the police?" Jake asked.

"Yes. Two of our girls came in crying that a man was showing his privates."

Fifteen-Ten, Ed Bartkowski and his partner had gotten the run to the school. The teachers were handing the information on the girls to Jake as their car pulled up.

Bart spoke as he got out. "Working plain clothes now, Jake?"

"Guess you could call it that."

"What you got?"

"A dick shaker. Can you take him in for me? I'll follow and make the report."

"What, not enough to do at the TMU?" Bart asked as his partner handcuffed the prisoner.

"Yeah, nothing better to do waiting for my next shift."

"You're nuts, Jake."

"I'll take that as a compliment."

243

Jake called home to tell Anne he was involved in an arrest, but he'd be home for dinner. "The girls get home from school okay?"

He felt good that Delbert Young was off the street. Bart wouldn't understand so he didn't say why he was there on that day.

He knew he couldn't say anything at home.

No sense in alarming Anne. She'd push harder to get me to quit and get the kids out of Detroit.

That day's mail had a letter for Jake notifying him that he was invited for an oral review board at the Northville Police Department, the 10th of November. He put in for that day off on comp time so he could make the 7 p.m. appointment.

Once he knew he made it to the oral board, he took the wife and kids for a ride. Northville was a small town just over a hour's drive from where they lived. Farms surrounded it. It was country. It was quiet. Anne liked it. The pay in Northville was somewhat less than Detroit, but there was overtime available during the race dates in the spring and fall of the year. Jake's only worry was that there wouldn't be enough for him to do. He liked putting crooks in jail.

The meeting with Chief John Horshig was scheduled for 4 p.m. on November 17th. Jake re-knotted his tie for the third time, wondering if wearing a suit was too much. The oral review board the week before went well, at least from Jake's perspective. A Captain from Royal Oak, a Michigan State Police Lieutenant and a member of the Northville City Council made up the board. There were four other applicants. One by one they were called in, then left. Of the five applicants only one other police officer had applied. Jake was the last one called. The parting remarks by those on the board seemed positive. Jake knew Northville had an opening they wanted to fill as soon as possible. There wouldn't be a need for a police academy if they chose him. A two-week notice was all he had to give, and with vacation he had earned, yes, he could be on the job at Northville whenever they wanted him. Things were moving fast. *Too fast.*

Jake walked in the front door of the Northville Police Department. The Chief was talking to a sergeant at the front desk. The chief cleared his throat before he spoke, a habit Jake picked up on during an earlier meeting. "Uh-hem. Officer Bush, good to see you again." With an arm motion he directed Jake toward his office. "Go on in. I'll be with you in a second."

Jake walked in the open door and stood for a moment looking at the pictures on the walls. In a frame among an array of photographs Jake caught sight of a younger Chief Horshig, wearing sergeant stripes. The badge clearly showed the name "Inkster" above the number. A minute later the chief walked in.

"Glad my secretary got in touch with you Jake. You don't mind if I call you Jake, do you?"

"Not at all."

The chief offered Jake a chair. "Uh-Hem. Can I get you a coffee or anything?"

Jake sat, unbuttoning his suit coat. "No thanks."

"Then let's get to the reason my secretary called." The chief rocked back in his chair. "Uh-hem. I want to offer you a position as a dispatcher. The pay is a bit less than that of a patrolman, but the next opening in the department will be filled from that position."

"Wasn't the test and the oral interview for a current opening?"

"Uh-hem." The chief's eyes went to the papers on his desk. "Yes, but I already filled that position." The chief fidgeted with a pen. "Uh-hem. I know you did real well on the written exam, and yes, the oral board did give you the highest marks, but…"

The rest of the words faded into the background as Jake remembered one of the men the night of the oral board saying he was an Inkster police officer. The picture of Sergeant Horshig on

245

the office wall was just over the chief's left shoulder as he was talking.

"Uh-hem," the chief cleared his throat again, bringing Jake back to the conversation. "Jake, I would really like you to consider that position. I have approval to hire a dispatcher the first of the year."

Jake stood. He knew the meeting was over. "Thanks for everything."

"Think about the dispatcher's job. And let my office know if you are."

"Yes sir." Jake turned and walked out. That was his last contact with the Northville Police Department.

Chapter 24

Duane was completing the log sheet after a night of nothing but traffic stops. "You never did say what happened to that Northville job."

"Just forget it."

"One day you wouldn't shut up about it, now forget it?"

"Yeah, just drop it."

"What'd they do, turn you down for someone else?"

Jake hit the brakes, jarring the pen out of Duane's hand. "I said drop it."

"Touchy subject, eh?"

"It was a set up. One ex-Inkster cop, hiring another. Me and the others interviewed were just there to make it look good."

"So much for people beating down the door to hire Detroit's top cop."

"Fuck you, Duane. You know you can ask the bosses for another partner."

"Easy Jake. I was just teasing."

Duane had the next two days off and Jake was glad Shaggert didn't know about Northville. Jake was cruising the curb with his lights out, only going out in the traffic lane when parked cars were in the way. Eight-Four was on Trumbull, near Tiger Stadium. A half a block ahead, Jake saw a figure moving under the streetlights. "Justin, is that guy checking car doors?"

Justin rolled down his window, took off his hat, hanging his head out. "Yes and I think he found one open."

Jake let the car slide to a stop while Justin kept his head out of the window, watching. Three cars ahead a car door opened and a man climbed out, stuffing something into his right coat pocket. "Time to take him," Justin said.

Jake hit the gas and drove up just as the man was trying another car door. Justin jumped out. "Hold it right there, mister."

Jake was out of the car to help. Justin had the man spread eagle on the hood of a Chrysler and emptied the man's coat pockets. In the right pocket were three packs of matches, a hairbrush, a roll of Tums, three quarters and an unused roll of film. In the left pocket was a small bottle of Aqua Velva.

Jake went back to the Mercury that they saw him climb out of and checked the glove box and came back. "Justin, where are the matches from?"

Justin checked. "From Stasik's Auto Body."

"Same name on the one he missed."

Justin finished searching the man. "What do you want to do with him?"

"Put the cuffs on him. He's just a street bum, but we can't let him keep on checking unlocked cars to see what he can pocket. Besides, he looks like he could use a warm place to sleep tonight. "

Justin slid in beside the prisoner. The man was white, in his fifties and in dire need of a bath. Jake was heading to Number Two to lock him up. Justin was questioning the prisoner with a strained voice.

"What's your name?" Before the reply came, Justin started having dry heaves. As he retched, Jake pulled to the curb. Justin stumbled out of the police car, hanging onto Eight-Four's back fender. He had his head close to the curb when his Chop-Suey supper gushed over the rear tire.

Jake stood beside him. When there was a pause in the puking he asked, "What's wrong?"

Shaggert spit a few times, knocking a string of saliva from his mouth. "I can't stand the smell of the guy. Sorry."

"You okay?"

"Will be in a minute. Just need a little fresh air."

Jake opened the rear door of their car. "Out, mister." The man slid out, arms still handcuffed behind his back. Jake unlocked the cuffs. "Okay, hit the road. I catch you in another car you won't see daylight for a month. Now get."

Justin was wiping his mouth with his handkerchief. "Sorry Jake. You didn't have to let him go."

"Hell, it was a bullshit arrest anyway. We'll take the matches and shit back to the car. I was just being kind; giving the guy a place to sleep for the night. Jail beats a doorway anytime." Jake drove in silence for a while, then spoke. "How long have you been on the job?"

"Two years."

"First time getting sick?"

"Yeah."

"Ever lock up a drunk who's been into a batch of moonshine?"

"No."

"Smells like someone shit in his mouth. You're lucky this guy was only drinking Aqua Velva. If you think someone needing a bath is bad, you haven't smelled anything yet."

"It won't happen again."

"Ever smell a dead body? One that's been dead for a week?"

"I said, it won't happen again."

"You sure?" Jake turned and caught the eye of his partner. "Justin, I got a bit of advice. Find a new line of work."

"I like what I'm doing."

"If this guy was a hold up man, a murderer or something, and we had to tussle with him, what then?"

"Hey, you're the guy looking for another job."

"Maybe 'cause I can't handle working with the partners they're giving me."

Jake thought as he drove.

Six years and all I can come up with are three cops I could count on. Mike, Ozell and Jess. Now I have Duane and Justin. I've gotta get out of here.

The next day Jake sent résumé's to two more cities and one to a corporation. *Maybe they'll need a security officer?* He laughed at the thought of not carrying a gun.

"Nah, I like the feel of a gun on my hip," he mumbled to himself as he licked the envelopes.

It was just after midnight on Thanksgiving Eve November 22, 1967, when Duane pulled into the alley behind the Taystee Barbecue at Woodward and Milwaukee. The place was their favorite lunch stop. Jake shivered a bit when he got out of the car. It was twenty degrees and he was going to the Lions-Packers game that afternoon. *I'm going to freeze my ass off.*

Jake and Duane grabbed and empty booth near the counter with its twelve stools. Jake was glancing at the menu when he noticed a man on a stool ten feet away looking at them. The man was chewing on a toothpick.

The waitress came up. "Two coffees and what else?"

"I'll take the rib special," Duane answered.

"Same for me," Jake said as he gave back the menu and headed to the men's room to wash his hands.

As he opened the men's room door, he was nose to nose with the toothpick man. The man jumped back wide-eyed.

"Excuse me," Jake said as he slid past. The door slammed shut behind him.

Was he hiding something? Drugs? Jake went to the toilet and removed the top. Nothing, just rust-stained water in the tank. He looked behind the stool and ran his had under the bowl. Nothing. Then he checked the wastebasket, finding only found wet hand towels and a couple of soggy cigarette butts.

The guy panicked, why? Jake washed his hands.

Jake slid back in the booth across from Duane. He caught the guy at the counter giving him another look.

"Duane, you remember anything about a guy that's wanted who always chews on a toothpick?"

"Toothpick? No."

"There's a guy on a circular I read that's wanted who constantly chews on a toothpick."

"I don't know what you are talking about."

"Ten seats behind you, at the counter, there's a guy in a maroon three-quarter length coat chewing on a toothpick. I am going to the car to check the book. If he starts to leave, stop him. I'll be right back."

"Jake, the food'll be comin'."

"Don't let him get out the door."

Jake left his hat and coat and banged out the door into the cold. He ran to the alley and unlocked the car door and started thumbing through the circular book under the alley light. He quick scanned each page as he flipped them. About the fifth page down the words jumped out. "Constantly chews on a toothpick." He quickly read some of the particulars, dropped the book on the seat and ran back to the front of the restaurant. Walking half a block north was the toothpick man. He looked in the window. Duane was gnawing on a rib bone. Jake broke into a run.

The man turned at the sound of Jake's feet.

"Hold on mister, I need to talk to you."

"Whatchew hassling me for?"

"Just need a few minutes."

"Man, I pay your wages. I don't need you wastin' my time."

"Yeah, I know, but I got a job to do. Come on for a walk." Jake grabbed an arm.

The man jerked back. "I got my rights. I don't need to go no where."

"You don't need to make this hard. We're goin' this way." Jake motioned his head back to the restaurant as he unconsciously rested his hand on the butt of his colt. The man saw the move and turned to walk with Jake.

"I don't need no bullshit. Got places to go."

"This won't take long." The cold night air chilled Jake as he guided the man around a frozen puddle on the sidewalk. He glanced in Taystee's window.

I'm freezing my ass off and Duane's filling his face.

Two plain-clothes officers were walking to the door of the barbecue joint from a car they parked next to a fire hydrant. They

251

stopped to let Jake and the man in the maroon coat walk by. "You supposed to eating?" one of them asked.

"Yeah."

"You some gung-ho hot dog?" were the words he heard as the two suits went in the door behind him.

"Yeah, you some kind of a hot dog?" His man repeated.

"Just shut the fuck up."

Jake walked the man to his car in the alley. His mind was running. *Is that what I am, a hot dog? Where in the fuck's Duane?* "Look, mister. I'll get your name and you're on your way." Jake's supper was waiting and he was cold. *Maybe they're right.*

He opened the passenger door and grabbed the clipboard. "Name?"

"Jesse Leander James Jr."

The clipboard dropped and Jake turned the man around pushing him against the car. He grabbed a wrist and slapped on a cuff, then grabbed the other hand, finishing cuffing the man behind his back. He remembered the words off the circular: *The man's name might be Jeffery or Jesse.* Jake opened the back door of his blue and white. "Lay down on the floor. You're under arrest for rape."

The word rape brought Jesse's head snapping back.

"Rape? I ain't raped nobody."

"Just get in. On the floor."

Jesse squirmed in on his belly with Jake helping by pulling on his arms from over the front seat until his head ended up behind the driver's seat. Jake looked around. *Still no Duane, the asshole!*

He slid in behind the wheel, grabbed the circular book and opened it, pulling the page out and put it over the visor. Jake started the car, then reached around and put his .38 in the ear of the man lying on the floor.

"Jesse, you move the wrong way and I will open up your ear drum. Understand?"

Jake felt a head nod at the end of his gun barrel and put the car in drive moving around to the side of the restaurant. He flipped on the blue lights and then gave a whir to the siren. No Duane.

A man was crossing Milwaukee in front of the car. Jake stuck his head out of the window. "Hey buddy. There's a cop inside eating. Tell him his partner wants him."

"Yes sir." Jake watched him stick his head inside the door and his lips move. He stepped back out, waved and continued walking up Woodward.

A minute later Duane stuck his head out of the door.

"Jake, your supper's getting cold."

I don't believe this. "Tell them to hold it. Bring my hat and coat."

Duane slipped in the passenger side of the car. "They put your dinner over the oven."

Jake squealed the tires as he made a left turn onto Woodward driving with his left arm. His right was still over the seat with his gun in his prisoner's ear.

"What's all the fuss about?"

"The prisoner in the back."

Only then did Duane notice Jake's arm over the seat. "What's goin' on?"

"The circular's over the visor."

Duane pulled it out and read. He turned it over, stopping as he read every line of the description to look over the seat.

"Black male, 22 to 25." He looked at the man. "Greased back hair." He took another look. "Three quarter length maroon car coat. Hush Puppy shoes." He spun to look at the man's feet. "Jake, how the fuck do you do it?"

"I told you not to let him leave the restaurant."

"I didn't hear you."

"You also didn't give a shit that I was out there freezing my ass off."

"Jake…"

"Just shut up. There's no excuse." Jake wheeled onto the ramp of the Thirteenth Precinct and led his prisoner up the side corridor to the bullpen.

Lieutenant Roberts turned when he saw Jake and his prisoner at the half door.

"What you got, guys?"

Jake handed the lieutenant the circular. Lt. Roberts read it over, his eyes flipping from the paper to the man. He smiled as he looked at the man in the maroon coat still working over a toothpick. "Book 'em and give Women's Division a call."

Duane was having a coffee when Jake got to the report room. "Can I get you a coffee partner?" Jake didn't answer. He just pulled up a chair and loaded a blank 3-copy report into the typewriter and banged at the keys without looking up. When he was done, he ripped out the report. He looked at the circular, grabbed the phone and dialed four numbers.

"Yeah, Women's Division? Jake Bush, TMU. Got a guy in on your circular WD#8A. Mary Fermonti's case. Thought you might want to know with the holiday and stuff." There was a pause. "Yes, at Number Thirteen. Thanks." Jake dropped the receiver into the cradle.

He turned the report toward Duane. "Here, sign it."

Coffee spilled as Duane put his cup on the desk. He quickly signed it. "It's your bust, Jake. I had nothing to do with it."

"Just sign it."

Jake was up dressing for the football game. His brother was going to pick him up at ten because the game started at noon. The phone rang. Anne answered it.

"For you, Jake." She handed him the receiver as he got to the kitchen.

"Officer Bush?" The female voice asked.

"Yes."

"Officer Mary Fermonti, Women's Division. Just wanted to make sure you had a happy Thanksgiving. We held a line up with your man. Seven out of twelve women picked him out as the rapist. Great catch."

Jake hung up the phone and sat down at the table. He felt like crying.

"Something wrong?" His wife asked.

"No, everything's right. A guy I busted last night was made on a bunch of rapes. Picked his targets riding a bus. Raped at least twelve at knifepoint." He paused. "I feel pretty good. I feel great, as a matter of fact."

"Jake, you promised next summer we'd be somewhere else. Not Detroit."

"Yeah, I know."

Yeah, I know.

At the game Jake could call the plays before they ran them. The Lions would run around the right end; one off tackle; one to the left and then punt. The Lions lost. Tobin Rote was no Bobby Lane. The football crowd was into their beer. Win or lose, they loved their Lions and no one, not Jake's brother, uncle and cousin ever heard about the man with the toothpick. But Jake knew about him and he felt good in the cold November air.

Anne, I wish you knew just how good it makes me feel to put a guy like that behind bars.

The Hudson's Christmas Parade ushered in the upcoming holiday season earlier that morning. Jake had given himself his own early Christmas present—a rapist behind bars. During the game's fourth quarter, he glanced at his watch and thought of Anne. She'd be playing with the kids as the turkey cooked. His mind wasn't on the game.

****

255

Jake checked the assignment board for December. He had asked to be on a new car. "Time for a change," is what he told Ski. He read the names for Eight-Four. Wattles, Bush and Shaggert.

Jake saw Sergeant Ski alone in the office.

"Hey Sarge, what about the change I asked for?"

"I had you penciled in on Ten. Wattles saw it and said you two get along great together." Sergeant Ski looked up at Jake. "Is there a problem?"

"No. Forget it."

No problem, I'll just work around them.

Chapter 25

Christmas came and went with nothing in the mail. There were no responses to the letters Jake had sent out two months before. Logical reasoning told him that the year's end meant they were holding off until after the first of the year to add to their payroll. At least he hoped that was the case.

Eight-Four neared East Grand Boulevard and turned onto Oakland. Jake and Justin made up the crew and it was New Year's Day, 1968. There were patches of ice where the thaw the day before froze and the temperature was predicted to be a high of 34 degrees. The low number cars were assigned to work the Thirteenth Precinct, Jake's old stomping grounds.

The 10:00 a.m. start of the shift found the streets of Detroit barren. "Musta been a hell of a New Year's Eve last night," Jake remarked as Justin drove north on Oakland Avenue. "Hardly a car moving."

"Yeah, nobody walking either."

Jake wondered if Justin still had a queasy stomach, but wouldn't ask. "Mind if we go past a couple of old haunts?"

"Like what?"

"Blind pigs. Let's see if they had parties last night."

"Just tell me where."

Justin followed Jake's directions and drove slowly down St. Antoine off of Harper. "The red brick house on the left," Jake pointed up the block. All was quiet. "Maybe Ol' Willie Coomer folded his tent, or Precinct Vice finally put him out of business."

Justin then headed up Harper toward John R as Jake directed. "There's a candy store on the right."

"Where all the cars are parked?" Justin drove closer. "Maybe the party's still going on," and slowed the blue and white. Cars were parked on both sides of the street on the block ahead of them.

"I think you're right. Pull in behind that car," Jake pointed to the Pontiac on the east side of John R.

Justin parked in the opening by the fire hydrant. They were a half of a block from the candy store. "The doorman should be pacing in front. I don't see him."

"Maybe he's at the party. Or it's too cold for him?"

"No. If it's the guy I remember, when the place is open, he's out front. I think he's the boss. Goes by Pappy Jack. His brother works behind the counter. The brother is the button man. You know, the police are coming and he hits a button. The buzzer alerts the guy running the games upstairs."

Jake sat watching and thinking as Justin turned the ignition off. *Lots of cars. A big party. Booze, broads and dice. Lots of money.*

Jake checked his watch. His mind was racing. *Ten thirty in the morning and the party's still going. But, no doorman. No Pappy Jack and his black stingy-brimmed hat and fur collared topcoat.* Jake broke the silence. "I want to play a hunch."

"Whatcha thinkin'?"

"We break up the party, or if something else is going on, then just doin' what we have to."

"Meaning what?"

"I'm thinking hold up. No doorman. Plenty of cars and plenty of customers. That means plenty of cash."

"You're dreaming."

"Maybe. But its time to end the party even if I'm wrong." Jake reached for the mic. "Eight-One and Eight-Two. Can you meet Four on Woodward and Piquette?" Jake listened for them to answer.

"Just back up, Justin—in case my dream is a reality. I don't want to drive past the store."

Jake had Justin drive him to Woodward and drop him off, then turn around to watch from the corner of John R and Harper. "Radio me if you see anything going on." Jake slipped out of the car and ran toward Piquette. He thought as he ran. *Dungy and Meredith. Cesarz and Garcia. Four of the best cops in the bureau.*

One and Two pulled onto Piquette as Jake got there. Jake told them what he thought was going on and outlined a plan.

Dick Dungy chimed in. "Let's get this thing going before someone spots us"

"You said just one way into the place?" It was Garcia asking.

"Yes, stairs on the outside, on the north side of the building. You can't see the stairs from the street, but they're wide open. I figure one crew can cover the back windows from the alley on the west side. The other crew, cover the stairs from the north. There's a side alley there that Tee's into the back alley. Shagg and I'll check out the candy store."

"We'll take the back alley," answered Meredith.

"What's the best way to cover the stairs?" asked Cesarz.

"From the ground north of the Tee alley. There's about a five-foot wooden fence that will parallel the staircase. You can take the alley to it. Oh, just so you know, the last time I was here people jumped out of the back windows into the alley, the less daring used the stairs."

"Shotguns Jake," rang in Dungy.

"Good idea. I'll cut between the houses to my car. Give me two minutes." Jake ran, heading toward Harper. He heard the racking of pump shotguns behind him.

Jake and Justin loaded their Winchesters with double-O buck as they heard the walkie-talkie crack on Jake's hip.

"Eight-One in position."

A pause, then "Two in position."

"Time to go kid. You all right with this?"

"Just lead the way."

Jake cut around the corner of John R heading toward the front of the candy store. It was two buildings down.

Still no doorman. Jake held up this hand as he reached to edge of the tall plate glass windows that sandwiched the recessed door on the front of the building.

"We both go in the door together. You cover the right side. I'll take the left. The candy counter and button for upstairs is on the left."

"If nothing else, we'll scare the shit out of them," Justin whispered.

"Them? Hell, it's me that's shakin'. Let's go."

Immediately, Jake saw four men sitting on chairs on the right wall as he and his partner burst through the full glass door with shotguns waving. Jake spoke. "Freeze. Nobody move!" Four sets of wide eyes and four open mouths froze in their chairs.

Jake recognized Pappy Jack and his bother Lannie. They were sitting between two men he'd never seen before. Those men had their hands in their coat pockets.

"Both of you, slowly, out with the hands and make sure they're empty." Jake waved the muzzle of his shotgun as he spoke. Justin took the cue and made sure his Winchester was pointed at the man on his end.

"Man, be cool with that thing," Jake's man said as he slid out an open hand.

"They got guns. Four more niggers are upstairs," Pappy Jack whispered.

Jake keyed the mic on his walkie-talkie. "One and Two, it's a holdup. Four men with guns are upstairs. We've got the downstairs secured."

"Everybody, just stay still," Justin went to his man and pulled a small blue steel automatic from the man's jacket pocket.

Jake turned the volume down on his radio just as a voice spoke. "Eight-Two to Eight-Seven-O. One, Two and Four are in the middle of a hold up, a blind pig on John R between Harper and Piquette. Requesting back up." Jake smiled as he heard Richard Dungy's voice.

Man, the guy is always thinking.

"I sho is glad to see you po-lice."

260

"Shut up, Pappy," Jake whispered as he took a revolver out of his man's pocket.

"All right everybody up and against the wall." He waved the barrel of his shotgun. "Lean and spread 'em." Pappy Jack and Lonnie were frisked as well as the two strangers. Jake motioned to Pappy Jack and Lonnie. "You two sit down and stay quiet."

He prodded his man with his shotgun barrel, "You two, on your bellies." Jake and Justin handcuffed them behind their backs as he whispered, "Make a fuckin' sound and this shotgun will make you wish you hadn't. Understand?" Two heads nodded. "Good." Jake Stood.

Jake thought for a while. "Pappy Jack. How many customers upstairs?"

" 'bout fifty."

"You say four men are up there with guns?"

"Yes sir. Six guys came up the sidewalk. I thought they were customers. They left these two with us."

"Still only the one way out, right?"

"Yeah. Top of the stairs and the back window."

Jake thought for a minute, and then keyed his radio. "All units, this is Four. There's four armed men upstairs. The only way down is the staircase. Let's just stay out of sight until they come to us."

"This is Eight-Seven-O, all units stay off of John R. Keep at least a half a block back. Four, I'll let Number Thirteen know to stay clear of the area."

Jake tapped the bottom of the foot on the man handcuffed next to him. "Gimme some names, some descriptions."

"Fuck you, po-lice," was the response.

"Pappy Jack, Lonnie, move behind the counter. Any shooting starts these guys might get hit. I got an itchy trigger finger." Jake waved his head to get them moving.

"Rawley Williams, Billy Talbot, Johnny Talbot and Jimmy Springer. I don't know what they're wearing. They're soul brothers."

"Thought you weren't talkin' to me," Jake said.

261

"I 'membered the Algiers Motel. You might be one of those killer cops."

The remark stung, but Jake shrugged it off.

"Smart man." Jake keyed the mic again. "Eight-One and Two. There's about fifty people up there. The bad guys are four black men. Don't have descriptions." Jake heard chairs scrapping the floor overhead. There was one gunshot followed by a long silence.

"Shagg, cover these guys. I'm goin' outside."

"Gotcha."

As Jake slipped out the front door he heard a whisper over his radio. "Door's opening. One, two, three guys on the steps."

Jake whispered into his keyed mic. "This is Jake. I'm at the front of the store on the street."

"The fourth guy just walked out." It was Dungy's voice.

Seconds ticked. Jake picked a spot behind a Buick parked in front of the store. He couldn't see the stairway except for the bottom step. His palms got sweaty as he knelt looking over the trunk, the bead on the Winchester was pointing toward the corner of the building at the base of the stairs.

"FREEZE," Meredith's deep baritone voice rang out. "Nobody moves and nobody gets hurt."

Jake could see Cesarz and Garcia's shotgun barrels pointing from behind the wooden fence up the staircase.

"Hands on your heads." It was Meredith again from the back alley.

Jake eased out from behind the Buick, short stepping to his right so he could see the whole stairway. There in front of him two steps from the bottom stood the first man, then two steps up, another. The third and fourth men were near the top. Jake could see their eyes jump from one shotgun barrel to another.

One at a time Rawley Williams, Billy Talbot, Johnny Talbot and Jimmy Springer were ordered down, disarmed and handcuffed. As Meredith handcuffed the last man, Jake heard him ask. "Who got shot up there?"

"No one. We just shot into the ceiling to put the fear of God into them. Didn't want anyone following us."

"You better be right. Murder's a long way from a robbery."

Brown evidence envelopes were filled with wristwatches, rings, and jewelry. A grand total of $22,474 in cash was also put in evidence. Not a bad take for a half hour above a candy store. Two extra crews of detectives were called in to take statements from the thirty-five men and twelve women. Some of the women were patrons with their boyfriends and some were whores that worked the place.

Jake overheard two men say they were from Persia and that they lived in Dearborn Heights. "We were just learning a dice game." They were talking to Detective Earl Walker. Each said he had invested $500 to find out what snake eyes were.

Jake had just finishing the arrest report when one of the Persians said, "Then these guys with guns come in. I thought it was a joke."

The other spoke up. "Yes, officer. I found out it was no joke when one put a gun barrel up my nose. I could smell death."

Detective Walker smiled as he took the statements. "Dupont powder sure smells a lot different than a whore's phoo-phoo juice, right Mr. Ahmed?"

"What's DuPont powder?" asked one.

"What's phoo-phoo juice?" asked the second.

Jake laughed as he pulled the report out of the typewriter and walked past Walker and his two Persians.

"Spend much more time on John R and you won't have to ask. One or both might get you killed." He left the detective's office area and turned in the report to the lieutenant on the desk.

Shaggert, Dungy, Meredith, Garcia and Cesarz were leaning on the end of it waiting for Jake. Cesarz spoke. "Kempf and Ski are waiting at Taystee's for us. They're buying the ribs."

263

During the ride over to the restaurant Jake replayed the morning in his mind. *Thank God Duane was off.* A shiver ran up his spine. *This could have been nasty.*

He always got a sharp pain in his back after tense times were over. Nerves he had guessed. Shaggert pulled into the alley behind the Taystee Barbecue and parked.

"By the way, Shagg, nice work this morning."

"Don't forget, there weren't any smelly drunks."

Jake just smiled at Justin's remark. *Thank God for that.*

****

"Heard you got lucky while I was off," Duane said as he cruised their assigned area the next day.

"Just a little action to start off the year."

"You never told me about them blind pigs in Thirteen."

"You don't remember me pointing out the candy store and doorman a couple of months ago?" A Buick turned onto Woodward in front of them and Jake's eyes went to the car board.

"How's your job hunt going?"

"Get that blue Buick." Jake's finger pointed at the car in the right lane. The Buick, two cars ahead, made a quick right.

"Make a right, Duane."

"Any replies to your letters?"

"Right, Duane. Make a fuckin' right. The Buick!"

"What Buick?"

Eight-Four passed the corner the Buick turned at. Jake saw it in the middle of the street with the doors open. "God damn it, Duane. If you'd pay attention…"

"What are you babbling about?"

"Go around the block. A Buick, license Boy David one, three, two, nine. It's stolen. The two guys in it are gone."

"Why didn't you say something?"

Fuckin' idiot were the words running through Jake's mind as Duane pulled up to the abandoned stolen car.

Jake was off. He sat at his portable typewriter drafting two letters. One he mailed to the Personnel Department, Dow Corning Corporation, the other to the Chief of Police, both of them located in Midland, Michigan. He was tired of waiting for answers to his first three letters.

At roll call on January 10th, Sergeant Kempf passed out subpoenas. Jake opened the first of the two he received. It read: "The People vs. Jesse Leander James Jr." He opened the small calendar book he carried in his shirt pocket and penciled in the name on the date along with "Recorder's Court, Judge Szymanski 8:00 a.m." on the lines for February 21, 1968. He remembered the rape arrest on Thanksgiving Eve and smiled.

Life in prison for sure. Jake put the notebook back in his pocket.

Chapter 26

January's day shift turned into the February night shift. Jake always looked forward to the 7 p.m. to 3 a.m. shift. There was more action. The hold up arrests the first of the year were all Eight-Four could lay claim to in January. Jake did not like just driving around. Duane hated nights, so he took a fifteen-day trip to visit his South Carolina kin to break up the winter.

Jake took full advantage with the car logging 13 felony arrests in the first three days of the month. Part of the haul included two stolen cars and a gun arrest. The man arrested for CCW had breath that reeked from moonshine. Justin didn't hesitate jumping in the back with the prisoner. He did roll down his window to let in some cold night air, but never let on that the smell was getting to him. Jake made sure he kept his eye on Justin through the rear view mirror. *Damn kid might make it yet.* They booked Henry Watson for Investigation of Robbery Armed with a hold for "Carrying a Concealed Weapon."

Jake was sitting in the small side room in Judge Szymanski's court behind the witness stand. It was a room used for jury deliberations when there was a jury trial. The subpoena had said 8:00 a.m., and he was there at 7:45.

Through the open door to the courtroom Jake could watch the people filing in. A head bobbed in the doorway. "Officer Bush?"

"Yes, sir."

"Assistant Prosecutor Joseph Paine. I'll call you when I need you." The head left the doorway before Jake could say anything. He positioned his chair so he could see into the courtroom. The prosecutor who stuck his head in the door was now face to face with another man. Paine turned and put his armload of folders and papers on the table in front of him. Two black women, one very young, Jake guessed at 18 or 19, the other older, maybe her mother, were seated to the right of assistant prosecutor. Paine said something to the women, and then continued his conversation with the man on his left. The rumpled suit, crooked tie and the stack of manila folders in front of that man spelled court appointed attorney to Jake. Fifteen minutes later, the rumpled suit moved to the next table.

Paine sat down and started talking to the two women at his table. For an hour Jake watched the prosecutor and the two women go back and forth. The women kept shaking their heads. *They don't want whatever he's offering.*

Jake re-read the Woman Division write-up that he received in the mail. It was on one of the rapes Jesse Leander James Jr. had committed. This victim was nineteen. Jake assumed it was the younger woman sitting in the courtroom that day. It read:

The complainant was returning from an evening part-time job at the Michigan Coney Island. She rode the bus, and was a full time student at Wayne State University. It was about 11:15pm. After she got off at her stop she felt like someone was following her. It was a man she had seen riding on the bus. She started to run, but he caught up to her, putting a knife to her throat. He forced her between the houses on Cass Avenue and raped her against a back porch. When he fled into the alley, she ran to her apartment on Willis. As she fumbled with the key to open her door, he was there again. He pushed her into her apartment with a knife at her throat and raped her a second time.

No plea bargains, we got him cold.

Jake looked up from the report from time to time as Paine talked. The lawyer waved his arms, shrugged his shoulders and talked some more. After another half hour, the older woman handed a handkerchief to the younger one. Both women were crying. Jake was glad he was there at the Taystee Barbecue that night. *Fuckin' animal.*

The bailiff brought in a handcuffed Jesse Leander James Jr. and Court was called to order.

The bailiff closed the door to Jake's room. More time passed. Jake, half asleep, was startled by someone calling his name. It was Paine. "We won't need you, Bush. The guy's copping a plea."

"To what?" Jake asked as he got out of his chair.

"Assault with intent to rape."

"You're joking?"

"No, I'm accepting the plea."

"Is that what you were doing, trying to convince the complainant to let you accept a bullshit plea?"

"That's none of your business. Your job is to arrest, mine is to prosecute. I'm here to expedite the case."

"So you're going to let him cop a plea and get what, two to ten? That amounts to eighteen months in jail after good behavior."

"That's still none of your concern. You can go." The attorney turned his back on Jake as if to brush him off.

Jake could feel the heat rise within him as he remembered Officer Mary Fiermonti's words: *Seven out of twelve picked your man out of a line up.*

"And when he's back on the street, then what?"

Paine looked over his shoulder. "I said you can go."

Jake picked up his jacket and rolled up the report, brushing past the Assistant Prosecuting Attorney. "I just hope that when he gets out, it's your mother, wife or daughter!"

Jake just caught the last of what Paine was shouting from behind. "I'm calling your boss!"

Jake turned as he reached the door of the near empty courtroom. "Sylvers. Inspector Sylvers. 835-7798 is the bureau number."

Lieutenant Orth was waiting for Jake as he walked into the squad room for the evening shift. "Bush, in here."

Jake could see the Inspector sitting behind his desk in the next office. *I see Paine made some calls.*

The inspector looked up when he heard the door open. "Here's Bush." The lieutenant held the door for Jake to enter. There was a wry smile on Orth's face.

The inspector wasn't smiling. "That's all lieutenant."

"Jake, what am I going to do with you?"

"Sorry sir. I just got pissed off."

"You know you can't go mouthing off to a prosecuting attorney."

"He was letting a rapist off."

"You should have kept your mouth shut."

"Inspector, I watched him haggle with the nineteen-year-old complainant and her mother for two hours. Somehow he coerced them into letting the guy cop a plea."

"You still should have just kept your mouth shut."

"Boss, I'm sorry I got you into this, but not sorry for what I said." Jake told about the report from Women's Division and the seven out of twelve ID's in the line up. "We had this guy cold turkey. If he beats one case, then try him on another. That's the way the law is supposed to work. Jesse Leander James Jr. does not belong on the street."

The inspector was leaning back in his chair. "I've got orders to take some action with you on this." Jake watched as the inspector shuffled some papers on his desk. "Still got a copy of the report Officer Fiermonti sent you?"

"Yes sir."

"I want you call her and get a complete run down on her total investigation. All the rapes. Every case. Then try to write up some kind of an apology." The inspector looked up waiting for Jake to reply.

"Yes sir."

"I will forward it to the prosecutor's office along with notes of our little chat here. I'll call it a verbal reprimand." He smiled. "Like I said, you should have kept your mouth shut. But, maybe Paine should have looked at the case a little harder."

"I'll have everything for you in a couple of days, sir."

"Good. One last thing, how about staying out of trouble for a while?"

"I'll try. No guarantees." Jake turned to leave.

"Did you really say you hoped it's his wife the next time?"

"Or his mother or daughter."

269

Jake let the door close behind him. "Now that's a boss," he mumbled under his breath. Jake knew that the lieutenant could hear everything that went on in there. Orth was not smiling as Jake walked passed and into the squad room for roll call.

By the end of February, Jake received letters from both the Midland City Police Department and Dow Corning Corporation. Midland City Police was not presently hiring, but would put his name on the list to be called when an opening arose. Dow Corning's letter gave their personnel manager's phone number for Jake to call. Jake made the call immediately.

Jack Harnick, the Personnel Manager, was interested in the services of John Anthony Bush. Through that one phone call, Dow Corning's personnel department arranged for a one-day visit on March 21st which would include a written test, oral interview and a complete physical at the Dow Chemical Medical Department. Jake made a note to take that day off when he put in for March's leave days.

There was a light blowing snow the last day of February. It was near midnight as Shaggert and Jake were patrolling the streets of the Twelfth Precinct.

"Thought Spring was right around the corner," said Justin as he turned the blue and white onto Santa Rosa.

"Yes, so much for winter coming to an end." Jake reached over and turned the temperature up in the car.

"What's with the woman in the blue robe?"

"I guess she wants to talk to us."

Justin pulled the car to the curb near the black woman who was waving her arms and rolled down his window. "Can we help you, ma'am?"

"Some kid broke into my house. I heard the door glass break. He made off with my portable TV. Took it right off the stand."

Jake and Justin got out of their car and followed the woman to her porch. "Did it just happen?" asked Jake as he threw the beam of his flashlight at some slight footprints in the light snow.

"Yes. I screamed and he made it for the door."

"Justin, get some info on the TV from her. I'll follow these tracks before the wind blows them away."

Jake went through the gate into the yard, then out the back gate into the alley. Twice he lost the tracks as the wind blew the light skiff of snow, but both times he found them again as a garage or a house shielded the snow from the wind.

Jake's radio cracked. "Walk-talk Four. He got a twenty-one inch Motorola. It's got a black plastic case trimmed in gold."

"Copy that Four. I'm south of you, now heading west. Let me get you a street name." There was a short silence on Four's radio. "Pilgrim."

"The lady is back in her house. I'll catch up."

"I'm in the alley west of Tuller, heading south." The tracks were blown away as Jake scanned the concrete beneath his feet. He backed up to the last track he could find. *Wind—the snow's too light.* His light beam caught a tall wood gate that left a slight scrape in the snow. Jake opened it.

Lights illuminated the kitchen area at the back of the house. There, sitting at a table was a young black male, sipping on a bottle of Faygo, leaning back in a chair. Jake crept in for a closer look. The man was watching TV. It was a black portable with a rabbit ear antenna and trimmed in gold around the outer edge.

"Eight-Four?"

"Go Jake."

"Go one block west of Tuller. I'm about five houses south of Pilgrim. I think I have our man."

Jake kept one eye on the man watching TV and looked for headlights between the houses. He spotted the blue and white slowly heading south and threw the beam of his flashlight that way.

"Gottcha, Jake," came Justin's voice over the walkie-talkie.

In seconds, Justin was leaning against the back of the house with Jake. "Go knock on the front door, Shagg. I'll be watching Jack Parr with our burglar and see what he does."

Justin rang the front doorbell and knocked. The head of an older man came into view in the kitchen, then left. The burglar. continued watching the TV. In a minute, Justin appeared in the kitchen with the older man. Jake saw Justin point to the back door. A porch light went on and the door opened.

"Come on in, officer. I just told your partner here," as the man walked up a short flight of steps to the kitchen, "mah boy has been here all night, watchin' TV."

Justin flipped the beam of his flashlight down under the table. "Then why are his shoes a little wet on the bottom? Melting snow, maybe?"

There was a pause before the older man spoke. "Johnny, I can't help you no more."

The man was talking as he walked over to the cupboard where a bottle of Jack Daniels stood. "Anyone want a drink?"

"Mrs. Roberts, we'll have to hold your TV as evidence for a while. The detectives will be calling you."

"I'm sho glad you come by when you did. We need to get these bad kids off'n the streets."

Jake looked at the snow, that was all but gone, blown just to the edges of Mrs. Roberts' lawn. "I'm glad we showed up when we did too."

Jake was filling out the log sheet for Eight-Four as Justin headed back to the bureau. "Sometimes we get a little lucky, partner. Being at the right place at the right time," he said.

Justin just smiled and nodded. "Still looking for another job, Jake?"

"Yep, still looking kid."

The first part of March flew by for Jake. He kept his appointment with Jack Harnick at the Dow Corning Plant in

Midland, Michigan. He found the main gate to the plant and saw that he had more than an hour until the scheduled appointment. He spent the time drinking coffee at the Chat 'n' Chew restaurant, a place he passed while looking for the plant.

The day was a long one. First he took a written test, and was driven over to the Medical Department. They drew blood, took a urine sample, and did eye and hearing tests. A doctor then checked him over from head to toe. Once that was over, a security guard returned Jake to the Personnel Director's office.

"I just went over the written test we gave you." Jack Harnick put the test into a folder he had in front of him. "You scored better than most engineers we've hired. Can I get you a cup of coffee?"

"No thanks. I've had plenty."

"I'm just waiting on a couple of more people to show up. We want this preliminary stuff out of the way so you can get home at a decent time."

Jake was introduced to Phillip Schwab and Michael Stinton. Jack Harnick was the most vocal of the three. They shot him a few questions, mainly about why he was looking to leave his present employer. Jake was as honest as he could be. "I love being a police officer, but I have a wife and four children to think of."

Jake was winding his way south on I-75, heading to Detroit with the final words from Jack Harnick resounding in his head, *We've got a contract coming due with the Union the end of April. As soon as that is settled, we'll call.*

Jake knew this would not be a repeat of the City of Northville fiasco.

Chapter 27

"How fast is that Buick going Jake?"

"55 right now. Flip on the lights and I'll pull it over." It was just over three weeks until Easter. Jake goosed his Plymouth and was closing in on the Buick.

Duane motioned toward the curb. "It's a woman."

"The blue lights don't mean a thing to her. I'll hit her with the spotlight." Duane pulled the spotlight out from under the dash and opened his window. He waved the beam of the light across the woman's face. She stared straight ahead.

"I don't think she intends on stopping." Jake gave his car more gas and pulled ahead of the Buick. "Hit the siren." The wail of the siren didn't seem to get her attention either. The Buick continued at a steady 55 mph. Jake pulled ahead and started easing into the woman's lane.

"Jake, she doesn't want to stop." Duane waved the spotlight beam across her face again.

"I'll stop her or put her over the curb." Jake was easing Eight-Four into the woman's lane. "Talk to her over the PA."

Duane cut the siren and grabbed the mic while flipping a switch. "Lady, this is the police. Pull to the curb. That is an order."

The Buick started to slow and eased toward the curb. "Watch out for her Jake, she looks like a zombie." Jake kept the nose of his Plymouth just ahead of the Buick, making sure he had her pinned against the curb, but Duane couldn't get out his side.

"I'll get her. I don't want her to take off. She'll have to go backwards if she does." Jake slipped out his door and moved quickly around the trunk and approached the driver's window. It was rolled up. He tapped on the glass with his flashlight.

"Roll down your window lady." She rolled it down three inches and the woman's eyes moved to look at Jake. "I'll need to see your license and registration, ma'am."

The woman searched her purse and found the license and registration. She eased them out of the slim window opening.

"Is there any reason you were driving 55 in a 35 mile per hour zone?" Jake waited for a response. There was none. "Didn't you see our flashing blue lights?"

She finally spoke, "I just got paid tonight and I was in a hurry to get home. My mom worries about me on payday nights driving through these black neighborhoods."

Her words were clear and concise. "Ma'am, I need you to step out of the car. Have you been drinking?"

She slowly opened her door and stepped out of the car. "That's absurd. Why would you think that?"

"Maybe because of your speed, and because it took me a half mile to get you to pull over." He watched her every move.

"Now walk to the back of your car, turn around and balance yourself on one leg." She followed his directions. *She's sober.* Jake reached in and pulled the keys from the ignition. "Okay, have a seat in your car. I'm going to move my car. Just sit still and wait until I come back with your license."

She got into her car and started to cry.

Jake backed his Plymouth out of the lane of traffic and got out his ticket book.

"Jeez Jake, you're actually gonna write a ticket."

"Yeah, for five over. Kind of a warning and it'll make Orth happy."

He was writing the name of Rosemary DeAngelo in the appropriate place on the ticket.

"Don't look now, Jake, but she's coming back to talk to you."

Jake rolled down his window as the woman approached. She looked down at Jake writing in his ticket book.

"You're writing a fuckin' ticket? Why you cocksucker!"

Jake started to open his door and gave it a quick heave. She jumped back. "I'd advise you to have a seat in your car ma'am and stay put. Unless you want to call your mother from the Seventh Precinct?"

The woman turned and got back into the Buick without a word. Jake watched as her head went out of sight, then finished writing the ticket on the hood of his car.

Jake walked up to her window and tapped on the glass. The woman was lying on the seat crying. She rose and rolled down the window.

"Note that you have the court copy of the ticket." He handed her the thin yellow second copy. "This one you cannot pay. You are to appear on the date noted on the bottom of the ticket. The judge will assess the fine. That's what your name calling bought."

Jake started to leave, then turned back. "I was going to write you for five over, just as a warning. Next time maybe you'll think before you talk."

He climbed back into his car and watched Rosemary DeAngelo drive off. "Kinda hard on her weren't you?"

"Yeah. I write my first mover this year and see what I get? Now I'm a fuckin' cocksucker." Duane laughed.

The next night Orth was holding roll call. "Eight-Three, Bohy and Lambert. Eight-Four, Wattles and Bush. Bush I have mail for you. Here, hand this back."

Jake took the envelope. It had ten postage stamps across the top and addressed to Patrolman John A. Bush, TMU, The Detroit Police Department. The words "Special Delivery" were stamped above his name. He opened it as the lieutenant continued roll call.

It was a card, a spiritual bouquet. He saw that 10 masses would be said, 10 rosaries, 10 Our Father's and 10 Hail Mary's. It was signed by Rosemary DeAngelo.

Jake was waiting for Duane to climb in the car. He was driving first. "What kind of fan mail are you getting, Jake?"

"A card from my girlfriend from last night."

"Already?"

"Yeah. It took about a buck to get it sent Special Delivery.

"What was so important?"

"She sent me a spiritual bouquet."

"What the hell is that?"

"It's a card that says someone is offering up so many masses and prayers for you. It's a Catholic thing."

"What, first you're a cocksucker and now she is praying for you?"

"That's what I can't figure out. She might be saying she is sorry for calling me names, or that I am such an asshole, I need the prayers."

"I don't think she's sorry."

"Neither do I." Jake put the car in drive and headed out of the garage.

The TMU was off the streets for a day of riot training on Belle Isle. It began at 8:00 a.m. Jake was bored by 9 practicing "Vee" formations that did not work the past July.

He went through the motions with the rest of the men. *There'll never be another riot.* The dust flew as the formation did their Step-Stomp, Step-Stomp.

****

Dr. Martin Luther King Jr. was assassinated in Memphis Tennessee while staying at the Lorraine Motel. The news shocked the country and put the Detroit Police on full alert again.

The Tactical Mobile Unit's day shift was called in to start at nine. "Plan on twelve-hour shifts," was the last thing the sergeant said as Jake hung up the phone. All days off were cancelled again.

No chance of a riot. Boy was I wrong. Jake packed a lunch.

Inspector Sylvers took the podium. Jake took note of the last thing the Inspector said. "We are going to be prepared for anything. Hopefully the city learned something from last July. If anything starts because of the King killing, we plan on stopping it as fast as possible. Any questions?"

There were none. The Inspector turned roll call over to Lt. Orth.

The Lieutenant went through the car assignment list. The three men assigned to each car were called. There was a full compliment of sixty men for the twenty cars.

"The low numbered cars will cover the Tenth and Thirteenth Precincts. We want two cars working together. One, you are with Two. The rest are to follow suit. The high numbered cars are assigned to Number Five and Seven. Pay close attention to business places. Any signs of mobs or crowds gathering let Eight-Six-O know immediately."

The crews were filing out into the basement garage. "'Bout time somebody shut that nigger up," Dick Whyser said as he lit his cigar.

Jake overheard the remark and responded, "Alive, King was just a voice. Now he'll be a martyr. That's not very smart."

"One of your hero's, Jake?"

"He's a whole lot better than Malcom X or Stokely Carmicheal. King was not preaching to get a gun and shoot a cop."

Jake reached his car where Shagg and Duane were checking the shotguns in the trunk. Duane spoke, "Now what are you and Whyser arguing about?"

"He's glad King got shot. I'm worried about another riot."

"All I see is that it means overtime. I need the money." Duane put the last of the two Winchesters in the box and closed the trunk.

"How long did it take them to pay us for last summer?" asked Shaggert.

"We did get paid though," answered Duane.

Jake climbed in behind the wheel. "I'm wondering if more of the coloreds are going to start listening to the rabble rousers."

Shagg didn't ask; he slid into the jump seat. Duane tried getting into the back. "Justin, can you move the seat up a bit? I'm kinda cramped back here."

"Back seats aren't really built for 250 pounders, eh Duane?" Jake adjusted the mirror to look at Duane as he asked the question.

"Just drive on chauffer, I'll be all right."

Eight-Three was the lead car. Bohy, Harrison and Conway made up that crew. Bohy was driving and chose Twelfth Street for his first slow cruise.

"I guess he wants to get right in there and see if there's any action where the riot started," Jake said.

He followed two car lengths back. "Shagg, keep an eye on the roof tops."

The street was very quiet. Too quiet No more than two people lingered here and there, watching the two blue and whites slowly drive north. "Four, this is Three. Grand River is next." Justin acknowledged the message on the car-to-car frequency. Four's radio scanned Central Dispatch. There were no calls on crowds. There was nothing to suggest how people were going to react to the news of King's death.

"Maybe we kicked enough ass last July," offered Duane from the back seat.

"Maybe it's the lull before the storm," answered Justin.

Just what will the people of Detroit do about a sniper attack in Memphis? I do need to get out of here.

Jake tried to focus on the people on the street and any car that might look suspicious. His thoughts kept going back to the hopes of a move for him and his family, away from the streets of Detroit.

Day two had the starting time rotating back an hour. The plan was to slowly work back to a 6 a.m. start for the day shift and 6 p.m. for the night shift.

Duane drove while Justin slid in the back. They were the lead car. "Any ideas where to go, Jake?"

"Let's spend some time on Woodward. Maybe we can talk to Ray Shoulders and see if he has a pulse on what is going on."

"Who's Ray Shoulders?" Duane asked as he took Chene to the Ford Freeway and headed toward the Thirteenth Precinct.

"He runs a TV repair business. He's also a Pastor at a small Negro Baptist Church."

279

Jake told Duane and Justin about his first meeting with Ray Shoulders at the TV repair shop. "I was walking a beat on midnights and found the back door unlocked."

He said he just got to talking with the last customer and forgot to turn the locks on it. "Thanks for the call, officer. And be sure to stop in anytime."

"I made it a point to stop when walking Woodward. Ray always had a pot of coffee going and usually had someone visiting. One time it was Willy Horton's brother. Willy's family lived just down the street from Ray's shop."

"Willy Horton, the Tiger's new left fielder?" asked Justin from the back seat.

"Yes, Willy Horton."

"Why would you want to talk to a preacher?" Duane asked.

"After the riot I saw in the paper that he was appointed to a citizen's committee. That's why I think we should stop and see what's going on. He might know."

A big "Closed" sign hung on the door of Ray's TV Repair.

"Try around the block on John R. He has a storefront church there," Jake offered.

"I'm not too sure we want to go driving around looking for some black minister to talk to."

"What harm will it do?" Jake asked.

"We might want to talk to Bohy and his crew before we go mingling with the enemy."

"What enemy? I just thought we might talk and see if he has a pulse on what might be going on."

"And he would tell you?"

"Hell, I don't know and I don't know if he would know anything."

Duane didn't make the turns to head toward John R. Jake went silent, reflecting on Duane's words.

Mingling with the enemy? By talking to a black man?

280

Jake knew that there was no arguing a black and white issue with Duane or some other police officers. He let Duane drive aimlessly around the Thirteenth and Tenth Precincts.

After seven days of twelve-hour shifts, nothing of note happened. The bureau went back to eight-hour shifts. By the middle of the month the TMU was back to two man crews and regular days off. *Thank God* thought Jake as the lieutenant announced the changes.

****

"Yes, I'll be right over." Jake hung up the phone. "Anne, mom wants me to come over. She's got a leaky faucet."

"Say good-night to the kids then. They'll be in bed by the time you get back."

Jake kissed the four kids, one at a time. "Say your prayers. And mind your mom." Jake stopped in his room and slipped his off-duty revolver in his back pocket.

"Think you'll need that at your mom's?" Anne asked, as Jake walked past.

"No, but you know I have to carry it when I am out of the house."

"I'll feel better when you don't have to carry it at all. How's the job-hunt going? You said in a year you'd be gone."

"You know mom'll be calling again if I am not there within five minutes. I've gotta go."

Jake went out the front door and crossed the lawn to make the trek to his mom's who lived across the street and ten houses down. He could see her porch light as his eyes adjusted to the darkness.

Why did I buy this house? Every time the wind blows or a faucet drips, she calls. "Jake, you need to come over right now." *I wish Dave lived a bit closer.*

Jake walked on his side of the street. These trips happened all too often since his dad died over two years before.

281

The sound of breaking glass broke his train of thought. He was in front of Marie Baluch's house and slowed, walking slowly to the driveway between Baluch's and the Pelka's house.

In the darkness Jake made out a figure reaching inside the side door window while propping open the storm door with his body. "Police," Jake yelled. The storm door slammed as the figure ran through the yard, jumping over the back fence into the alley.

Jake leap-frogged the fence, trying to keep up with the running figure. He pulled the .38 from his back pocket.

"Stop you son-of-a-bitch or I'll shoot." The words just made the man run faster and jump another four-foot cyclone fence into Glen Sather's yard. Jake followed suit and cut around the darkened house. He stopped.

No one was running. He stood, straining to hear footfalls. Nothing. Jake listened. Minutes passed. He turned and slowly walked back into Glen's yard. *Did he go over the fence next to the garage then back into the alley?*

He strained his ears and heard nothing. Jake stood still knowing whomever he was chasing might be doing the same.

He might be in the next yard or long gone.

Jake's heartrate slowed. He leaned against Glen's house. Glen and Linda, his wife, went to bed early. Their house was dark.

Jake knew the neighborhood as well as the back of his hand. Two houses down to his left was the corner of Bringard and Strasburg. He played Hide and Seek or Blind Man's Bluff many times with Hank, Jerry, Jack, Dave and Tommy under the street light. This house, Glen's, was only two doors down and across the street from his mom's.

Mom is talking to Anne on the phone by now. Now, both of them are wondering where I am.

Jake waited, wanting to light a cigarette. He thought better. He was going to give it ten minutes.

Jake heard a rustling in front of the house and peered around the corner. There, standing next to the porch, was a dark figure that slowly started toward the sidewalk. He had, no doubt, been lying on the ground on the other side of Glen's front porch. The figure's back was to Jake as he walked casually on the sidewalk back in the direction of the Balluch house.

Pistol in hand, Jake broke into a run. As the figure turned, Jake hit him with a cross-body block, rolled and thrust the Colt into the man's left eye.

"Move and you're dead."

The Bogucki's and the Schultz's porch lights went on. People on Strasburg always heard things outside.

Tina Bogucki stuck her head out the door, yelling, "What the hell's going on out there?"

Jake did not look away from his prisoner. He knew the voice.

"Tina, call the police. It's me, Jake. Tell them I'm hanging onto a burglar."

Jake rolled the man onto his stomach and put his knee in the man's back. "Hands straight to the side and open wide. Grab some concrete."

In minutes a black police car pulled to the curb where four porch lights illuminated the neighbors standing on their porches. Jake still had one knee in the middle of the man's back. The two men in uniform approached with their flashlights. "Bush from TMU. Can one of you put some cuffs on this guy?"

The handcuffs were in place and the prisoner was put in the back seat of Fifteen-Ten. Two small pry bars were found in the man's pants pocket. He had no identification and wasn't talking.

"I'll be back in a minute. I need to tell my mom I won't be over to fix her faucet."

Two hours later Jake was finished with the Number Fifteen detectives at the Baluch house. He walked in his house to find his wife sitting up in a dark living room.

"Thought you'd be in bed by now," he said as he turned on a light and saw her.

"Jake, we're raising four kids. We cannot…I cannot sleep at night worrying about what is going to happen next. Your mom told me you arrested someone."

"A burglar." Jake sat down next to Anne and put his arm around her, pulling her head onto his shoulder.

"Aren't you even a little happy I caught the guy?"

"No. I want out of this town." Tears finished the sentence.

"I'll make some calls tomorrow. I'll see what's happening in Midland."

"What about that job your brother talked about?"

"I'm a cop, Anne. I'm not going to sell insurance."

"And when one of our kids gets hurt or killed, how will you live with yourself?"

Jake got up. "I'll go tuck them in." He stopped in the doorway and looked back. "Just give me some time."

I'm a cop woman. I like being a cop, can't you understand that? He quietly opened the door to Mike's bedroom.

Four tries and a week later Jake did get a call through to Jack Harnick, the Personnel Director at Dow Corning in Midland. "Sorry to say, Jake, they went out on strike the end of April. That's why we haven't called you. Check back in a month or so and I may know more."

Jake hung up the phone. In one sense, breathing a sigh of relief.

Chapter 28

Jake and his crew were back on afternoons. It was a warm, sunny day in May and they were working the First Precinct. Shagg was driving.

"What I can't figure out is how you get so lucky?"

"What are you talking about?"

"Catching bad guys. Duane says you just fall into shit."

"That's 'cause Duane doesn't have his eyes open. Hell, as a matter of fact, he doesn't hear too well either."

Justin drove Eight-Four up Woodward off of Michigan. Downtown Detroit was home to J.L. Hudson's, Sanders Bakery, S.S. Kresgee's and all the shops that a woman could ask for. They passed the Fox Theater.

"There are people all over the place. Like ants crawling from store to store."

"You should have seen it before a clerk got killed about two years ago. Then there was last year's riot."

Jake thought a while then started reminiscing aloud. "Back when I was a kid, my mom would load us up on a streetcar and come all the way downtown to spend the day so she could look at everything at every counter on every floor at Hudson's." He let out a chuckle. "At least it seemed like that to me. It was not a fun time, me tagging along with an older sister and a younger brother that I fought with all the time. The only salvation was the lunch counter at Sanders, if we behaved ourselves. I always had a slice of the ice cream chocolate cake roll covered with thick,hot chocolate sauce."

"You're avoiding my question?"

"What question?"

"On how you just happen to fall into things?"

"First off, you have to want to be a cop."

"Duane said you're looking for another job."

"That doesn't mean I don't want to be a cop. Second, you have to keep your eyes open. What else has Duane been telling you?"

285

"Nuthin, really. I think you're his hero. He always talks about not wanting to lose a partner like you."

"I'm flattered." Jake checked the hot sheet on a car that passed. "Justin, I am going to tell you what an old partner told me a few years ago. That's to watch the street people. It's as simple as that."

"Man, there's a hundred people on this block in front of us. How can you watch all of 'em?"

"Pick one. Pick someone who is out of place or is real concerned about our blue and white driving by. Like at this bus stop." Jake pointed to the crowd of people waiting for a bus. "What do you see?"

Justin was driving by the Central Methodist Church at the corner of Woodward and Grand Circus Park. There were twenty people waiting for the next bus heading north. Justin scanned the crowd. "I see a bunch of women waiting to catch a bus."

"What about the guy?"

"One white guy. Seems to be walking with a limp."

"Where was he looking?"

"He looked away as we drove by."

"Before he saw us, his eyes were going from woman to woman."

"I didn't see that."

"Well, maybe I'm reading more into it than what it really is. But that's me. Take the next corner and let's end up on the other side of Woodward out of sight of the bus stop. I'll slip out of the car, grab a cigarette and watch him for a while. You take the car and lay low around the corner."

Justin made the turn saying, "I'll get out of the car." Jake slid in behind the wheel as Justin got out, talking the portable radio.

"He's probably just a guy heading home to Highland Park. I'll give you two buses unless he gets on the first one." Jake drove and found an open spot in front of a fire hydrant two blocks south. He could not see the bus stop, but he could watch the street traffic. He watched one northbound bus go by. Justin did not radio that the guy got on it.

Five minutes later, a second bus was passing in front of Jake. A minute passed.

"Four. I'm in foot pursuit of a white male heading west across Woodward. Now north on First."

The Plymouth engine roared as Jake flipped on his blue lights, made a U-turn and drove in the direction Justin was chasing his man.

"Just crossed Park, heading west again," were words coming out between Justin's panting.

Jake cut off a Checker Cab made a right, a left and then took another right.

Eight-Four approached Temple when the man appeared suddenly running into the right front fender of Jake's car. He flipped over the hood, hitting the ground and took off again.

Jake was out of his door running. The man headed back south, then west again. Jake was losing ground. His sides ached. His lungs burned. The man was now a half of a block away from Jake as he slipped between northbound cars.

Jake opened a door of a car stuck in traffic. He slid in beside the elderly black woman that was driving. "I need some help, lady. I am trying to catch that white guy that's in front of us." Jake pointed toward the man.

The man slowed to a walk when he did not see a uniform behind him. At the next corner he turned north. Jake slid out of the car and ran to catch up to the man. The sound of Jake's footfalls made the man take off again. He cut across the street, dodging in and out of cars. Jake was falling behind, but kept the man in sight. The man jumped a four-foot cyclone fence into a parking lot. He was running for the open gate at the attendant's booth.

Jake saw Justin running from the left, hitting the man in full stride with a hip check. The man went head first into the wall of the attendant's booth.

Jake got to the prone man as Justin was squeezing on the handcuffs. Jake bent over putting his hands on his knees, trying to catch his breath.

"You might be getting too old for this, Jake," smiled Justin as he lifted the prisoner to his feet.

"I, I gotta give up them damn cigarettes," Jake said pushing the words out between gasps.

"I would have had him right at the get go, but he threw the purse at me. It gave him a head start."

"That what he did, grab a purse?"

"Yeah. Must not have liked the first group waiting for the bus. Just after it left five other women showed up, one with three bags and a purse hanging down. When she was repositioning the bags he grabbed her purse." Justin was beaming. "By the way, he lost his limp in a hurry as he ran across Woodward."

"Where's the purse?"

"The front seat of our car. I carried it as I ran. Musta looked real cute, me carrying a red purse." He smiled. "I hope the woman is still there waiting for us."

The scanner picked up the run for "One-Eleven, Central Methodist Church, meet a woman on a purse snatching."

The woman was standing in front of the church when Eight-Four crossed Woodward. One-Eleven had just pulled to the curb. They said they'd make the report.

John Harvey age 22 of 1522 Cass was taken to Number One and booked for Robbery Unarmed.

"How'd you know he was going to grab a purse?"

"Didn't. But he was the only guy at the bus stop. Hell, he might have been looking for a date. I guessed right this time."

"You know you almost ran him over."

"Too bad I missed." Jake smiled as he looked at his partner. "Damn, I'm even thinking like Jess."

"Who's Jess?"

"The guy who taught me to watch the street people. A good cop."

"Where's he now?"

"Mora Minnesota. Running a bulk oil business."

"He quit?"

"Sometimes good cops have to quit to keep their sanity."

It was June 3rd just after lunch. "All right kids, get your sweaters It's a little cool out. We'll take a walk to the store and get an ice cream."

Jake had just hung up the phone after talking to the Personnel Department at Dow Corning. He'd promised Anne to call. They were still on strike.

"Daddy, can we ride our bikes?" asked Debbie.

"Yeah, daddy, we want to ride our bikes," chimed in Michelle.

"Me too, me too," Mike was yelling as he found the sweater Jake laid out for him on the couch.

Jake was watching the kids since it was a Monday. Anne worked at the Detroit Bank and Trust on Mondays and Fridays. Jake was bundling up Jeanette for a ride in the stroller. "Oh, alright. Go get them out of the garage."

The older girls were home from school. Pulaski students had the day off. A teacher's conference is what Anne's note had said.

Jake led Jeanette by the hand and put her in the stroller outside the side door of their house. She was almost 16 months old. Michelle came out of the garage on her bike, followed by Deb with Mike lagging behind on his tricycle.

"Let's go dad. I want chocolate swirl," called Michelle as she rode past to the corner.

"I'm getting Strawberry," said Deb, her bike whizzing by.

Mike was pedaling as hard as he could to keep up. "I want two scoops of V'nilla."

All three stopped at the corner and got off of their bikes to walk them across Collingham. "Wait up, kids." Jake cautioned them as he approached with the stroller. He looked both ways, then up and down Strasburg. "Okay, walk your bikes."

Mike hurried pushing his tricycle around the outside of the girls. "Beat you guys across." Deb and Michelle got to the other curb before he did after cutting him off. "Dad, they cheated…"

The older girls were eight and seven. Mike was going to be six that fall. The parade of two kids on bikes, one on a tricycle and Jake pushing the stroller with Jeanette, proceeded toward Eight Mile and the store where they hand dipped ice cream cones. Deb and Michelle turned the corner heading toward the store and stopped. They straddled their bikes, not saying a word. Mike, Jake and the stroller caught up.

Jake saw what stopped them. Two black police cars with their red lights rotating were in front of The Eight Mile Grocery a half block away.

"Kids, wait here. Deb, here, keep and eye on Jeanette. I'll see what's up."

Jake walked in the front door. "The store's closed," yelled a police officer from the back. His partner came out of the walk-in cooler. Two other police officers came out of the back room beyond the cooler.

"Bill, get on the radio and call for the detectives," said the first officer of the two. "And no one touch anything."

"Bush, TMU," Jake said to the approaching officer as he flashed his tin.

"Well pal, looks like the lady working here is dead in the cooler," answered Bill. "Stop here often?"

"All my life," answered Jake. "I grew up down the street."

"I'm Miller, 15-5. You say you know the people that work here?"

"Yes. Mrs. Lagorio is the owner. Her husband died last year. She's generally here most of the time. Lives upstairs."

"Take a quick peek in the cooler. But don't touch anything."

Jake walked toward the back of the store. The walk-in cooler door was propped open with a case of Stroh's.

Lying on the floor with her head twisted, facing the door in a pool of blood was Margaret Lagorio wearing her trademark meat cutter's apron. He walked back to the front door where Miller was waiting for him. "Yes, that's the owner Margaret Lagorio."

"Can you stick around? The Dicks are on the way. They may want to talk to you."

"My kids are at the corner. We were coming here for an ice cream. I need to get them home."

"Will you be there for a while?"

"Can be. 20322 Strasburg. I'll take the kids home and wait around for a while."

"Give me your name again and a phone number."

Jake walked back to his children waiting on the corner of Eight Mile and Strasburg. Michelle was the first to speak. "Can we get our ice cream, Dad?"

"Not right now, kids. There's been an accident. The store is closed."

"Aw, Dad. I want an ice cream. You promised." Mike's bottom lip was puffed out as he spoke.

"Later, kids. We have to go home and wait. The police may want to talk to me." Jake grabbed the stroller and turned it around. "Come on. We'll go to another store later."

Jeanette started crying in the stroller. "I' crea, daddy I' crea."

"Later, Jet. I'll take you to another store."

The parade of two bikes, a trike and the stroller headed back down Strasburg. Jake was silent as the three older kids jockeyed for position ahead.

"I want chocolate chip," yelled Mike.

The voices of the older girls were drowned out by Jake's thoughts.

Yes, Anne is right. I have to get these kids out of Detroit. A murder one block from the house. Mrs. Lagorio. No more "Hi Jake. I know, Pepsi. Twelve full ounces that's a lot."

He heard that old advertising jingle every time he stopped in there when she was behind the counter. She started doing that eighteen years before when he was collecting for his route with the Detroit Free Press.

Jake just finished shaving and was putting on his uniform when he heard the phone ring in the kitchen.

"There's a Jack Harnick on the phone for you. It's Dow Corning."

Jake's heart was beating rapidly as he went to the phone. The call was short and sweet. The strike was over. There was an opening on the Security Department for the midnight shift.

"Would you like to come up and talk with the department people before you make a decision?"

Jake checked his calendar. "I'm off on Wednesday the 12th. Can we set something up for that day?"

"Let's set it for 10 a.m. at the personnel office."

"I'll be there." Jake hung up the phone.

Midland Michigan. Three hours from here. Anne will be happy and the kids 'll be safe.

Jake already had checked on the town. Midland was a city of about 25,000 with little or no crime. He was guessing that the starting pay would less than what he was getting in Detroit. He put on his tie and badge and headed off to work.

Jake knew they could make it even at less pay. He had money in his police retirement fund.

His wife agreed. "Promise me you'll do this."

"I guess we've talked about it enough." He kissed the kids and his wife goodbye.

From being a police officer to a night watchman. He laughed at the thought as he drove to work. *Well, just maybe the Midland Police Department will have an opening soon.* That was his outside hope. Someday being a cop again, doing what he loved.

Chapter 29

The return address on letter was from the office of District Inspector Lincoln Walsh. Jake's hands were shaking as he opened it. He read the paragraph twice.

"You are scheduled for a termination interview at 10 a.m. on June 24, 1968."

Jake had submitted his resignation papers. His final day wearing badge number 2441 would be June 28th.

It was hard enough for him to fill out the forms, now someone from the department was going to ask him why he was quitting.

Oh well, its all part of saying good-bye. At least I won't have to face Tony Bertolini.

District Inspector Bertolini was now in charge of the Western District. The TMU came under the Central District. He knew it would be easier to talk to someone he never worked for.

As the days went by Jake's biggest concern would be that Inspector Walsh would ask him to stay. Jake's dreams were punctuated with the words, "We need men like you." But Jake knew he had to leave. He promised his wife. He owed it to his children.

Deep within, Jake liked being a cop more than anything else. He liked wearing the badge, carrying the revolver and bearing the responsibility that came with both. Above all, he liked slamming the barred door on a bad guy.

The closest thing to orgasm. He laughed at the thought, but knew that's how he felt.

At 9:55 a.m. Jake was standing at the receptionist's desk. "I'm Officer Bush. I have a ten o'clock appointment with the Inspector."

"Please have a seat. I'll let him know you are here."

Jake sat in the chair against the wall next to a stack of magazines on an oval table. To his right was the inspector's office. Jake never met Inspector Walsh. He could see that the inspector, a gray haired wrinkled neck man, was standing with his back to the door. He was looking out at the Detroit skyline from the fifth floor office. Jake knew that somewhere on the mahogany desk was a file on John Anthony Bush. In that file Jake knew were copies of the 14 citations and 15 commendations he had received since 1962. The receptionist stopped at the doorway.

"Patrolman Bush is here for his exit interview, sir."

Jake could see the inspector didn't turn his head. He continued looking out the window as he spoke.

"Get a statement from him. I don't have time for quitters."

The words stung as the receptionist returned to her desk.

So much for his record. So much for being asked to stay.

"I'm just to get a statement from you," she said as she slid back into her chair. "Can you tell me why you are resigning?"

Jake stood and walked to her desk. He tried to hide the tear rolling down his left cheek. His voice cracked, "Because of people like him." Jake turned and took the three steps to the door. It quietly closed behind him.

During the drive home Jake realized that he was just a number. In seconds Inspector Walsh dashed his fantasy that Detroit wanted men like him. When he got home he checked the count-down numbers in his pocket memo book. He had four days to work.

Jake withdrew from the card games and the groups of officers retelling their war stories before and after his shifts. The days became a blur as Duane talked endlessly on how Jake would never make it as a "Night Watchman."

As the days were going by and the clock was ticking, Jake was stuck working the day shift.

"How many more days Mr. Night Watchman?" Duane asked.

That doesn't even deserve and answer.

Jake quietly kept driving, heading north on Chene Street. It was just after ten in the morning. In the distance he could see a gray Corvair turning off of the Edsel Ford service drive to head south toward their car. It was a block away.

The car did not straighten out of the turn. Instead it crossed over into the northbound lane, jumped the curb and crashed into the concrete overpass railing.

"Jezus Christ, a drunk first thing in the morning," Duane mumbled.

Jake gave the Plymouth some gas pulling crossways in the northbound lanes to block traffic. He jumped out of the blue and white, running to the driver's door.

The window was down. Jake reached in and moved the head of the black man that was behind the wheel. The man's lips were turning blue and saliva was running out the corner of his mouth. He opened the door and pulled the man out, laying him on the sidewalk next to the Corvair.

"Duane, call Fire Rescue. Quick!"

Jake tilted the man's head back, pinched off his nose and put his mouth over the man's mouth. He blew three quick blasts of air into the man. There was no response. Jake took another deep breath and repeated the blasts of air into the man's mouth, then started pumping on his chest. On the third attempt Jake heard a siren in the background and smelled a foul odor. The man had soiled himself. Jake held him.

The Fire Rescue Unit put the man on a stretcher and wheeled him into the back of their unit.

"He's dead. We'll take him to Receiving Hospital. I'll call you with a doctor's name as soon as they make it official."

"We'll be at Number Seven. We're Eight-Four." Jake turned and climbed back behind the wheel of his car. He grabbed the mic and spoke, arranging for a tow truck at the accident scene. Death was not new to Jake, but he did not expect it this day.

The ride to Number Seven was quiet. Duane never bothered to start a report. He knew Jake did all the typing.

At the station Duane went to the coffee pot while Jake grabbed a blank PCR and found a typewriter.

The Fire Rescue team called to relay the information to complete the report. Anderson Peach was 62 and lived at 8742 Leland. Receiving hospital would notify the family. Jake pulled the short report out of the typewriter.

Jake rejoined Duane in the car. Duane was behind the wheel. It was near noon. "Ready for lunch?" Duane asked as he started the car.

"You're driving." Jake added the entry on Anderson Peach to their log sheet. Duane headed straight to Biff's restaurant at the corner of Grand Boulevard and Jefferson. At the counter Jake gave his quick order to the waitress and got up.

"Goin' to wash up."

"Scrub up good. You need it."

"Meaning what?"

"If you don't know—Oh forget it."

Duane's words fell into the background noise as Jake found the men's room. He lathered up his face and hands, wondering what Duane was going to say next.

He'll miss me. That brought a smile to Jake's face as he toweled off. *I won't miss you, buddy.*

Duane turned Eight-Four onto the bridge leading to Belle Isle after lunch. "Time to get a fishing report."

"The bosses said to stay off of the island."

"What are you worried about? You only got a couple of days left."

"I'd rather be working the street than killing time on Belle Isle."

"I'm driving, I make the choices." He let out a grunt. "Just pretend it is next week and you don't have that badge."

The car slowly crept around the road that circled the island park. It was the end of June, school was out and the sun was hot. The beach was crowed with kids running and jumping into the Detroit River.

At the first fishing pier extending out into the water, a father was baiting a hook for his son. The kid was jumping up and down, no doubt trying to get dad to hurry. The next dock had two men leaning back in canvas folding chairs. They had bells attached to the ends of the poles in the rod holders they clamped to the pier railing. Empty beer bottles were at their feet. One was offering the other a light for his cigar.

The strong odor of hops filled the island air as the warm breeze brought the unmistakable smell down river from the Stroh's and Black Label breweries to the west.

On a second cruise around the island Jake saw more kids lined up to get into the bathhouse and onto the beach. The dad was trying to untangle the line on a reel at the first fishing dock. Before Eight-Four got to the second dock that faced the Canadian side of the island Jake piped up. "Don't you think it's time to check our area?"

"Hey, you're the guy moving up north. Getting out of the city. This is my up north. This is my fresh country air."

"Well the smell of the breweries is getting to me. Let's get off the fuckin' island."

"Alright, alright." Duane's voice dropped into a whisper "The quitter wants to do some police work." He made a quick U-turn and jumped into the right lane. It led to the approach to leave the island.

The word "quitter" hurt, but Jake let it go. His eyes were on a traffic jam at the midpoint on the bridge. People were outside of their cars on Jake's side of the bridge.

As Eight-Four approached, Jake spotted a woman's head towering above the crowd. "Duane, there's a woman on the rail that's going to jump."

Duane looked over. "Who cares? It'll be just another nigger in the river."

Jake did not wait for Duane to stop. He jumped out of the slowly moving police car and ran, pushing his way through the twenty or so people watching the woman teeter on the rail.

Voices were heard as he moved through the crowd. "Po-lice. Po-lice."

The woman, wearing a nurse's uniform, heard the voices and looked over her shoulder. She saw Jake and his badge. "Don't come any closer. I'll jump."

Duane's words were still echoing in Jake's mind. He repeated them.

"Who cares? It'd just be another nigger in the river."

Jake's cutting remark froze the woman long enough where he could grab her and pull her off of the railing. With his other arm he reached down and grabbed the purse and the white cap at the base of the railing before pushing through the crowd to his car.

He could hear the rumbling around him.

"Man, he called her a nigger."

"Honky fuckin' Po-lice is all he is."

Jake pushed the woman into the back of his car., sliding in beside her.

"Quick, Duane. Let's get the hell out of here."

"Where to, Mr. Hero?"

"Receiving Hospital. Anywhere but here. The mob's pissed."

Duane gunned Eight-Four over the low divider hump in the center of the bridge to cut around the cars at the scene. At Jefferson he made a left, heading toward downtown and Receiving Hospital.

In the back seat the woman was screaming and started swinging at Jake. He caught her arms and held them.

"White honky son-of-a-bitch. Why didn't you let me jump?"

"I couldn't..."

"What I do ain't none of your business. Remember, I'm just a nigger."

She pulled her arms free and turned to stare out the side window.

"I just called you that to distract you."

"Yeah, sure. A white mutha fuckin' is all you are." Tears were rolling down her cheeks. She turned her face into the seatback and sobbed.

Duane turned the rearview mirror to look at Jake.

"That's your typical thank you, Mr. White Honky, in case you missed it."

Both of their words had Jake reach his piss-off point.

"You know what lady, why don't you come back and jump on Saturday? Ol' Duane here and someone else may not stop you..." He found himself shouting. "...but today, while I'm still wearing this badge, I can't and won't let you jump."

It took a few moments, but the sobbing stopped. The nurse pulled her face out of the seatback and started to wipe the tears with her hand. Jake offered his handkerchief. She dried her cheeks and blew her nose.

"Can I have a cigarette?"

Jake offered her one from his pack of Pall Malls. He lit it for her. "You're a nurse?"

"Yes."

"Which hospital?"

"Grace. Grace hospital." she answered, just above a whisper.

"Got any kids?"

Her eyes widened and her voice rose. "My babies. My babies. I forgot about my babies." She started crying again burying her face into Jake's handkerchief.

"Where they at?"

"My momma's. A block from where I live."

"Give me her number. I'll call her to make sure they're all right."

"Promise me you'll do that."

"I will. How old are they?"

"They're twins. Five and a half."

"Mine are from eight down to one. I have four. Three girls and a boy."

"You're probably a good daddy." She dried her eyes again.

"What brought about this trip to the bridge?"

Jake's question unfolded a tale of a registered nurse who worked in surgery. She went in to work after dropping her boys off at her mom's. Her husband left for the Chrysler Plant an hour before. She got sick, a touch of the flu or something. The hospital put her in a cab and sent her home.

When she got there she found her husband screwing the neighbor from upstairs on their living room floor.

"I just panicked and ran. I had to get away." She turned and looked at Jake. "Mister, I love that man. Loved him since I was sixteen and he loved me. At least I thought he did. To see him there..." She buried her eyes into the handkerchief again, sobbing softly.

"Forget him. You've got a couple of boys to look after. What's their names?"

"William and Benjamin. After my daddy. Do we have to go to the hospital? I'm okay now. My boys need me."

"Yes, we have to. Formalities. Once the doctor says you can go, you'll be on your way. I'll call your mom so she won't worry."

"Don't tell her about the bridge."

"I won't. Just promise me you'll be there to take care of Benjamin and William and to watch them grow up."

Eight-Four pulled into the back of Receiving Hospital near the emergency entrance. Jake escorted Leona Hart up the stairs. Duane lagged behind. Jake found the ward used for mental patients and directed Leona to a chair beside one of six gurneys along the wall. The gurney's had thick leather straps dangling off of them.

In a corner behind a desk sat a black nurse filling out papers. "Uh-uh, honey. Put her on the gurney and strap her down." She stood and headed toward Jake. "All patients have to be strapped down."

"She'll be okay. She's fine now."

"I ain't wrasslin' with some crazy bitch. Strap her down." The ward nurse pushed a button on the wall.

Leona started to climb onto the gurney. Jake gently grabbed her arm. "I'll stay here with her 'til the doctor comes."

"Then you're gonna do the wrasslin', not me."

In two minutes two black men entered the far end of the ward. They brushed past Duane who was leaning on one side of the doorway. One was an orderly. The other Jake judged to be a doctor by the long white coat and the stethoscope hanging around his neck.

While the orderly stood next to Leona, Jake explained to the doctor what had happened and told what he knew about Leona Hart. Dr. Isaacs nodded as Jake talked. The doctor looked at the orderly. "Russell, she'll be all right. Miss Booth, I'll take Mrs. Hart to my office."

Jake looked at Leona, then at the doctor. "I have a call to make. If you're done with me, I'll get out of here." Jake turned to leave.

Leona jumped up from the chair, and Russell instinctively grabbed her arm. "I just want to thank the officer." She shrugged off Russell's hand. "Mind if a colored woman says thanks and gives you a kiss?"

Jake stopped and smiled. "I never pass up a kiss from a pretty lady." Leona stood on her tiptoes and planted a kiss on the cheek he offered. She gave him a hug for good measure and he hugged her back.

Cold stares from the doctor, the orderly and the nurse turned to smiles. Jake was a white man in a black world at Receiving Hospital.

He stopped at the nurses' station and made out the paperwork. Before he left he made the phone call he had promised.

Eight-Four was done for the day. Jake walked out to his car with Duane right behind him. "Jezus Jake. Twice in one day, kissing niggers."

Jake's head snapped as he turned and looked into his partner's eyes. Duane understood the non-answer—the look.

301

Duane, you had better shut the fuck up.

Duane drove to the bureau in silence as Jake hand wrote a report on an "Attempted Suicide," and filled in the details. He knew that *if* he were not quitting, he and Duane might get a citation for meritorious police work for grabbing Leona Hart off of the Belle Isle Bridge.

He shrugged his shoulders. He was sure that Leona was glad he came by.

One day maybe, she'll tell Benjamin and William about the cop that called her a nigger.

Jake walked through the roll call room to the bosses' offices. Lt. Orth was collecting the log sheets, reports and tickets. Sergeant Ski was filing some old reports behind the lieutenant. Orth looked up as Jake got to the desk.

"How many more days do you have Bush?"

"Two, why?"

" 'cause I am tired of carrying dead weight."

Sergeant Ski dropped the papers he was filing.

Jake paused with the reports in his hand. He remembered the smell of Anderson Peach as he died in his arms, then the smile on Leona Hart's face as she reached up to kiss him.

Jake wanted to scream and at the same time, cry. *Dead weight?* Jake just dropped the reports on the desk, turned and left. *No, the asshole is not getting to me today.* Jake never looked back.

It was June 27, 1968 and Eight-Four was working Number Thirteen, a proper place for Jake to work his last day.

"Thirteen Five and Thirteen Cruiser, Second and the Boulevard at the Detroit Bank and Trust, hold up in progress."

Eight-Four's scanner picked up the replies. "Five on the way."

" Thirteen-Cruiser on the way."

"Right turn, Duane, now!" Jake flicked on the blue lights, but not the siren. "The Northwest corner, next to the Fisher Theater." Duane hit the brakes and Jake bailed out of the car.

Jake paused long enough to look through the glass door before entering with his .38 out in a crouched short step, looking from the left to the right.

Five people were on the floor covering their heads. Jake could not see anyone behind the four teller cages. He reached the first woman, a black elderly lady. Jake whispered, "Where is the robber?"

The woman rolled her head to see the man in the uniform crouched over her. "He-he j-just went out the door. Told us not to move."

Duane moved in the door as Jake holstered his revolver. "Alright, people, the police are here," Jake announced in a normal voice. "I need a description." Heads appeared behind all four cages and more came up from behind the desks in the customer service area to Jake's right.

The woman from behind the second window spoke. "He was at my window and showed me a note."

Jake cut her off. "Two other cars are on the way. Can you give me a quick description so we can start looking?"

"He was a Negro. 'bout twenty-five. Had a red 'do-rag', or was it black? He wore sunglasses. Kind of a red sateen shirt."

"Did you see which way he went?"

"No, he had us lay on the floor. Oh, something else, he had a gold left front tooth. He was smiling as he handed me the note. But, it wasn't a tooth. More like a metal blade."

Suits and uniforms came in the door as Thirteen-Five and the Cruiser crew arrived.

"I'll get a description over the air," Jake said as he yanked Duane's arm and headed out the door. "The woman, second from the left was the one held up."

Duane jumped behind the wheel as Jake grabbed the mic. "Duane, drive in circles. Eight-Four to Radio. We've got some information on the bank hold up, Number Thirteen."

"Go ahead Four."

Jake proceeded to repeat what the teller gave him. "Thirteen-Five and the Cruiser are there now. They'll follow up with further information." Jake hung up the mic.

Gold tooth, not a tooth, reverberated in Jake's mind. He kept repeating this to himself, searching his memory bank. "Wider circles, Duane."

Gold blade instead of a front tooth. Where have I seen that? Damn. Harris Harris.

"It's Harris Harris, Duane."

"Who?"

"It's Harris Harris. A guy with first and last names the same."

"What the hell you talking about?"

"I'll tell you later. Head toward Hamilton Avenue. Somewhere in the back of my mind I remember that he lives off Hamilton."

"Jake, you got two days, that's what you should remember."

"Just shut up and drive. Try Calvert. Calvert and Hamilton. Drive slow and look for a Negro with a 'do-rag' and a red shiny shirt."

"Jake, tomorrow you turn in your badge…"

"Just keep your eyes open."

Duane turned right onto Hamilton off Boston Boulevard. "You sure about this? How long ago did you run across this Harris guy?"

"Couple of years ago, Jess snatched the gun from him before he could shoot me. You don't forget shit like that."

Jake was checking the alleys as they drove slowly in the curb lane, then the storefronts.

"Hell, if he is walking, it'd be an hour before he got this far."

"He's not walking. Look for anyone getting out of a car or a cab."

"How do you know so much?"

"I'm guessing. Shut up and keep your eyes open."

A Checker Cab was driving south on Hamilton coming out of Highland Park. It pulled to the curb at Englewood.

Jake watched the cab stop and the man getting out. The man was a young black male with a black shiny shirt. He had a new "Do," wavy and shiny with pomade. The man walked west on Englewood next to a bar, toward the alley.

"Let me out, Duane, and make a U-turn and head around the block. I want to talk to that guy in the shiny shirt." Jake bailed out of the car.

He heard Duane in the background, "It's black. Not red." Jake ran between oncoming traffic onto the sidewalk and cut around the front of the bar onto Englewood. At the alley he caught sight of the man in the black shiny shirt cutting back east on Rosedale.

Jake ran. When he reached Rosedale he spotted his man crossing Hamilton. At the alley paralleling the east side of Hamilton, the man went south.

Jake grabbed the mic off of his walkie-talkie. "Four, he's in the alley east of Hamilton, heading south from Englewood." Jake started running and turned into the alley. He came to a dead stop. The man was gone.

With nothing else to do, he started walking with his .38 in his right hand and the radio mic in his left. He looked into the yards of the homes that backed up to the alley he was in. A noise had Jake turn as the man in the black shirt arose from behind some garbage cans and started running.

"Four, he's heading east in the alley between Rosedale and Harmon." Jake was guessing the street names from the beat he had walked five years before as he ran. Another garbage can fell onto the concrete alley two houses in front of Jake as the black shirt cut south through a wooden gate.

"Duane, get the Cruiser here. He's heading toward Calvert."

Jake cut into the yard, slowing as he neared the front of the garage. There was a jog to get to the side of the house and Jake could not see the walkway that led to the street.

He pressed against the shingled siding on the rear of the house and inched closer to the edge to peer around, jumping into the opening landing in a crouch. A tall wooden gate was closed. A hinge squeaked behind him and he turned to see the man door to the garage partially open.

Maybe he made it out the front gate? But he chose to check the garage first.

Jake's heart thumped as he inched toward the door.

It was broad daylight, but dark inside the one car garage as Jake peered into the slightly ajar door. The sliding door opening to the alley suddenly threw some light into the garage; enough where Jake saw the black sateen shirt slip back into the alley.

Jake hit the small opening, dove through it and rolled into the alley.

Two garbage cans fell and the man in a black sateen shirt stood, gold tooth interrupting a wide smile as his right hand came up pointing a pistol at him.

Jake's .38 fired at the same time the man's pistol discharged. The man fell into the garbage cans rolling behind him as Jake fell backwards among the tin cans and glass on the alley floor.

Duane, where are you? His mind went blank.

Eight-Four, turned west into the alley off of Second Avenue and Duane saw the rolling garbage cans and two bodies on the ground. One had on a blue shirt.

"Officer down! Officer down!" Duane screamed into the car's mic.

"Car calling radio. Give a location on the officer down."

"Alley running east of Hamilton. Maybe between Rosedale and Calvert."

"Radio to all units. Officer down in an alley east of Hamilton. Possibly between Calvert and Rosedale. Unit calling, identify yourself."

Four's radio blared into empty seats and an open door. Duane was running toward Jake and the man in the black shiny shirt.

"Jake, Jake. For Christ's sake, talk to me."

Duane knelt down. Jake's badge had a hole in it. One of the fours off on the badge was gone and the other bent inward. There was blood slowly oozing onto the light blue shirt behind the badge.

Sirens sounded. Black cars and blue and whites filled the alley. Thirteen-Seven had a stretcher next to Jake. Lt. Orth started to help put Jake on the stretcher when Sgt. Ski bumped him out of the way.

"Lou, I'll got him." The Sergeant grabbed and arm and Jake's Sam Browne belt. "Come on guys let's get him to Ford Hospital." Breedlove and DiPonio helped Ski put Jake on the stretcher and in the back of Thirteen-Seven.

Their siren wailed as Breedlove floored the Ford Wagon and headed for Hamilton. The car slid sideways when Jim took the ramp onto the Lodge Freeway.

"Easy partner. Don't get us killed."

"I let him down once, Ronnie. Not again. I am going to get him there alive."

The stretcher lurched forward, then back as Thirteen-Seven cut through afternoon traffic on the Lodge Freeway.

Harris you son-of-a-bitch. Still in my dreams.

Jake coughed and felt the pain in his chest.

Just one more day, Anne.

Ronnie steadied the stretcher.

"Hang on, Jake. We're almost there."

Epilogue:

The medical team at Henry Ford Hospital quickly stopped the bleeding. Jake's badge, namely the two fours, deflected the .32 caliber lead projectile upwards. The slug glanced off of the third, left-side rib and shattered Jake's left collarbone. The deformed slug was removed by surgery.

Jake's left arm was immobilized with a sling for six weeks while the clavicle grew back together. His treatment put him on disability leave for eight weeks. The badge, number 2441, was repaired and returned to him.

On August 30, 1968, Lieutenant Alan Orth walked to the podium as Sergeant Kempf shouted, "Roll Call."

"Eight-One…" The lieutenant stopped and looked up when he heard the door open.

"Hey Jake, you're lookin' fit," whispered Garcia as the man in civilian clothes walked around the ranks.

Jake stopped in front of the podium and looked the lieutenant in the eye offering his badge in a trembling right hand.

He then turned and walked to the door of the Detroit Police Tactical Mobile Unit. As he grabbed for the handle, Sergeants Ski and Kempf started a slow round of applause. The forty men in the ranks joined in.

Jake turned and took his last look at what he no longer was a part of. It was then that he saw Lieutenant Alan Orth give him a sharp salute and start to clap.

About The Author

The author is a 76-year-old retiree (since the end of 1997). He is a married father of four grown children, has one stepson, eight grandchildren and eight great grandchildren. His wife of 25 years, Edie, is his partner, friend, biggest fan and critic. Her subtle suggestions after he retired started the long journey that resulted in this book.

T.A. Novak retired from the Dow Corning Corporation with nearly thirty years of service. He had been a technical writer, specializing in emergency response procedures for the company's products and equipment.

As a young man, the author was a police officer in Detroit, serving there for 6 ½ years. This was a job he lived and loved. He resigned, knowing that he would always be a police officer at heart. As the author worked at Dow Corning, he often told stories about being an "Alley Cop." Many of his listeners would remark that he should write a book. He'd always end the conversation with, "I'll do that when I retire."

One of the author's avocations has always been writing, starting in high school with the encouragement of an English teacher, Mr. Conrad Vachon. At age 35, he started on a quest to get an Associate of Arts Degree from Delta College in mid-Michigan. There he took all the English and writing classes available. One such class on radio and television writing brought forth a story that had his teacher searching for a list of agents and suggestions that the story would fit the then popular series called "Police Story." Security was one of the reasons the author resigned himself to put off any serious writing while raising a family until later in life.

The author took up bird dogs and hunting in 1966. Since the early 1970s the author had been reporting several bird dog field trials a year to the American Field Publishing Company of Chicago. The Christmas Issue of the "Field" has even featured a few of his short stories on bird dogs, hunting trips and even some poetry over the years. In the late 1970s, the author had two short stories published in Hunting Dog, a magazine out of Cincinnati, Ohio.

"Among the Tin Cans and Broken Glass" is the author's first attempt at a novel and is based on his own personal experiences.

Author T.A.Novak and Children

44705756R00176

Made in the USA
Middletown, DE
13 May 2019